'The trench raid episode is a sta
terrors of trench warfare. Gritty and well researched, this novel avoids the common clichés that surround novels about the Great War. *Starlight* contrasts life on the Home and War fronts in a way that allows the reader to experience the emotional conflicts and problems experienced by a combatant moving between home and safety and the trenches and comradeship and danger.'

ANDY ROBERTSHAW
Director of The Royal Logistic Corps Museum

'Terrific. I was utterly engrossed by the slowly and delicately budding love affair in Cornwall and the intercut descriptions of the war. I loved the characterisations and the details of life and loss in the trench. I really felt I was there. I just thought it ended too soon. I wanted to know more. I was gripped throughout.'

FIONA BRUCE
BBC Presenter

Starlight

FERGUS O'CONNELL

paper & celluloid

ISBN 978-0-9569706-0-2
British Library Cataloguing in Publication Data.
A catalogue record for this book is available from the British Library.

Editing by Dan Leissner
Book design by Fiona Raven

First Printing August 2011
Printed in Ireland

Published by Paper & Celluloid
The Boathouse, Moatstown House
Athy, Co. Kildare, Ireland

www.PaperAndCelluloid.com

Part way through the writing of this,
my beautiful and extraordinary wife Clare,
died tragically. Starlight *is in her memory.*

When I set out for Lyonnesse,
A hundred miles away,
The rime was on the spray,
And starlight lit my lonesomeness
When I set out for Lyonnesse
A hundred miles away.

What would bechance at Lyonnesse
While I should sojourn there
No prophet durst declare,
Nor did the wisest wizard guess
What would bechance at Lyonnesse
While I should sojourn there.

When I came back from Lyonnesse
With magic in my eyes,
All marked with mute surmise
My radiance rare and fathomless,
When I came back from Lyonnesse
With magic in my eyes!

Thomas Hardy

Part 1

I

$\mathcal{E}$nd of September 1918. Late afternoon.

It was Helen's birthday. Lieutenant Lewis Friday, who counted himself as her lover, was spending the day at the bottom of a ten foot deep trench in Northern France. He had done the same last year in a trench less than fifty miles to the rear of where he was now. At this rate it would take at least ten more of Helen's birthdays before they got to Berlin and the War would be over. Nineteen twenty eight. He put the thought out of his head.

There had been no change in the weather. The white, dripping fog, which had been there when dawn broke, had not lifted at all. Instead it lay above the trench, unmoving in the still air. It was as though Death had snagged his shroud on the barbed wire.

Everything was wet – the mushy wooden revetting, the soggy sandbags, the slimy mud walls of the trench. The duckboards were covered in mud, ankle deep, with the consistency and suction of wet concrete. The sponginess under foot spoke of ghastly horrors buried in the trench. Lewis assumed it had been used as a grave at one time or another. The French were always doing that but since the Somme the British had done the same. There were just too many bodies so that if the men were tired and hungry or under harassing fire and there was a ready made grave, why not use it? There was a spot along the trench where, when he stood on the duckboards, they pivoted slightly acting as a bellows pumping out puffs of vile-smelling air. He preferred not to think of what lay beneath.

The fog meant that he couldn't see beyond the parapet and that made Lewis very frightened. He had a constant vision of giant men in grey suddenly appearing out of the milky whiteness, standing with one booted foot on the sandbags above him and shooting down into the trench as though shooting rats in a barrel.

In reality, it was unlikely that this would happen. The Germans had all but ceased attacking but all it took was one over-zealous commander. Just in case then, the British had put sentries out in no-man's-land as well as the usual ones on the fire step. Not that they would see much in this. As an added precaution, he had ordered his men to tie empty bully beef tins to the wire to act as alarms in case anybody did try to get through. That still didn't stop him being frightened.

He had just returned from inspecting his section of the line and was turning a corner of a traverse when he collided with a man hurrying in the other direction. As they pulled back from each other, Lewis recognised Byrne, one of the battalion runners.

'Sorry, sir,' said Byrne, breathless and trying to salute.

Given how on edge he was, Lewis was tempted to be angry. Instead, he said, 'Got a rendezvous with a young lady, Byrne?'

'Nossir. Sorry, sir.'

Best runner in the battalion, Lewis had heard. Byrne had only been here a couple of months, so he was probably just turned eighteen – a fact attested to by his podgy cheeks and smooth chin. But the deep hollows beneath his eyes, and the eyes themselves told another story.

'Permission to continue spreading a rumour, sir?'

Lewis smiled a fraction. He liked Byrne. He reminded Lewis of himself when he had first come here – calm, reasonable, rational, keeping a tight lid on his emotions. He had tried then to view the War as a series of problems to be tackled and solved. One problem at a time. Live in the now. Don't think about the future.

For a while, it had worked. The problem might be just trying to stay warm – assuming you couldn't stay dry – in a waterlogged trench with your feet and legs permanently under a foot or two of water. And this was ignoring the fat rats, the lice, the constant weakness from lack of sleep and bad food. But then a shell would land on the line killing or wounding some men and collapsing part of the trench. So now the problems came. Evacuate the wounded. Bury the dead, assuming there was something to bury. Otherwise clean up the bits, stick them in a sandbag and try to find some place to bury them where they might stay buried. And while this was going on the Germans might send over gas. So you had to get your respirator on. Which made any kind of movement or seeing or breathing or giving orders or any other fucking thing immensely difficult. And what if, in the midst of all that, an attack came? Or there was more shelling?

You prioritised and dealt with the problems, one at a time, in rapid succession. But there seemed to be no end to the problems. Every day brought more than yesterday, so that eventually the never-ending problems wore you down. There were too many. They came too frequently. And sometimes, while in the midst of one problem, half a dozen more emerged that had to be solved at the same time. Each day of doing this took away reserves of strength and energy that could never be replaced by sleep or food or time out of the line. Lewis knew he was getting very close to the end of his tether. Maybe he was already there.

'Permission granted, Byrne.'

'Rumour is the Germans are finished, sir.'

'Been on the phone to the Kaiser, have you?'

He often exchanged banter like this with the men. Some took to it more than others. Byrne seemed to enjoy it.

'Nossir, rumour is that the Germans are deserting in droves.'

'Ah. So we'll be seeing a white flag any day now, will we? Very good, Byrne. Let me know if they call you back, won't you?'

'Yessir. Excuse me, sir. Must go.'

'Carry on, Byrne.'

'Thank you, sir.'

Byrne saluted and disappeared at speed around the bay.

Rumours. There were always rumours. But this one? Lewis dared not think about it. After all this time. That it might actually end. Could it be true?

It was late afternoon and the light was starting to fail. It was as though somebody had punctured the sky and the colour was draining out through the hole. The soggy air was glacial and the clothes Lewis wore – long underpants, vest, tunic, trousers, puttees, greatcoat, leather, fleece-lined gloves, muffler, woollen cap and steel helmet – seemed little protection against it. He couldn't remember the last time he'd changed them and knew that he stank. His socks were wet and he couldn't feel his feet. Lice patrolled his underwear, needling his groin and armpits, crossing unreachable areas of his back, goading him to scratch and give himself trench fever. He arrived at the entrance to his dugout. He should really have gone down into it but felt safer out here. In the dugout he would be cornered. At least out here he could run. He didn't want to die now. Not now. Not if these really *were* the last few days.

He took a cigarette from his case and placed it his mouth, noticing again the slight tremor in his hand. He couldn't remember exactly when it had begun but now it was always there. It caused the yellow match flame – bright in the gathering gloom of the trench – to shiver as he positioned it beneath the end of the cigarette and lit it. The shaking wasn't going away. He took a first deep, calming drag.

When he had come to France last year it had seemed like an impossible ambition that he would live more than a couple of weeks. He remembered those first shocked, stunned days. The unbelievable violence and squalor around him. Impossible to believe that men could live – and die – like this. Looking back on it now, he was astonished that he either hadn't been carried off in a straight jacket screaming, or killed outright, given that he had made so many mistakes. But he had learned that you could get used to anything. And the letters from Helen, the link to her, had carried him safely through those first few days. So that gradually he had the feeling that she was watching over him – just as she had said she would.

And so Lewis learned the craft of soldiering in the trenches. He quickly realised that it wasn't courage or daring that would enable him to survive. Of course there was a certain randomness to war – especially this war of artillery – against which there was no defence. So you needed luck. But there was also something much more mundane.

You needed attention to detail. Because there were lots of things that could get a man killed. Carelessness, a head raised an inch too high above a parapet. Thoughtlessness, no harm in lighting a fag here – what red glow in the dark? Lack of fore-thought – which way is the way back to our lines when both sides look the same at night, a silhouette of stakes and wire and rotting corpses, against a starlit background?

He had become conscious of the details, of how everything could be broken down into its constituent parts and how these parts needed to be understood and made as simple and as idiot-proof as possible. His men liked him for it. He became known as an officer who knew his onions. They felt they were in safe hands with him. Well, as safe as could be, anyway. That's why there had been no problem earlier today when he had looked for men to take the bully beef tins out into no-man's-land. They saw the sense of it – a detail that might turn out to be all important.

So the War might end. The Germans were clearly in a bad way but could it really, actually, end? Could it really happen that he could go home, be with Helen, they could get married, have a future. Maybe have a child. A son. Or a daughter as beautiful as Helen. Life. Long years stretching off into the future. Years of being with her when, so far, the time he had spent with her could be counted in weeks. He hardly dared hope.

He was lighting another cigarette, his hand shaking even more, when he heard the sound. It was like the dull tinkling of mess tins or the sound of cow bells in an Alpine meadow. Jesus Christ – the bully beef tins. The Germans were coming.

2

'Like to read a book, Lewis?'

'Yes please, Mum. I'll get one from my shelf.'

It was something they often did together, during the long afternoons after lunch and before Dad came home. He was four and it was winter. A blazing coal fire burned red and yellow in the grate. Mum had lit it before lunch so that the room was warm and cosy. Outside the wind rattled the window panes and threw squalls of rain at them. It sounded like handfuls of gravel were being thrown against the glass. They had already done their lists, sitting at the dining room table. Mum had written 'cat' and then Lewis had written a whole lot of other words – 'rat', 'sat', 'bat' and so on. Then Mum had tried 'dog' and again Lewis had written a list of words that sounded like it. They had done nine or ten lists like this.

'These are words that rhyme,' she explained. 'That's poetry.'

'Sometimes, he would say words that she said weren't words at all. So 'dog', 'bog', 'log' and then 'rog.' Then she would laugh or tickle him and say, '*That's* not a real word.' Sometimes she would say words that weren't real words too and they would both end up convulsed with laughter.

'No, don't do that,' she said. 'I have one here from my shelf.'

'A grown-up book?'

'Well, sort of, but I think you'll like it.'

Lewis settled himself on Mum's lap. She had thick dark hair the colour of chocolate. When he touched the skin of her face, which he often did, it reminded him of peaches. She smelt of flowers and the drawers in her bedroom. She opened the book's black cover.

'Treasure Island,' she said. 'By Robert Louis Stevenson'. He loved her voice. When she read it was like music. She turned some more pages, laying her fingertips on the pages she had turned, then catching the corner of the next one with her thumb, lifting it up and turning it over. She had long fingers that seemed to stroke the pages. Mum played the piano. She pressed down gently on both pages of the book with the palm of her hand. She wore two rings on her third finger, one with a stone and one that was just a ring.

'Part 1, The Old Buccaneer.'

She turned another page.

'Chapter one. The Old Sea Dog at The "Admiral Benbow".'

'Oh, it's about a dog,' said Lewis excitedly.

'No, it's not about a dog,' she said. 'It's about a pirate, a sailor. A sea dog is another name for a sailor.'

'Like Dad,' Lewis said, looking up at her.

'Yes,' she agreed, lifting her eyes from the book and looking into the fire. She had green eyes. 'Like your father was.'

She was silent for a heartbeat. Then she said, 'Anyway, I think you'll like it. Here we go.'

Here we go. It was like sliding down the side of a mountain.

'*Squire Trelawney, Dr. Livesey, and the rest of these gentlemen having asked me to write down the whole particulars about Treasure Island, from the beginning to the end, keeping nothing back but the bearings of the island, and that only because there is still treasure not yet lifted, I take up my pen in the year of grace 17——, and go back to the time when my father kept the "Admiral Benbow" inn, and the brown old seaman, with the sabre cut, first took up his lodging under our roof.*

I remember him as if it were yesterday.'

Outside the wind howled and the rain continued to spatter on the glass. The clock on the mantelpiece ticked in the background. Mum's voice was soft when she was telling the story but she would do the voices. A bluff, man's voice for the captain. Her own voice returned when telling the story. The pages rustled gently as she turned them.

They were still in the first chapter when she read about Jim Hawkins's father being sick – a sickness that eventually 'took him off'. Before Lewis could think too much about this, Mum began to sing the captain's song in the captain's voice. 'Fifteen men on the dead man's chest – Yo-ho-ho, and a bottle of rum!'

'Why were they sitting on the dead man's chest, Mum?' he interrupted.

It was hard to imagine how so many people could fit on such a small space. She looked at him, puzzled for an instant, and then understood.

'No, it's not that kind of chest,' she said, touching Lewis' chest with the palm of her hand. 'It's a chest like the captain had. A trunk. Like Dad's one upstairs in the bedroom.'

After the first page Lewis was enthralled. Mum had said they would read a chapter every day but today they had read two. In the first chapter the captain arrived at the 'Admiral Benbow'.

It was just Jim Hawkins and his father and his mother – just as it was for Lewis. And just as with Lewis, Jim's father wasn't in the story very much. Since leaving the Navy, Lewis' father had worked as a salesman for a company that sold meat slicers and other kitchen equipment. He spent a lot of time working. Lewis liked the way Jim wasn't afraid of the captain. He liked the fact that Jim's father had said that the captain's presence would ruin the inn whereas Jim knew that it was actually good and brought in customers. Lewis didn't really like Jim's father and the way he wouldn't ask the captain for the rent. Lewis liked that Jim seemed to be really the man of the house and the way he took care of his mother.

Mum was coming to the end of a page and had already lifted its corner with her thumb.

'How that personage haunted my dreams I need scarcely tell you. On stormy nights, when the wind shook the four corners of the house —'

'Just like today,' said Lewis, burrowing in more closely to her.

'Yes, just like today,' she said.

When she reached the end of the chapter, Mum held the book in a V between her fingers and thumb and then closed it with a soft 'plip'.

'Oh, Mum can we just read a little more – another page, please?'

'I've got to get tea ready. Daddy will be in.'

'Just one more page, Mum – please.'

She reopened the book.

'I'll just read a little bit more – just to give you a taste of what's to come.'

'Thanks, Mum.'

She was beautiful when she smiled.

'Chapter two. Black Dog appears and disappears.'

'Gosh, this story's full of dogs, isn't it Lewis?'

He nodded.

'Are you enjoying it?' she asked.

'It's the best story I've ever heard,' he said.

'It was not very long after this that there occurred the first of the mysterious events that rid us at last of the captain, though not, as you will see, of his affairs. It was a bitter cold winter, with long, hard frosts and heavy gales; and it was plain from the first that my poor father was little likely to see the spring. He sank daily, and my mother and I had all the inn upon our hands; and were kept busy enough, without paying much regard to our unpleasant guest.

It was one January morning, very early – a pinching, frosty morning – the cove all grey with hoar-frost, the ripple lapping softly on the stones, the sun still low and only touching the hilltops and shining far to seaward.'

In the days that followed, Black Dog came and went. By now, Lewis was imagining that he was in charge – with Mum – of the

'Admiral Benbow'. She wasn't quite like the mum in the story, though. Lewis got the impression that that mum was a bit dowdy. In his imagination the mum who owned and ran the 'Admiral Benbow' was beautiful and hard-working. And she was strong and honest, as Jim's mum showed herself to be, when she counted out exactly what was due to her from the captain's chest. The only time Jim's mum showed any weakness was just after they had left the inn and the pirates arrived. Then she fainted and Lewis had to pull her in under the little bridge so that they could hide.

Lewis had asked her, soon after she had started reading, where Black Hill Cove – the site of the 'Admiral Benbow' – was.

'It's not a real place, luvvy – it's only a story.'

'But these things could have happened, couldn't they?' he asked.

'I suppose they could. Actually I'm sure things like this did happen when there were pirates around.'

'And so where do you think they happened?'

She thought a moment and then said, 'Cornwall, maybe. There are lots of little coves down there. When we were kids, Nana and Grandad – my Mum and Dad – took us to Cornwall. I remember there was a place called Readymoney Cove. I think it was called that because pirates or smugglers used to land their cargos there.'

'Could we could go and live in Cornwall?'

'Oh, I don't know think so. I don't know if Daddy would like it – or if he could work down there.'

Lewis thought – though he didn't say it – that maybe he and Mum could go. They could find an inn at Readymoney Cove or some place like that and it would be just like in *Treasure Island*. Lewis and Mum would run the place.

Sometimes Dad had to stay away overnight. 'Daddy's got to go to a meeting in Birmingham,' Mum would say. Lewis wondered what would happen if Dad never came back. Or if he died like Jim's dad did in *Treasure Island*. Lewis would become the man of the house then. He wouldn't go to school but instead get a job and sleep in Mum's bed. He often did this when Dad was away, always finding some excuse – a bad dream or he couldn't sleep.

'Come on so, sleepy head,' she would say, lifting the covers, opening up the warm, dark cave.

He loved to climb in beside her and snuggle up to her. He loved the faint smell of perfume or soap or whatever it was. Or maybe this was the smell of her. Her hair that tickled his nose if he pressed up against her so that they were like two spoons in a drawer. The feel of her thigh through the fabric of her nightdress, if he rested his hand on it. Or her buttocks pressing into him. Or his head on the softness of her breasts if she cuddled him to her.

Someday, if Dad really died or didn't come back, Lewis would marry Mum and they would go to Cornwall and buy an inn and live together just like Jim Hawkins in *Treasure Island*.

3

*L*ewis had heard it for the first time the previous day. He was at home in Acton, lying in the back garden reading, and wondering whether he would go to the trouble of going down to the shop to get an ice cream. He lay in shorts, shirt off, sun on his skin, a large square of canvas that Dad had brought back from the sea, beneath him. The canvas smelt dusty. Birds twittered in the garden. Beyond the house, out in the street, he heard the sound of a horse clip clopping as a deliveryman's dray went past. Somewhere off in a neighbouring house children shouted as they played. Then, beyond all these, Lewis heard another sound. It was faint, so faint at first that he wasn't sure whether he'd actually imagined it. He put the book down and listened again. It was like very distant thunder or heavy drums. But the sky was blue. It was hard to imagine any place not bathed in sunshine. And then he knew what it was.

'I'm almost certain it was the guns in France,' he said to his father at tea time. 'Bombarding the German trenches. I read about it in *The Times* today.'

'With luck this push will end the War and you won't have to go,' said Dad.

His father had a wide, friendly face and hair that was starting to show grey in patches. There were photographs of him in his naval uniform looking slim and handsome. Since giving up the sea he had become a bit more beefy and jowly. Lewis wondered what it must be like to be the men under those guns. The sound went on right up to the time he fell asleep.

Next morning was the first of July. Lewis was awake and out

of bed very early – he had hardly slept at all. At the foot of the bed was the leather travelling bag that Dad had bought for him for the trip. His dormer window looked out onto Horn Lane where there was hardly anybody stirring at this time of the morning. He went to the bathroom, had a quick bath and returned to his room to get dressed. His desk was in front of the window. He had tidied it up and cleared everything off the top, so that the only things left were a pot of pencils and pens and a bottle of ink. On the wall beside it were prints of *The Defence of Rorke's Drift* by Elizabeth Butler and two pictures, one of Nelson and one of the *Victory* at Trafalgar. Along another wall was his bookshelf with its copies of Stevenson, Hardy, Buchan and all the others. Lewis had agonised endlessly over what books to bring on his trip. Eventually, he had limited himself to three. Any others he would buy in Cornwall.

In some ways he was sad to be leaving. He had been enjoying the endless days of sunshine and lemonade and reading and losing track of what day it was. But he would be leaving in November anyway. This was by way of a rehearsal.

It had been Dad's suggestion that Lewis go on holiday by himself. Dad had been in the Navy and had been recalled with the onset of the War. He now worked long hours somewhere in the Admiralty, so Lewis saw him less and less.

'Cornwall,' Dad had said. 'There's a place down there called Fowey. It's a nice spot. I remember we put in there one autumn and went ashore. There's a pub there called "The King of Prussia". We all had a bit too much to drink and when we came out we were trying to find our way back to the boat. We came to a flight of steps and there were leaves at the bottom – you know, fallen leaves, like you see in autumn. I thought the steps led to some kind of pathway.

"Come on. This way," I said, as I went down the steps. They were leaves that had blown off the trees alright but they were just floating on the surface of the water. I was in it up to my knees before I realised what was going on.'

Lewis laughed.

'So go down there and ask if they remember me.'

'When was it?'

'Oh, about 1895, I think. Just before I gave up the sea. Anyway, you could go for July, August and September, if you like. It would be a chance to fend for yourself'.

Lewis knew what Dad really meant by this. Dad was gregarious, outgoing, hail-fellow-well-met. Lewis was solitary, shy, a loner. Dad wanted him to lose some of his shyness – to better prepare him for what he might face in the Army – and presumably, for life generally. Lewis wanted this too. He hated the shyness. In the last year or so, had been trying to do something about it himself. He had started by asking – every night in his prayers – that he be cured of his shyness, as though it were some form of disease. He had done this for several months. Nothing had happened.

His big breakthrough came when, lying in bed one night, he realised that shyness wasn't a disease at all. Rather it was just an act. Just as confidence was an act, so too was its opposite. Dad appeared confident because he behaved in a certain way. He would always exchange a cheery word with somebody in a shop, or a neighbour on the street. He took an interest in people, asked about their lives. He didn't think people were looking at him all the time, as Lewis did. If Dad made a mistake he laughed it off. If he didn't know something he asked. It was just an act. Not that he meant that Dad was acting or pretending. No, Dad was like this. But Lewis realised that it was the things you said and did which made people think you were confident or not. If Lewis did things that would make him appear confident then he would *be* confident.

And so he had started to do that. It took a lot of effort to create the thin shell of confidence and it didn't take much to shatter it, but he was getting better at it. This morning, after he had said his goodbyes and left the house to begin his journey to Cornwall, he headed towards the Tube station, feeling strong and confident and powerful.

The morning was still cool but overhead the bright blue sky promised another hot day. The trees cast long shadows. At the far end of the road, where it turned slightly to the right, the air seemed to be almost a misty blue. Most of the houses still had their blinds down or curtains drawn. A few houses ahead, Lewis saw a man emerge from a house and walk along the short path to his front gate. He was smartly dressed – for the City Lewis guessed – prosperous looking and carried a briefcase. Lewis reached his gate just as the man did and their eyes met.

'Good morning, sir,' said Lewis.

It was definitely the kind of thing Dad would have done. But more importantly it was what a person who wasn't shy – or rather, didn't care what people thought – would have done.

Surprised, but pleasantly so, judging by his face, the man replied, 'Good morning, young man. Another fine day.'

'Isn't it lovely, sir?' said Lewis and then he had passed by, another layer added to the onion skin of his confidence.

Lewis was tall – five foot ten, with hair and eyes the same colour as his mother's. He didn't think he was particularly good-looking but he certainly wasn't ugly. He was finished school and would be eighteen on November the tenth. Then he would have to join the Army. He wanted to enlist, to do his bit but he didn't want to be killed. If the 'push' whose guns he had heard the sound of, was successful, then maybe he would be alright. This time, the War *might* be over by Christmas or early in 1917. If he enlisted in November, presumably it would be several months before he was trained and shipped to France. The War might be coming to an end or be over. He might see little or no action and then be discharged. He would be able to say that he had done his duty. He would have had a bit of an adventure, worked in a career, made some money – and lived.

So in some ways, this morning was the start of that whole great journey. He thought of the next few months as preparing for the Army. He would become physically strong in Cornwall – he would walk or run or climb hills – and he would become mentally strong. He would increase his endurance somehow – though he didn't know how exactly yet. He would become better at building the confidence shell. Maybe it would become a permanent thing. He had never kissed a girl, but maybe he would meet a girl in Cornwall. When he imagined her, it was somebody like himself, down on holidays from London. He would meet her and they would fall in love and he would leave her behind when he went off to the Army.

Lewis made his way to Paddington. The sound of the guns was gone now. What did that mean? The wind direction had changed? Or the bombardment had stopped? And if it had stopped, what did *that* mean?

He queued at the ticket office and bought a ticket to Truro. The man behind the ticket desk looked like a warm and jolly uncle. As he handed over Lewis' ticket and change, he said, 'Lucky you, sir. Getting out of the city in weather like this and getting down to Cornwall.'

'I believe it's beautiful,' said Lewis.

'You won't be disappointed, sir. Enjoy yourself.'

'I will,' said Lewis.

He bought a copy of *The Times* at Wyman's bookstall and browsed through the books. He hoped there would be a bookshop in Fowey. He imagined a dusty second hand bookshop in a quaint back street and pictured finding some delights there. Maybe that would be where he would bump into the girl he dreamt of meeting. How nice it would be if they both shared a passion for books.

He was suddenly hungry now in a way he hadn't been when Margaret, the housekeeper, had pushed tea and toast on him this morning. He bought some coffee and a scone from a very pretty young girl who smiled at him when she took his order. He tried to think of some chatty thing to say to her but was unable to. Still, it didn't matter. He smiled back and said, 'Thanks very much,' to which she replied, 'Thank *you*, sir.'

After he had eaten he set off to find his platform. The concourse was crowded and noisy under the high glazed roof. He threaded his way through the throng. Suddenly, just ahead of him, he saw that a gap had opened up in which a group of women stood. He wondered what sort of trip a group of women would be going on. Then one of them noticed him and began to come in his direction. He wondered for a second if he knew her. Was she one of those distant cousins whom he saw every couple of years and whom he never recognised because they always seemed to have grown so much? She was a girl really – small, in a summer hat, blonde – probably in her twenties. He scanned her face but didn't recognise her. The other women followed. He thought they were coming to ask for directions, about a particular platform or train and he hoped he would be able to help them. But he noticed that they all had angry expressions on their faces. The small blonde stopped right in front of Lewis, a foot or so away from him, and looked up at him.

'Why aren't you in khaki?' she demanded, in a voice that had an electric snarl to it. It was possible she might have been pretty but right now, her face was contorted with fury. Lewis felt his face redden.

'I'm not eighteen yet, Miss,' he began. As he did, the women spread around him like the horns of a bull. He had a sense that there were perhaps two or three on either side but there could have been more because they spread beyond his field of view. Uncertainly, he continued.

'I won't be until November. Then, I am enlisting.'

'You're a liar,' she sneered, and Lewis felt his face burning, he was blushing so much.

The woman to the left of the blonde joined in. She was taller than the blonde, well-built and older. She wore an ugly, black old-fashioned hat. Again Lewis was struck by how faces are changed by anger. In normal circumstances, this woman's might have had a kindly look about it – she looked like a mum or an auntie – but right now her face was red and she was furious.

'Plenty of boys haven't waited until they were eighteen.'

Her voice was deep, almost manly.

'You're tall – the Army would take you right now, if only you had the courage to go to a recruiting office.'

'Come with us,' the blonde said, her angry face suddenly transforming into a smile. 'Right now. The nearest recruiting station isn't far from here. We'll take you there. You could be in the Army by lunchtime.'

She sounded big sisterly.

Lewis was suddenly terrified. He couldn't end up in a recruiting station. He had a panicked picture of himself arriving home in Horn Lane saying that he'd joined up. He had to go to Cornwall. He wanted to go to Cornwall. He would join the Army – but not today.

'Please – let me pass,' he said.

His face felt like it was on fire.

'No. Come on. Come with us.' said the blonde, softly, cajoling, like a lover asking for a favour.

'No … really … not today. I can't. I have a train to catch.'

Lewis said this as though it was suddenly the solution to the problem.

The blonde held out her hand and took his. He allowed her to do it without resisting. He couldn't think what else to do.

'Come on,' she inveigled.

Her voice was even softer now.

'Never mind the train. This is more important.'

He was vaguely aware of cries of encouragement and 'well dones' coming from somewhere. Was it the other women? Suddenly he pulled his hand away and said, 'No really, sorry I can't. Not today. I will in November. Honest.'

It struck him how outrageous the whole conversation was. Why should he be having to justify himself to her? The blonde's face suddenly contorted again.

'Coward,' she said, spitting out the word. 'Coward.'

Lewis moved to the right, to try to get round one of the tips of the horns but yet another woman moved to block his way. He was hemmed in by the women and now there was a curtain of onlookers beyond that.

'Coward,' the blonde spat again, and then taking a white feather about five inches long from her pocket, she pushed it into Lewis' lapel.

'Please, I must go,' he said, as he tried again to get past them. He was conscious now of the feather in his lapel. He could see it on the edge of his vision. He would have tried to push his way through the women, but how was he to do that? They were women – he couldn't lay hands on them; he couldn't push them.

'Coward,' said the blonde again, still blocking his way, still looking up at him with eyes full of hatred. The other women took up the word and began to chant 'Coward! Coward! Coward!' The well-built woman turned to face the crowd and tried to get them to join in, directing them like an orchestra conductor. He attempted again to get past them, this time by turning away from them and going off to the side, but again there was a woman there. She had a man's face and dull hair.

'My son is in France,' she said, looking at him with hatred on her face.

It occurred to Lewis that he should say, 'So you're his father, are you?' to the woman but fear chased the thought out of his head again.

'Come on now, ladies. Leave this poor lad alone.'

The middle aged man who spoke had a florid face, mutton chop whiskers and wore a top hat and morning coat. Lewis felt a strong hand take his arm and somehow steer him past or through the women. Suddenly they were behind and the man was saying, 'You should be alright now, son. Go and catch your train.'

The man's breath smelled of mints.

'Thank you, sir,' Lewis had begun to say, but already he was wondering what the man must think of him. 'I'm not eighteen yet,' he blurted out. 'When I'm eighteen I'm going to enlist.'

'You don't have to justify yourself to me, lad.'

Lewis wasn't sure exactly what this meant – whether the man believed him or not.

'If I had a son I'm not sure I'd be keen to see him go.'

The words didn't really make Lewis feel any better.

'Stupid bloody cows,' the man added. 'Get along now and catch your train.'

Lewis turned to go.

'Oh,' said the man, reaching for the white feather and pulling it from Lewis' lapel, 'you won't be needing this.'

The man placed the feather on the air, and let it go. It began to float softly to the ground. Lewis thought he should have said thank you again, but he was in too much of a hurry to get away from anybody who had witnessed what had just happened. His face burned as he made his way to the platform where the train was waiting. The words 'Cornish Riviera Express' were written on a wide band along the edge of the roof of each carriage. Lewis just wanted to be by himself, to find a compartment with nobody else in it, to escape.

But it wasn't going to be possible. It was high summer and, even with a war on, people were going to the West and to the sea. The delay the women had caused him meant that many of the compartments were full. Eventually he found a seat in one of them, wedged between a fat woman and a young man in his twenties. Lewis put his bag on the rack overhead, took out his newspaper and buried his face in it.

Carriage doors were slammed, whistles blew and there was a hissing of steam. The train pulled out of the station and began to pick up speed. He wondered whether any of the other people in the compartment had seen what had happened in the station. It had been a huge commotion and he thought it most unlikely that somebody here hadn't witnessed it. What if somebody remarked on it to him? And even if nobody did remark on it, and even if nobody had seen, surely they must all be wondering why he wasn't in uniform. His face burned so much so that his eyes stung. He realised that he was sweating. He wanted to stand up and take off his jacket but was too embarrassed to do it and draw any further attention to himself.

It was a long time before he was actually able to read his newspaper. Even though he tried several times, the words refused to have any meaning. The incident in the station still consumed him, crowding everything else out of his mind. Finally, the gentle rhythm of the train seemed to calm him a little. He turned to the War news.

'Determined British Bombardment' ran the headline. 'The activity which has prevailed for the last three days has now assumed the character of a definite and determined bombardment of the enemy's positions along practically the whole of the British front'.

Lewis had been fifteen when the War had started. He had been as excited as everyone else about it, suddenly taking to reading the papers assiduously and following the troop movements on a map of France that had come free with one of them. Now, nearly two years later, he had come to the conclusion that a lot of what was in the papers was sound and fury, signifying nothing. Things happened, but ultimately nothing happened – except that lots of men seemed to die. There were no advances, there was no sense of progress towards an objective. For almost all of 1915, he had lost interest. But when 1916 dawned, his interest was renewed. He would be enlisting at the end of the year, so now he wanted to get a sense of what was going on and what it would be like.

Between what he had heard yesterday afternoon in the garden and what he was reading here, it sounded like something big was up. But some of the phrases in the paper made his blood run cold. *'Gas Attacks Claimed To Be Unsuccessful'*. *'Liquid Fire On Verdun Salients'* was a headline and beneath it, *'A series of very violent local attacks, preceded by intense bombardments and accompanied by jets of liquid flame, was directed by the enemy against the principal salients of our line.'* Maybe whatever was happening now would be successful and he would never have to face these things.

Lunchtime came and went. Margaret had made sandwiches of fresh white bread, thick, delicious ham and mustard for the journey. But he didn't want to draw attention to himself by standing up to get them, or by eating them with all these people around him. So he sat there hungrily while all the other occupants of the compartment either ate the food they'd brought themselves or went off to the dining car. Outside the day was glorious and the train rattled along through the green countryside. Later, whether from hunger or the heat of the compartment or the shock of what had happened in Paddington, he felt a terrible weariness and wanted to sleep. But he didn't want to fall asleep with all of these people around him, so he struggled to stay awake. The train passed through Devon and into Cornwall, but Lewis could take no pleasure in it.

The train pulled in to Truro in the late afternoon. Lewis was relieved to escape the compartment. Maybe in doing so it would help him to escape what had happened in London. The sun was still very hot. While he waited for the next train he finally ate the sandwiches.

4

'Fowey – last stop.'

Lewis had dozed. The motion of the train and the heat inside it, coupled with everything that had happened earlier, had overtaken him in the end. He got up hastily, took his bag from the luggage rack and got off. A few minutes later, he was standing outside Mrs Middleton's guest house.

It was a fine three-storey building painted pink with two bay windows on the first floor. The front looked out onto the river. Lewis entered and found an attractive, middle-aged woman bustling around behind a wooden counter. Her hair looked like it had been newly done, she wore fresh make-up and was smartly dressed. It was the first time Lewis had ever checked into a hotel or boarding house by himself.

'Mrs Middleton?' he asked.

Her face blossomed into a warm smile.

'Ah, you'll be Mr Friday. I've got your room all ready, sir. I think you'll like it – you've got a river view. I've given you one of our nicest ones since you're staying with us for so long. Now, if you'll just fill in your details in my book.'

She turned a large ledger towards him and handed him a pen.

'How was your journey?' she asked, as he wrote.

'Fine, thank you,' he said. Then added, 'Tiring.'

'Yes, London is a long way,' she said.

You've no idea how far, thought Lewis. He finished writing and turned the book back to her. Without looking at it, she said, 'And you're all paid up, bed and breakfast and evening meal, for the first two weeks. After that you can just pay me a week in advance as you go. That alright?'

'Oh yes, that'll be fine, thank you.'

'Now, if you'll just follow me, sir.'

The stairs had a bright red carpet with yellow and green flowers on it and creaked occasionally as they went up. A smell of meat roasting came from the back of the house. As if reading his thoughts, Mrs Middleton said, 'Dinner will be at seven, so you'll have time to freshen up. It's every evening at seven so if there's some evening when you're not going to be here, just let me know that morning before you go out, won't you?'

'Of course. Thank you. Though I can't imagine a situation where that might arise.'

'Well whatever you say, but just in case. Best to be on the safe side's what I always say.'

They reached the second floor and walked along a short carpeted corridor. Then she opened a room with the number '6' on the door and walked in ahead of him.

He was thankful to put the bag down. The room had a large window which overlooked the estuary. The top pane was down, the bottom one up and a tiny, warm breeze, smelling of salt and fish and the sea, stirred the net curtain.

'I hope it's to your satisfaction,' said Mrs Middleton.

He wasn't sure what he was meant to do to verify this, so he parted the curtain and looked out the window at the water and the gentle hill opposite.

'It's lovely,' he said, 'really lovely.'

It was as though he had passed a test, because now, suddenly, he wasn't 'Mr Friday' or 'sir' any more.

'Here's your key, my darling – there's a room key and a key to the front door. Not that you'll need the second one. Our door is hardly ever locked. No, no need for that, you'll be as safe here as if you were in God's pocket. Now, I'll give you time to freshen up and then I'll see you at dinner. We all eat at the one table – well, that is, you do – my guests, and we've got a full house, so lots of interesting people to meet.'

With that she went out and closed the door.

Lewis' heart sank at the mention of more people. He had hoped it would be more like a restaurant where he could have sat at a table by himself. Still, time to think about that later.

The room was furnished with a bed, a wardrobe, a washstand with a jug and bowl, a dressing table and a kind of desk. There was a spacious feel to it. On the walls were tinted prints of three English cathedrals – Salisbury, Wells and Winchester. Lewis leant on the window sill and looked out. There was a narrow quayside and then a flight of stone steps, just like the ones Dad had described, leading down to the river. A number of small boats bobbed around on the river. Most of them seemed to be rowing boats while one or two had a single mast in the centre and one had a triangular sail raised. Turning back into the room he bounced onto the bed and stretched out on it. It was very comfortable.

Opening his case, he took a framed photograph from it. The photograph was of a woman in her mid twenties. She was looking directly into the camera with an expression of great determination on her face. Lewis placed it on the bedside table. Then he took his diary from his case. The cover was dark green with a red embossed label on the front with the words 'Lett's No. 9 Diary 1916' touched out in gold. He opened the marbled inside front cover, flicked through the pages and found today. Then he began to write everything that had happened.

Dinner at a table with a group of strangers turned out to be quite pleasant and not at all the ordeal that he had feared. Mrs Middleton had been so friendly towards him and he found that this was always good for his own confidence. He felt he was fitting in to this new world. That was the thing about shyness – you felt you didn't belong. And so you didn't want to draw attention to yourself. It was so stupid, of course, because by being shy, you drew enormous attention to yourself.

The other guests were all holidaymakers, but since Mrs Middleton had fed the children at an earlier sitting, there were only adults at the table. Also, since the guest house was quite big there were actually three long tables in the dining room. Lewis sat at a table with six others. Happily, the issue of his Army service came up almost immediately and, this time, in a very pleasant way.

There was a couple in their fifties, and as soon as Lewis sat down, the man said, 'So – you're on your own young man. Finished school, are you?'

'Yes, sir,' said Lewis, 'I'm eighteen on the tenth of November and I'll be joining up then.'

'I say, well done, young feller. That's the spirit. So you've got a few months to enjoy yourself before you go.'

'Yes, sir.'

'Wine, women and song, eh?'

'George!' said his wife admonishingly.

But she was smiling. Lewis could see she adored her husband.

'Do you think I've come to the right place?' asked Lewis.

He wondered if the man would think he was being too cheeky.

'Of course, you have. No place like Cornwall, is there, Mrs Middleton?'

The landlady had just swept in from the kitchen carrying a large tureen of soup.

'What's that, m'dear?'

'Our brave young man here will be going off to France in November. I was telling him that there's no better place than Cornwall to enjoy himself before he goes.'

'No, no better place at all,' she agreed.

She reached in over their heads and placed the tureen on some cork mats in the centre of the table.

'Now – help yourselves, m'loves.'

'George – call me George' – turned out to be a bit like Lewis' Dad. He did just what Dad would have done – involving everybody in the conversation, asking just enough about them to appear interested but not nosy. When the wine came, he got the table to drink a toast to 'brave Lewis'. Lewis enjoyed the evening immensely and the memory of the morning in the station began to fade. He was exhausted when he finally fell into bed and slept the sleep of the dead.

Next morning, he was up early and came down to breakfast just after seven. The dining room was deserted. Everybody else seemed to be lying in, but Lewis was anxious to go off and begin exploring. Mrs Middleton was already up and about and Lewis ordered from her. As she brought in a plate of delicious smelling sausages, bacon and eggs, she said, 'I don't know if you needed to know about the church, Mr Friday, it being Sunday and all, but the first service is at eight. You should just be able to make it after you've eaten. If you want to, that is, of course.'

Church had been the farthest thing from Lewis' mind, but he took Mrs Middleton's remarks as an instruction rather than information. After breakfast, he headed out the front door following the directions she had given him.

The air smelled of tar and rope and tidewater. At this hour birds still owned the town. Overhead seagulls laughed shrilly or ba-ba-barped. On a slipway, swans preened themselves while mallards moved among them or sat concentrating silently. Ahead of him in the street, two seagulls were having a tug-of-war with a brown paper bag. The contents suddenly spilled out and they dived into it, oblivious to Lewis as he stepped past them. He went down to the quayside before going into the church. There, on the top rail of an iron railing, a dark coloured bird sat, looking out at the estuary and the low sun, singing beautifully.

It was just before eight as he entered. A small crowd of mostly elderly people was scattered around the seats. The organist was playing. The interior was cool and had a musty, watery smell to it. Lewis took a seat midway up the church just to the right of the centre aisle. He hadn't really intended to do this, this morning but he had already resolved – once the trip itself had been decided on – that he would explore every junction in the road, every seemingly interesting doorway, every seemingly random event that happened. As Mrs Middleton had opened this particular doorway, he had just stepped through.

As the congregation waited for the vicar to emerge, Lewis heard, from behind him, the sound of heels on the paving stones of the church. He glanced to his left and was just in time to see a woman walk past. He felt a tiny gust of perfume as she did so. He saw the curve of a cheek, an eyelash and heard the rustle of the material of her dress. In contrast with most of the other occupants of the church, she was brightly dressed. She was slim and wore a white, long-sleeved dress that came down to her calves. The sleeves were made of see-though, lacy material so he could see the outline of her arms. Beneath the wide brim of her hat with its orange ribbon, her hair was blonde and tumbled onto her shoulders. He watched her hips as her heels clicked on the flagstones. She chose a pew not quite at the front and six rows ahead of Lewis. She stepped in. He watched as she knelt, bowed her head and stayed like this for several minutes. Then she sat back on the seat with her spine very straight and waited with everybody else for the vicar to appear.

Lewis watched her for the rest of the service. The hat covered much of the back of her head so that only a few curls of golden hair peeped out here and there. There were the tiniest of indentations on each of the shoulders of her dress. He assumed these were from the straps of whatever she wore underneath. He wondered what her face was like and willed her to turn so that he could see it. He wondered whether she was alone – or had a husband – and whether he was at the Front. And did she have children? And where did she live? From the brief glimpse he had had of her, he thought she might have been in her thirties. She sat, knelt and stood at the various points during the service but always with her head facing forward. He thought she might be singing the hymns instead of mouthing them as Lewis was doing, but it was impossible to tell from the back. Only when the vicar spoke from the pulpit did she turn slightly to the left where the pulpit was, but even then her hair obscured any view he might have had of her face.

Finally, the last hymn was sung and people began to file out of the church. Now he would see her, when she got up to go. But instead of leaving she just sat back down. He waited in the hope that this would only be for a short period of time. But the time dragged on and the church emptied. Still she sat there. The vicar returned from having greeted his parishioners outside the front door and disappeared into the back of the church. The place was echoingly empty now except for the pair of them. But still she didn't move. Finally, tiring of the whole business, Lewis got up and walked out into the sunshine.

He went back to Mrs Middleton's, changed his clothes and put on boots more suited to walking. He went to a shop and bought some bread, cheese and a bottle of lemonade. Having placed these in his pack, which also contained a large scale map of the area and a compass, he headed off to explore. It would be his first 'route march'.

By the end of the day, he reckoned that he had covered about ten miles. He hadn't particularly pushed himself – he would do that on later walks. Rather he had been happy to explore and find out what was where and get a sense of the place. He had stood on three beaches – Readymoney, Pridmouth and Polkerris. Readymoney – the beach Mum had told him about all those years ago. He had climbed to the top of the Gribben Head. A local man he met there told him that the red and white striped marker was nearly a hundred feet high and had been erected in the last century to guide mariners into Fowey. Beside the Gribben, overlooking the sea and bathed in sunshine, Lewis ate his sandwiches and drank his lemonade. Afterwards, he took off his shirt and lay on the grass and dozed and only the build up of heat on his skin woke him. Then, rousing himself, he struck inland and later turned eastwards to arrive back in Fowey around six.

The woman in the church came back into his head over dinner. He wondered where she was tonight. What was her name and what had she been thinking about in the church? Some great happiness? Or sadness? He wondered what was she like and tried to imagine her personality based on what he had seen of her.

She wasn't shy – that was certain. He could tell from the way she had entered the church that she was confident, her own woman. She dressed how she liked. She dressed so that she looked good – and she knew that people noticed. He wondered about where she lived. Was her house very tidy? He imagined that it was – that she would have been very clean and neat. He thought she was probably very relaxed, happy, easy going. She laughed and smiled a lot and probably had a beautiful smile. She would have had no time for those stupid women in Paddington yesterday. What would she have done if confronted by them? Probably dismissed them with some withering remark.

'So what did our young soldier do today?'

Lewis suddenly realised that George was speaking to him. Before he could think of anything to say, George answered his own question.

'Met a young lady, by the look of things.'

Everybody at the table laughed and, to his own surprise, Lewis wasn't embarrassed or didn't blush. Instead he smiled and said, 'Now that would be telling, wouldn't it?'

'Oooh,' exclaimed George's wife to more laughter.

'That's right, lad,' said George. 'Don't you be telling any of these people your business.'

Then he added with a big wink, 'You can tell me later in the bar.'

As Lewis was going up the stairs later he found the woman in the church coming back into his head yet again. He pictured her in bed now or getting ready for it. What did she wear in bed? Did she wear the same long white nighties that Mum wore when he was a child? Did she brush her hair out as Mum did as she got ready for bed? Did the woman in the church have a job, he wondered. Or was she rich and maybe just came down here for the summer? Maybe they had that in common – just here for the summer. He had decided she probably did live alone. Or maybe it was that he hoped she did. He didn't want to think of there being a man in her life. Of course, he thought, he would probably never find out the answers to any of these questions. But that didn't stop him thinking about her right up to the time he fell asleep.

Some time during the night he woke from a dream. He was laughing. Not just laughing silently but laughing out loud – a noise that sounded almost sacrilegious in the silence of the guest house and the dark harbour outside. The women from Paddington were in the dream. They had surrounded him and were trying to give him white feathers. But it wasn't a nightmare, and he wasn't frightened or embarrassed. Instead, as several hands were extended, pushing feathers towards him, he said, 'Ladies, could I suggest you take your white feathers, insert them in your generous bottoms and fly away home.'

After his laughter had died down – and it took a while, because every time he thought about it he laughed again – he lay for a long time looking up at the ceiling. Dreams came from the heart of you, the real part of you, the essence of you. Mum always said that. And this was who he was – this was his essence. He wasn't shy and blushing all the time. He was funny, confident, not taking life too seriously. 'Ladies, could I suggest you take the white feathers ...' was what she – the woman in the church – would have said if she had been faced with the same predicament. He needed to remember this. He *would* remember this. Now if only he could hold onto it.

5

*L*ewis drew his pistol and looked up at the parapet but all he could see was the low sandbag wall. Above it the mist and oncoming darkness were mixing to form an opaque soup. The tinkling went silent but then it started again. Oh Jesus, oh Jesus, not now, please not now. Along the fire bay, a few paces away, a sentry, standing on the fire step with his rifle out through a loophole in the sandbags, tensed. Lewis was sweating now despite the cold. The lice, pleased with the rise in body temperature, began to fan out. He felt them down the arms of his tunic.

'What can you see, Wilson?' he asked the sentry, trying to keep the panic out of his voice.

'Nothing, sir.'

The bully beef tins tinkled again. Oh sweet Christ.

There was a pair of loopholes, side by side. Lewis stood on the fire step and looked out through the second one. With the fog and darkness it was like looking into a bag. Oh Jesus, they were coming and without any bombardment. A surprise raid. There would be grenades first and then hand-to-hand, knives, bayonets. Oh Christ, oh Christ. How could Wilson be so calm? He had been in France much longer than Lewis – since 1915. There was some small arms fire further down the trench line. Sweet Jesus, they were in the trench.

'Think it's just the breeze, sir,' said Wilson, calmly.

'What breeze?'

Lewis hadn't meant to snap but it had come out like that. He felt Wilson turn sideways to look at him.

'Breeze's come up, sir. Can't you feel it?'

And now Lewis did. A foul-smelling breath of air wafted in through the loophole.

'Just the bloody breeze,' he heard Wilson chuckle to himself. 'Bloody breeze.'

Wilson relaxed his finger on the trigger and then his whole body relaxed as he settled back to gazing through the loophole.

'Should clear the mist anyway,' he said, contentedly.

Lewis got down from the fire step. He had been windy and Wilson had seen it.

Lewis had never been this frightened before. It was all these rumours of the end of the War. The thing was that men would die between now and whatever day the War finally did end. He had seen one go only this morning – Winter – half his face sliced off by a white-hot shell fragment that then lodged, still smoking, in what remained of his head. And men would continue to die after that – through accidents, unexploded bombs, booby traps – the Germans had been spreading them about liberally as they retreated. Lewis didn't want to die now.

Could it be conceivably possible that they were living through its last few weeks? Most men, including Lewis, believed that the only end that would come would be *their* end. They felt that sooner or later everything would go black from a bullet or they would be vaporised by a shell and that would be how the War would end. It was virtually impossible to believe that this huge machine that had been running for more than four years would itself, stop. Impossible to believe it actually *could* be stopped.

The cold was becoming too much. He stamped his feet to try to get some warmth or circulation back into them. He would finish the cigarette and go and write to Helen.

Even though he couldn't be with her for her birthday he had wanted to celebrate it. Apart from sending her some gifts he had bought in Amiens, he had just wanted a quiet day that he could spend thinking about her. And today *had* been relatively quiet – that's if you could call the on-off artillery duel between the British and the retreating Germans quiet. It was quiet, he supposed, in the sense that only one shell had landed in his sector – the one that had killed Winter.

He had wanted a little bit of beauty – a sign that it still existed in the world and something that might remind him of her. He had hoped there might be a sunset – pink seen through diaphanous blue maybe or enraged reds and oranges like a forge of the gods or the passion of lovers. But there had been no sky today and now the trench was becoming dark and vile and sewer smelling. He still hoped that some hot food would come up from the rear and he would have that with a few inches of whiskey that remained in a bottle Dad had sent.

The dugout Lewis occupied had been built by Germans and was like the Ritz in comparison to its British counterparts. The Germans built theirs as though they were staying, the British as if they were passing through. It was a delusion which had lasted three and a half years, and which the red tabs at GHQ had finally only abandoned when the Germans began to retreat in the spring. The dugout had a tongued and grooved ceiling, floor boards, wood panelling and had once boasted electric light, though this no longer worked since the Germans had blown up the generator. A bunk that wouldn't have looked out of place on a ship was in an alcove on one wall. The place was dry, warm in comparison to the arctic conditions outside and – so far – had proved free of rats' nests. Some food and drink and time to reflect on the fact that he might now survive the War and have a life after it – that was the sort of birthday he wanted. And there might even be some letters – from Dad or Helen – brought up with the food.

He threw the cigarette butt onto the duckboard where it fizzled out in small pool of water in the mud. He was just reaching for the gas curtain that hung across the entrance to the dugout when a soldier appeared around the corner of the trench, came towards him and saluted. In the dusk it took Lewis a moment to recognise that it was Byrne again.

'Got a message for you, sir. Got it from one of the C.O.'s runners on the way back. C.O. wants to see you, sir. In his command post at six pip emma.'

Lewis felt his hand start to shake again. He straightened up and he clamped it to his side. He was suddenly sweaty again – and he was angry – very, very angry.

'He didn't happen to say why, did he?'

It came out almost as a snarl.

'No, sir.'

'But you know anyway, Byrne, don't you?'

'Yessir.'

'And?'

'Trench raid, sir. Tonight.'

Now, the anger ignited.

'A trench raid? For Christ's sake, the Huns are running back to Berlin as fast as their legs will carry them. What possible reason could there *possibly* be for a bloody trench raid?'

'Dunno, sir. Orders from above, sir?'

Lewis extinguished his anger. There was no point in it. Not in front of the men. They just thought you were windy. Instead he reached once again for humour. The restorative properties were powerful – they restored both him and the men around him. There was a time when he had given of it freely. But now that well was almost dry. Now, whenever he drew from it, he wondered whether any would remain, whether these few drops might not be the last. And he found himself resenting the fact that other people benefited from this elixir.

'Very well, thank you for the message, Byrne. You can inform Colonel Ogilvy that I shall be delighted to attend his little soiree at six o'clock.'

The faintest of smiles appeared on Byrne's face. It had

worked – as it almost always did. Lewis scraped around for a few other drops.

'Will cocktails be served?' he asked.

'Doubt it, sir.'

'No, indeed,' said Lewis, thoughtfully. 'So I suppose then Byrne, it's going to be another night requiring matchless valour, consummate strategy and a proper handling of sticks.'

'Sir?'

'Nothing Byrne. Nothing.'

'It's a quote, sir. About the "proper handling of sticks," I mean. It's a quote, isn't it?'

'It is Byrne. And if I happen to get back alive from tonight's little effort, I shall tell you what it's from.'

'I'd appreciate that, sir. Will that be all?'

Lewis nodded.

'You should probably leave now, sir. Takes nearly an hour to get here.'

'It can't take that long.'

'Mud's very heavy further back, sir.'

'And you're going there now?'

'Yessir.'

'Very well then. I'll just get my things.'

Lewis pulled the gas curtain aside and went into the dugout. In reality, there was nothing he had to get – everything he needed he had on him. But, just inside, in the dark, he whispered, 'Please Helen, protect and watch over me, so that I will leave this place in one piece.'

When he had first made up this prayer, he had said 'alive' but now he said 'in one piece'. He had seen men who in theory were 'alive' being taken away on stretchers. He didn't want it to be *that* kind of alive.

He went out to re-join Byrne.

6

*I*t was summer and they had gone for a picnic in the country – Lewis, Mum and Dad. They had been on the train and now they were swishing along a path under a canopy of trees. Pigeons cooed somewhere in the distance. Other birds twittered and called and whistled, high up in the trees or the sky. Occasionally, the bird calls sounded as though they were coming from very low down. Lewis wondered if the birds were actually on the ground and he pictured a little woodland glade with lots of birds hopping around in that jerky movement of theirs. Everything smelt green and earthy. It was cool under the trees but outside in the sun and on the train, it had been baking.

'Wouldn't be surprised if it was in the nineties today,' said Dad.

The path was bordered by ferns that were chest high on Lewis and he ran his hand through them as they went along. They rustled dryly by. He led the way, with Mum behind and Dad at the back carrying the picnic basket.

'Are you sure you know where we're going?' Mum asked.

'Of course. I used to come here when I was a boy. But not many people knew about it even then. It should be nice and quiet. I'd be surprised if there was anyone here at all here except us.'

The path between the ferns became a rutted lane of hardened, cracked mud, with grass growing up the centre and overhanging branches through which the sun shone. Lewis ran ahead through the dappled patches of light.

'Be careful, Lewis darling,' Mum called. 'Mind you don't trip.'

'I will,' he called back.

The track ended but there was a path off to the left through some more ferns. They followed this and came out at a wide stream which they crossed on a bridge made of railway sleepers. The sides of the bridge consisted of rusty iron railings driven into the wood. A ruined building of grey stone clothed in ivy stood on the far side amongst the trees. It had once been a mill, Dad explained and they walked around to the other side to see the mill race. Nettles and bushes and a sapling choked what remained of the wheel, a skeleton of damp decaying wood.

Close by, shaded somewhat by the canopy of trees, there was a grassy bank dotted with daisies.

'What do you reckon, me hearties – good spot for a picnic?'

'It's a handy cove, Dad.'

'It is, lad. It's a handy cove, indeed.'

Dad sprawled at full length on the grass. He lay on his back and closed his eyes. Mum lifted up the lid of the wicker picnic basket. It had compartments for different things, and straps for holding plates and bottles. Lewis had helped Mum pack it this morning, carefully stowing things in their places.

'I'd forgotten you had that basket, Susan,' said Dad.

'I bought it the first summer after I finished school. I had made some money from my dressmaking and thought it would be a good thing to have. I thought I'd be having lots of picnics with friends. To the beach. Into the country. That sort of thing.'

'And instead you met me,' he said.

'That's right,' she said. 'I did.'

Mum shook out the table cloth and spread it. Then she took out all the mysterious packets one by one and arranged their contents in due order. When everything was ready, she said, 'Now, pitch in, everybody.'

Lewis helped himself while Mum asked Dad what he wanted in his sandwich. There was a bottle of white wine and Dad opened it. Mum took a little; Dad emptied his first glass and refilled it.

Afterwards Dad played with Lewis, rolling him down the

bank and then tumbling after him to knock him down just as he was getting to his feet. Lewis screamed with delight and Dad shook with laughter. Mum was lying on her elbow watching them when suddenly Dad ran up the bank, lifted her up in his arms and carried her to the edge of it.

'No, you're not throwing me down that,' she squealed. 'You'll ruin my skirt.'

'Come on,' he said, 'it's your turn.'

'No, Nick. No.'

She had sounded serious when he had first lifted her but now she began to laugh.

'Everybody's had their turn. It's yours now.'

'No please, stop,' said Mum, laughing uncontrollably.

Dad placed her gently in a lying position on the edge of the bank. Mum was laughing too much to resist. Then he pushed her and she tumbled down. He rolled down after her so that he ended up beside her. Through her laughter, she said, 'My hair. It's ruined. And look at my blouse.'

'Never mind your blouse,' he said, 'give us a kiss.'

She did.

'I love you,' Lewis heard Dad say softly.

He kissed her again and this time, they let it go on. Loudly and theatrically, Lewis said 'Uhhh!'

7

*L*ewis had always hated Mondays; hated that doom that descended on him on Sunday night knowing that he was going through the last few hours of the weekend before school on Monday. So today, a Monday when there was no longer any school, when a golden summer beckoned and an empty book waited to have its pages filled up – he had written this in his diary that morning – there was only one thing for it – a day on the beach.

In his room, he put two of the three books he had brought with him into his pack: *Greenmantle* by John Buchan and *The Drama of Three Hundred and Sixty Five Days: Scenes in the Great War* by Hall Caine. Mrs Middleton had made him two Cornish pasties – one for lunch and a second one, with apple in it for dessert. With these and a bottle of lemonade, he headed off towards Readymoney.

He had come here yesterday with a strange mixture of anticipation and excitement and wonder. His Mum had been here, as a little girl, with her parents. As he got closer, past the grey stone house with its imposing gateway and then down the gentle hill towards the beach, he thought of her here. He pictured her holding her mum's hand and chattering excitedly as they got nearer and the smell of the sea got stronger. How carefree she must have been then – and full of life.

Readymoney. Boats pulled up on the beach while a ship rode at anchor just offshore. Masts and sails and the black hulk of the vessel in the starlight. Lanterns swaying in the darkness; dark figures unloading boats; the jingle of gold coins. Readymoney. You could see how suited the place was to such nocturnal undertakings.

The cove was shaped like it was embraced between two arms of land. He imagined Mum standing here catching her first glimpse of the beach and the speckled sunlight on the water. How thrilled she must have been. He pictured her wonderment at the sensation of sand under her feet – at first warm, powdery, yielding and then damp and hard-packed. He saw her playing on the sand, paddling in the water, running in and out and squealing because of its coldness.

It was like a circle – Mum had come here, and then there had been *Treasure Island* and now he was here himself. The circle closed. He felt very close to her. He saw the little girl on the beach, sitting in the sand in her summer clothes with a bucket and spade all those years ago. Readymoney had probably changed very little since she had been here.

It occurred to him that the course her life had taken from that day had probably not been at all what she had intended. Of course, neither would his be now. Was that how life worked? There were things you wanted to do, things you wanted to achieve in your life. No, no – it wasn't so much achievement. It was about happiness. That was it. You wanted to find happiness. The same happiness that the little girl with her skirts spreading out around her on the sand knew. But how did you do that? And did anyone ever? Maybe the problem was just that you grew up and entered the adult world with all its difficulties and complications and unknowns. Or maybe it was that life just had a way of taking you and tossing you around and doing what it wanted with you.

Still, it had been strange and wonderful to stand here yesterday. A moment of almost mystical significance and closeness to her and communication with her, was what he had written in his diary.

Today was another day of blue sky and Lewis was one of the first to arrive. The tide was out. He chose a spot over on the right, roughly halfway between the back of the beach and the sea. He had put on his swimsuit beneath his clothes so now he was able to take down his trousers, unbutton his shirt and he was ready. He rolled out his towel, lay down and opened John Buchan.

But he couldn't stop thinking about the little girl on the beach. Was it that she hadn't known what she wanted, that she didn't know what would make her happy? Was that the problem – that we tried certain things hoping or expecting that they would make us happy? Sometimes they did but more often they turned out to be not what we wanted after all. And what then? You'd made your bed so lie in it? Or move on and do something different? At least Mum had had choices, he supposed. With this War, he – his generation – were being given none.

He picked up his book again. Best not to think about all this. Anyway, it was only the third of July – lots could happen between now and his birthday on the tenth of November. And lots more before he might actually be trained and shipped to France and in danger. Best just to enjoy the day.

He spent it in and out of the water. He would read for half an hour or so. By then his body was so hot that he would have to run into the water to cool off. Then it was back to the book again. By lunchtime the beach had filled up and he was ravenous.

He was sitting up, eating the first of his pasties, looking at the sun on the water when he saw a figure walk down towards the sea. She wore a floppy straw hat, a flouncy white skirt that came down below her knees and a white blouse. She carried a straw basket with the handles looped over her shoulder. She was barefoot and her shoes were in her hand. There was something about her that looked vaguely familiar but it took him a few moments before he realised that it was the woman from the church. He hadn't realised how tall she was. She found what she seemed to think was a good spot – it was pretty much in the centre of the beach – took a towel from her bag and rolled it out. She was closer to the sea than Lewis and probably twenty yards away with her back to him. Her hands went to the side of her skirt where she undid something and then she stepped out of it to reveal the trousers of a neck-to-knee swimsuit in a mauve colour. She unbuttoned the blouse and removed it showing the swimsuit's top with its round neck and sleeves that came down to just above the elbows. Then she took a swimming cap from her bag, and with what seemed like one deft movement, she rolled her blonde hair up into a bun and slipped the cap down over it. She walked across the sand, into the water and, when it was up to her thighs, plunged in. He saw quickly that she was a good swimmer as, after a few casual strokes, she began to swim back and forth parallel to the shore.

Lewis wrapped the partially eaten pasty back up in the brown paper it had come in, put it in his pack and stood up. He hurried into the water.

He wanted to get closer to her, to see her face. He had failed to do it yesterday but by heaven, he was going to do it today. At some stage she would stop swimming and go to get out of the water and then he needed to be close enough to her. But right now she was showing no sign of stopping and continued to plough back and forth. Lewis decided that he would do the same and he would stay closer to the shore than she was, so that he could intercept her, if he had to. As casually as possible and when the water was up to his waist, he slid into its cooling embrace.

He stayed a bit behind her so that she wouldn't feel that he was following her and pulled through the water. Up ahead he saw her turn. He went on for a few strokes more and then turned himself. He had just taken a stroke or two and she was a good eight or ten yards ahead of him, when she suddenly turned to her right and began to make for the shore. He had to keep going himself. Otherwise it would have been obvious that he was following her. He swam a few more strokes and then stopped and allowed himself to sink and his feet to touch the sand. By this time she was already standing up. The bits of her arms that showed, were brown from the sun. She waded out of the water and back to where her towel was. Lewis waded out himself. She pulled off her bathing cap and shook out her hair. Then she began to dry herself with the towel. He tried not to look directly at her. He could hardly walk past where she was so he headed to where his things were. When he did look over at her, he saw that she had lain face down on her towel and was basking in the sun.

She didn't go into the water again after that. At least not that Lewis saw. But at some time during the afternoon, the heat of the day caused him to nod off. His head dropped onto the book and he dozed for what would afterwards turn out to be over an hour. When he woke, she was gone.

8

The church bell tolled six o' clock.

'Goodness, is that the time. I must put your father's dinner on.'

'Can we read some more?' asked Lewis.

'Not today. Tomorrow. Promise.'

Mum went into the kitchen and put on her apron.

'Want to help me peel some potatoes?' she asked.

'Yes please,' said Lewis. He pulled one of the kitchen chairs away from the table and half carried, half dragged it across the floor to the sink. Just then, they heard the front door open, some steps in the hallway and then the kitchen door opened.

'Hello me old mates!'

'Daddy!'

Lewis rushed into his father's arms. Dad lifted him up and carried him over to where Mum was bent down, taking a dish from the cupboard. She straightened up, turned slightly towards Dad and proffered her cheek which he kissed.

Mum made dinner consisting of steak and kidney pie, peas from her small vegetable patch and potatoes, yellow with butter. Lewis had a grown up knife and fork and he manipulated them awkwardly.

'How are things at work?' asked Mum.

'I've made quota – and it's only the twentieth.'

'That's wonderful. You'll be able to go a bit easier now.'

'Oh, you can't really rest in our business, you know. If you do, someone will get in ahead of you. If you're not going forwards you're going backwards – all that sort of thing.'

'I was down at Turners today. Mr Turner asked if we could clear some of his account.'

'Tell him that the commission I get this month will more than pay his bill.' Robert poured himself some more of the bottle of wine he had brought. He offered some to Mum but she declined, covering her still half-full glass with her hand.

'We said that last month, and even though we paid off some of his bill, we owe him more now than we did then.'

'I don't know where all the money goes. I'd have thought I must have one of the best paid jobs of anyone around here.'

'Perhaps if you could let me have some more for the house-keeping.'

Dad lowered his knife and fork and placed them carefully on either side of his plate.

'There isn't any more. I'm working like a dog as it is.'

'I know you are, dear, but I can show you the bills.'

'Never mind the bills,' he said angrily, 'The bills are your responsibility. I'm bringing in all I can. Maybe you should have married that accountant fellow. Maybe he could have made the pennies go further, though quite frankly, I don't see how.'

'Perhaps if you didn't go to the pub quite so often.'

Lewis glanced at Mum's face. She seemed to have shrunk.

'You were in there this evening, for example.'

'Christ, you'd think I was a bloody alcoholic the way you go on. Yes, I sometimes go to the pub for a drink and yes, I was there this evening. I've made quota half way through the month and I was having a small celebration. Do you begrudge me that? Do you?'

Dad seemed to have forgotten his dinner now. The plate looked like a boat, the knife and fork like two oars dangling over the side.

'Some of the fellows in there never make quota. I do – consist-ently. Do you think that's easy? I'd like to see you roll into that bloody office on the first of each month, with an empty order book, and wondering where in God's name, in the tiny territory I have, I'm going to find enough people to buy bloody bacon slicers. Just how many bacon slicers do you think one shop will buy? And yet I do it – month after month after bloody month.'

Mum spoke very softly.

'Look, why can't we talk about this reasonably? I was just saying —'

'I know what you were just saying. You were just saying that I drink all my salary while you and Lewis here starve. That's what you were saying. And I won't have it. What do you think keeps this roof over your head? I work as hard as any man, harder than most; and if what I bring in isn't enough to keep you in the style to which you've become accustomed, then I don't know what is.'

Dad pushed back his chair. It grated harshly on the black and white linoleum squares of the kitchen floor. He stood up and stormed out of the kitchen. They heard his heavy footsteps on the stairs. Lewis looked at Mum. At first she wouldn't meet his eyes, and when she did, he thought she just looked sad and broken. A short while later the front door banged. Lewis continued looking at Mum, wanting her to say something. Eventually, she did.

'It's all right, my darling. Daddy's just tired. Finish up your dinner, there's a good boy.'

Lewis thought Mum looked like she was going to cry. He put his head down and resumed eating.

Mum said, 'Excuse me a moment, my love – I just need to go to the bathroom.'

She disappeared and Lewis sat at the table by himself. He remembered that bit in *Treasure Island* where Jim's father used to ask the captain for money and then wring his hands when he was refused. It was like that now, except that Mum was the one who was being rebuffed.

9

*L*ewis returned to Readymoney the next day in the hope that she might be there. But for that day and for several days after there was no sign of her. He knew it was a silly obsession. The woman was a stranger; she was old enough to be his mother, he suspected. But he just wanted to see her face. After that he would be satisfied and would let it go. Anyway, it had become a 'mission' – at least that's the way he had been thinking about it. He couldn't fail on his first mission as a soldier. It would set a bad precedent, be a bad omen for the future.

After three days in a row at Readymoney, he thought that maybe she was frequenting one of the other beaches. Maybe she had only been trying out Readymoney and maybe the swimming or something there wasn't to her liking. So the next day he tried Pridmouth and Polruan the day after that, but there was no sign of her. Eventually, towards the end of the week, he was getting fed up of the whole silly business.

It was Monday, a week since he had first seen her. He had gone for a long walk, returning along the coast. It was just before five as he was passing Readymoney. The day was hot, he was sweaty and the chance of a cooling swim before dinner was too good to pass up. He had packed his swimsuit and a towel, just in case, so he went down to the beach. Because it was getting close to teatime, it wasn't as crowded as it had been the previous times he had been here. There were people leaving, carrying their things and heading homewards.

And there she was – sitting on her towel, in the mauve bathing suit, blonde hair loose, looking out to sea. Lewis went down the beach and positioned himself about twenty yards away on her right and slightly behind her. He tried to give the impression that he had just chosen the spot at random. He made a skirt with the towel and changed into his swimsuit. If she was aware of what he was doing she gave no sign as she continued to gaze out at the sun-drenched water.

Lewis ran past her into the sea and dived in. He hoped she was watching him. He swam a few strokes with his face down in the water, revelling in the coolness. But when he stood up, he saw to his dismay that she had already packed up her things and was walking up the beach. He hurried out of the water. By the time he reached his towel she had bent down and was putting on her shoes. As he lifted up the towel and shook off the sand, she straightened up. The she turned to the right towards Fowey and was gone.

The next day he came in the morning and she arrived about mid-day. He knew now that he wasn't going to let today go until he had seen her face. She went into the water several times, as did he. Sometimes he went in when she did. But when this happened he was sure to stay ten or fifteen yards away from her. Sometimes he went in first, as though doing so would entice her in. Finally, as it was getting close to tea time and he knew she would be disappearing soon, he decided on a bolder course of action. She was sitting on her towel on the sand and he was in the water. He had gone in one last time in the hope that she would follow him in but it hadn't worked. Now, daringly, he came out of the water and walked towards where she sat reading. He saw his shadow on the sand. As he did so and as he got closer she looked up.

He saw fine skin, pale lips, the blonde hair, the eyes shadowed beneath the straw hat. She was sitting with her left knee flat on the sand, her right knee raised and her elbow resting on it. She held the book in her lap with her left hand. He wondered what she was reading.

And then she smiled. Smiled at him. Her face which had merely seemed pretty, was suddenly the face of an angel. He knew that she must be kind and generous, warm and loving. Whoever she lived with – husband or children or both – were blessed. Here was a beautiful presence in their lives. But did he also see a hint of sadness there – loneliness, perhaps or vulnerability?

He hadn't been expecting this and was too surprised to smile back. By the time it had registered with him that he should, he had walked past her. He looked back and saw her head bow as she returned to her book. He had let her down. She had shown friendliness towards him and he hadn't returned it. What a fool. Dad would probably have walked back at this point. He would have apologised, said that his mind was elsewhere. They would have begun to talk. In no time at all, Dad would have been sitting on the sand beside her or asking her to come for a drink, more likely.

Lewis couldn't bring himself to do that. He knew he should but he couldn't. And so later, she stood up, packed up her things and, without looking in his direction, went away. He felt crushed and spent the rest of the evening brooding over his failure. She must think him cold and unfriendly. Or was she wise enough to understand how it was to be a seventeen year old? What had she been like at that age? He tried to picture a younger, more willowy version of her. He couldn't imagine her uncertain and shy. To be born beautiful like that must mean you were always confident. He replayed what had happened endlessly in his head and imagined how it should and could have been so different.

The next day they were both there again. Again, just as yesterday, he waited until late to walk near to where she sat. Again she looked up and again, to his immense relief and wonder, she smiled at him. This time he smiled back. Their eyes held for Lewis knew not what amount of time but it was a delicious feeling. Then he had walked past her.

He reached his towel in triumph. Mission accomplished. After this all he would need would be a few more days and he would start speaking to her. He suddenly realised he had a new mission. He would talk to her, just as Dad would have done. Maybe he would offer to buy her an ice cream. Yes, once he had thought of it, he had resolved that that would be his new objective.

It was about five when she packed up her things to leave. Lewis watched her movements. She was graceful. The way women moved was so different from men. He wondered what it must be like to be her, to inhabit that body. To bathe it, put clothes on it, move around in it throughout the day, lay it down at night to sleep? He pictured her sleeping, hair scattered on the pillow.

She walked up the beach, without looking to right or left. His eyes followed her. Now that she was leaving, there was no point in his staying and so Lewis began to get dressed himself. She turned to the right, past the low stone wall topped with ivy. Then she came to the taller wall of the big grey house and was gone from view. He finished dressing, put everything into his pack and made his way back up the beach to the road. Maybe she was walking into Fowey and he could walk behind her. Or catch up with her? Did he dare to talk to her? But on what pretext?

He turned the way she had gone and there, a couple of hundred yards up the road, he saw her. She was standing, looking down at a bicycle which leant against the high grey stone wall. As he walked towards her she squatted down putting a hand on the front wheel. His heart was pounding. As he got nearer, he could see that the front tyre was flat. She looked up.

She had green eyes, high cheekbones and lips that were parted slightly. Her teeth were very white and peeped out through bright red lipsticked lips. Her face looked inexpressibly kind. Lewis thought that he had never seen anyone more beautiful – not even his mother. Should he walk past her or say hello? It seemed ridiculous on this deserted road with just the two of them that he should just pass her by. But he was suddenly terrified by the prospect of speaking to her. In the end, the decision was taken out of his hands, when she smiled and said, 'Hello. I'm afraid my tyre is gone flat. I think it must be punctured. Do you know if there's a place in Fowey where I can get it fixed?'

A small furrow of worry showed between her eyebrows.

'I could probably fix it for you,' he said.

He had blurted out the words before thinking. It was true that he knew how to fix a puncture because Dad had shown him how to do it. Lewis wasn't normally good at things like that, but he had enjoyed watching his father going through the various steps of the operation. It had all seemed very simple – and there were some very clever bits in it. And this was the *front* tyre which made it a bit less complicated.

'Could you really?' she said.

Her voice was gentle and tender and hopeful.

'I think so. I know what to do. Do you have a puncture repair kit?'

She thought for a moment.

'Yes, I do. I got it when I bought the bike.'

'Alright then. Here, let me wheel it for you.'

'Oh, you're so kind … Mister?'

'Lewis. I mean Lewis is my first name. Lewis Friday.'

She held out a hand.

'Helen Hope.'

Lewis took her hand in his. Her grip was firm but the skin and fingers felt warm and soft.

'I'm renting a house just up here,' she said, indicating the hill that rose away from the sea. 'It's only a couple of minutes. Oh, I do hope I'm not taking you too far out of your way. Or delaying you.'

Lewis was struck by the fact that she was treating him as an adult, even though he felt more like a youngster in the presence of a grown-up. Her skin was pale and peachy under the straw hat. He guessed her to be in her early thirties.

'No, it's no trouble. I'm staying in town.'

'So you're on holiday?'

'Yes.'

'Are you here with your family?'

'No, by myself. My Dad suggested I come down here for the summer.'

And then he added, to put the issue out of the way as quickly as possible.

'I'll be eighteen in November and joining the Army. I'm just really waiting until then. I don't know – it's the calm before the storm, fattening me up for the kill, that sort of thing.'

'Oh, don't say that,' she said. 'I think you're very brave.'

'Or very stupid. One of our neighbour's sons was killed in 1915 – and another came home blind.'

Her hand went up to her mouth. She had perfect nails – Lewis always bit or picked at his.

'I shouldn't like to die,' he said lightly. 'I like living.'

'Yes, it's nice,' she said, 'isn't it?'

Again that smile. He would do anything for that smile. He hoped now that he would be able to fix the tyre. He didn't want to make a mess of it or find out a few days later that he hadn't done it properly. He suddenly felt fearful. How good he would feel if he could do this for this goddess – and how terrible if he failed.

10

*I*t was dark and fetid in the trench as Lewis followed Byrne back to the battalion command post. The occasional lantern, hanging from an iron stake driven into the trench wall, gave inadequate light. There was the acute smell of a sewer but added to that the chronic, sweet smell of things rotting. Away, in the distance the artillery grumbled and crashed as it always did and occasional flashes made the fog lighter from time to time. Was it Lewis' imagination or was it thinning?

Jesus Christ, a bloody trench raid. Oh Christ. Lewis had a bad feeling about this. Why couldn't those stupid staff bastards just call it a day? Why did they have to go on killing people? Hadn't enough men died? In a few more weeks it could be all over. What was the fucking point of a trench raid? What possible difference could it make?

'Mind the sump, sir,' called Byrne, in a monotone.

Lewis stopped, looked down, just about saw the waterlogged hole in the trench floor and stepped across it.

He tried to subdue the anger he felt. It only clouded things. Made you miss details and out here, missing any detail, no matter how small could be fatal. He patted his tunic pocket through his greatcoat just to reassure himself that he had his notebook.

'Telephone cable overhead, sir.'

Byrne lifted some cables that were draped across the trench and handed them back to Lewis. He took them, stepped under them and dropped them back where they'd been. Lewis would concentrate on the briefing. He would get through this. He wasn't going to die now.

'Low trench, sir – possible sniper.'

'In this weather, Byrne?'

Lewis ducked anyway, following Byrne's lead. A few moments later Lewis tripped on something and put his hand against the wall of the trench to keep his balance. He had expected his leather gloved hand to land against wooden revetting but instead it sank up to his wrist in some malodorous mush in the trench wall. Whatever it was leaked inside Lewis' glove and the smell came with him the rest of the way, despite taking off the glove and trying to shake out whatever was in there.

The battalion command post was in a dugout near the reserve line. Stepping inside, Lewis found himself in a single room that contained one undamaged chair and a table upon which two storm lanterns burned. Some maps lay scattered on the table along with some glasses, a revolver and an almost full bottle of whiskey that glowed golden in the lamplight. The place smelt of sweat and paraffin and bad breath and faintly of whiskey. Colonel Ogilvy, the CO was there along with Major West and three other lieutenants. With his tall, thin frame like a stork, thinning hair and glasses perched on the end his nose, Colonel Ogilvy had the air of a school principal. Major West had black hair, a black moustache and a swarthy complexion that made him look like a pirate.

'That's everybody,' somebody said.

'Very well, let's make a start,' said Colonel Ogilvy. 'Major West?'

The sound of the artillery was much duller in here. West swished a map out from under some others, smoothed it out with his hands and weighed down the corners with the whiskey bottle, the revolver and two of the glasses. He moved the lanterns to improve the light. The map was carefully hand drawn in blue and red ink on a piece of foolscap. It showed a section of the British and German front line trenches. Even shell holes had been faithfully reproduced.

'Alright gentlemen, have a look here. Division wants us to send out a raiding party tonight.'

In this fog, thought Lewis.

West said, 'According to Division's met people, the fog is due to lift in the next hour or so. They're expecting a clear night.'

'And if it doesn't, sir?'

The speaker was Lieutenant Redman – small, reminding Lewis of a terrier – smoking a cigarette in a way that managed to make him look important.

'Lift, I mean?'

'The raid will go ahead anyway, Lieutenant.'

Lewis tried to remember what time the moon had set last night. Again West was there ahead of him. Lewis liked West. He was careful – careful with men's lives.

'There will be no moon.'

Colonel Ogilvy looked round the occupants of the room over his glasses. West continued.

'We're to enter the enemy's front line trench here' – he pointed at a spot marked 'C' on the map – 'on a frontage of about fifty yards. The objectives will be the usual. Capture prisoners, get identifications, papers, titles, any article of military use and – as always – cause havoc to the enemy.'

West sounded like he was reading from a script that he had memorised many years ago.

'Division wants to get a sense of the strength and morale of the people opposite us. You may have heard rumours of an armistice. I expect Division wants to see how real these might be.

The wire is reported to be in a broken condition but we know that Jerry renews it every night by throwing out large bundles of coiled wire. So our people will shell it with two inch mortars in the next hour or so. Oh, we also have reason to believe that they have machine guns at these points here and here.'

Of course they bloody do, thought Lewis.

'Lieutenant Redman will lead the raid.'

'Thank you, sir,' said Redman cheerily.

'Lieutenant Friday will be second in command and will lead the Body Snatching Party.'

Oh Jesus, this was going from bad to worse. Lewis had been on several trench raids before. But he had never led the Body Snatching Party. These were the men who jumped into the enemy trench and had to subdue the prisoners. It was ghastly, close quarters work, done with knives and knuckle dusters and clubs but also with fists and knees and boots and teeth. Anything could happen and the success of the trench raid was measured by what the Body Snatchers achieved. If they didn't bring back the requisite prisoners they would just be sent out again. Lewis would have to lead by example but he had hated fighting in school and had avoided it whenever he could. He had been hopeless at tackling in rugby. Tonight he would have to tackle men who were fighting for their lives.

'Lieutenant Friday?' West asked.

'Sir?'

'You'll be leading the Body Snatchers.'

'Yessir. Er, thank you, sir.

11

'Lewis. Lewis. It's me – it's Mummy. Wake up. Wake up, Lewis.'

Lewis was groggy from sleep. Where was he?

'You must come and help me – it's your father.'

She peeled back the bedclothes and he felt a wave of cold. He moaned and pulled at the blankets to try to pull them back over his shoulder, but he couldn't find them. There seemed no other option now but to wake up. He opened his eyes. Mum was there in her long white nightie with an anxious look on her face. He thought she looked much older than she had earlier this evening.

'I'm sorry to wake you up, luvvy,' she said, 'but I need you to help me.'

He was awake now – still a bit muzzy, but awake. She had left his light off, but the light was on in the hall and the bedroom door was open. He climbed out onto the familiar rug and then stepped from there onto the floorboards. They went out onto the landing. Lewis blinked against the bright light. He rubbed his eyes. They went down the short stairs from his bedroom at the top of the house and then across the landing until they reached the top of the main stairs. At the bottom his father lay on his back. His eyes were closed but he seemed to be awake because he was talking to himself.

'What's wrong with Daddy?'

'Come on,' said Mum.

She took his hand and they started down the stairs. As they did his father's eyes opened. He watched the two of them descend.

'He ... should ... be ... in ... bed.'

He said each of the words very slowly, as if there was some difficulty in remembering them or getting them out. The words sounded very soft and floury.

'Lewis,' he said, in the same strange way. 'You should be in bed.'

'Come on, help me lift him.'

Lewis' mum took one of Dad's arms and Lewis took the other. With Mum doing most of the lifting – Lewis found Dad was just a dead weight – they managed to get him sitting upright. Then Mum gave a huge gasp and lifted, and Dad seemed to help a little bit by shaking his arm free from Lewis' grasp and putting a hand on the floor to lever himself up. However it was done, they got him into a precarious standing position.

'We're not going to get him upstairs,' said Mum. 'Come on. In here.'

With his arm slung across Mum's shoulder, and Lewis holding Dad's hand and pushing against his leg, they managed to get him into the sitting room. They steered him to the couch and he collapsed onto it. Mum knelt down to untie his shoelaces and, as she did so, she said to Lewis, 'Fetch some blankets from the cupboard upstairs, there's a good boy.'

'You're a good boy, Lewis,' said Dad in the same funny voice he'd used earlier.

Lewis ran from the sitting room, up the stairs and returned with the blankets. By this time Dad's shoes were off, his jacket and tie were thrown on a nearby chair and he was lying on the couch, head on one arm, feet on the other. Mum arranged the blankets over him. He appeared to be sleeping already.

'Is he sick?' Lewis asked, frightened.

'No, he's not sick,' said Mum, concentrating on what she was doing.

When Mum had finished, she put an arm around Lewis and led him out of the room. She turned out the light and shut the door. They heard a snore through the door.

'No, he'll be fine now,' said Mum. 'Come on.'

He tucked in beside her as they climbed back up the stairs to his bedroom. He could feel her legs moving beneath the nightdress. She settled him back into bed and knelt there, stroking his face and hair, until he drifted off into a warm sleep.

Next morning Lewis hoped he wouldn't have to see his father. But while Lewis was eating breakfast he heard heavy steps on the stairs and then the sound of the toilet flushing. Dad came into the kitchen.

'So how're all my crew this morning?' he asked.

Lewis looked up and said, 'Fine, Dad', softly.

Mum stood at the sink with her back to them and said nothing. Dad wore his trousers and braces, slippers and a vest. His face was red and he was sweating. His black hair looked oily. Mum poured a cup of tea silently, put it at Dad's place and returned to the sink. Lewis saw that she was looking out the window. He stared at his Dad.

'I'll just have a couple of raw eggs in a glass please, Sue.'

Without indicating that she'd heard him, Mum took eggs from the cupboard and broke them into a glass. She mixed the result with a fork.

'I'll be going away for most of next week,' Dad announced. 'There's a trade show on in Newcastle. I'll have to go up there on Sunday. Probably be back on Thursday.'

Mum placed the yellowy glass in front of him and returned again to the sink and the window. Dad drank down the contents.

'You'll take care of Mummy until I get back, won't you, Lewis?'

He smelled of oily stuff on his hair, and his breath didn't smell nice.

'Yes, Dad.'

'That's a good boy.'

12

*H*elen's house was a small, two-storey cottage with a flag-stoned path all round it, a lawn of rough grass at the back and a freshly cultivated vegetable patch on one side. A gate led in from the road. Lewis wheeled the bike through the gate and round to the back door. Here there was a double line of flagstones that made a small patio. The cottage looked out over Readymoney towards the sea. He turned the bike upside down, resting it on its handlebars and saddle. He tried to feel strong and manly and knowledgeable. In fact, he was quaking. *Oh please don't let me make a mess of it. Please let it work.*

'I'll need the puncture repair kit, the pump and a bowl of water,' he said.

'Yes, doctor,' she said.

He looked at her uncertainly. Was she teasing him? But her face was smiling as though she had some secret she wasn't going to tell.

'Just kidding,' she said. 'A bowl of water?'

'Yes, a big bowl, like a washing up bowl. About three quarters full.'

'Really?' she said, grinning.

'No, really,' he said, realising that she thought *he* was joking. 'You'll see.'

And then. 'Trust me.'

It felt good to say that. She disappeared and returned almost immediately with the bowl of water. She had taken off her hat. The colour of her hair made him think of honey and gold and wheat fields towards sunset. Her face and throat were tanned.

She went inside again, he heard some drawers being opened and shut and then she was back with the puncture repair kit in a little tin box. Finally she went in a third time and brought back two glasses of lemonade on a tray and the bicycle pump under her arm.

'Do you mind if I watch?' she said.

'Not at all,' he said with a nonchalance he didn't feel. He took the lemonade and almost emptied the glass. He was very thirsty.

He got the tyre off easily and extracted the tube. He pumped it up and then put it into the bowl of water, squeezing it while running it through his hands a piece at a time.

'Why are you doing that?' she asked.

With perfect timing he saw the tiny stream of tell-tale bubbles.

'See,' he said. 'In the water. The bubbles mean there's air coming out. That's where the hole is.'

She squatted down beside him. She smelt of flowers.

'Yes, I see it,' she said. 'That's so clever'.

'It is, isn't it? My dad showed me how to do it,' he said, turning to look at her.

What perfect skin she had. He noticed the tiny lines on her lips. He wanted to keep looking. He wanted to study her face – the straight nose, the curve of her jaw. He wanted to reach out and touch her cheekbones. He felt a mad urge to kiss her.

Instead he took the tube from the water, holding his thumb on the punctured spot. Then, bending the tube around his forefinger, he blew on it until it dried. He marked the area around the hole with chalk from the repair kit. Rummaging in the little box, he found a small piece of sandpaper and sanded the area he was going to patch. Finally, he applied the glue and pressed down the patch. He stood up.

'Now we have to wait a few minutes,' he explained. 'For it to dry.'

'More lemonade, Lewis?' she asked.

It was the first time she had said his name.

'Yes please.'

'Are *you* on holiday?' he called as she disappeared into the kitchen and returned a few moments later with a jug.

'A sort of long holiday.'

He wasn't quite sure what she meant by this but before he had a chance to think about it, she said, 'So they packed you off here by yourself?'

'That's right. I'll be going away in November anyway. My Dad thought it would be a good idea for me to do this. Get used to being on my own, fending for myself, that sort of thing.'

'You probably won't be on your own much once they get you in the Army,' she said.

'No, I suppose not,' he agreed.

He didn't know what to say next, so he said. 'It doesn't take long for the glue to dry.'

'That's good.'

'Oh, and I'll need two spoons.'

She cocked her head slightly and looked at him.

'Spoons.'

It was a statement rather than a question.

'Yes, big ones. Not teaspoons. Dessert spoons or soup spoons.'

'Whatever you say,' she said, as she went back into the house, returning with the spoons.

'Now this is the tricky bit. You have to get the tube back in without pinching it between the tyre and the wheel. That could just puncture it again.'

He repositioned the tube on the rim and then, using the handles of the spoons, levered the tyre back on. He was sweating by the time he'd finished but he wasn't sure whether this was from the heat of the day or the exertion or the fear that he'd messed it up. He pumped up the tyre, squeezing it from time to time between thumb and forefinger. Finally, he was happy with it.

'You'd better test it. We should take it back out on the road.'

'Oh, we don't want to do that now,' she said. 'It's time for tea. I'll try it here.'

She stepped through the frame of the bike, her skirt fluttering. She put a foot on one of the pedals and hoisted herself onto the saddle. Wobbling crazily, she began to pedal. Terrified that he had made a mess of it, Lewis stared at the front tyre, trying to see if it held its sausage-like shape. Helen reached the corner and disappeared round it. He heard her squeal and laugh and he went to the corner. But when he reached it she had already disappeared. He turned back and a few moments later she came round the other corner of the cottage. She was beaming.

'Is it holding up?' he asked, anxiously.

'Perfect,' she said. 'You're wonderful, Lewis. Thank you.'

He felt a surge of pride and happiness. She wobbled to a halt and as the bike toppled over, she put a foot down to brace herself. She stumbled and he held out his arms to catch her and the bike. He caught it with one hand but then realised he was going to need both hands to catch her. He let the bike go just as she fell into his arms. He smelt her perfume and her hair tickled his face. He could feel her soft shape against him. For an instant he felt the soft mounds of her breasts on his chest.

She stepped back, still laughing, and he picked up the bike. They stood facing each other, the bike between them. He marvelled at her soft green eyes and the arches of her eyebrows.

'Thank you,' she said. 'You've been so kind.'

And then after a pause, 'And now, we must have tea. You'll stay, of course.'

It was more than he could have hoped for. But now he realised that he wouldn't be able to. He hadn't told Mrs Middleton that he wouldn't be back. Helen must have seen his hesitation. Her smile faded.

'Is that alright? Tea, I mean. You will stay, won't you?'

Bugger it – he would worry about Mrs Middleton later. But

when he spoke, he found himself saying, "I'd love to. It's just that well, I'm afraid I can't. You see, the place where I'm staying – I have to tell them if I won't be back for dinner. And I never told them.'

He thought he sounded like a little boy. He was stupid. He should have said nothing and just accepted and got to spend all that extra time with her. He could have dealt with Mrs Middleton later.

But Helen said, 'Oh, is that all? Well, don't worry about that. I thought you didn't want to stay.'

'No,' he blurted out. 'I'd love to. I'd love to have stayed. Could we … could we do it some other day?'

He thought he was being incredibly presumptuous. She shrugged.

'How about tomorrow, then?'

'That would be wonderful.'

'Very well then, it's all agreed. And now I'd better let you go so that you'll be back in time. We don't want to keep your landlady waiting, do we?'

He wondered if this was more teasing but there didn't appear to be any trace of it on her face.

'Will you be down on the beach?' he asked eagerly. 'Tomorrow, I mean?'

She thought for a moment.

'No, I don't think so – not tomorrow. I've got lots to do around here. Washing, tidying, that sort of thing. But never mind that. Just come up when you're finished. You know the way.'

They shook hands when he left. Lewis walked back to Mrs Middleton's in a daze of delight. He had always hoped to meet a girl when he came down here. Insofar as he had imagined her, she had probably been just finished school like him, slim with blonde hair and a pretty face. He had seen them having lots of interests in common, going for long walks around Fowey, talking endlessly, lingering in little coffee shops or watching the sun set.

But this? This was so much more than he could have hoped for – and so much better than meeting some silly girl his own age. Here was a woman who had experience of the world. She was someone from whom he could learn things and – maybe, he hoped – talk to about his innermost fears, especially the fear of what lay ahead in November. She could become his friend. They could write to each other when he was in the Army. He would probably get ragged for it, he thought with a smile. Other men would think he was writing to his girlfriend or getting letters from her. Little would they know. She could give him advice and he could talk or write to her about his problems. When he came home on leave they could see each other. He found himself wondering again who else was in her life, but he put that thought away for the moment, as he floated back to Mrs Middleton's. He wondered if he would dare, at some stage before the summer was over, ask Helen for a photograph of herself.

13

*T*hey moved house. Lewis was four or five at the time. It happened all of a sudden. Nobody said anything to him. But suddenly they weren't in the old house any more and they were living in the house in which his grandmother – Dad's mother – lived.

The new house was much bigger and on a wide street. In the front a low wall with green railings mounted on it, enclosed a hedge and then a small patch of grass. The house had two bay windows and a door with a round arch over it. Three wide steps led up to the door with a stained glass window in it. On the roof was what Dad called a dormer window.

Lewis quickly got the lie of the land. The dining room was in the back of the house with the kitchen. The living room was in the downstairs front room while Grandma slept in the corresponding room upstairs. His parent's room was at the back of the house over a reasonably sized garden. Lewis had the room at the top of the house with the dormer window.

Lewis only met this grandma once. He thought it funny that she spent all her time in bed. Dad went with him, knocking gently on the door and opening it timidly when a croaky voice called, 'Come in'. It was summer with lots of summer sounds outside. Inside the room was very warm and the curtains were closed. The room smelt dusty and old. Lewis was reminded of the Captain's chest in *Treasure Island*. The air felt thick like breathing in soup. It was a tiny bit frightening, except Dad was there. The old woman in the bed said, 'Hello Lewis. Give your grandmother a kiss, there's a good boy.'

Dad picked him up, the heavy smell got stronger and he felt

a froggy kiss on his cheek. Lewis thought it was all a bit peculiar. He didn't see his grandmother again after that. In time he would learn that she had died.

That night, curled up in his old bed but in a strange new room, he could hardly sleep with excitement. New sounds came up from the street below. Several times he crept over to the curtains and looked out. On one occasion, a man and a girl walked hand in hand on the other side of the street. The man stopped and swung around the gaslight. When he swung back onto the pavement, he happened to glance up. His eyes met Lewis' and the man smiled and waved. The girl looked up too and laughed. Lewis waved back.

Next morning, Mum went out with Lewis to do some food shopping. The little porch with its curved arch was irradiated with sunlight as they stepped out into the heat of late morning. Mum wore a fawn skirt and a white blouse and her dark hair fell below her shoulders from a straw hat with a cornflower blue ribbon. They crossed to the far side of the street where the trees gave some shade.

The shade was gone by the time they got to the shops and it was a relief to walk into the cool saw dusted interior of the grocers, with the name 'Barton & Son' painted in copper on the large plate glass window. The shop smelled of bacon. A man with large moustaches smiled at them from behind a marble counter.

'Morning Ma'm, lovely morning again. Can I be of any assistance?'

'Yes please, I have quite a long list of things.'

'Never fear Ma'm, we'll take care of all that and have it delivered to you.'

'Thank you, that's very kind of you.'

She began to run down her list.

'My, you are stocking up, aren't you?'

'Yes, we've just moved in – in Shalimar Terrace.'

'And who is this little gentleman?'

Lewis gave his name to the tall figure in a blue apron with white stripes.

'Well, here we are young sir, this is for you,' said the man offering him a large red apple.

When she had finished, the man asked if she would like to pay or open an account.

'Oh, I'll pay,' said Mum enthusiastically, taking some bank-notes from her purse. The groceries would be delivered in the next hour or so. They left the shop and walked back home.

'What do you think of the new house, Lewis?' asked Mum.

'I like it. I like my room. I like where it is on the top of the house.'

Then he said, 'Do you like it, Mum?'

'Do I like it?' she mused. 'Well, I loved our other house. I really loved that. And there's a lot of extra work now having to take care of your grandma. But yes, it's nice I suppose. And we have some extra money now, so that's good.'

They walked on in silence until she said, 'But I miss the old house. I really loved that house. I felt that that house was *my* house.'

Lewis looked up at her. She looked very sad and her eyes were wet.

'Are you alright, Mum?' he asked.

She sniffed and reached into her bag for a hankie. She looked down at him, and said, 'Yes, I'm fine, darling. I'm fine.'

She blew her nose and put the hankie back in her bag. She was silent as though she was thinking about something but as they approached the house and Lewis saw the green railings, she said, 'So – what would you like to do this afternoon?'

'I was going to take my fort and soldiers out into the new garden.'

'That sounds like a good idea,' she said. 'Maybe I'll do some work in the garden myself this afternoon. It could do with a good tidy.'

14

*L*ewis woke in the middle of the night. He was in his bed in Mrs Middleton's. Outside the seagulls shrilled as usual and somewhere a lone duck quacked as if to say, 'I'm here too, you know'. A memory had come back to him – something he had forgotten about completely but now, suddenly, for some reason, it had come back to him with startling clarity. As far as he could place it, it had happened when he was six or seven.

Dad had announced that they would be going to the beach for a summer holiday. So a few days later, at breakfast, Mum said to Lewis that they would have to go into town to get some things. Mum had a bath and got dressed and then they walked the short distance to the bus stop.

It was the beginning of the summer. The morning was already hot so that Mum wore just a white blouse and a long skirt. The material swished as they walked along. She felt so tall with her dark chestnut hair tied up. The sky was already a rich blue and the birds sang. On the bus, the conductor whistled as he went up and down the aisle clicking his ticket machine. 'Any more fares please?' In London, they went into a huge shop where Mum began to browse among the swimsuits on a rail. An assistant hovered nearby and smiled at Lewis. Eventually Mum chose a couple from the rail and the assistant showed the way to the changing rooms.

'Come over here, darling, where I can see you,' said Mum.

Lewis did as he was told. Mum went into the changing room and left the door ajar. There was a full-length mirror right inside the door and she and Lewis could see each other in it. She

75

unbuttoned her white blouse with its puffy sleeves, took it off and hung it on a hook. Underneath she wore what looked like a vest to Lewis, except that it had lacy pieces that ran over her shoulders. The skin of the lower part of her arms was tanned from working in the garden. Mum put one foot on a chair that stood to one side of the mirror and hitched up her skirt a little. Beneath the blue skirt was a froth of white. She untied her lace and eased off the shoe, placing it on the floor. She wore white stockings. She took off the other shoe in the same way and placed it beside the first one. One shoe stood up while the other one fell on its side.

Next Mum undid the wide belt she wore around her waist and dropped it onto a chair. She unbuttoned her long blue skirt and stepped out of it, draping it over the back of the chair. Now Lewis could see that the lacy vest was actually part of a single garment with legs that came down below Mum's knees. The ends of the legs were also lacy and there were lacy looking flowers on the front of the vest part.

Lewis thought she looked very beautiful but also he got a sense that she needed to be taken care of – just like Jim Hawkins did for his mum in *Treasure Island*. There was something defence-less about her as she stood there. She knew so much about so much and yet, at that moment, Lewis felt stronger than her; older than her, in a strange kind of way. In her normal day-to-day clothes, she was a woman, his mum. But it was as though he was seeing her now as the little girl she had been when she had been his age – dressing as *her* mum watched over her.

Lying in his bed in the darkened bedroom, Lewis realised that it was the little girl on the beach again. But he remembered clearly how he had felt at the time. He realised that up to that day, it was only Dad who had seen her undressing like this. But now Lewis had seen her too. It was a new bond between them. She was his Mum and he was her little boy and she took care of him. But now he realised that he had to protect her too; in some ways she was a little girl and he was the man. He would do his best to make sure that she was never sad – especially as she was sometimes with Dad.

The first swimsuit was navy blue with white trim on it, so that it looked a bit like a sailor suit. Mum put one leg into the pants of the swimsuit, then the other, pulled it up, over her white lacy thing. Now she put the top on – a sleeveless jacket that wrapped around and tied with a belt. She looked in the mirror, turned to one side and struck a pose. Then she did the same on the other side. She saw him looking at her.

'What do you think?' she smiled.

'The other one is a nicer colour,' he said, indicating the second one she had brought with her.

'Let's try that one, then,' she said, beginning to undo the belt on the jacket. As she did, she glanced at the tag hanging on a short white string that gave the price.

In the end she took neither of them. She thanked the assistant and left the shop.

'Fancy some coffee?' she asked.

It was what she always said, to which he always replied, 'Yes, please' with the emphasis on the 'yes'. Then they would both laugh and head for the nearest ABC Tea Shop.

'Why didn't you buy one of the swimsuits?' he asked.

'I didn't really like them,' she said, looking down at him. 'And anyway, they were very expensive. I could make one for a lot cheaper than those. And we should be making the money that Daddy earns go as far as possible.'

In the ABC, she ordered coffee and a slice of cake for herself. Lewis had his favourite – circular shortbread biscuits with strawberry jam in between and white or pink icing on top. Today she let him have two, one white, one pink. The aroma of freshly roasted coffee was overwhelming and the hissing of the machine that frothed the milk made the place sound like a railway station.

Their order arrived.

'I wonder what you'll be when you grow up,' said Mum, as she lifted her cup and saucer, took a sip of coffee and lowered them again.

'A soldier,' he announced immediately.

'Gosh, I hope not,' she said, putting an alarmed look on her face.

'Why not? I like soldiers. It's my favourite game.'

'But suppose something happened to you?'

'Nothing would happen to me. I should be a good soldier – brave and strong.'

'But even if nothing happened to you, I should be worried while you were away – in case anything did.'

'Did you always want to be a mum – when you grew up, I mean?'

She thought for a moment.

'No, I didn't actually. But now that I am, I love it. I love you. I wouldn't have met you if I hadn't decided to become a mum.'

He thought about this for a moment, realising the truth of it.

'So what did you want to be?'

'Well, I had a little dressmaking business before I met your Dad. Just in the front room of your nana's house, making wedding dresses and things like that.'

Her voice had changed. It sounded distant, dreamy.

'Or even a musician. When I was younger my piano teacher said that I had a lot of talent. She wanted me to go to music school.'

'And why didn't you?'

'I met your daddy.'

'And that was more fun than music school.'

'Yes, it was more fun then,' she said. 'He made me laugh. He was great fun to be with.'

'How did you meet him?' asked Lewis.

'He and your uncle John were serving on the same ship. They docked in Chatham and John was coming home for a few days. He asked your Dad if he would like to come along. So they came back to where we lived in Gillingham – you know, Nana and Grandad's house?'

Lewis nodded.

'I was out walking my dog and I bumped into them coming from the station.'

'What was you dog's name?'

'He was called Chappie.'

'And you really liked him?'

'My dog?'

'No,' said Lewis laughing. 'Dad.'

'Oh yes,' said Mum, laughing too. 'I really liked him.'

'And so then you got married?'

Lewis could see that Mum was enjoying this conversation.

'Well not straight away but about a year later. Your Dad was still at sea then. I really missed him when he had to go away again. I did a very silly thing.'

She sounded as though she was about to share a secret with him.

'He was sailing to New York and back so I said I would follow his progress on a map. Then I would know when I could expect to see him again. He told me the speed of the ship and so every day, I would work out how far they had travelled, measure it and mark it on the map. Well, your Dad showed up one day *weeks* before I expected him to. I was thrilled but I couldn't understand how I'd gotten it so wrong. He asked me to explain how I had been working it out. So many knots per hour, I said, multiplied by twelve hours. Twelve, he asked. Why twelve? Well, you have to sleep don't you, I said? He started roaring with laughter. The *ship* doesn't sleep he said. Wasn't that silly?'

Lewis agreed that it was.

'After he gave up the sea and started the job he has now, he would often come home unexpectedly. He might be far away on a trip but would do all kinds of things to try to get home. I'd be there – in the last house – and suddenly late at night I'd hear the key in the door and there he'd be. "I sailed through the night," he'd always say and we'd laugh.'

After they had finished, they went into a material shop and bought some white material with small yellow and blue flowers on it. That afternoon, while a small garrison of his favourite soldiers defended the fort against overwhelming odds, the sewing machine clattered away on the dining room table. In a couple of hours the swimsuit was ready. By then it was getting close to tea time.

'I'll just try it on before your father gets in,' she said. She went out into the kitchen.

'Don't come in,' she called, before emerging with the swimsuit on. She had long legs and these were very white in comparison to her arms.

'How do I look, Lewis?'

'You look beautiful.'

'My little darling,' she said, extending her arms. He stood up and ran to her, pressing himself against her. He faintly smelled her perfume and his hands could feel her body through the thin fabric. He stayed there until she said, 'Alright, we'd better start tidying up.'

Outside the window of Mrs Middleton's guest house, the sky had lightened a fraction. Lewis yawned and turned over. He was sleepy again now. His last thought was how strange it was that he remembered almost nothing of the holiday itself.

15

*W*est continued the briefing. The dugout and its occupants made Lewis think of a pirate's den.

'The raiding party will consist of the following. Covering Party – Lieutenant Redman, two NCO's, two tape men, two blanket men, two ladder men, two scouts with revolvers. Left and Right Blocking Parties – each two NCO's, four bayonet men, four bombers in each. Body Snatching Party – Lieutenant Friday, two NCO's, six men. Connecting Points – One NCO and two men. There will be an additional Support Party consisting of Second Lieutenant Harris, one NCO, four bombers, four bayonet men and two men on the Lewis Gun. Alright, so far?'

There was silence and some nodding.

'You'll rendezvous at this dugout 'J' here in the Support Line at Zero minus one hour thirty minutes. You'll then proceed along this sap to the front line trench here and assemble in no-man's-land on our side of the wire, along this line.'

West traced out the various movements with his forefinger. Somebody had picked out their route in little red dashes on the trench map. Lewis pictured them in the darkness going silently along the trench. What if he was killed on Helen's birthday? It had a terrible irony to it. And not just an irony – but a logic. An awful, warped logic. He began to feel very afraid.

He tried to concentrate as West unfolded the plan. It was the standard one for trench raids. An artillery barrage would box off a section of trench isolating it from the rest of the German trench system. The blocking parties would go into the trench to further ensure that no Germans got through into the boxed-off

81

bit. Then Lewis and his men would capture as many prisoners as they could and return them to the British lines. Everyone would retire, the artillery barrage would stop and that would be that. Despite the fact that it was such a standard operation, there were so many things that could go wrong, so many ways it could end in horror.

'Previous reconnaissance has established a prominent clump of brushwood here' – West stabbed his finger onto the table emphatically – 'and this will be the marker for your point of entry.

The Covering Party will take up a position here on the German parapet at the point of entry. They will hold same until all of the other parties have reported clear. It will be the responsibility of the NCO's in charge of each of the other parties to do this. Lieutenant Redman will accompany and remain in direct charge of the Covering Party.

The Right Blocking Party will enter the hostile trench at the point of entry. Four men each will go to this point and block the front line trench running south and the communications trench running east. Similarly, the Left Blocking Party after going in at the entry point will move towards this point and block the front line trench going north and also block the communications trench. NCO's will remain at the junction of these two trenches. The bayonet men of both Blocking Parties will watch over the parapet for an overland attack by the enemy.'

A nightmare – trapped in an unfamiliar trench with the enemy coming overland. There would be grenades first and then, if you survived those, the enemy in the trench with bayonets. Dying with a foot and a half of steel in your belly in the dark in a squalid ditch. He didn't want to die tonight. He didn't want to die now when it might be just a matter of a few weeks and the killing would stop.

'The Body Snatching Party will seize all enemy, printed and written papers, any identification and portable articles and bring same back when ordered to withdraw. The Connecting Party will remain halfway along the tape. This party will take the prisoners back and hand them into our trench. It will also guide the other parties back. The Supporting Party will take up a position in our trench and bring such fire as is necessary to protect the raiding party's right flank. They will remain out until ordered to retire by the OC Raiding Party, Lieutenant Redman. Lewis Guns will accompany the Supporting Party, Second Lieutenant Harris commanding.'

There were no cushy assignments here. Any of them could die. They could all die. Men were going to die between now and any armistice. Why should Lewis not become one of them? There had been so many times since he had arrived in France just before Easter of last year when he had thought that the game was up. Messines, Passchaendale, the German Spring Offensive were the big ones but there had been things every day. A Calvary of days, all equally terrifying and differentiated only by the scale of death and maiming. His first encounter with the enemy had been a night-time trench raid just before the Battle of Messines. It had been petrifying because he hadn't known what to expect. Everything after that had been terrifying because he *had*.

'No time is to be wasted and having entered the trench, each party will proceed to its objective at once. The Body Snatching Party will take as many prisoners as possible, disarm them and immediately pass them back to the Covering Party. These will get them back to the Connecting Party who will get them back to our trench. Lieutenant Smith will be waiting here, and will accompany the prisoners to Centre Company where they will be handed over to the Regimental Police.'

The order to retire will be given by Lieutenant Redman fifteen minutes after Zero.'

All told, it would be less than half an hour. Less than half an hour and it would be over. That's all it would be. A small number of minutes that could change everything. Oh that it were over. That he was back in his nice warm cosy dugout with whiskey and food.

'You will retire in this order across the tapes laid. Body Snatching Party, Left Blocking Party, Right Blocking Party. Then will come the Covering Party and the Connecting Points. When all the Raiding Party is in, Lieutenant Redman will withdraw the Support Party. After roll-call in the dugout here, he will proceed to Battalion for debriefing.'

Lewis doubted if it would all turn out to be as neat as that in practice. He had seen trench raids that had turned into routs with men running for their lives.

'The OC Machine Gun Company has arranged for one of his guns to open fire at plus three minutes on the German front line. They will cease fire at plus seventeen. This will be a protection to the left flank of the Raiding Party and will therefore continue after plus seventeen, if required.

All identification is to be removed from all ranks in the party before leaving the dugout. Each man will wear service tunic with the buttons dulled, trews, puttees, steel helmet and Bomber's Shield.'

Jesus, the so-called Bomber's Shield. It was like a padded waistcoat, the padding being about an inch thick and covered in brown muslin. The padding was made up of different layers of tissue, scraps of linen, cotton and silk. The lot was said to be hardened with some form of resinous material but nobody believed that. It might stop a pea from a pea shooter though Lewis wasn't convinced. Still he would wear it. He would wear anything if he felt it would help him to get through this.

'Each man will carry a field dressing and two bombs, one in each trouser pocket. Bombers will carry eight bombs in bomb carriers. Riflemen will carry fifty rounds in canvas bandoliers and nine rounds in their magazines. All safety's to be locked and bayonets fixed. Bombers will carry knobkerries. The two scouts in the Advanced Party will carry a revolver and a wire cutter each. Bayonets will be blackened, faces and hands darkened, all luminous watches to be hidden. Officers to carry revolvers and ten rounds of ammunition. Officers and scouts to carry compasses. Officers of the Raiding Party to carry torches. Rations not to be carried. Six hand ropes to be carried by Body Snatching Party.

Here's the timetable. At Zero minus one and a half hours, the raiding party will leave the dugout "J". The rear of the party will pass this point "F"' – West pointed at it on the map – 'in the front line trench at minus thirty minutes. The whole party will be on our side of the wire, in no-man's-land, ready to go forward at minus three. Zero hour and the signal for the attack will be the beginning of the artillery barrage. Machine gun fire will commence at plus three. I expect everybody to be back in their own trenches by Zero plus fifteen at which time the artillery fire is scheduled to cease. The code word to withdraw will be "Whitby". Zero hour will be at one thirty ack emma tomorrow.'

'Fifteen minutes, gentlemen,' put in Ogilvy. 'Fifteen minutes. That's all it should take from the time the artillery starts. Five minutes should be more than enough to gain entry to their trench, five minutes to find the people you want and get them out, five minutes to get back to our lines. There's plenty of contingency in there. Major West?'

West looked around at the circle of faces.

'Any questions, gentlemen? No? Well, in that case it only just remains for me to wish you good luck and to synchronise our watches.'

'And remember,' said Ogilvy as they broke up. 'The thing is to bring back prisoners, not casualties.'

He looked around at them over his glasses again as if to emphasise the point.

'Good luck gentlemen.'

16

$\mathcal{I}$n the end, Lewis didn't go to the beach either. He went for a long walk in the morning and had lunch in a pub. He spent the whole time thinking about her. He looked endlessly at his watch and was repeatedly surprised at how little time had gone by. When would it be time to go back to Mrs Middleton's and get ready?

He returned there about three – much earlier than he had intended, but he just couldn't wait any longer. He bathed, washed his hair and shaved, even though he had shaved yesterday and didn't really need to. Then he put on fresh clothes. He agonised briefly over whether or not to wear a tie, but in the end he decided he should. Dad had always said that it was better to err on the side of caution in things like this. Anyway, Lewis could always take it off later.

He told Mrs Middleton he wouldn't be back for dinner and whatever she thought about this and the way he was dressed, all she said was, 'Alright, m'dear, see you later on.' Lewis found a florist's and bought a bouquet of flowers. He knew nothing about flowers so he asked for a mixture and the florist arranged them beautifully. He carried the flowers cradled in his arms. It was very warm and he hoped they wouldn't wilt before he got there. As he left Fowey he was in a fever of excitement. Helen might be much older than him, but she didn't seem like that. She seemed young, carefree, full of fun. And she treated him as though there were no age difference between them. And she was so beautiful. He tried to picture her face now but found that he couldn't, other than a generally pretty face framed by blonde hair. He would be more observant when he was there this time.

When he arrived he pushed through the gate and came round to the back of the cottage. The back door was ajar.

'Hello,' he called, and a few moments later he heard her coming through the house and she appeared in the little porch. Her hair seemed to shine when she stepped into the sunlight. She wore a white blouse and a light blue skirt that came down below her knees.

'Lewis!'

She came to him and kissed him on the cheek. He could smell her perfume and her hair which had a fragrance of its own. Then she said, 'My, you *are* looking smart.'

'I wasn't sure how posh we were going to be,' he said, but it was more in good humour than embarrassment.

'I shall have to change,' she said, picking up the thread.

'Or I could take my tie off,' he said.

'Better idea,' she confirmed.

He had almost forgotten that he was holding the flowers.

'Oh, these are for you,' he said, handing them over as though he were passing a baby.

'Oh Lewis,' she said. 'They're beautiful. Thank you. You're such a darling. Come in. Let's put them in water.'

She led the way through. There was a small porch and then a large room. It had a kitchen part that had a sink under a window, a range against one wall and a table and chairs. Then, beyond that, were a fireplace, a couple of armchairs, a small sideboard and an open stairs. On the table was an empty vase.

She took the paper wrapping off the flowers and placed them one by one in the vase, testing the effect after each one. Lewis was glad he had brought them. There was something about women and flowers – fragility, fragrance, beauty. When she was finished she placed them on the kitchen table.

'They're absolutely gorgeous,' she said.

And then he thought the smile in her eyes seemed to soften and be replaced by vulnerability or even sadness.

'It's a long time since anybody's bought me flowers.'

If you were mine, I would bring you flowers every day.

'I was feeling a bit down,' she said. 'But this has cheered me up no end.'

'Why were you feeling down?' he asked, not sure whether he should or not.

'What? Oh, no reason. Never mind. I'm not now – that's the important thing. I thought we'd eat outside,' she said, changing the subject. 'That's if we can get the table through the door.'

'It shouldn't be a problem,' he said, hoping, as he went to pick it up, that it wouldn't be as heavy as it looked. She lifted the vase of flowers from it.

As it turned out, the table *was* as heavy as it looked. But it was too late to turn back now. He took hold of it as she said,' Here, let me give you a hand.'

'No, it'll be fine,' he almost groaned.

'Mind you don't hurt yourself,' she said.

He managed to turn the table on its end. Then, face red, lifting it with his arms and pushing it with his knees and feet, he was able to get it through the first door into the porch. He paused for breath and then pushed it out onto the flag stoned patio. He was pleased. He had never been particularly good at these practical kinds of things but here, he seemed to be able to do whatever she needed doing. It was like being the man of the house. He supposed he was in a way – there seemed to be no other man here. Helen brought out a tablecloth which she shook out and floated down onto the table. Then she brought the vase with the flowers, a plateful of scones, little pots of butter, jam and Cornish clotted cream.

'What I've done is a bit of a mish-mash really. I made scones because I asked you to tea. But then I realised that you've been having your dinner in the evening. So I thought we'd have omelettes and salad and I bought a cake for afters.'

'It sounds lovely,' he said.

He felt overwhelmed with happiness to be in her company. She made tea and they sat at the table and drank and ate. She had long fingers and she wasn't wearing any rings. She asked him what he'd been up to since she'd seen him last. He told her about some of the guests at Mrs Middleton's, about George conducting the 'ensemble' every evening. She smiled at some of Lewis' descriptions. Then he thought that since she had asked him questions and been interested in him, he should do the same.

'So where did you live before you came here?'

'Shropshire.'

'When did you come?'

'About a month ago. I've been here since the beginning of June.'

'Are you married?'

He had asked the question lightly. He hadn't expected it to have the effect that it did. The light seemed to go out of her eyes. They became far away and glazed over. The question seemed to have flustered her in some way.

'I am.'

She hesitated.

'Yes, I am. Yes, I am married. My husband's in the Army – in France. Now, I'd better go and see about those omelettes. You stay here. I shan't be long.'

She disappeared into the kitchen. He didn't know what he had said wrong but he had clearly said something. Better to deal with it now, he thought. He got up and went inside. She was standing at the range with her back to him. He thought she looked frail and deflated. She glanced over her shoulder when she heard him.

'I'm sorry,' he said. 'I didn't mean to pry – to upset you. It's none of my business. I shouldn't have asked.'

'Oh, don't mind me, Lewis. I'm just having a bad day. But there's no need to apologise. You didn't do anything wrong.'

'Are you sure?' he asked uncertainly.

She turned completely to face him. She was wearing an apron over her skirt and had opened an extra button on her blouse. The skin beneath her throat was brown against the white fabric.

'Absolutely,' she nodded. Don't give it another thought. Now let's see to those eggs.'

She went to the range and poured half the beaten eggs from the bowl into the frying pan where it sizzled on the butter.

'The first night I stayed here,' she said. 'I arrived in the evening. Mr Paige, who owns the cottage, had left a little food for me. Just the basics, tea, milk, sugar, bread, butter, cheese, eggs. I made a cheese omelette – just like these. Have you ever noticed how cold cheese is just a snack, but cook it, heat it and it's a feast? That's what it was for me that night.'

He thought of her arriving here alone. That must have been difficult. Was she lonely here all by herself? Was that why she had been having such a bad day today?

'Now you take that out and eat it while it's hot,' she said. 'I'll be there in two minutes.'

He waited until she joined him. The omelette was light and slightly runny, just the way he liked it.

'At home,' he said. 'Since I was a kid, we've had a succession of housekeepers. They cleaned the house, did the washing and the cooking, that sort of thing.'

'And were they good cooks?'

Lewis laughed aloud.

'They were all *terrible* cooks. The second one – she wasn't so bad and she was only a couple of years older than me. I thought she was nice, but after she left my dad told me that she had been stealing things. Anyway, after that, I asked Dad if he could find a good cook this time. He said he would. And so, a few weeks later, this woman arrived. Her name was Lil. I think she must have been in her sixties. Dad said she had been cooking in a convent for nuns. So I thought well, nuns must be fairly choosy. She must be a good cook.'

'And she was?'

'Terrible.'

Helen laughed.

'Really, really terrible. By far the worst. I came home from school the first day,' Lewis continued. 'She put a plate with meat and potatoes and peas in front of me. I tucked in – I was starving. Except then I noticed that the peas had black marks on them. They were burnt. How do you burn peas? I mean, is that actually possible?'

Helen laughed.

'And the potatoes?'

'They were sort of floury on the outside and looked really nice. But biting into them you found that the insides were hard as golf balls.'

'The meat?' said Helen hopefully.

Lewis shook his head.

'Oh, dear.'

'She asked me if I'd like some "brown gravy", she called it. I thought anything to soften the rest of it. So she poured the gravy over everything. Of course, the gravy had been burned too and the meat was hard as the sole of my boot.'

'Did she ever improve?' asked Helen.

'No,' said Lewis, shaking his head and putting a mournful look on his face.

'Poor Lewis,' she said. 'You're very funny, Lewis. Funny ha-ha, I mean. You've got a good sense of humour. You've got a funny way of looking at the world.'

He had never thought of it before. Dad had a good sense of humour and Lewis thought he might have inherited it a bit, but it had never seemed to him that anybody else had noticed. He would never feel shy again, he thought.

'Thank you,' he said. 'I wish you had been our housekeeper.'

He wanted to say, 'I wish you'd been my Mum', but he felt there would be some kind of betrayal in it.

'Mmm, I think we should have had a lot of fun together. If I'd been your housekeeper, I mean. I think we'll have a bit of a rest before the cake.'

Lewis had never had such a wonderful evening. He had thought at first that it would be like going to tea at an auntie's house. But as it turned out, it was more like visiting a friend. He didn't want it to end, but when they both began to yawn, Helen laughed and said, 'I think it's time for us to call it a day.' Lewis jumped up.

'I hope I haven't kept you too late – I didn't mean to.'

'No. Don't be silly,' she said. 'I've had a lovely evening. I hope you enjoyed yourself and didn't mind spending time with an old woman like me.'

'You're not old,' he said. He wanted to say 'you're beautiful', but couldn't summon up the courage to do so. And he was suddenly anxious that he would never get to do anything like this again. 'Are you going to the beach tomorrow?' he asked, hopefully.

She thought. Lewis wondered if she could hear his heart pounding with anxiety as he waited for her answer.

'I hadn't decided – but if the weather's fine, why not?'

'Readymoney?' he asked. 'Or would you like to try one of the other ones?'

'You choose,' she said, and he thought that, for a moment, she looked and sounded like a girl. The suggestion that he would decide for the pair of them suddenly seemed to bring them closer together.

'Pridmouth,' he said. 'It's the next one along the coast.'

'Would we need to go by bike? Do you have one?'

'No, but it's not much of a walk. We could easily do it,' he said, hoping he wasn't sounding too presumptuous.

'Why don't you call for me when you're coming past in the morning? I'll make a picnic.'

'Oh,' said Lewis suddenly.

'What's wrong?'

'I just realised – tomorrow's Sunday. Don't you – er, did you want to go to church?'

She thought about it for a moment.

'No, I don't think so. If the weather's nice and we're out enjoying creation, I'm sure that'll be as good as any dry old sermon from a vicar. Don't you think?'

He did.

With this agreed, they headed for the back door. She opened it, and they stepped out onto the little patio. There were stars overhead. They could see and hear the sea. The air smelt of foliage and salt and the heat of the day.

'Thank you again,' he said, as he stood facing her.

'You're more than welcome, my love. I enjoyed it. It was a lovely evening.'

She touched one of his cheeks gently with the palm of her hand and leaning forward kissed him on the other.

'Good night,' she said.

Then she stood with arms folded at the back door, until he had disappeared around the corner of the house. He went out through the gate and down the dusty laneway that was the way back to Fowey. She had called him 'my love'. But then aunties often called him 'my love'. He walked home in another blur of happiness. He could hardly believe the night he had spent and that she was in his life. He realised that he still knew very little about her. In fact, it was funny that she had talked so much yet revealed so little about herself. But there would be plenty of time.

The sky overhead was full of stars and he stopped several times to gaze up at them. He tried to remember her fragrance but it was gone. But he could see her face now and that was the last thing he pictured later before he slid away to sleep.

17

After lunch on Christmas Eve Dad took Lewis to the station to catch an Underground train into London to see the lights and the shops. It was the first Christmas after they had moved house. It was very cold and Lewis wore a scarf around his neck and the lower parts of his ears. The train was crowded and stifling after the chill of the platform. Dad found them seats and Lewis studied the flushed faces in the compartment as the train rocked its way into the city.

It was already dusk when they came up the steps from the Underground station. The yellow globes of the gaslights glowed and illuminated shop windows spilled brightness out onto the pavements. Through the windows Lewis could see people standing at counters paying money or talking with shop assistants. On the pavements there was a great bustle of shoppers hurrying past carrying boxes or with armfuls of things. In one or two windows he saw men working at desks with pens and large books. A man on crutches stood in the gutter selling matchboxes. Carriages and other vehicles bowled by in the roadway. They went into a jeweller's where Dad asked to see some necklaces.

'If sir could give me a rough idea as to price,' said a weary looking man who did his best to smile.

Dad told him and the weariness suddenly became animated interest. The decision quickly came down to one or two circlets of gold and Dad seemed unable to decide. He asked if he could see both necklaces on a girl with black hair who worked in the shop.

'This lady is going to try on each one,' Dad said. 'And whichever one looks prettiest, we'll take for Mummy.'

The girl smiled at Lewis, and with each one she leant her head back slightly pushing her neck and her chest forward a little so that both Dad and Lewis could see the effect.

'What do you think, Lewis?'

'She's not as pretty as Mummy,' said Lewis.

'Lewis!' said Dad in mock outrage, enjoying the girl's reaction.

'I'm sure I'm not,' she said, laughing good naturedly.

'I think we'll take this one,' said Dad indicating the wider of the two. 'And thank you for your help, Miss, even if some of us appreciated it more than others.'

Lewis saw Dad wink at her.

After the jeweller's they went into a pub. Dad seemed to know a lot of people there. They stayed for several hours. Lewis was afraid that they'd be late putting up the Christmas tree and the Christmas decorations and that then Santa Claus won't come. He kept asking Dad when they were going to leave so that Dad became annoyed. Each time it looked like Dad had finished his drink, a new one arrived.

Finally, they went back out into the street where the strains of carol singers singing 'Once in Royal David's City' could be heard. The air smelt sooty and felt thick in his nose and throat. It seemed incredibly late to Lewis. They hurried to the Underground station and caught the train.

'Wake up, Lewis. We're here.'

Lewis woke to see people whizzing by on the station platform. They gradually slowed to a halt. Lewis rubbed his eyes.

'Is it still Christmas?' he asked drowsily.

'Of course it's still Christmas,' said Dad. We'll have some tea and then it'll be up with that tree and those decorations faster than you can say Jack Robinson. Then we'll have to get you to bed early before Santa comes.'

There was still a lot of traffic on the street as they approached home. The gas lamps on the far side shone like blocks of golden ice. They met several of the neighbours and compliments of the season were exchanged. The wrought iron garden gate squealed open and Lewis saw excitedly that there was a wreath of holly and laurel on the door. As they walked up the path, the door opened. It was Mum – she must have heard them. She wore an apron and stood there in the yellow light. She was smiling and Lewis was delighted to see her looking so happy.

She had transformed the house. The hallstand and banisters and parquet floor gleamed from the recent polishing. Brightly coloured paper chains crossed from the four corners to meet in the centre of the ceiling of the living room. Sprigs of shiny holly rested on all of the pictures on the walls. The tree was up though only partially decorated.

'I hope you've left some for us to do,' said Dad.

'Yes, I didn't get a chance to finish the tree, so you two can do that while I get tea ready.'

A fire blazed in the hearth, fire irons shone and the table and sideboard reflected back a warm woody glow. The Christmas tree stood in the bay window. Paper decorations and tinsel and brightly coloured balls lay tumbled out of a box on its side beside the tree. Magic had invaded the house and Lewis thought his heart would burst with joy. When Mum came in to call them for tea, she complimented them on the tree. While Lewis draped the last piece of tinsel over the lower branches, she and Dad hugged.

The kitchen window was thick with condensation. Wire trays of sausage rolls and mince pies lay on the table. For tea they had sausages, bacon and eggs. The bacon tasted salty and smoky and juicy. The eggs had been fried in the meat juices. There was one further job to be done before Lewis went to bed. That was to leave a plate of sausage rolls and mince pies on the dining room table along with a bottle of lemonade and some carrots. The carrots were for the reindeers, the rest was for Santa Claus. Dad had suggested a bottle of beer but no, Lewis didn't want Santa getting drunk and losing his way.

It was like no other night, Lewis thought, as he lay in bed wide awake. The rest of the year the world just got along with its business, but at Christmas Santa Claus came and visited every house in the world. Tonight he would be here in 4 Shalimar Terrace. How did it work? Did the night get stretched so that Santa had time to visit each house and spend some time there? What time would he come here? Where was he now? Faintly, downstairs, Lewis could hear the sound of Mum in the kitchen. Baking trays and crockery were clanging and knocking in the kitchen sink. Mum and Dad had better come to bed soon. Otherwise, if they were downstairs, maybe Santa wouldn't come at all.

Dad had hung stockings on the mantelpiece over the fire, but Lewis had hung another one on the end of his bed, just to give Santa a choice. It was dark in the room. Lewis jumped out of bed and pulled back the curtains a fraction. This would give some light by which he could see Santa if he came into the room. Lewis lay in bed trying to fight off sleep. Several times his lids drooped heavily and he shook his head to restore a wakefulness which only seemed to last for a few moments. He looked continually at the end of the bed, and once or twice he thought he saw movement there but it was nothing.

Lewis was awake early the next morning. Despite his best efforts he had fallen asleep, but no matter. It was Christmas Day. He ran across the landing into his parent's room. Dad took a while to wake up but eventually, he said, 'Right-ho, I'd better go down and make sure Santa's gone.'

He went downstairs while Lewis and Mum in their dressing gowns waited at the top of the stairs. They heard the rattle of the door handle and then the door opening. .

'There's no one here,' Dad called. 'You can come down.'

Lewis hurtled down the stairs.

Dad had turned up the lights and the first thing Lewis saw on entering the sitting room was the remains of Santa's meal.

'He's been, he's been,' he shrieked joyously, and then dived under the glistening tree, growing out of a heap of brightly coloured parcels.

Lewis got books from his aunts and uncles. He got books and boxes of toy soldiers from Mum and Dad. As well as that Mum had knitted him some mittens and a scarf and a woolly hat for the cold weather. But the most wonderful present of all was a brand new wooden fort that his grandfather had made. The fort stood on a raised wooden base. There were towers at the four corners, two tall ones at the back and two shorter ones at the front. Low walls ran around three sides while at the back, a higher battlement with rooms built into it, served as accommodation for the troops. There was a gate tower with a portcullis and a separate piece consisting of a ramp which rose to the same level as the wooden base. A drawbridge connected the ramp to the main castle and could be raised and lowered. Lewis began to deploy his soldiers onto the towers and battlements. This small force would defend the castle against the hordes of his existing armies.

Looking up he saw Dad standing amongst the opened wrappings, scattered like large, colourful autumn leaves. He handed Mum a long thin box.

When she opened it, she said, 'It's beautiful, Nick. But you really shouldn't have. It's too much. We can't afford it.'

Lewis thought her voice sounded quiet in an odd way. She wasn't really excited like he was. Maybe Christmas was different for adults.

'I've had a good year,' Dad said. 'And anyway, you deserve it love – for having to put up with me.'

Later they went to church. Lewis was reluctant to leave his soldiers and the service seemed interminable. When they returned, the smell of roasting meat filled the hall as they came in the door.

For dinner they had goose with sage and onion stuffing, apple sauce, roast potatoes, brussels sprouts with pudding and mince pies for dessert. Lewis ate so much he thought he was going to be sick. Dad settled into his armchair by the blazing fire and, after a couple of glasses of brandy, dozed off.

Later the three of them went for a walk in the short chill afternoon. The weather was raw and dry with a grey sky. An occasional bird flapped in the bare trees, and the houses with their smoky chimneys had a whitish look about them as though seen through muslin. They were glad to return to the warmth of the banked up fire. For the rest of the day Lewis played with his fort and the battle around it was still raging when Mum kissed him off to bed at ten o'clock.

18

*T*owards the end of the summer, Mum has to go into hospital.

'It's only for a few days, she says, as she kisses Lewis and goes down the steps to the waiting cab. One of Lewis' aunties – Dad's youngest sister, Edna – comes to stay with them and mind Lewis and cook their meals.

'It's only while Mum is in hospital,' Dad says.

Then one school day, when he gets up Lewis is told that he won't have to go to school that day. It is a horrible day anyway, cold and raining, so Lewis is happy to stay in front of the fire with his fort and soldiers. Some time later that morning, Dad comes in and scoops him up and sits him on his knee.

'You know how Mum is so beautiful,' he says.

Lewis nods hurriedly. He wants to go back to the game.

'Well God decided that Mum was so wonderful he'd like to keep her with him.'

Now the game is forgotten and Lewis is puzzled. He can smell Dad's cigarette smell.

'When is she coming back?' he asks.

It seems the best and quickest way to get an answer.

'That's what I mean, Lewis – she's not coming back. She's gone to stay with God.'

Lewis starts to cry.

'She's got to come back,' he says through tears.

And that is when Dad holds him so tight that it hurts and maybe Dad is crying too.

Lewis stops crying after a while. He is still on Dad's lap.

'I'm going to go back to my game now,' he says.

He slides off Dad's knee, goes back to his soldiers and plays away for the rest of the day. Some of the shortbread cakes that he likes appear and he is allowed to have as many as he wants. He has three before deciding he has had enough. He is told he won't have to go to school for the rest of the week. Since it is Wednesday that means three days off including today. He isn't too upset now. He has decided how he can see Mum again.

Nobody pushes him to go to bed that night, and when he volunteers to go right on his bedtime, if anyone is surprised they don't say anything. 'A good night's sleep will do you the world of good,' somebody says as he does the rounds of his grandparents and the handful of other aunts and uncles that have materialised during the day. He dutifully kisses them all, smelling the mothballs from the women's coats. Then he is upstairs, teeth brushed, pyjamas on and into his room. Dad comes and tucks him in and asks him if he is alright. Lewis says that he is. Dad kisses him goodnight, closes the door and Lewis hears his feet receding on the stairs.

Lewis' bed lies along the wall. Opposite his bed is a wardrobe and on the inside of the wardrobe door is a full length mirror. Now he opens the wardrobe door and positions it ajar so that he can see the mirror from where he lies in bed. It takes several adjustments to get it right. He moves the door and mirror a fraction then goes and lies on the bed. He jumps up and adjusts it again. Finally he is happy, hops into bed and waits.

She will come and visit him through the mirror. That will be her gateway from wherever she is now, to him. Whether it will be her ghost or her, he doesn't really know. But if it is a ghost he isn't afraid. After all, it's Mum. She won't harm him. The light from the street shines through the curtains and make the mirror silvery and shimmery. He waits and waits. Once or twice he sees the pattern of light on the mirror shift and he thinks that she is about to come, but it's only a trick of the light.

The wallpaper on his wall is light blue with white stars on it. One time he tried to count all the stars but he had to give up. He lies and tries not to think of heaven and space and infinity but they tease at the edge of his thoughts. The world seems so vast.

He only wants to say goodbye to her. Just for a few minutes. There are some questions he wants to ask. Where is she? What is it like? Are there other people there that she knows? Is she happy? What happened to her? Why did she die? And he hopes that she will give him some advice for the future. What should he do now? He hopes that she will have some wisdom for him – she knows so many things. More than anything else he just wants to say a proper goodbye to her. He wants to hold her and hug her and remember her fragrance. He doesn't know if you can hug a ghost but he supposes that God can make all things possible.

He is falling asleep now and fighting to stay awake. It is like Christmas Eve. Eventually he does sleep and when he wakes the next morning the birds are singing and the early morning sounds of the milkman are coming from the street and the wardrobe door is still open.

He's not at all disappointed nor does he give up hope. He reasons that she is just settling in to wherever she is. There must be lots to do and new things to learn. He isn't quite sure when she went there but if it was only yesterday then she mightn't have been able to get away. Maybe it's a complicated business coming back to Earth to see people. Maybe she has to get permission. And maybe she only discovered last night that he was waiting for her and about the wardrobe and the mirror and how that would work. He will look again tonight. Now that she knows – and she must know by now – that he is waiting for her, she will surely come.

But she doesn't – on that second night.

He is not downhearted. In fact, if anything he is probably most confident the third night. He knows the saying, 'Third time lucky'. So he sleeps late the morning after the second night so that he will be wide awake and able to stay awake tonight. He has done the most planning and the most preparation for this third night. Surely this will be the one.

That night, he remembers hearing the church bell chiming midnight. She has still not come. Some time after that he falls asleep. When he wakes the next morning the room is cold with the usual ice on the inside of the window panes. He knows then with a certainty he has never known before in his life that she will not be coming. She has left him. Deserted him. Abandoned him.

He is desolate. He lies in the bed stunned, empty, disbelieving. He was sure that she could see him wherever she was, that she could read his thoughts and that she would come to him. Now, he knows he will never see her again – never hear her voice, see her face, smell her. He will never get to speak with her again, to hear her laugh. The woman who looked so defenceless that day in the changing room has turned out to be exactly that. She has been seized, taken away and is not coming back. And she has left him – just suddenly, out of the blue, just like that.

He lies there and knows he has some decisions to make. If she isn't going to come then a few things are clear. Life can change in an instant – he'd better get used to its unpredictability; he'd better be ready for it. And he knows that from now on he can't rely on anyone else. He must take care of himself, just like a soldier, those soldiers that he plays with every day. He will become strong, so that – if necessary – he can take care of other people. Everything else can't be trusted, but if he relies on himself, if he became strong and grown-up, then he will survive.

19

*L*ewis sped out to the cottage and Helen answered his knock almost immediately.

'I've bought some food we can have for a picnic,' she said. 'It's on the kitchen table. I just need to put it in my bag.'

On the table were mysterious packets, all wrapped in white or brown paper.

'I can take them in my pack,' volunteered Lewis. 'It would be handier.'

'As long as you don't mind,' she called as she ran up the stairs. 'Shan't be a moment.'

They went to Pridmouth, where they swam and basked in the sun and ate their picnic. They had books but neither of them read. The beach wasn't very crowded. Lewis felt proud and confident being with her. He wondered whether the other people on the beach wondered about the relationship between them. Mother and son? The ambiguity of the situation pleased him.

When they were walking back she asked him if he would stay for tea again.

'Are you sure you don't mind?' Lewis asked. 'Maybe you have other people you want to see or things you would like to do.'

'There's nothing I'd like to do more,' she said.

They ate outside as they had the previous night. Then, when the sun had dropped below the horizon, and the light began to grow dusky, she said, 'Come inside. There's something you might like.'

They went into the living room part of the downstairs room. There were several rugs which softened the coldness of the flag stoned floor. Apart from the fireplace and the two armchairs there was a small sideboard.

'I think it will be cosy in the winter,' said Helen. 'And there's a big stock of firewood against that wall there,' she said, indicating with a nod the wall which housed the fireplace.

'Does it need chopping?' asked Lewis. 'I'll be happy to do it.'

'You're sweet,' she smiled. 'We're a long way from the winter yet, but yes, maybe some day, if you wouldn't mind. Come on, sit down. This is what I wanted to show you.'

In the corner – he only noticed it now that she stood beside it – was a gramophone. It was tall, on four squat legs with two sets of doors on the front of it – two large ones at the bottom and two smaller ones above them. On top was a wooden lid that hinged upwards. She raised it now and a jointed steel arm locked, holding the lid in position.

'I was so surprised that first evening I arrived here and found this. I thought it might just have been dumped here, that it was junk, but it actually works. And there are recordings.'

She opened the bottom two doors to reveal a cupboard. Inside was a collection of recordings in brown cardboard sleeves. She selected one from it and then opened the two other, smaller doors where the loudspeaker was. She took the recording from its sleeve and holding it carefully between the palms of her hands, she placed it on the turntable.

'It's already wound up,' she explained and started the music. 'Now, listen to this.'

He sat in one of the armchairs while she took the other one. Some notes on a violin began. They were sad and plaintive.

'Do you know it?' she asked, softly.

He shook his head.

'It's called *The Lark Ascending* by Ralph Vaughan Williams. It's the sound of lying in a field in summer looking up at the sky.'

She closed her eyes, her blonde hair framing her face, her

mouth in a faint smile. He watched her face and listened as the music unfolded. But then, afraid that she would open her eyes and catch him staring at her, or maybe he was just taken by the music anyway, he shut his own eyes. It was the music of Mole and Ratty and Badger. He could see them trotting along the River Bank with the glistening river in the foreground. It was his childhood and the life he had lost – those summer days that would never come again. It was being with Mum. It was the music of being in love. He imagined himself and Helen in a wheat field – in a small bath of trampled down wheat, lying on their backs. Their bodies would be hot from the sun. Lying in an X he would reach out and find her hand and their warm fingers would intertwine. He suddenly found there were tears in his eyes.

He reached for his handkerchief and opened his eyes. She had just opened hers. He saw the startled look on her face.

'What's wrong, Lewis? What's wrong, my love?'

She came over and knelt beside his chair. The tears were pouring down his cheeks now and he was crying and he couldn't stop. He felt her arms encircle him and she drew him to her. He continued to sob and sob, his chest heaving. He was unable to speak. She began to sooth him like a child and rock him very gently, all the while kneeling beside him. Once, twice, he tried to speak but after a word or two, the crying just took over and the words wouldn't come out.

'Shhh,' she said softly. 'There's no need to say anything. Just let it all go. Let it all out.'

Lewis felt incredibly stupid. Eventually, the sobbing eased. Gently, he pulled away from her though he would have happily stayed in her warm, fragrant embrace forever. She released him but stayed kneeling, looking at him tenderly as he dabbed one eye and then the other with his handkerchief.

He smiled wearily.

'I'm sorry,' he said. 'I'm so sorry.'

She shook her head and touched his arm.

'There's nothing to be sorry about, you know. I've often cried to that music.'

'It wasn't the music,' he snuffled. 'Well, I suppose it was really. It just made me think of my childhood ... and my mother —'

'Do you miss her a lot?' asked Helen.

'No,' he sniffed. 'You don't understand. I'm not ... it's not homesickness. My mum ... my mum died when I was eight.'

Helen's hands went up her mouth. He began to shake his head. 'And I just found there ... that music ... it made me think of her. Made me realise how much I missed her and how much I'd lost.'

'Oh Lewis, I'm so sorry. So, so sorry.'

He smiled and waved her away weakly,

'I'm better now. Thank you. Sorry to have been so stupid. You must think me a terrible cry baby.'

She squeezed his arm.

'I don't think anything of the sort,' she said. 'I think it must have been a terrible thing to happen to you.'

'Anyway,' he said with what he hoped would be a final snuffle. 'It's lovely music.'

She stood up.

'Shall I make you some tea?'

'No, I'm fine,' he said. 'Honest.'

'Nonsense,' she said. 'I think you need a bit of mothering.'

Then, as though alarmed by what she had said, she asked, 'Do you mind me saying that, Lewis. Do you?'

'No,' he said with a grin. 'I'd love to be mothered by you.'

'Tea, it is, then,' she said. 'I'd offer you something stronger but I'm afraid I have nothing in the house.'

'Tea will be fine,' he said. 'Thank you.'

As she waited for the kettle to boil, he said, 'Do you play music?'

'I do actually,' she said. 'I play the piano. I used to be a music teacher before I got married. In some ways it's the thing I miss most,' she said, more to herself than to him.

'My Mum used to play the piano.'

'Did she indeed? And what sorts of things did she play?'

He could hardly remember now. In fact he realised he couldn't picture her sitting at the piano or remember anything that she played.

'She had the music for lots of classical pieces. And popular songs as well. She sometimes accompanied people when they sang – at parties or family gatherings.'

'And she sang,' added Lewis. 'She had a lovely voice.'

'She must have been very talented,' said Helen.

Helen made the tea and poured it out. When they each had a cup, she said, 'Have you had enough music for tonight?'

'No, I'd love to hear some more,' he said, 'and I promise not to cry this time.'

'Well, you can cry if you want,' she said. 'And if you don't, maybe I will.'

She changed the recordings.

'This is a piece called *Summer Night on the River* by Delius.'

She didn't say any more but just let the music play. She didn't have to say anything. It was all there in the music. It *was* a summer night by the river. A couple of lovers walking hand in hand in the warm darkness. Fireflies. Trees drooping over the river bank and a grassy path for them to walk. Starlight overhead.

When it finished, he said, 'That was *so* beautiful.'

Then, after a pause, 'Do you know the book, *The Wind in the Willows*?'

It was the third book he had brought with him from home.

'I've heard of it,' she said. 'But I've never read it.'

'I'll loan it to you,' he said. 'I have it back at Mrs Middleton's. In theory it's a children's book, but I'm not so sure. A lot of it happens on a river. You should read it while listening to that.'

'Well if you wouldn't mind loaning it to me.'

'I'll bring it tomorrow,' he said.

Then suddenly realising that he might have sounded too presumptuous, Lewis added, 'Or whenever I see you again.'

'Tomorrow will be fine,' she smiled.

'And you're sure there aren't other things you need to be doing? Places to go? People to see? I feel like I must be taking up all of your time.'

She looked at him.

'Lewis, I've been alone for a lot of my life. If you don't mind spending time with an old woman, then you're welcome to be here as much as you like.'

It was the same thing she had said the previous night. He repeated what he had said then, that she wasn't old.

'No,' she said, in a strange, distant, thoughtful sort of way. 'No, I suppose I'm not.'

20

The twins were called Victoria and Sophie. They were both blonde, lived just around the corner from Lewis, who was then aged sixteen, and he thought they were the most beautiful creatures he had ever seen. They were not identical. He had worked that out even from a distance – he had never seen them close up. They had to pass his house on their way to school and sometimes, if he dawdled in the morning, he would see them pass at about ten to nine. They didn't seem to be very punctual though – or to have a routine. Occasionally they were earlier. More often they hadn't appeared before he had to leave.

But on the days when they did appear, he would immediately grab his satchel and run out the door as quickly as he could with hurried goodbyes to Margaret the housekeeper, and Dad, if he was there. His route followed the twins' for about five minutes before they turned off for the girls' grammar school. From behind, on summer days, their hair was radiant in the sunlight.

He didn't know which was which, but one of them had a thinner face than the other. For some reason which he couldn't remember, he came to the conclusion that the thinner faced one was Sophie and the other one Victoria. He decided that he preferred Victoria. On Sundays they always went to church with their mother. When Mum was alive, she, Lewis and Dad had gone to church regularly, but after she died the practice had lapsed. So Lewis told Dad he would like to start going again. Lewis thought Dad looked momentarily alarmed – Sunday was the one day in the week when he slept in. But Lewis explained that he was happy to go by himself and said something about 'pray for Mum' and 'those fighting in the War' and Dad seemed happy enough with that.

So Lewis would go to church and try to sit near them, ideally in the row behind. From there he could glory in their hair, particularly when sunlight came though the stained glass windows and irradiated them. Or he could wonder what they were whispering about which they did from time to time until a disapproving gaze from their large and stern mother caused them to stop. Or he could try to kneel forward while they were still sitting, enabling him to get so close that he could smell their fragrance.

There was always only ever the three of them and so Lewis came to realise that there was no father in the family. He assumed that the father was dead. So – they had something in common.

He spent endless hours thinking about them. He reckoned they were his age and there was that thing that girls were more grown up than boys of the same age. But that didn't bother him. He was one of the smarter people in his class so he didn't think that that would be a problem. There were some days, he had established, when they always came home later than him from school and he always tried to be in the sitting room or in the front garden on those days. They always passed on the far side of the street and if they did happen to glance over it was without interest in Lewis or what he was doing.

They had a friend who had dark hair, who was often with them. She was also beautiful but it was the twins that Lewis had fallen in love with – Victoria especially, but either one would do. He imagined himself as their friend, going places with the three of them. He would be Victoria's boyfriend but he would be friends with all of them. They could talk about not having a parent and what it had meant to them growing up. He saw himself holding Victoria's hand as they walked along the street. He imagined the sensation of kissing her, and the scent of her blonde hair as he did. At night – this was the period when he was praying to be cured of his shyness – he also prayed that some event would happen that would make all this come about. They had this huge hole in their lives, this missing parent. Surely God owed it to him to bring them together. Or maybe that was too strong. Maybe you couldn't say that to God, but surely He could see the sense of it – how perfect it would be. Maybe that was the reason why they found themselves living near each other – because they were going to *be* together.

During the summers there were dances in the local church hall. The money raised was used to send gift boxes to the troops. In the summer of 1915, Lewis went to his first one. He wore his best trousers, a new white shirt and a tie that he bought specially for the occasion from hoarded pocket money. The dance was due to start at eight. He was going with James, his friend from school who lived further along Horn Lane. Dad wished him good luck as he went out the door.

The evening was still warm after the heat of the day. The sky was blue and the streets were green and leafy and shaded. He rendezvoused with James as they had arranged and they walked together in the direction of the church hall. They were both apprehensive and tried to disguise it with chatter. Part of Lewis wished he was back in his room or out in the garden reading. As they approached the church hall they could hear music and see young people arriving there like swallows onto telegraph wires in autumn.

Inside, the stage had been decorated with balloons and strings of small union flags. A three piece band – piano, violin and cello – played light classical pieces, songs from operettas and popular songs. There were a few couples on the floor but mostly the girls were sitting on benches around the edge of the hall and the boys were clustered together in groups.

Once he got there Lewis wished that James hadn't come. He felt embarrassed with him there and if a girl was going to refuse him he didn't want James to witness it. Also, he got no sense from James that he would ask any girl to dance and was happy just to mooch along with Lewis and let him make the first move. They were like a hunter and his faithful dog, Lewis thought. They wandered around the edges of the hall where the girls all sat on benches. There was no sign of the twins and Lewis' heart dropped at the thought that that they might not be coming.

The hall filled up quickly and the dance floor became more crowded. Lewis and James bumped into Albert, a classmate of theirs.

'Oh, hello lads. Haven't seen you here before.'

'This is our first time,' said Lewis.

'Well have a good night,' said Albert, and – as he dived into the crowd – 'good hunting.'

Lewis suggested to James that they split up and James agreed. He was a person who seemed happy to agree to most anything and while Lewis was happy with this most of the time – because it made Lewis the leader – sometimes, like now, he found it intensely irritating. After James had wandered off, Lewis made another concentrated effort to see if the twins were there. He wondered about dancing with some other girl just to get some practice in actually asking somebody to dance. But he decided against it. It would be the twins or nobody. Then suddenly, in the crowd ahead, he saw Victoria. She was wearing a summery blouse with short sleeves and a long skirt. She stood a few people back from the edge of the crowd that was watching the couples who were dancing. She appeared to be by herself – there was no sign of Sophie or their friend with the dark hair. This was wonderful – it made it so much easier to approach her.

The little ensemble was playing a fast number and Lewis was going to wait until they played a waltz. But he realised that she might not be alone for that long so he took a deep breath and threaded his way through the crowd towards her. He hoped she might sense him coming and turn her head towards him and that he might see a flash of recognition on her face. But she seemed unaware of his presence until he arrived beside her and tapped her on the shoulder. His touch on the white fabric of her blouse and the feeling of skin underneath was like an electric shock that ran from his fingertips. He smelt freshly shampooed hair. She turned to him and above the sound of the orchestra, he said, 'Would you like to dance?'

If she recognised him she made no sign. Her lips were very pink, her eyes blue and her skin smooth. Her face was every bit as beautiful as it had seemed from a distance. He thought it was a kind and loving face. She didn't smile, but said yes. He wondered whether he should lead her onto the floor or whether it was ladies first, and while he was hesitating, and without looking at him, she led the way. He smelt her perfume as he followed in her wake.

As they reached the edge of the floor she turned to face him. He extended his arms, putting an arm around her waist and taking her hand in his. He felt her waist beneath the material of her dress and he thought that he had never felt anything more thrilling in his life. They began to move away from where they had started. She was still not smiling and was looking away from him.

'Have you been to these dances before?' he asked.

She looked at him as though seeing him for the first time. She hadn't heard what he said, either because it was too noisy or her mind was someplace else. He repeated the question. She smiled faintly and shook her head. He wondered what to say to her next. He was going to ask her if she knew that they lived nearby to one another but it seemed like a silly thing to say. Then he was going to say that the orchestra was good but he suspected that all she would do would be to smile again. He thought he should tell her his name but what if she then didn't tell him hers? He thought to ask whether her sister was here as well and then he hoped that that could lead into a discussion about twins. But he didn't want it to appear like he was interested in her sister rather than her. And the volume of the musicians seemed to prohibit any kind of conversation anyway, although when he looked around he could see that some other couples were chatting easily. All the time they moved around the floor.

While all of this was going on in his head, she was looking over his shoulder. Their eyes met once and she smiled at him. It was a smile that would have been described in books as a sweet smile. But he thought it was the smile of somebody trapped in a place that they didn't want to be; a make-the-most-of-a-bad-lot smile. They had only been on the floor for no more than a minute or two. Suddenly the music came to and end. She took her hand from his and extricated her body from his other hand.

'Thank you,' she said blankly and walked off the floor.

He followed her and saw her disappear into the press of bodies. Albert's face floated up in front of him.

'You did well there,' he said.

Lewis smiled weakly and nodded. He wasn't sure if Albert was being sarcastic.

'Good man,' said Albert, slapping him on the shoulder before wandering off again.

Lewis drifted around a little more. The twins were together again and the girl with the dark hair was with them now. The three of them were talking very seriously about something. He turned away and went and got a lemonade – he had been hoping to have been buying the lemonade for Victoria. It was very hot and stuffy by now and he was sweating. He downed the lemonade in one gulp and then went and watched the dancers. He was hoping to see the twins again, to see what sort of boys they were with, but there was no sign of them. James appeared and Lewis asked him how he got on. 'Fine' was James's laconic reply and Lewis reckoned he hadn't danced with anyone. He wasn't sure that James was interested in girls at all. If Lewis came to another dance here he would come on his own.

Neither of them danced again and they left just before ten. There was a gaggle of people around the door of the church hall. One or two couples could be seen walking hand in hand down the short tree-lined drive to the gates, their silhouettes black against the street lights beyond the trees. There was a tree with a large trunk only a few steps from the church hall door and there was a small gap between it and the tall hedge that encircled the church hall and its grounds. Lewis saw a couple in the shadows and when they moved into the light of the street lamps, Lewis saw the veil of blonde hair and realised that it was Victoria. A boy was holding her and they were locked in a kiss.

'They're having fun,' said James cheerily.

Lewis said nothing and they walked home in silence. He was glad when James said good night and he was able to make the remainder of the journey on his own. To his annoyance, Dad was up when Lewis got in and he had to talk to him for a few minutes. But then pleading tiredness, Lewis headed upstairs to his room.

He lay for a long time in the darkness. 'All the illusions gone.' The phrase kept repeating itself in his head. He had pictured himself and Victoria together. He had seen himself with her and her sister and their friend. He had seen himself as the boy in their lives – friendly with all of them, in love with Victoria. All of that was gone now.

He wondered where he went from here. There had been no other girl there tonight that he felt the remotest attraction to. And he couldn't go back now to Sophie or to the girl with the dark hair. What was wrong with him? He knew that Albert had already had several girlfriends. And lots of other fellows that he knew were the same – you'd see them around town any Saturday. Why was he different?

Was it his looks? He had looked in the mirror that night and yes, he wasn't as handsome as some of the boys, but he wasn't ugly. Why couldn't Mum have helped him? She had left him. She had run out on him. He had gotten over that now but why couldn't she help him? Surely she owed him that much. Surely she owed him something. That was all he asked – a bit of luck where girls were concerned. A bit of love and kissing and female company with all their softness and fragrance.

But of course Mum was gone. There was no point in asking her. He existed and so *she* must have, but he felt no link to her. How was that possible? She had borne him inside her body – could there be any greater closeness? And yet now she smiled out from photographs and was … just a person in photographs.

21

*L*ewis emerged from the dugout into the darkness of the trench. A cold crab of fear clung to his heart. He was sweating despite the intense cold. He would die tonight. He was convinced of it. The mocking logic of it. Born on his birthday, died on Helen's. He couldn't get the idea out of his head. The crab's claws gripped and scored and sliced his heart. He felt faint and stopped, resting his arm against a piece of angle iron that held revetting in place.

He still remembered his first trench raid – and Sergeant Bennis, his first sergeant. Long dead now, cut in two by a machine gun at Arras. He was still the most foul-mouthed man Lewis had ever met and no respecter of rank. They had emerged from a similar briefing before Lewis was due to go on his first trench raid and Bennis had said, 'Are you afraid, sir?'

It was an outrageous question for a sergeant to ask his senior officer. It was also obviously some kind of test and Lewis didn't know how to answer.

'No, sergeant. Well, yes. Nervous, you know. Butterflies and all that.'

Bennis's eyes drilled into him.

'You're not half afraid enough, sir' he said, the last word spoken as though it wasn't deserved.

And there had been that moment after it was all over when Bennis had said, 'You did well, sir.'

Lewis thought it was the first time Bennis had called him 'sir' and actually meant it.

But now Lewis was scared enough. He took a deep breath

to try to calm himself. And another and another. A soldier went past in the other direction carrying an oval dixie from which a greasy smell of food issued. Lewis thought the soldier might have glanced at him – it was hard to tell in the darkness – but if he did, he said nothing. Lewis knew he couldn't stay here. Get back to the dugout. Write to Helen or read her last letter. That would help. He needed to shake off this feeling of doom. Maybe there would be a new letter from her – it might come up with the food.

It was nearly eight by the time he got back to the dugout; it had taken him a lot longer to get back without Byrne to guide him. He pulled aside the gas curtain and stepped in out of the dank iciness of the night into the relative warmth of the dugout. The place was in inky blackness so with hands extended and one foot leading, he inched forward gingerly until his thigh met the table. He groped for the candle in the bottle, found it and lit it with the lighter from his greatcoat pocket. A ball of cosy yellow light expanded above the table where socks hung from an improvised washing line slung across the dugout.

'Alright, girls?' Lewis said to the photograph of the two girls left by the previous German occupants. It was pinned to a supporting pillar of the dugout just beside the table. Lewis called them Victoria and Sophie. The two girls looked to be the same age as the real Victoria and Sophia would have been now. But there the similarity ended. The picture was taken with the two girls standing in profile and almost naked. Victoria – that was she on the left – wore cavalry boots while the other wore ankle length boots and stockings held up by garters. They stood facing each other, leaning forward at the waist so that, between them, they formed a sort of 'A'. Victoria had her hands over her head with her fingertips on top of her head. She was pouting. Sophie was leaning forward and was in the process of kissing Victoria's pout with one of her own. Talking to them eased Lewis' terrible fear a little.

Currently he had the dugout to himself. Wilson, the previous occupant of the other bunk, had been blown to spots a few weeks ago and his replacement had yet to arrive. There was also a problem with the second bunk in that the ceiling area above it smelt foul and maggots kept dropping from above. There was only one reason why there might be such a concentration of maggots in the earth. When Wilson was alive he had tried to work out how the maggots got through the wood panelled ceiling since it was expertly tongued and grooved. Eventually he had given up and had solved the problem by hanging his groundsheet overhead to catch them. Each morning when he woke he gathered up the four corners of the groundsheet and carried the collected maggots outside and emptied it. The night he was obliterated it had been raining and he had been on duty with his groundsheet draped over him. So now there was no Wilson, no groundsheet, only a steady fall of maggots and the lingering stench.

'Dinner, sir?'

Private Chase's face appeared at the door, with a tin plate in his hand.

'It's hot, sir.'

'Thanks, Chase.'

Chase deposited the plate on the table. The food appeared to be some kind of stew with potatoes and carrots and a greasy film over it. An hour ago Lewis had been hungry and looking forward to his dinner. Now he couldn't eat. He never could before something like this. He wouldn't want to anyway – better to have an empty belly in case he got a stomach wound. His gut felt like it was tied in knots. He was tempted to finish the whiskey but he knew it would slow his movements and make him clumsy. He took Helen's photograph from his wallet and propped it against the bottle. She was smiling – impish and innocent all at once like she had just proposed that they do something that they had never done before and was waiting for his reply. In one of his letters to her a few weeks ago he had written about the lack of any beauty in the trenches. He had been thinking then of her and of all things feminine. Stray strands of long hair, red lips, skin like peaches, ribbons, lace, frilly things, sheer stockings, straps, bows, fabric pulled taut, her curves against him in bed, fragrance on a pillow or sheets.

With her reply she had sent him one of her stockings, sprayed with perfume. Grossmith's *Shem-el-Nessim*. He remembered the first time he had seen the exquisite little bottle on her dressing table. 'The Scent of Araby', it said on it. He took the stocking from his inside pocket. The scent of the perfume was almost gone now – just the faintest hint of it lingered. He inhaled it deeply. Smell. The most evocative of the senses. He covered his eyes with the stocking as though it were a blindfold. She *had* blindfolded him with one once. Then he touched it to his cheek and held it there for several moments.

He stroked each of her cheeks in the photograph with his fingertips; then the cascade of her hair with the backs of his fingers. Finally he ran his index finger down her nose. He opened his greatcoat and took out the pen from the side pocket of his tunic.

My dearest, darling Helen,

It's your birthday. Happy birthday, my darling love. Of course this means that that silly age difference between us has opened up a bit again – but I'll close it in November, never you fear.

I don't know how it is where you are, but there are rumours that the War might be coming to an end. Of course, we have heard such rumours for years but maybe this time it's true. Certainly the signs are encouraging. And if it were would it be too much to hope that we would spend this Christmas together? We never have. And your next birthday. And mine. And all our birthdays & Christmases after this together & never be apart again.

If the War is over, what shall I do? I shall have a little money so maybe there will be time to think about all of this. Maybe we shall return to where it all started – though no, maybe we cannot go there. But we shall find some place & be together.

We have a little job to do tonight, but don't worry, it's nothing serious. After it I shall go to bed & dream of your lovely face & your body – the body of a goddess. My goddess.

Sleep well, my darling until we hold each other in our arms.

Your adoring,

Lewis.

He folded the letter and kissed it, put it in an envelope and placed it on the table. He felt better. It was like he had invoked a spell. The certainty that he would die had receded from his mind somewhat. The talk of a future together had driven it away. Eight thirty, his watch said. Another three and a half hours. He ate a couple of spoonfuls of the food – he didn't want to feel weak from hunger later. It was slop. He pushed it away and found the remains of a bar of French chocolate that he had bought in Amiens.

Some time later Sergeant Robinson and Corporal Jackson came in. Robinson had none of the extremes that Bennis had. He was balanced, practical, level-headed. Lewis knew that Robinson had a wife and two children and imagined that before the War, he probably adored his wife, was a good father and did everything he could to provide for his family. He was the same here – caring about his men, resourceful, a good man to have beside you in a crisis. Jackson, Lewis was less sure about. He was new, young, pimply and didn't say very much. He looked far too young to be in uniform, never mind a corporal. Lewis wondered what the men thought of him.

'Drink, Sergeant, Corporal?'

Lewis lifted the bottle from the table, uncorked it and offered it to them.

'Thank you, sir,' they said in unison.

The bottle was passed around and back to Lewis. Without wiping the top of it, he took a deep swig. He considered what remained and handed it back to them.

'May as well finish it.'

There was only one chair so Lewis got the other two to sit on the edge of the bunk while they decided how they would deploy their men. Lewis' right hand began to shake again. If they noticed, they said nothing.

They were to bring back documents and prisoners. On entering the trench, Robinson, Jackson and two men would go left. If they found Germans they would subdue them and make them prisoner but their main job was to find documents. This would involve going into dugouts. Standing orders were not to throw in any grenades in case valuable documents were destroyed. Nobody ever obeyed these orders. Go into a dugout not knowing what was there? Those staff people were out of their fucking minds. Robinson would bomb first and look for papers afterwards.

Lewis would take the remaining four men and go right. They needed to bring back at least three prisoners. That was the minimum Division would settle for. As Lewis' party found Germans they would subdue them, tie their hands and then each would be accompanied back to the entry point by one of Lewis' men. When the third German was captured, Lewis would issue the order to withdraw. The man who would accompany the third prisoner to the entry point would then find Sergeant Robinson's men and tell them to withdraw. He would also do the same with the Left Blocking Party. The fourth man with Lewis would communicate the order for withdrawal to the Right Blocking Party and then return with Lewis to the entry point.

If it all went according to plan then, Lewis and the fourth man would return to the entry point where they should find Robinson, Jackson and the five other men. Ideally, the prisoners would already be on their way back to the British lines, taken there by the men of the Covering Party. With all nine of them accounted for, they would then exit the trench and return.

There was nothing else.

'I'll go over it with the men, sir,' said Robinson.

He and Jackson saluted and went out.

22

*T*he next day Lewis brought *The Wind In The Willows* with him and gave it to Helen. She said she would start reading it that day. He hoped she would like it and wouldn't find him stupid for having recommended it. With anybody else he might have talked about more serious, adult books, but with her he could say exactly what he felt.

Later on the beach, she said to him, 'Tell me about losing your Mum at such an early age.'

'You must have thought I was a real cry baby yesterday,' he said. 'You know, when you thought I was crying because I missed home and my Mum. Anyway, I'll tell you what I can remember.'

He told her about Mum going into hospital and the day that Dad told him she was dead. He told Helen what he had never told anybody – about the wardrobe, and that Mum's ghost would come back and about his devastation when she didn't. She touched his hand.

'You poor boy,' she said so softly that it was almost a whisper.

Her fingers were warm on his skin. They looked so graceful and beautiful.

They were sitting on their towels looking out at the water. A couple of swimmers in the water were silhouettes in a pool of sunlight-splashed sea.

'You know that expression, he said. '"Every cloud has a silver lining"? Well, I really think that's true. Because even though it was a terrible thing to happen – terrible for my Mum, for my Dad, for me – it had some good effects. It made me terribly independent. I remember so clearly thinking after that third night, when she didn't come back, that I would have to look after myself from now on. I think it'll hold me in good stead in what's to come. And I suppose, after something like that, you feel that nothing worse can happen. Though maybe I'll have to revise that opinion after I join the Army.'

'But you've lost so much.'

'I suppose you don't miss what you never had,' he said, with a lightness he didn't feel.

She was looking at him and it was as though her green eyes could read what was written on his heart.

'I think I don't actually know what I've lost, and maybe that's what is worst of all. I think there are many things that she should have taught me but didn't get the time to. I don't know what they are, but they are things that mothers teach children. About the world. About people. I think in many ways I am innocent of the world. In some ways my growing stopped or got stunted when she died.'

He paused.

'I've never spoken to anyone like this … about these things before. I don't think I even knew I felt like this.'

The sunlight shone on her hair showing tints of gold and honey.

'Maybe that's why you've come into my life,' Lewis said. 'To teach me these things – whatever they are.'

'Maybe I have,' she said.

'How long are you going to stay here for?' he asked.

The sun illuminated a silver pathway on the water out to where the shoulder of land that marked the right hand side of the cove dropped to the sea. Beyond the entrance a ship moved slowly past on the horizon. She turned away from him and faced out to sea, pulling her knees up to her chin and circling her arms around them.

'I don't know,' she said.

He knew she didn't want to say any more but he pressed on regardless.

'It must be terrible for you having your husband at the front.'

'It would be nice to know whether he's going to come back alive or not,' she murmured.

'When was the last time you saw him?'

'Easter. But he writes every day – and expected me to write back.'

The use of the past tense sounded odd.

'You must miss him terribly.'

She said nothing more. The silence lengthened and Lewis thought he'd better give up on it. He too began to look out to sea. A small boat with a mast and a sail set appeared round the headland and turned into the cove. He heard her snuffle and glanced across at her.

Helen's shoulders were shaking and her eyes and cheeks were wet with tears. Lewis was suddenly guilty. He shouldn't have probed so much – shouldn't have been so nosy. He had upset her now. And he wouldn't have wanted to upset her for the world. Daringly, he put an arm around her shoulder and left it there. She made no attempt to push it away.

'I'm so sorry,' he said. 'I shouldn't have brought the subject up. I've been an unfeeling clod.'

She rummaged in her bag, took out a small handkerchief and blew her nose. She shook her head.

'It's not that. It's not you.'

She wiped the tears with the back of her wrist and looked at him.

'It's not you. It's him – Robert, my husband. I hate him.'

And then with a venom he would not have expected of her.

'I hope he never comes back.'

Her green eyes were pools of tears.

'And even if he does – well, I've left him. He doesn't know I'm here. He doesn't know where I am. You must think I'm terrible.'

Lewis wasn't quite sure what to say. It struck him how sheltered a life he had been living at home. This was life in the real world.

'I don't think you're terrible. If you left him you must have had a good reason for doing so.'

He had half intended it as a question but she didn't answer. Instead she had gone back to looking at the boat with the sail which was now making its way towards the shore. The figure on board lowered the sail. He moved in that casual way that people who know boats have. Then he sat down, swung out first one oar, then another and began to row the boat the last few yards in. When it had beached he jumped out and, in rolled up trousers and bare feet, dragged the boat up the shingle until it was clear of the water.

'He didn't used to beat me,' she stated.

'You don't have to tell me any of this, Helen. Not if you find it too upsetting.'

'I have to tell somebody,' she said.

'I've never been lucky with the men in my life. I don't think my father really liked me. He certainly didn't like my mother and I think he saw me as being on her side. So everything I did – I was good in school, I had a real talent for the piano, I started my own little business giving piano lessons – everything I did, I got no praise for it. Not that I wanted much. But it would have been nice if, once in a while, just once in a while, he had said, "You've done well" or "I knew you could do it" or "That's my girl." But no, there was nothing.'

Her voice had become very tear-sodden.

'He never once told me he loved me.'

She turned to face Lewis. Her face was red from crying.

'Can you believe that? Not once?'

Lewis *couldn't* believe it. After his mother died, all of his relations had showered him in love. It would never have even occurred to him that all these people didn't love him. He found it hard to imagine the sterile world she was describing. She turned away again.

'So when I wasn't married by the time I was twenty, I think it gave him a certain satisfaction. Do you know, I think it actually pleased him? And as I went through my twenties unmarried, it was like he was sitting there with this mixture of smugness and contempt. I had a really enjoyable time in my twenties. I had money from my piano teaching, I had lots of friends, I had boyfriends. But none of that was enough for him and occasionally he would slip in snide remarks about my not being married.

I suppose by the time I was into my thirties I was starting to believe these remarks myself. Or maybe it was just that he had opened up a tiny crack of doubt in my own mind. Whatever it was, it didn't take much to push me down the marriage road when I met Robert.

It was only five years ago. It seems a lot longer. I met him at a cocktail party. He seemed so handsome in his uniform. He was a few years older than me. I felt young around him and not at all the aged spinster that my father kept telling me I was. We were married within a year. And that's when it all changed.

As I said, he didn't used to beat me. But there are others ways to break a person. You can stop them from being themselves; from living the life they want to live. You can take away their hopes, their dreams. You can criticise them until they stop believing in themselves. Until they start believing that the good things about them aren't actually good at all or even that they don't exist. You take away everything that was good about them. Why do people feel that when they get married it gives them the right to say whatever they like to the other person? There's no politeness, no respect. They say things that they would never say, for example, to a neighbour or somebody in a shop. And once that starts happening it's a short hop to all kinds of hurtful and abusive things.

He got me to give up my piano teaching, my pupils. Told me I didn't need to earn money – he had plenty of it, which he did. But then it meant that I lost all that human contact as well, never mind the creativity that went along with it.'

'So why didn't you leave him then?' asked Lewis.

She paused. Then she spoke slowly.

'I hope, Lewis, that when the time comes and you meet somebody and you marry them, that you'll be completely and utterly happy. I really, really hope that. Because if you don't I think you'll find that there are many reasons not to leave somebody.

First of all, there's the money. Robert is very well off. What was I going to do if I left him? Where would I go? How would I start? I had saved a little of what he gave me but it didn't seem a lot, not in comparison to what I was used to. And there's routine. You know – you just get used to things. And the notion of starting again in a new place, where everything is new, where you don't even know where your toothbrush goes. Well – it's daunting. And, the fact is, it's not all bad all the time. Robert could be charming when he wanted to be. We had some nice times together. And then there was my father. I suppose I just didn't want to give him the satisfaction of seeing me back on the shelf again. And finally, there's the fact that everybody just wants to be loved. And I suppose that some love is better than no love at all. And if I Ieft I would have to start looking all over again. I'll be thirty-seven in December, Lewis. I'm a spinster with all the sad things that that word implies. Where would I find love now? As I say, there are all sorts of reasons why it's easier to stay.'

'If I was married, I would never criticise the other person,' said Lewis. 'At least I'd like to think I wouldn't. I'd like to think it would just be live and let live. And anyway that I would love so much about them that these other things, whatever they were, wouldn't matter.'

'I hope you find that Lewis. I really do. It's the rarest thing – a marriage like that. Mine wasn't like it and I don't think my parents' was. What about your parents? Were they like that?'

It was a long time before he answered.

'I don't know,' he said. 'I wish I did know. I don't really remember a great deal about their relationship. If I'd known she was going to die so soon in my life then maybe I would have remembered more. I wish I had.'

The man who had arrived in the boat had walked up the beach and disappeared. After another long, thoughtful silence, Helen continued.

'It was like he had a picture of how he wanted his wife to be. And I had to conform to that. And his picture wasn't me at all. He must have known that when he married me. I made no secret of it.'

She sounded like she was talking more to herself than to him.

'He shouldn't have been surprised. But he was – and once he realised it he wanted to change me. I had to change.'

'I can't imagine why anybody would want you to change,' said Lewis. 'You're beautiful as you are.'

She turned to him, smiled weakly and held his gaze for a few moments. Then she turned away again.

'I tried for a while. I really did. I remember I used to lie awake for hours at night, wondering how I'd done that day and how could I improve the next. But no matter what I did it was never enough. And that's when the War came along. I know it sounds terrible but I was so happy the day that War was declared.'

She paused.

'I was so, so happy. I was walking on air for the next few weeks. My torture was at an end. There was a period after the War started when he was still about the house. But then came the day when he had to go off. It was like a huge dark cloud had lifted. All the tension was gone from the house. I had never liked the house – it was his family home that he had inherited, but now I could see its beauty. There was a wonderful sense of peace there. It was such a pleasure not to have him in the house. Or in the bedroom. I felt lighter. Like I'd been born again.'

Lewis felt a peculiar stab of jealousy as she mentioned 'the bedroom'. He wondered where it had come from.

'When I married him I had lots of friends of my own. But if we met them for a drink, he would criticise them afterwards. Only small criticisms – a dig here, a snide remark there. Or if they came to the house, he'd be in one of his moods. Or he'd be bright and cheery while they were there but then I'd pay for it for days afterwards. So I started to see them by myself. I would make some excuse about Robert not being able to come. But then he didn't like me going out on my own. The result was that, one by one, they just dropped away.

But now I was able to start calling them up again. It was glorious. Like being released from prison. They all remarked on it – how it was marvellous to have the old Helen back.

"We shall write every day," he told me, when he finally went off. But what he really meant by that was that I was to write every day. And I did. I was happy to do it. That hour I spent every day, packing my letter full of all the little happenings in my life, was a small price to pay. There was lots I didn't tell him, of course – things that I was doing that I never could have done when he was there. He came home on leave once or twice but I didn't mind. I knew he'd be going away again.'

Lewis felt the jealousy again. He wondered if, when he came home, she had to – 'submit to him' was the phrase that came into his head. She looked at him.

'Do you know what I found myself hoping?'

'No.'

'I know you'll think this is terrible but I found myself hoping that he would be killed.'

She reached out and took his hand. Her eyes seemed to be boring into him.

'That's terrible, isn't it?

He didn't know what to say. He thought it *was* terrible.

'And do you know what my only fear was?'

Lewis saw fear in her face now. Her grip on his hand had tightened.

'That the War would end?'

'That he would be wounded. Maimed. Disabled in some way. And that they would bring him back and that I'd have to take care of him. For the rest of my life. A life sentence.'

'Why didn't you just divorce him?' asked Lewis.

She let go his hand.

'Yes, it sounds easy, doesn't it? Just get a solicitor to send him some letters, go to court, sign some papers and it would be all over. Several times I nearly did. I called up solicitors, made appointments, but then I would phone up and cancel. I thought it wasn't fair to do it to him while he was out there. After all I was part of what he was fighting for. What more noble thing can a man do for a woman? I decided I'd wait until the War was over. He would come back and then I would do it.

But this thing of him coming back wounded began to eat into me. I knew that if he came back like that – blind or in a wheelchair or needing to be fed or taken to the toilet – I knew that then I would never be able to leave him. It got to the point where I dreaded the postman coming or seeing a telegram boy. Finally, at the end of May, I couldn't take it any more. I left. I left on the first of June. I decided I would leave first, find a new place and then I would write to him.

The letter is actually written. It's on my dressing table. Every morning I look at it and wonder, is today the day?'

'But why wait? You've done the difficult bit now, haven't you? And surely he'll be worried that he hasn't heard from you.'

'Because I'm a spineless coward, that's why. I'm still taking his money. As soon as I send that letter he'll stop giving me money.'

'But surely if you go to a lawyer?'

'Oh Lewis, what grounds do I have for a divorce? Does he beat you, Mrs Hope? No, not at all. I live – or used to – in a nice house. I have more than enough money. What do I have to complain about? My husband is grumpy sometimes. He likes things to be a certain way … to be just so. No solicitor would take the case. And if I did I wouldn't get a penny off him.'

'But you could get a job. Start your piano teaching again. Or once I go into the Army, I can give you money.'

Her eyes widened. She took his other hand.

'Oh Lewis,' she said, 'that it one of the kindest things anyone's ever said to me. Of course I couldn't take your money. I'm not your wife, for goodness sake. No, with you, it's enough that I have you to talk to. Come on, I've had enough of this gloomy talk. Let's go and swim.'

He stood and she allowed him to pull her up.

'Race you,' she said, and they splashed into the surf together.

23

_L_ ewis and Helen walked home in the still-warm evening. She was silent, responding to anything he said only in monosyllables. He wondered whether she was embarrassed because she had talked so intimately about her marriage. He wondered whether this would be the end of it; that she wouldn't want to see him again now that she had bared her soul like this. She asked him in and fed him but it seemed to him that their evening was without the enchantment of the previous day. He was surprised and upset by this. He thought that after the intimacy of today they would have been closer than ever. He was saddened to think that this might be the last time he would be here. She seemed sad or distracted or something. She moved the food around her plate but ate very little. At one stage she looked across at him and said, 'I'm not very good company this evening, am I?'

'Talking about all that today – it must have brought back lots of unhappy memories.'

'Things are better now,' she said. 'Thank you for listening. You're a good listener.'

The compliment delighted him.

Later, in the hall, she kissed him goodnight on the cheek. He had waited all evening for her to talk about what they would do tomorrow. When she hadn't and now that they were at the door, he said, 'Will you be going to the beach tomorrow?'

'Maybe not tomorrow,' she said. 'But you know where I am. Drop in if you're down there.'

It was hardly an invitation at all. She opened the door and let him out. She said goodnight, her body half hidden by the door. Then the rectangle of yellow light collapsed and she was gone.

It was as though the happiness of the day had evaporated. Since he had met her, she had seemed to be enjoying his company as much as he enjoyed hers. Now, whether it was because of the confidences she had shared today, or for some other reason, she didn't really want to see him any more. He wasn't sure he would ever call in on her uninvited. And he didn't want to become an irritation to her, like a puppy dog following her around.

'Good evening, Mr Friday?' asked Mrs Middleton cheerily as he came in.

She was fussing around her little office. Lewis wondered whether it was to see who was coming back and in what state and whether they were bringing anybody with them.

'Yes, thank you, Mrs Middleton.'

He was in no mood for her chit-chat. He took the stairs two at a time and went to his room. In bed he lay awake for hours thinking about Helen until sleep claimed him.

In the morning he told Mrs Middleton he wouldn't be home for dinner. He would eat in one of the restaurants in Fowey. But he decided to spend the day at Readymoney. If nothing else, he would be near Helen. Maybe she would be in a better mood today and she would come down to the beach. As he passed by the lane that led to her cottage, he looked up along it but there was no sign of her. At the beach he read, swam and ate his sandwiches. Towards evening, he lay on his back with his shirt over his face, drifting between sleeping and wakefulness.

The waves lapped and birds twittered in the trees above the beach. There was a gentle murmur of conversation and occasionally louder bursts of chatter. Swimmers splashed or squealed in the water. The sounds of summer.

He had wanted to meet a girl during this holiday but then along had come Helen. Now all he wanted was to be with her.

In some ways it was stupid, he knew. There was a huge age difference between them but what did that matter if they enjoyed being together? Couldn't they be friends? Couldn't they be best friends, even if they couldn't be anything else?

But he would have liked something else. To be with her – always, every day. To be married to her. They could do it if she got divorced. To wake up beside her in the morning, to eat breakfast with her, to spend the day with her, to help her cook, to read and laugh and go for walks. And then, when it was dark, to go to bed with her. He had seen her tall, statuesque figure in the bathing suit; had seen the shape of her breasts and the lines of her thighs – at least as much as he could because the top of the swimsuit came down to just above her knees. But he wondered what it would be like to remove her clothes. He could feel himself becoming hard, as he thought of unbuttoning her blouse slowly, button by button and then peeling it off her shoulders.

'Hello stranger. I wondered if you'd be here.'

He was instantly awake. He pulled the shirt from his face and sat bolt upright. He dropped his hands to his lap wondering whether she had seen what was happening to him. He blinked against the brightness. She knelt on the sand beside him.

'Sorry, I didn't mean to startle you.'

'No – it's lovely to see you. Absolutely wonderful. Sit down – have some towel.'

He stood up, shook out the towel and spread it out for the two of them. Her face was bright and happy. Radiant, he thought.

'Well, I've done it.'

'Done it?'

'I've done it. I've posted the letter. I took the train to Plymouth and posted it from there. It says in it that I'm giving it to a friend of mine to post and that she's touring the West Country.'

Lewis must have looked puzzled. She tossed his hair with her hand.

'Wake up, you silly boo. If I'd posted it here, he could find me from the postmark. This way he never will.'

'No, of course. I see, I see. That's wonderful,' he said. 'Well done. Congratulations.'

'Isn't it? I'm really happy. I'll have a think about all this divorce and solicitor business later … soon. I'll probably do something at the end of the summer but right now, we should just enjoy ourselves.'

She suddenly looked anxious.

'That's if you'd like to spend more time with me.'

Was she mad? How could she doubt it?

'Of course. Of course, I would.'

'But maybe you want to be with people your own age. Find yourself a girlfriend amongst all these holidaymakers.'

'Who do I know here? We're both strangers here. What could be better than that we spend the rest of the summer together?'

'I want to treat you,' she said.

'Why, what have I done?'

'You just listened, Lewis. And in the end, that made all the difference. I heard myself yesterday, just moaning on about how my life was so terrible. I just thought – I can leave it as it is or I can do something about it. And I thought about you. I think I have problems but you're going off in November and who knows what terrible dangers you might face. We should enjoy life while we can. Who knows if we'll have a tomorrow? There's only today and we should make the most of it.

So that's why I want to treat you. Let's go back, get washed and changed and I'll take you to dinner at the Fowey Hotel. What about that?'

24

'So what did you say in the letter?' Lewis asked.

They were eating soup at a table by the window, overlooking the estuary. There was a candle lit on the table even though it was still daylight. The dining room was busy and Lewis felt proud to be with her. There were a man and woman at a neighbouring table and Lewis noticed that the man was taking every chance he could to look at Helen. Lewis felt happy and jealous all at once. Helen wiped her mouth with the heavy linen napkin. Some of her lipstick came off on the fabric.

'The letter that I had originally written – the one that was on my dressing table – that was a long tirade about all the hateful things I felt he'd done to me. But after talking to you yesterday, and thinking about it all … well, I tore up that letter.

I realised that I had allowed him to treat me the way he had – out of fear maybe, or insecurity, or that he would leave me without any money. But you know, thinking about it now, maybe it wasn't that. Maybe I thought that by trying to be the person he wanted me to be, that I would be showing him that I loved him. That this was what love was – adapting to the other person, dedicating your life to making them happy.'

'Isn't it?' asked Lewis. 'If I was married to you, I would dedicate my life to making you happy.'

She smiled at this but shook her head at the same time.

'But don't you see. It's not that at all. And I'm telling you this because when you find a girl that you love, you don't want to make the mistake that I made.'

The waiter came to clear away the soup. He was a portly man in his late fifties or early sixties, balding with a streak of greying hair combed over. Helen looked up at him and smiled.

'Thank you,' she said. 'It was lovely, really lovely.'

'Why, thank you, Madam,' the waiter – seeming somewhat surprised – beamed back at her. 'I shall tell the chef.'

As he walked away past the palm tree in the centre of the room, Lewis thought the waiter had the walk of a much older man. It was as though he had spent too many years, and walked too many miles in other people's service. He thought the man looked frail and vulnerable and not at all the commanding figure he'd seemed when they had first arrived in the dining room. It was the same sensation, Lewis realised, that he had felt when he had seen his mother undressing in the changing room all those years ago.

'He's a lovely man, isn't he,' said Helen.

'He is,' Lewis agreed. 'I wonder if he enjoys his job, if he's had a happy life.'

'I wonder,' said Helen. 'Have you noticed how in posh restaurants, most people treat the staff as though they were invisible? The food appears and disappears but there is no acknowledgement of the people who do the bringing and the taking away. Take that man, for instance. I wonder how long he's been doing this – and how many miles he walks each evening.'

'I had just been thinking that,' said Lewis.

Her eyes smiled back at him.

'My father acknowledges the staff in restaurants,' he said. 'But it's usually because he's flirting with the waitresses.'

She laughed.

'Do you think I'd like your father?'

'I think so. I hope you'll get to meet him some day. But don't say I didn't warn you about him.'

'I'll be careful,' she grinned. 'Anyway, where was I?'

'The mistake you made,' he said. 'You were going to talk about the mistake you made.'

'Yes, you see, love is *not* dedicating yourself to making the other person happy.'

'It's not.'

He said it as a statement but it was really a question.

'No, it's not.'

'What is it then?'

'It's about being happy in yourself. About having your own life that's fulfilling and happy and wonderful. Once you have that – once you wake up every day and can't wait to jump out of bed and start doing – then you're ready for somebody else. And if they are the same. Actually – they have to be the same. If you're both like that, then you don't need the other person to be able feel wonderful about yourself. You just feel wonderful anyway.'

'But then surely, you don't need the other person at all,' said Lewis.

He was enjoying this conversation. He had never had one like it before.

'No – that's just it. Then the whole becomes more than the sum of the parts. You are like two magnificent animals – lions maybe, or eagles. Each person has a separate life and then they are part of the life together. It is like being doubly blessed. Can you imagine it – a marriage like that? My parent's marriage wasn't like that. And I know you said you can't remember much about yours. Your father sounds like he was a good man.'

'I can only remember some little pictures or scenes – like bits of a roll of film that has been mostly destroyed. Money always seemed to be a problem. I remember that. So anyway – the letter – what did you say?'

'I said simply that I was writing to tell him that I was leaving him – had, in fact, left him. That I realised now that I wasn't the person he thought I was or wanted me to be. I hoped he would stay safe and find somebody else. I told him that my solicitor would be in touch in due course to work out a divorce.'

'Do you have a solicitor?'

'No, I'll have to find one. I'm sure there's one here, but for the moment, I don't want him to know where I am.'

'Why, what would he do if he found out?'

'I don't know. I don't know what I'm afraid of but I am. Maybe that he'd come after me.'

'And hurt you?'

'No, not so much that. At least I don't think so. More that he would try to use guilt to make me come back to him. I'm not strong enough to deal with that yet.'

'What will he do when he gets it?'

'He'll be furious. Apoplectic. And the first thing he'll do is to stop my money. So I'm going to have to start looking for a job.'

Later, the waiter brought the bill. He hesitated for a moment, unsure of whom to hand it to. Then Helen reached up and took the little silver tray with the paper on top. Her eyes widened fractionally when she unfolded the little piece of paper.

'Please let me pay for some of this,' said Lewis.

'Nonsense,' she said, as she reached into her handbag. 'I asked you out.'

'But you need to save your money now.'

'That's as may be. But some things are special and have to be celebrated.'

'Well, thank you so much. It was a lovely evening. Wonderful food. Beautiful company.'

'Why, thank you, sir,' she said.

'I've had another idea,' said Lewis, as the waiter took the tray and money away.

'What?' she said, resting her head on her hands.

'Well, remember I said I could give you some money – once I was in the Army?'

'Which you're not going to,' she said.

'No. But right now I'm paying Mrs Middleton at the bed and breakfast. Supposing instead I paid that money to you?'

She looked puzzled for a moment.

'I mean I would become your lodger. I would stay at your house. I haven't seen it all but it looks like there must be room. I would have a place to stay and you would have some money. Some income – so that you wouldn't be eating into your savings. It would give you some breathing space while you looked for a job.'

He looked at her expectantly.

'What do you think?' he said.

She hesitated and he was sure she was going to refuse him.

'Lewis,' she said. 'There was a time when I would have thought, "That's going to raise eyebrows. What are people going to think?" But you know – I don't care now what anyone thinks. I've let what people think run my life for too long. We're out here, we're away from town, we're not doing anyone any harm. Let them think what they like. I don't care.

So your idea is marvellous. How clever of you to have thought of it.'

25

*L*ewis sighed, took a deep breath of the stale air and began his preparations. He touched the photograph of Helen again, caressing her cheek. Then he began to say the words. There was a time when he had had to read them. Now he didn't need to reach for the tattered volume. He knew them by heart.

'When it began to grow dark, the Rat, with an air of excitement and mystery, summoned them back into the parlour, stood each of them up alongside of his little heap, and proceeded to dress them up for the coming expedition. He was very earnest and thoroughgoing about it, and the affair took quite a long time. First, there was a belt to go round each animal.'

Lewis took a knife in its sheath from his pack and, opening his belt, slid it on. He retied the belt and positioned the knife comfortably on his left side.

'And then a sword to be stuck into each belt, and then a cutlass on the other side to balance it.'

He took off his boots and socks and put on a pair of dry socks from the line overhead. Then he put his boots back on and re-tied the laces carefully in double knots. Placing his right foot on the chair he re-tied his puttee. Then he did the same with the left one. The boots and puttees felt tight and comfortable.

'Then a pair of pistols, a policeman's truncheon, several sets of handcuffs, some bandages and sticking plaster, and a flask and a sandwich case.'

Lewis slipped a couple of hand ropes into his tunic pocket and made sure that he had his first field dressing. He checked his revolver and that he had extra ammunition in his pocket.

His watch showed just after nine thirty. He was starting to get anxious again.

He had always found the words comforting. He read them before any operation and he felt that their effect was to armour him, to give him some form of magic protection. They didn't seem to have had much of an effect this time.

He lay on his bunk and closed his eyes but sleep wouldn't come. He tried to read, write in his diary. He started to make a list of things he might do after the War. But then he decided that that might be an unlucky thing to do, so he put the paper in the candle flame and watched it blacken, catch fire and crinkle up. He shook it from his fingers. Private Chase looked in to take away the plate and Lewis gave him the letter for Helen. Lewis didn't need to say anything – Chase knew.

With the letter to Helen gone, Lewis feels that he has 'passed over to the other side'. He is in the ante-room to hell, the waiting room for death. It is a place not of the old, comfortable, everyday world, but neither is he dead. It is another no-mans-land, paralleling the one between him and the Germans. Here he will spend the next few hours and with luck he will return. But now all he can do is to complete his preparations.

Opening a tin of shoe polish, and propping a small mirror against the whiskey bottle, he blackens his face and his hands. He checks that he has his compass and slips a torch into his other tunic pocket. It is nearly ten o'clock. Now he must just wait.

The minutes crawl. At ten thirty he goes outside to relieve his bladder. The Divisional weather people were right. The mist is gone but it's cloudy overhead. He can see no stars. When this was a German front line trench the sap to the latrines lay to the rear of the trench. Now that the British are using it as their front line trench, the sap to the latrines runs out into no-man's-land and ends just short of the wire. Lewis is reluctant to venture out there before he has to, so he just moves a little away from the dugout entrance and urinates against the revetting. Judging by the smell of urine and excrement and the soggy mess underfoot, it is what most people do. He tries but not much comes. He will try again before he leaves.

At eleven Lewis picks up the photograph of Helen, kisses her image on the lips and speaks to her.

'Darling Helen, I'm going out soon,' he murmurs. 'And I'm not going to be able to do this by myself. I need you to take care of me, so I'm going to give you my life to mind. It's going to be in your hands while the raid lasts. Please take care of it so that I will see you again.'

Then he puts her picture in his pack and ties the straps.

Just before eleven thirty Lewis has just finished putting on his Bomber's Shield when Sergeant Robinson looks in.

'It's about time, sir. The men are waiting outside.'

Lewis nods in acknowledgement. He finishes dressing and follows Robinson outside to where Jackson and the six men are waiting. The men have removed their greatcoats and wear steel helmets and Bomber's Shields over tunics. If nothing else the Shields keep them warm. The eastern end of the sky overhead has cleared and some stars are visible. It is very cold. There will be a frost tonight and the men blow on their hands. Apart from that they are silent.

Now he must be the leader. He must be physically strong when he has to grapple with Germans. He must be brave and make all the right decisions and accomplish the mission and bring his men back safely. He knows they are thinking this as they look at him. It seems an impossibly tall order.

'All set, men?' he asks, trying to keep his voice neutral, ordinary; trying to keep the quiver out of it.

There are muttered 'yessirs.'

Lewis says, 'Very good. Sergeant Jackson?'

Jackson speaks the order softly and, with Lewis leading, they move off.

26

*L*ewis gave Mrs Middleton a week's notice and a week's rent but moved out the next day. As he carried his bag up the laneway, he phrased in his head the letter he would write to his father to tell him of his new address. He would say – truthfully – that he had found 'nicer lodgings at the same price'.

When he arrived Helen showed him around the upstairs, where he had never been before. The open stairway came out onto a small landing with two bedrooms off it. Both doors and the upstairs windows were open to let the warm air circulate through the house. Her bedroom was at the back of the house looking out to seaward.

'This is my room,' she said, stepping just inside while he stood on the threshold. There was a neatly made bed, a dressing table with some jars, small bottles and a hair brush, a chair, a wardrobe, a low, narrow chest of drawers, a washbasin and a jug. He thought of her sleeping here, in this bed. He wondered again whether she had been lonely.

'And this is your room.'

The room had a view out onto the front of the house and the gate that led to the lane. It was furnished very much as hers.

'It's lovely,' he said.

'Well, it's not the Ritz,' she said smiling. 'But it's all nice and dry and airy. You unpack and I'll make some tea.'

'Was your old place – I mean the place you lived with your husband – much grander than this?' asked Lewis, as they sat drinking tea outside the back door.

'A *lot* grander,' she said. 'It was a small country house. It had been in my husband's family for generations. We even had a couple of servants when the War began – a cook and a maid.'

'Ooo, very posh.'

'Wasn't it just? Far too posh for me. I had been brought up in an ordinary suburban house. So there was all of that to learn as well – running the house, managing the servants, choosing menus. A whole lot of other things that I would end up not doing right.

Both of the servants left at the beginning of this year. They found jobs that paid better, working in a factory – munitions, I think or building aeroplanes. In one respect, it was a blessing that they did go. I should never have been able to escape with them there. Or at least it would have been much more difficult and he would have found out almost immediately. But then that left me rattling round this big house on my own. I nearly went crazy at that point.'

'You can tell me to mind my own business —'

'You're my friend, Lewis,' she interrupted. 'My very dear friend. There shouldn't be too many things I need to keep from you.'

Then she added, 'Just a couple maybe.'

Her eyes lit up. 'A girl has to have some secrets after all. Go on – what was it you were going to ask?'

'I ... I was wondering whether it would have all turned out differently if you'd had a child – or children.'

She looked away from him, down the garden towards the hedge that was the border on that side.

'I'm sure it would,' she said. 'But we didn't.'

The way she said it, it sounded like she might have wanted to say more. Instead, she turned back to him.

'But then again maybe it wouldn't have made any difference and it would have been much worse if there had been children. I wouldn't have been able to leave him then. Not with children involved. I don't think I could ever have done that.'

'Still – it must have been very hard when it came to it – to leave, I mean.'

She nodded.

'You know how it is. You get into habits. You have a routine. Simple things like how familiar the bed is and knowing where everything is and just, one's comforts I suppose really. You're going to have to give up all of that – swap the familiar for the unknown.

For days before I left I went through everything I had – having to choose. Did this matter so much that I had to bring it? Did I really want that? The first time I did it I was left with a pile of things that would have needed a truck to carry them all. So I did it all again and finally got it down to two suitcases.

I'm lucky this house came furnished and with linen and crockery and everything, because a lot of the things I brought with me weren't too practical.'

She shrugged – a hopeless expression on her face.

'A lot of the things were things from my childhood. While I was going through a trunk in the attic I found an old sketch pad of mine and some coloured pencils. I had forgotten about it until I found them, but when I was about thirteen I used to paint and draw. Mainly landscapes. I thought that maybe I would start to do that again. I used to love it.'

'Maybe you could earn some money doing it,' said Lewis. 'That would be a good way to make a living.'

'I would need to practice and practice and practice but yes, you're right – it would be a nice way to make a living. Especially down around here where there is so much beautiful countryside.'

'And holidaymakers who would buy your pictures,' offered Lewis. 'We should go and buy you some paints so that you can get started.'

He jumped up.

'Let's do it now. Let's go into town. There's a stationary shop down there. I'm sure they'd have paints.'

'Hold your horses,' she said, laughing. 'I'll get to it. The more immediate thing is to get a little income going. I need to start giving piano lessons again. I don't know how much call for them there is in a place like this, but I could go to peoples' houses and teach their children until I can afford to buy a piano of my own. And I would probably need to live in some place that was a bit more central to town. But it's probably best to leave that until the children go back to school. So for right now, I just want to enjoy the summer and this lovely place that we're in. I want to explore and swim and lie in the sun and eat some nice food.'

'Do you know how to cook?' she asked, changing the subject.

He loved this about her – how she could jump to some entirely new and unexpected thing.

'I can make bacon and eggs. I used to do it for my Dad and myself on Saturdays. When he was at home, that is.'

'Hmm. Bacon and eggs. It's a start. Can you boil an egg?'

'Yes. Eggs became a bit of a staple in our house. After another catastrophic day trying to survive the housekeeper's latest attempt to poison me, eggs would always hit the spot. So I can fry them, poach them, boil them, scramble them.'

'My, I *am* impressed. What else?'

'Well, that's about it really.'

'Stew?' she asked hopefully.

He shook his head.

'Well, let me teach you – right now. It sounds like it would be a useful thing to know when you're in the Army. All you need is a pot, a cooker or a fire, and some things to throw into it. Come on – no time like the present. Oh, and I've got a bottle of wine. Do you drink wine?'

'I've had little drops from time to time. When I used to go to family parties, my cousins and I would be dragooned to clean up glasses. We used to take them into the kitchen and empty them into one glass. Wine, beer, stout, sherry – all in together.'

'Uhhh,' she said.

'You have to keep tasting it,' she said later as the pot simmered on the range.

She had poured generous glasses of white wine for each of them.

'That way you'll become an instinctive cook. You won't need to follow recipes. You'll just know what to do. So have a taste of this now.'

She took a spoonful of broth from the stew and held it out to him. Steam rose from it. He blew on it to cool it.

'Come on, don't be such a baby,' she said. 'It's not that hot.'

'It's bloody boiling,' he exclaimed. 'Just because you have a fireproof mouth.'

'Come on.'

He drank the broth.

'So?' she asked.

'More salt and pepper, I'd say.'

'Alright – off you go.'

He added some of each. Then he dipped the spoon in again and this time brought up a piece of meat. It steamed and he blew on it. Then taking it between his finger and thumb he bit a piece of it off.

'Oh, that's very good,' he said, as he chewed. 'Try some?'

'Yes,' she said eagerly.

He went to dip the spoon back in to get another piece but she nodded, indicating the piece in his hand.

'That'll do fine,' she said.

He extended the hand and her lips closed around the piece of meat and the tops of his fingers. Then she sucked the meat into her mouth, along with the juice that clung to his fingertips. When her lips came away it was as though she had tried to peel his fingers.

'That's wonderful,' she said.

Her eyes held his for a moment or two longer and then she snapped out of it.

'Time to lay the table,' she said.

Later, after they had eaten and listened to more music, Helen said, 'Well, I'm off to bed. Feel free to do whatever you want. Stay up. More music. Whatever you like.'

Lewis rose too. She came towards him and embraced him.

'It's good to have you here,' she said. 'Good to have company. There were times when it was very lonely.'

He loved the sensation of being held in her arms. Then she proffered a cheek and he kissed her goodnight.

27

*L*ewis woke from a deep sleep and it was a while before he remembered where he was. The window had curtains on it but he always liked to sleep with them open. It was much darker here than it had been in town and he could see stars low in the sky. A faint smell of honeysuckle drifted in through the window. The sheets still had the fresh smell of having been newly washed. The bed was comfortable and the pillows deep. He lay on his side gazing at the stars trying to see if he recognised any of them.

He thought of her in the other bedroom – they were separated only by the small landing. Was she asleep or was she looking at the stars too – and what was she thinking about? 'There were times when it was very lonely,' she had said. Yes, he could imagine there must have been. Between her marriage and now coming here, it sounded like she had spent a lot of time on her own. Just like him really.

He heard a sound and he thought first it came from outside. It was a human sound, not an animal one. Like a sniff. Then he heard it again. And then, like the introduction to a song before the words start, the sniff was replaced by tears. They were coming from her room. She was crying. It went on for several minutes and then seemed to ease up a little, as though she was trying to stop.

He wondered what he should do. Go to her? Knock on her door? But if she said, 'yes?' what would he say then? 'I thought I heard you crying.' And supposing she said she wasn't. And what business was it of his anyway? He wished he could do something but he didn't know what. While he was agonising over all this, her crying picked up again and continued for, it must have been nearly ten minutes, until it seemed to run out of steam. He heard a few more sniffs and then there was silence.

He said nothing to her the next day and she seemed happy. They went to the beach and came back and had salad and cold meat for tea. But that night he heard it again, not long after they had gone to bed. This time he got up, opened his door and went across the landing in his pyjamas. It was louder now – deep, anguished sobs. He stood near the door, hesitating. Then he went back closer to his own door and called across, 'Is everything alright, Helen?'

There was a long pause and several snuffles before she said, 'Yes, I'm fine. Sorry if I woke you. I'm fine.'

'Anything I can do?' he asked.

'No thanks, Lewis. Go back to bed, won't you?'

He called goodnight to her to which she responded and then there was silence.

She said nothing about it the next day and he decided it would be better for him not to, unless she mentioned it. She was subdued and when he suggested going to the beach, she told him that he should go by himself. It was phrased in such a way that he really felt he had no choice and so he spent the afternoon there reading and wondering what, if anything, he should do. When he came back, there was no sign of her. But the back door was open so he assumed she was in the house and not gone into town. He made himself a sandwich and sat outside watching the sea and the sun. He was still there and it was late – nearly nine o'clock – when he heard movement behind him.

'Hello,' she said.

Her hair had been half-brushed and she wore no makeup. She had put on the clothes she had been wearing yesterday. He stood up and turned to face her.

'Is everything alright?' he said. 'Has something happened? Are you ill?'

Her smile was somewhat sheepish. She shook her head.

'I'm sorry. It's just that – marriage … feelings. You can't just turn them off like a tap. I loved Robert one time. And I care about him now. I can't bear to think of him being hurt.'

'He hurt you,' said Lewis baldly.

'Yes, but that doesn't mean I should hurt him. And what I'm doing – what I've done – will.'

'Have you changed your mind?' asked Lewis.

'No,' she said, with a huge sigh. 'I haven't changed my mind, but that doesn't make all of this any easier.'

Lewis wanted to go to her. To hug her. To hold her. She was just as kind and gentle and generous as he had thought she was, that first time he had seen her face. He doubted if he would have been as noble in a similar situation.

'You're a good person,' he said.

'I don't know about that,' she replied. 'I don't know about that at all.'

28

*T*he days of July and August fell into a regular pattern. They got up around seven but by then – most days – it was already starting to be warm. There would always be a hug and a kiss on the cheek. Helen showed Lewis how to bake bread and make scones. While whatever it was they had made was baking in the oven they sat outside looking at the sea. They had breakfast while the day was still young and dewy and birds twittered in the foliage that surrounded the cottage and its little patch of land.

Helen bought paints and a large block of paper. In the afternoons they would go to a cove or up on the cliffs or to a headland or to some place that overlooked Fowey and here, she would paint or draw. She wasn't happy with her first efforts but she improved quickly. Lewis had decided that he'd better start becoming fit. So he began running and by the beginning of August he was able to do three or four miles each day, cruising up and down the local hills.

'I was terrible at sports in school,' he said. 'But I suppose the nice thing about running is that everyone can do it. You don't need any special equipment or technique or skill.'

Helen was a strong swimmer, so she set herself to improve Lewis' swimming. In the evenings she cooked dinner while he helped, chopping, cutting and fetching. Some memories of his childhood, long forgotten, surfaced. Standing on a chair at the sink doing the washing up – in reality more playing boats with the cups in the sudsy water. Helping Mum to mix the Christmas cake, the mixture like cement so that he was unable to make much headway in it. Then watching her slim, strong arm take over. Being allowed to lick the bowl afterwards. He didn't mention them to Helen. He didn't want her to think that he thought of her as a mother.

After dinner, they would talk or listen to music. Sometimes they read – but not very often. There was too much to talk about. Too much – he felt – to find out about her. Always too, at the back of his mind, was the feeling that the days were numbered. He deliberately hadn't counted them but he was conscious of them moving on. Soon it would be possible to count them on his fingers and then there would be none at all. He tried, as much as he could, to put these thoughts out of his mind.

'When are you going to start selling your paintings?' he asked.

'Oh, not for a while yet,' she said. 'Maybe in September.'

'And what about you, Lewis? The War can't last forever. Who knows – hopefully it'll be over by the end of the year and you won't have to go to France. What are you going to do then?'

'I've no idea,' he said. 'Way way back before the War began, I had planned to go to University. Then the War came along and I knew I would have to go into the Army. There didn't seem much point in planning anything after that. What if I'm not around?'

'Oh Lewis darling, don't say that. You'll get through it. I know you will.'

He liked it when she called him darling.

'Do you like writing?' she asked.

'I suppose I do. I won an essay competition in school a couple of years ago.'

'Well, there you are then.'

'There I am then?'

'You should take up writing. Just as I'm painting. You could start keeping a diary and when the War is over you could publish it as a book. "One Young Soldier's Experience In The War".'

'But I'm not a soldier yet.'

'That's alright. You can talk about your feelings as you enjoy your last few weeks before going into the Army. The preparations you're making. Your fears and hopes. I'm sure there will be lots of people writing books after the War. Why shouldn't you be one of them?'

'I keep a diary anyway,' he said.

'There you are then,' she said.

'Maybe I just need to put more in it that might be interesting in a book.'

'Of course, you're missing one very important element,' she said.

'What's that?' he asked.

'A girl. A love interest. You've got to have that for your story to be really exciting. You know – the girl you leave behind as you head off to the War to fight for her honour.'

'You're teasing.'

'No, not at all. The story would be so much more exciting if there was a woman in it. It's Romeo and Juliet. Do the lovers and their love survive? The eternal question.'

'So what did you think of it?' Lewis asked when Helen handed him back *The Wind in the Willows*, saying that she had finished it the previous night in bed.

'I think it's the way the world should be – the way England should be. All beautiful countryside and where bad people always get their comeuppance. I thought that the chapter called *The Piper at the Gates of Dawn* was utterly beautiful. Mystical. Religious – at least the kind of religion that I should like to be part of.'

'I used to think you were a churchgoer,' said Lewis.

'Why on earth did you think that?'

'Because the first morning I was in Fowey I went to church.'

She raised her eyebrows, questioningly.

Oh, I didn't really want to go, but when Mrs Middleton – my landlady – asked if I was going, I felt I had to. Anyway, as it turned out it was a good thing because you were there. I saw you. That was the first time I saw you.'

'Ah yes, I did go once. I don't remember seeing you.'

'Well, I was there. You wore a white dress with some blue on it. It had long sleeves. And you had a sort of yellowy hat.'

'I made a big effort that day,' she said, smiling at the memory. 'I'm not sure what I was thinking. Perhaps that I would meet some interesting people there. Or maybe *an interesting person*.'

'But you just sat there where the service was over.'

'I did,' she said dreamily, as though remembering it. 'I got very sad during the service. It was the music, I think – the singing. I was close to tears when it was over. I wasn't fit to meet or talk to anybody. I was terrified the vicar would come and speak to me, especially as I was so obviously a stranger. I think I should have just burst into tears.'

'And how is your sadness now?' he asked.

'It comes and goes,' she said. 'It's only been three months after all. It'll get better, I'm sure.'

The tone in her voice didn't sound that convincing to him. He thought he would change the subject and take her away from any unhappy thoughts.

Have you ever read *Treasure Island*?' he asked.

'Can't say that I have,' she said. 'It's a boy's book, isn't it? Pirates and buried treasure and lots of swashbuckling, that sort of business.'

'Yes, that's right. My mum read it to me when I was four.'

'Four! That was a bit young to be hearing about bloodthirsty things like that, wasn't it?'

'I suppose it was,' said Lewis. 'But I loved it. I really liked the beginning – the first five chapters. It begins in a lonely cove. I imagine it as like one of the coves around here. The hero is called Jim Hawkins and his parents run an inn. It's perched on a cliff, maybe and a track leads from somewhere past the inn and on to Bristol. His father makes just one appearance in the book and then he's gone.'

'He dies?'

'Yes.'

'That's pretty grim, isn't it?' she said.

'I suppose it is. Anyway, after that, it's just Lewis and his mother. He sort of becomes her protector and in the end – of the five chapters, I mean – he saves her from the pirates.'

'Is that what you're reading now?'

He nodded.

'I often re-read the first five chapters. They're so atmospheric. And a lot of the countryside around here reminds me of it. I think it's my favourite book.'

'So now when you read it, you're Jim Hawkins and I'm playing the part of your mother.'

He blushed.

'No, I didn't mean that,' he said, hastily. It was exactly what he had meant.

'I know what you meant,' she said. 'Anyway, for what it's worth, I'd have loved to have had somebody like you as my son. And if I had, I should have read *Treasure Island* to him, just like your mum did.'

There was only once during this time where there was any degree of friction between them. It happened one evening when Lewis asked her when she was going to see about her divorce. He had expected that they would talk about it in the way they talked about most things. But instead, she said, 'Why are you asking me this?'

If he noticed the strange tone in her voice, he didn't respond to it.

'No reason in particular,' he said. 'It's just that I'd been thinking about what you said – about your husband using guilt to get you back. If you got a divorce it would be one step further away from him. It would be more final. Well, it would be final.'

He realised that he was gabbling on.

'Well, that's hardly any of your business, is it?'

Lewis was shocked.

'I didn't —'

'Look Lewis, I'll get a divorce when I'm good and ready. What are you anyway? Do you want to be my new husband, is that it?'

'No, I —'

'I'm going to bed. I'll see you in the morning. Good night.'

And with that, she stormed off.

Lewis sat there stunned. He went to bed himself shortly after that. He lay awake for hours, cursing himself for having raised the subject. He had ruined everything. He wondered if she would throw him out in the morning. In the end he drifted off into a deep sleep.

When he awoke, the room was warm and filled with sunlight. It was late. The memory of last night hit him like a falling rock. He could hear her downstairs. She was alternately singing and humming a song. He dreaded having to go down to face her. He dressed slowly and went down the stairs. She was at the sink and turned when she heard him.

'Morning, sleepy head,' she said, brightly.

'Helen,' Lewis began slowly, 'I'm really sorry about last night. I didn't mean to … I shouldn't have …'

She turned to face him, drying her hands on a towel and then holding it in her lap in front of her.

'Dearest, darling, Lewis. I'm the one who should be sorry. I shouldn't have flown off the handle like I did.'

'No, I shouldn't have mentioned it. I was only trying to be —'

'You were only trying to be a friend to me. Which is what you have always been – a true and dear friend. Come here.'

He went to her and she embraced him and held him tight.

'I behaved dreadfully. It was unforgivable. Will you forgive me?'

'Of course I'll forgive you.'
'Now,' she said, 'let me get you breakfast.'

29

'Do you mind if I ask you something?' asked Helen one evening.

'Anything you like,' replied Lewis carelessly.

'Why did your Mum die?'

'She got leukaemia. Why do you ask?'

'No, I don't really mean what did she die of. I meant why did she die?'

'Is there a difference?'

'Some people believe that we chose when we want to die. I remember I had an uncle and he was very sick. I can't remember exactly what was wrong with him but he'd had a whole series of operations over a short period of time – less than a year. I remember the last time I visited him in hospital – the last time I saw him alive, actually – he told me that he was tired.'

'Tired of the operations? Of being sick?'

'No, tired of life. Of living. He'd had enough. He died a few days later.'

Lewis thought for a moment.

'But you could see how if he was sick, if he was spending all his time in hospital, how he might want to die. But my Mum was very healthy. We had gone on a holiday only a few months earlier and she seemed fine. She was full of life.'

'And then she caught leukaemia.'

Lewis nodded.

'Why did she catch leukaemia, I wonder?' said Helen.

'I don't know. I'm not a doctor. These things happen, I suppose.'

'Some people think it's all connected – our body, our mind,

our feelings. So that if say, we weren't feeling happy, it can appear as something in our body. So, for example, when I was married to Robert I used to get a lot of headaches. Maybe three or four times a week. Some of them were mild but some of them were so bad that I would have to go and lie down. I don't get half so many now. And I remember the first week that I was here, I got this terrible pain in my stomach. Now, I've never had pains in my stomach. So what was that all about? I think it was my body reacting to the huge thing I had just done. '

'But those are headaches, stomach aches. Lots of people get those. There's a bit of a difference between getting a headache and getting leukaemia.'

'Is there?'

Then, after a pause, she added, 'What's the difference?'

'One's a serious illness. The other's just … well, an inconvenience.'

She began to raise her eyebrows so he added hastily, 'Well maybe it's more than an inconvenience —'

'You've obviously never had headaches like I had them.'

'I know, I'm sorry,' he said. 'All I'm saying is that there's a bit of a difference between a fatal illness and something that passes after a couple of hours or a couple of days.'

'What's the difference?'

'I don't know. Like I said, I'm not a doctor.'

'Maybe the difference is to do with how unhappy you are. Or how well you can cope with that unhappiness. Maybe a small unhappiness produces a small illness and a big unhappiness produces a big one.'

'Do you think my mum was unhappy?'

'I don't know. I didn't know her. What do you think?'

'I think she was happy when she was with me. I don't think she was so happy with my dad.'

He paused.

'But if she was unhappy being with him, why didn't she divorce him?'

'And do what? Go where?'

'Back to her mum. My grandmother is still alive. My mum had had a little dressmaking business. She could have gone back to doing that.'

'Mmm,' agreed Helen, 'I suppose she could. But maybe there were other reasons rather than practical ones why she couldn't bring herself to leave your father.'

'Like?'

'Maybe she didn't want to upset you.'

'So she died instead? That hardly makes sense.'

'Maybe she felt responsible for him; for his happiness. She would have felt guilty to have left him. Like I feel about Robert.'

'Is that why you're asking me this? Because of Robert?'

'I hadn't thought about it,' she said. 'But yes, I think it probably is, now that you come to mention it. Is he a strong man, your father?'

Lewis thought about this for a moment.

'I don't think he is actually. Not in the way that I feel I'm strong. He relies a lot on other people.'

'Nothing wrong with that.'

'But no, what I mean is that he expects other people to do things for him. And they generally do. So then he feels good that there are all of these people who care for him.'

'So if your mother had left that would have been a huge blow to him?'

'I think so. He told me that when he first met her she was engaged to be married to some other bloke. Dad moved in on him was how he put it.'

'So she was a trophy to be captured?'

'Yes, I suppose she was really.'

'So your father was weak. Was she the strong one?'

'I think so. Anything she wanted to do, anything she put her mind to – she did it.'

'So she was afraid that if she left him he would fall apart.'

'But even if she was, you can't be responsible for somebody else's happiness.'

And then he added, 'Can you?'

'No, you're right, nobody should feel that way. But lots of people do.'

'Do you? Do you feel that way about your husband?'

'I certainly did. I'm not sure if I still do. But I certainly feel guilty about leaving him. Or I don't know if it's guilt. Maybe I feel bad because it didn't last forever like it's meant to.'

'But you feel happier now,' said Lewis, suddenly anxious.

'Oh yes, I do. Of course I do. But that doesn't mean that I don't feel sad. Or unhappy for him. I suppose I was the strong one in our relationship.'

'So if you're the strong one, that should make it easier to leave.'

She smiled a weak smile and looked directly at him.

'You'd have thought so, wouldn't you? But strangely enough, it turns out to be the opposite. At least in my case. When you're strong you feel you can take on somebody else's burden as well as your own. Their unhappiness – that you'll carry that for them. Because they don't have the strength to carry it. Do you know what I mean?'

'I think so,' said Lewis. 'It sort of makes sense.'

'So maybe that's what your mum did with your father. She thought that she was responsible for his happiness and carrying that became what she did.'

She paused. It was as though she was letting him think about it. Then she continued.

'But she eventually found that not only could she not make him happy, she was now carrying too big a load, trying to find her own happiness as well. Eventually, it all became too much for her.'

'And so she got leukaemia?'

'And so she got leukaemia.'

Helen went silent, like she was thinking.

'Was your father faithful to your mother?'

He hadn't expected this.

'I'd have no way of knowing,' he said neutrally, trying to defuse the question. He definitely didn't want to think about it. Simultaneously he was amazed that he could have this relationship with her – where they could talk about these things.

'I know that,' she said. 'But what do you think? Knowing the kind of man he is.'

Lewis tried to dodge the question. 'Do you think your husband – Robert – was faithful to you?'

She replied immediately.

'I've thought about this a lot and I think he was, in fact. That sort of thing didn't actually interest him that much'.

The ball was back in Lewis' court. He began to speak slowly.

'If he had wanted to, he would certainly have had plenty of chances. He was away a lot.'

'And if he had, would it have upset him, would he have felt guilty? Would he have told your mother – confessed – if he had?'

'You know, I don't think he would actually – have confessed, I mean. Or felt guilty. Or been upset by it. I think he probably had a wild enough life when he was at sea. Maybe he wouldn't have seen it as that serious a thing. Providing he loved and cared for us – which he did – I suspect he would have seen that as relatively unimportant.'

'And your mum – how would she have seen it?'

'If it had happened … if she had found it … I think she would have been devastated. I think she loved the way I —'. He hesitated, found different words and went on. 'I think she loved the way I feel I would love. That I cared for the person above anything else. That I would do nothing to hurt them.'

'It sounds like she could have been deeply unhappy,' said Helen.

'Enough to die?' asked Lewis.

She looked at him and said simply, 'Who can say?'

30

*I*t is just coming up to midnight when Lewis reaches the dugout known as 'J'. There are over thirty men already there. If a shell landed here now there would be carnage, but any sound of artillery is distant but angry. Always angry. The dugout cannot accommodate them all so they mill outside in the trench and Lewis has to jostle his way through to where Lieutenant Redman and the commanders of the various parties are assembled. On his way Lewis hears somebody say, 'I 'ear ole Fritz is on starvation rations now, so he shouldn't be too 'eavy if we 'ave to carry 'im back.' There is soft, nervous laughter. Several men are carrying knobkerries – clubs like medieval maces. They are made by wrapping a length of barbed wire around the top of a pole about the length of a cricket bat, until it forms a knob. They are vicious looking things.

Redman asks the commanders to carry out a roll call and quick inspection of their men. When this is done, and everything is reported in order, the entire party moves off. Lewis is at the head of his own group of men. *The hour is come. Follow me.* Behind him is Lance Corporal Jackson, then six men with Sergeant Robinson bringing up the rear. Lewis follows the steel helmet and back of the man in front of him.

They go along the support trench and after about fifty yards, turn right so that they are now heading directly towards the German lines. There is no talk, only the clink of equipment and sound of boots on duckboards or squelching through patches of mud. The smell of trench is all around. Wet earth, sweet decomposition, chloride of lime, the sharp smell of human waste. The well constructed wooden revetting holding the trench walls moves by on either side. Overhead, half of the sky is still covered in cloud but there are stars in the other. The stars are always very intense when seen from the bottom of a trench. Fear gnaws at Lewis like a rat in his brain. Fear that he will not do a good job; fear that he will freeze as he has seen men do; fear that men will die and it will be his fault, fear that he will die or worse still, be blinded or crippled or left as a vegetable or castrated.

Eventually they stop and Lewis checks his watch. It is just before one o' clock. They are right on time. Up ahead he knows that Lieutenant Redman is feeding his men out into no-man's-land. They shuffle forward slowly like a crowd at a turnstile for a football match. Finally, Lewis reaches the head of the queue.

'You know where to go?' whispers Redman.

Lewis nods. He doesn't like Redman who is patronising, especially when he is in command. But there is no doubt that he is a good officer and Lewis feels that at least they are in good hands tonight. Lewis clambers up a ladder and over the lip of the trench. He tries to move silently, crouched down as though this will help. He sees shadows ahead and these materialise to become the Right Blocking Party, in line and lying on the wet, turned earth. There is a gap between these and the other blocking party and Lewis begins to line up his men in this gap. Eventually everyone is in place – Lewis at the head of the Raiding Party with the Left and Right Blocking Parties to either side and the Covering Party spread out in front. When all this is done, Lewis lies on his belly.

More of the sky has cleared and a good two thirds of it is now star-studded, though the stars are fainter out here on the open ground. He sees the 'W' of Cassiopeia. There is only a small amount of light but Lewis feels fearfully exposed. There is less than five minutes to go. A shower of Very lights goes up and waterfalls to earth. Everybody hugs the ground trying to become invisible. Out here, the earth has a different smell – the stench of decomposition is mixed with the chemical smell of explosive.

Lewis locates the clump of brushwood that West spoke about and takes compass bearings on it. This is not really his job as it is up to Lieutenant Redman and others to guide him back to the British line. But that will be small consolation if it all goes horribly wrong. Lewis prefers to rely on his own resources. He wants to get this over with before any more of the sky clears and the night gets any brighter. Starlight. He has loved it all his life but here it is a treacherous enemy. His eyes have adjusted somewhat to the darkness now and he scans the open space they will have to cross. Artillery is crumping all up and down the line but it is remote, unimportant.

He checks his watch. There is less than a minute and a half to go. He feels his heart pounding. Despite the cold he is sweating. His stomach feels like it has fallen through his groin. The luminous second hand on his watch sweeps past twelve. They are into the last minute before the artillery is due to start.

His watch registers one thirty exactly and as it does so, there is a distant thump of a gun being fired. Lewis jumps. Even though he knew it was coming, it still startles him. The thump is followed by an express-train roaring that becomes the shriek of a shell and then a crashing explosion on the German front line. Other heavy guns join in as well as lighter Stokes guns in a cacophony of sound. Yellow and red flashes of fire and, in their light, billows of black smoke erupt on the German side of the wire. The Covering Party rises from the ground and crouching, begins to move forward.

31

'Thank you,' said Lewis the next morning.

He had just come out of his bedroom onto the landing and she had emerged from her room.

'What for?' she asked, her face breaking into a smile. He loved her smile. He loved the way she always smiled in the morning when he first saw her.

'For telling me about my mother.'

'I don't think I told you anything you didn't already know.'

They began to go down the stairs, Lewis in front.

'I suppose I'd never thought about it. But once I did ...'

'Do you think she was *very* unhappy?' she asked, as they reached the bottom of the stairs. Lewis turned to her.

'Yes, I think she was. I don't mean this to sound the wrong way, but I think I may have been the only happiness she had. I know that sounds awful but —'

'It doesn't sound awful at all. I could see why that would be the case.'

She paused.

'And how do you feel about your father?' she asked.

'I don't know,' he said. 'Resentful? Angry? I feel I should hate him but I can't. I don't.'

She shook her head.

'You shouldn't hate him. He doesn't sound like a bad man. Maybe they just shouldn't have been together.'

'But surely he should have seen what he was doing to her?'

'He probably saw himself being a good and loving father, husband and provider.'

'A loving husband? Being unfaithful to her.'

'I'm sure he just saw that as fulfilling a need, that it was nothing to do with love. And he was a good father?'

'He was,' agreed Lewis.

'And you never lacked for anything?'

'No.'

'I suppose people do what they can,' she said. 'He did. She did. It's all any of us can do.'

'What were Vestal Virgins?' asked Lewis later as they lay on the beach. They were on towels, side by side, lying on their backs, eyes closed against the hot sun.

'Something in Ancient Rome, weren't they?' she said. 'They helped with sacrifices or something like that. They wore long white dresses with belts at the waist and V necks.'

Lewis started laughing.

'What's so funny?' she asked.

'It's history as fashion,' he said.

She began to laugh too.

'You'd have looked good in one of those dresses,' he said.

'That's very kind of you,' she said. Then added, 'You'd have looked good in one of those short skirts the Roman centurions wore.'

They were flirting, Lewis realised.

Lewis was in the jungle in the land of the Amazons. A hunting party of women, each with one breast bare, had captured him. They tied his wrists together, then his heels. Laying him on his back and raising his limbs, they passed a long bamboo pole underneath the bindings. He was hoisted up and the pole was shouldered by four women, two at the front and two at the back, all in a line. They were all beautiful and all had dark hair – black or brown.

They set off at a pace through the jungle and eventually came to the palace of the Amazon queen. She was blonde and

Helen. She sat on tiger skin on a raised throne at one end of a long hall. Lewis was dumped onto the floor in front of her and the pole removed.

'We found him in the jungle,' said the leader of the hunting party.

Helen was completely bare-breasted. She stood up and stepped slowly down from the dais upon which the throne was mounted. She wore a short skirt of animal skin and shoes tied with criss-crossed thongs that came up to her knees. She came down and stood over him. He saw columnar thighs and above him the heavy breasts.

'He shall be mine,' said the Queen of the Amazons. 'Take him to my quarters.'

Lewis woke in the middle of the night. The luminous hands on his watch showed two forty in the morning. The air was warm. A night bird called somewhere. From outside came the faintest sighing – a sound that was either the sea or the air moving in the trees – he could never be sure which. As always, the stars. Across in Helen's room he heard a creak of the bed as she turned in it.

He heard another creak and another. Then he thought he heard a faint whimper. Then silence. Then a whimper again. The sounds continued intermittently. Silence for a few moments. Then a creak in the bed. Silence. A whimper. Then a louder sound almost like a sob. Was she crying again? He thought of going to her. He wanted to. The bed creaked again. Then there was a gasp and a long sigh. Silence. He listened intently. Nothing. Was she dead? Should he knock at the door? A long silence. And then the comforting sound of somebody turning in a bed.

Lewis was already in the kitchen when Helen came down. She had slept later than usual. Lewis looked at her face, remembering what he had heard in the night. It had a sleepy happiness about it.

'Hello, sleepy head,' he said. 'Sleep well?'

'Very well,' she said.

Even though her eyes were wide open, she still seemed half asleep. She came over to him and embraced him and kissed him on the lips.

'Good morning,' she said.

The kiss was not in any way lingering. It was as brief as the ones that Lewis used to plant so delicately on her cheek. But it was on the lips. After that their good night and good morning kisses were always on the lips.

Lewis had been captured by pirates in a sea fight. He was thrown in the hold of their ship and the ship eventually dropped anchor. When he and the other captives came blinking up into the light, he saw a sun-blue harbour surrounded by high, parched hills. It looked like the Caribbean or the Mediterranean. Densely packed, ochre coloured houses with red tiled roofs climbed up the hillsides and there were palm trees along the seafront. It was a sight that Nelson must have seen.

They were taken to a prison, a fearsome place built of great stones and iron. Lewis was thrown into a cell where at first he thought he was alone. But as his eyes grew accustomed to the gloom, he realised that there was somebody else in there. A woman. Helen. She was dressed in eighteenth century clothes – a dress that had once been white with short sleeves and a low neckline.

'We are to be sold as slaves,' she told Lewis.

They were taken to the slave market in a cart drawn by a bullock. A large crowd had gathered about a raised stage. It was like an execution except there was no gallows or block. As each slave was taken up onto the stage, they were stripped down to their underclothes. Helen struggled but the slave master pulled off her dress, tearing her bodice in the process. It hung open and she held it shut with her hands, standing in only her knickers. The slave master used a whip, folded back on itself, to prod her, turning her around and lifting her head.

But then Lewis overpowered the guards and seized Helen from the slave master. At this all the other slaves broke free and Lewis led them to the harbour. They seized a ship and sailed off. It was a different sort of *Treasure Island*.

Some nights Lewis was unable to fall asleep as he thought about her. Or he would wake in the middle of the night and listen for her. He willed her to come into him. And imagined the scene as the doorknob turned and she was there in her long white nightgown – which he had seen on the line – and came to his bed and got in.

32

The *Titanic* was sinking and Lewis was on it. Passengers, crazed with terror, fled towards the stern of the ship as the bow slipped beneath the waves. But now the great stern of the ship began to rear up into the starlit night sky. People clung to the railings or threw themselves over the side, hoping to swim away and avoid the suction that would take everything with it when the great ship went down. Lewis' eyes were wide with terror. Somebody pulled at him, holding onto his arms and his clothes. It was a woman with a shawl over her head and a child in her arms. He tried to tear himself away but her fingers bit into him like talons. He could feel the ship moving beneath his feet, Rearing. Sliding. He would not be able to escape. She would drag him down when the ship went down.

He was in an underground station, on the platform. Trains kept coming into the station. They pulled open carriages into which were crammed those who had died on the *Titanic*. The people were still wet and shocked from their experience. On the curved wall of the station, a film was being projected. It showed the sinking of the ship, the great stern now beginning its final death slide into the frigid waters of the North Atlantic.

Lewis was back on the ship. The water washed around him, bitterly cold, biting into every part of him. He thought his body would shut down, it was so cold. The woman and child still held onto him. He tried to pull himself free. He was being sucked under. He couldn't breathe. His nose and mouth were blocked. He was gasping.

'Lewis! Lewis!'

He felt arms around him. The woman with the child was trying to pinion him. But no, suddenly now he was warm. He opened his eyes.

He was sitting up in bed, his pyjama jacket cold and stuck to him with sweat. The room was in darkness but some starlight came in through the open window and curtains. Helen sat opposite him in her nightgown, her hair untidy. She held him by the upper arms.

'You were having a nightmare,' she said.

As his eyes adjusted, he saw that she was frowning, her eyes intense, lips parted slightly. She lowered her hands to her lap.

'I was,' he said weakly. 'I dreamt I was on the *Titanic* – and it was going down. I was in the water and I was suffocating.'

'How awful,' she said. 'I wonder where that came from.'

'I was reading in the paper yesterday about a gas attack somewhere in France. I think it may have been that. You know – gas, suffocation. I'm afraid, Helen. I don't want to go.'

'Oh, my poor boy,' she said. 'Come here.'

She pulled him towards her, moved closer and held him. He could feel her breasts pressing against him. She smelt of sleep. She stroked his hair and rocked him gently. She held him for what seemed like ages. He didn't want it to end. Eventually, she lay him down as one would a child. She pulled the bedclothes up under his chin and then continued to sit there, her hands in her lap. She was still there when he drifted off to sleep.

It was late when he woke the next morning. Sunlight poured through the window and the air outside was alive with birdsong. He dressed and went out on the landing. Her bedroom door and window were open and he could hear her doing her usual mixture of humming and singing downstairs. He came down the stairs. She was at the table mixing what looked to be bread or a cake in a bowl.

'Hello Lewis,' she said, brightly. 'How are you feeling?'

'Better. I fell back into a deep sleep. I'm really sorry about last night.'

A look of tenderness came on her face.

'Don't be silly. You've nothing to be sorry about. What you're facing into – it's awful, horrible. If it was me I'd be scared out of my wits.'

'I know I said last night that I didn't want to go, but I have to, of course.'

She nodded.

'I'll make us some tea.'

He pulled a chair out and sat down at the table.

'I feel cursed,' he said. 'Maybe my whole generation is. That we have to go and do this. Why us?'

He joined his hands on the table as though praying.

'With you —' he said, looking down at the table.

He paused and then looked up. She was holding the kettle and had turned to look at him.

'I don't know if this sounds stupid or strange but – with you – I feel like I've got a mother again; that she's been given back to me. And now, just when this happens, it's all about to be snatched away again.'

Helen put the kettle on the range to boil. She came over and sat at the table opposite him.

'We're so happy here,' he went on. 'What should happen now is that I should find a job or go to university or something and that we would live close by one another and be able to meet like this. It's not fair. This War isn't fair.'

She reached across the table, took his hands and looked into his eyes.

'I don't think anyone ever said anything about life being fair. But you're right – what you and your generation have been asked to do is appalling, unspeakable, unjust. If you were my son, I think I'd be telling you not to go. To become a conscientious objector.'

Lewis shook his head. He tried to speak but thought he might burst into tears if he did. She squeezed his hands.

'I know. I know you wouldn't. You're in a position where you've got no other real choice. And there's nothing I can say, there's nothing anyone can do to make that easier for you. All I can suggest is that you try to put it out of your mind for now. Yes, continue your training and get fit. But let's enjoy the rest of our time together. Who knows what will happen? Maybe the War will end. And you should start thinking too of what you want to do when it's over. Be positive. You're going to come back. You know you are. So make plans for that.'

Later he went out for a run. He went further than he had ever gone before – he reckoned it was about five miles. The last mile was tough – especially in the heat and on the uphills – but he pushed on. Endurance would be something he would need in abundance from now on. By the time he got back the dark cloud that had been hanging over him had lifted; he had managed to push November to the back of his mind. She was right. There was no point in thinking about things that might never come to pass. If something was going to happen to him, all the worrying in the world wasn't going to change that. And supposing nothing did? Then he would have a future. She was right about that too. He needed to start thinking about what he would do when he got out of the Army. He just knew one thing for certain. Now that she was in his life, he didn't want to lose her. He wanted to be near her. Maybe they could live together if he did go to university. It's not like she had any roots here in Cornwall. They could go anywhere that they both decided to go. Other people might wonder about their relationship but he didn't care. If he was going to live through a war, that would be the least of his concerns if he survived.

When he got back from the run, Helen had washed her hair and was sitting outside in the sunshine, brushing it as it dried.

'Would you like me to brush it for you?' he asked on an impulse.

She looked surprised but said, 'That would be nice.'

She straightened up in the chair, hitched up the towel that was draped over her shoulders and handed him the brush. He stood behind her and began to pull it in long, slow strokes through her hair. She tilted her face up to the sun. Even though he couldn't see them, he knew that she had closed her eyes. He continued to stroke with the brush and occasionally, she made low, purring-with-satisfaction kinds of noises.

'That's lovely,' she said, dreamily.

'You look so much younger than thirty six,' he said.

'Flattery, flattery, flattery.'

'No, it's true. I really mean it.'

In bed that night, he thought about her. She was thirty six, nineteen years older than him. She *was* old enough to be his mother. When she would be forty, he would be twenty one. When she was fifty, he would be thirty one. But she looked and acted a lot younger. And if he went to war and came back safely – say, next year – he wouldn't be a normal nineteen year old with no experience of the world. He would have been in a *war*, for heaven's sake.

He imagined them living together and sharing the same bed. He saw himself undressing her. Undoing her skirt so that she stepped out of it. Then unbuttoning her blouse. Taking down her stockings. He had seen her underwear on the clothes line. Bodices and knickers and one or two things that she called brassieres. He would unbutton the bodice slowly unveiling her breasts – and finally, he would kneel down in front of the goddess that she was, kiss her groin through the fabric and then take down her knickers. They would make love and after that drift off to sleep, warm and all cuddled up together and wrapped around each other and naked.

The next day Helen cycled into town to do some shopping while Lewis weeded the small vegetable patch that she had created. Once she had gone, he went to the back door, took off his boots and socks and went inside in his bare feet. He washed his hands at the sink and went upstairs. He stood in the doorway of her room. The bed was made and everything tidied away, except for her bottles and jars and a hairbrush which lay on the dressing table. The temple of the goddess.

He went inside. There was a faint smell of perfume. He looked at the labels on the bottles. 'Shem-el-Nessim', one of them said, along with a picture of a beautiful woman dressed for a harem. Helen in a harem. There was a thought for later. Outside the birds twittered. In the distance he heard a dog barking and a seagull shrieked. He went to the chest of drawers and opened the top drawer of three. It contained stockings, mainly white but also a couple of black pairs, each pair wrapped around each other in a ball. He took a white pair, separated them and stretched one between his hands. It was as insubstantial as air. How was it possible to make something so delicate? He stroked it against his cheek. He had shaved the previous day – he needed to every two or three days now – and the fabric was like the whisper of the wind against his skin. He held the stocking across his eyes like a blindfold. Everything was filmy, gauzy. She wore these on her legs. On her thighs. He smelt them and wondered if the smell was of her. He replaced the stockings carefully and took a black pair. Again he unrolled the ball and stretched a stocking. Holding it to his lips he kissed it, near to the top. The white ones spoke of summer and wine and tennis; the black ones were secret. Intimate. He replaced the stockings and closed the drawer.

The second drawer contained the bodices – buttons, ribbon, frills, bows, clips to hold the stockings – a froth of white. He inspected the clips. So simple yet so clever. The garments were shaped to her body. He took out a brassiere. She had tucked one cup into the other and the straps lay in the hollow of the cup. He pictured the wide straps straining around her sides, the narrow ones over her shoulders and down her back. The clasp where it all came together on her spine. To lay his head upon her breasts. To touch them. To hold them in his hands as though weighing them. To kiss them.

In the third drawer were the knickers. Again all white. The most sacred garments. He took a pair out and held them up by the waistband. He saw the curve of her body at the front and imagined the twin rounds of her buttocks at the back. He looked at the gusset from the outside and then from the inside. The fabric was different here – slightly thicker, wool unlike the rest of the material which was some kind of silky thing. Maybe it was silk. This was where the centre of her rested. The place where he had come from. Where everybody came from. But also the centre of her pleasure. He stroked the fabric against his cheek. He buried his face in the material but there was only the smell of clean washing, dried in the sun. He kissed it, letting his lips linger. He breathed her name.

'Helen. Darling Helen.'

Then he carefully replaced it. The rite of adoration, the ritual of worship was over.

33

They were in the kitchen. The day was fine and Lewis pushed up the window over the sink. Behind him he heard Helen say, 'I've been dreading to ask this, Lewis but when are you planning to go back to London?'

'The end of October,' he said, turning round. 'That was what I originally agreed with my dad.'

She said nothing and the silence between them lengthened.

'I suppose I could delay it,' he said. 'I'm not actually eighteen until the tenth of November. So maybe there's no need for me to be back there until say, a week before. 'I'll write and ask Dad. See what he says.'

'Would you like to stay longer?' she asked.

'You know I would. There's nothing I'd like more.'

Later that afternoon, Helen said that she needed to go into town as she had to get some things.

'I'll get them for you,' said Lewis.

She shook her head.

'No, I'll go. They're woman things.'

He blushed. She smiled.

'Won't be long,' she said. 'Have the kettle on when I come back. I'll get some cakes.'

Lewis filled the kettle – he would put it on in a while – and laid the table. Some time later she returned. She went to the kitchen table and began to unload what she had bought.

'I bought scones,' she said, 'and some other cakes. The bakery was selling them off cheap to get rid of them before they closed.

I've got clotted cream, there's jam in the cupboard so I think we shall have a Cornish cream tea.'

'You're so good at this,' he said.

'Good at what?' she asked, turning round.

'I don't know what you'd call it. Providing, I suppose. You always buy such nice things. And cook such nice things.'

'Why, that's a lovely thing to say, Lewis. Thank you.'

'You do,' he said. And then added, 'I'll make the tea.'

'Food's important,' she said, as she returned to her unpacking. 'It's life, isn't it?'

He took the kettle off the range and poured some of the boiled water into the teapot to warm it. He put the lid on and swilled the water around in it. He was about to pour it down the sink when something occurred to him that he wanted to say to her. He turned and, as he did so, he saw a shadow pass the window to which Helen had her back.

'Oh, we've got a visitor,' he said with some surprise.

They had hardly had anyone call while he had been here.

'I wonder who it is,' he said, putting down the teapot and going to the back door. Just then there was a firm knock on it. Lewis got to the door and opened it.

The man who stood there was tall, well-built with ruddy cheeks and a small grey-brown moustache. His dark suit looked like it was his best one and Lewis thought he looked very overdressed for a day that was still warm and sunny. The man took off his hat and there was sweat glistening on his forehead and upper lip. Underneath the hat the man was bald with just the finest fringe of grey hair above his ears and a tuft on top at the front. He held the hat in his hands and had a confident air about him, like he was used to calling at doors.

'Good evening, sir. I was looking for a Mrs Helen Goddard and hoped I might have the right address.'

'I'm sorry,' said Lewis, 'there's no Mrs Goddard here. Maybe she was a previous tenant,' he suggested helpfully.

The stranger hesitated a moment.

'What about a Mrs Helen Hope, then?'

After that a few things happened together. Lewis heard Helen calling from the kitchen, 'Who is it Lewis?' He thought her voice sounded high and strange. Simultaneously, Lewis realised that this must be Helen's husband, despite the civilian clothes. Lewis went to close the door but found that it wouldn't close. For a second he couldn't understand why but then he looked down to see that the stranger's well-polished black shoe was wedged against the bottom of the door. By then Lewis heard Helen behind him in the little porch. He half-turned and saw that she was standing there with her hands hanging down by her sides.

'Hello, Helen,' said the stranger, in a voice that Lewis thought, sounded warm and friendly.

'Hello, Bill,' she said.

It seemed as though everyone had become frozen. Nobody moved. The colour was gone from Helen's face and Lewis thought she gave the impression of being ill. He looked at her for some sign or guidance as to what he should do.

'May I come in, Helen?' the man she had called Bill asked.

'Yes,' she said. 'Yes, of course. Come in.'

Lewis released the pressure on the door and Bill stepped in past Lewis.

'Come through to the kitchen,' said Helen, turning.

Bill followed her with Lewis bringing up the rear. By the time he got into the room, Helen seemed to have composed herself somewhat.

'Would you like some tea?'

'That'd be nice. It was a long journey down here.'

'And I'm sorry,' he said, turning to Lewis. 'We haven't been introduced. Bill Goddard. Detective Inspector Bill Goddard.'

He reached out a hand. Lewis took it. It was a worker's hand, not calloused exactly but sandpapery. They shook hands.

'Bill is my brother-in-law,' said Helen.

Then she added, 'Lewis is my lodger.'

The lady doth protest too much, thought Lewis. He saw that she was blushing.

'Ah,' said Bill.

He let the sound hang in the air before adding, 'This is a nice little place you've got here, Helen.'

If he'd said 'love nest' the remark couldn't have sounded more suggestive.

'Though nothing in comparison to home, eh?'

'Sit down, Bill,' she said.

'I'll make the tea,' offered Lewis, taking a step towards the sink.

'Lewis,' said Helen. 'I need to speak with Bill privately. Would you mind leaving us alone for a little while?'

If Lewis was about to protest, he thought better of it. Or maybe he couldn't think of anything else to say or do. He nodded and went out of the room, leaving them together. As he pulled the door shut he held it for a moment and looked back in at Helen. Her eyes met his but there was only blankness there.

Lewis stood in the little porch for a moment, uncertain what to do. Then he went as loudly as he could out through the back door, shutting it behind him. He hesitated a moment or two more and then tiptoed round to the side of the house where the window was open. He paused just before the window and listened. He had missed the beginning of the conversation.

' … don't know how in God's name he managed to get to a telephone out there, but he did.'

'He has a staff job, for heaven's sake, Bill. Of course he can get to a telephone.'

'He's devastated, Helen. Absolutely devastated. He asked me to tell you that, to begin with.'

'He'll get over it,' said Helen.

Her voice was cold.

'But, why, Helen? Just answer me that – why?'

'Look Bill, you know I'm very fond of you and I don't want us to have a row. But – he was killing me?'

'What, was he beating you?'

'No. Of course, not.'

'Well what then? What was it?'

'I can't explain it in a way you'd understand.'

Bill's voice was suddenly steely.

'Well, I'm afraid you're going to have to – that is, if you want me to go away. Because here's the way I see it. You had a lovely home, plenty of money, a husband that loved you and that was always faithful to you. If that wasn't enough, he's off in France risking his life for you —'

'Oh spare me, Bill. He's not risking his life'.

'— Risking his life for you. And it still wasn't enough for you. I have to say that sounds pretty selfish to me. Selfish – or crazy. Most women would love to have been in the situation you are in.

And he's prepared to take you back. He asked me to tell you this. He's prepared to overlook your whole ... this whole thing and just carry on with life as it was. He loves you, Helen. That was what he said to me on the phone. "Please make it clear to her that I love her".'

'He doesn't love me, Bill. He loves an image of me that he wants me to become.'

'Oh, come off it, Helen. What does that mean anyhow? To be honest, that's just a lot of clap-trap.'

'It's not clap-trap. It's my marriage, Bill – or, at least, was. You weren't there. You don't know what it was like – how suffocating it was.'

'You should see some of the people I come across in the course of my work. If you did, you'd see how bloody lucky you were.'

'Look, he doesn't own me, Bill. He may have been my husband but he doesn't own me. I just want to get my own life back. To go back to being me. I've been doing that since I came down here. I've had some of the happiest weeks of my life since I got here.'

'What – with that "lodger" of yours?'

Bill said the word with a sneer in his voice. For a second Helen said nothing. Then Lewis heard her say,' How *dare* you? How *dare* you?' And this time the 'dare' was said in disbelief. 'How dare you accuse me of something like that?'

Lewis heard a chair slide across the floor as if someone was getting up.

'Bit too close to the mark, eh Helen?'

'Get out of my house now,' Lewis heard Helen say.

There was fury in her voice. Lewis pulled away from the window and hurried silently down towards the rear hedge. Next moment he heard the back door open and first, Bill and then Helen were there.

'Please Helen,' Bill was saying. 'I hadn't meant for us to quarrel but you're making a terrible mistake. One that you'll regret for the rest of your life.'

Lewis began to walk up towards them.

'Why don't we let me be the judge of that,' said Helen, with icy fury.

Then she slammed the back door and disappeared inside. Bill looked at Lewis for several moments and seemed to be about to say something. But then he just turned towards the front gate and was gone.

34

$\mathcal{L}$ewis came back into the house. Helen was at the sink, hands on the front edge of it, facing the window. Her head was bowed and she was shaking. She was crying. Lewis went to her, putting an arm around her.

'Here, come and sit down.'

She looked at him. Her face was red and sodden with tears and she looked bewildered, as though she didn't recognise him. She reeled a little and Lewis thought she was going to fall. He turned her, guided her to the chair and she half-fell, was half-pushed into it. He knelt beside her.

'How did he find you? I thought you said you posted the letter in Plymouth?'

'I did. That wasn't how he did it. He didn't need the postmark.'

'Then how?'

'He's a policeman,' she said with annoyance in her voice.

Lewis still look puzzled and Helen flared into anger.

'Think about it. Because he's a policeman he was able to check my bank account and find out where I was withdrawing money. Once he'd tracked me down to Fowey, a photograph and a few questions did the rest.'

She sat slumped in the chair. Lewis took her hand.

'But it's over now. He's gone. You told him you weren't going back.'

He paused and then hurriedly added, 'Didn't you?'

She looked at him and he thought, for a moment, she was going to explode into anger but she just said, 'That won't be the end of it.'

'But what can he do? He may be a policeman but he can't force you to go back. It's a free country. You can do as you choose.'

'Oh, it's been stupid this game we've been playing here. Playing house just like a couple of children.'

'We haven't been playing. It *hasn't* been a game. This is real life.'

But she was shaking her head.

'No, it's not. No, it's not,' and now she was angry again. Her cheeks were wet with tears. She pulled her hand away and spoke very slowly, deliberately.

'Real life is me married to Robert. This has been – oh, I don't know what it's been. A holiday romance without the romance. An interlude? A piece of madness?'

'It —'

'Look,' she said, her face turning bright red. 'Will you shut up and listen to me?'

She had never spoken to him like this before. She had never told him to shut up. He did as he was told.

'I was crazy to do this. Mad. It was pure madness.'

For an instant it ran through his mind that she *was* mad. She was almost unrecognisable from the Helen he knew.

'This isn't how life works – you try a marriage and if you don't like it, you leave it like a bad meal in a restaurant. Marriage is for life. Robert and I are for life.'

She paused and then said, 'I've made my bed, Lewis. I'll have to lie in it.'

Lewis was at a loss for words.

'And you know,' she said. 'Maybe it wasn't so bad anyway.'

Lewis stood up slowly and took a step away from her.

'He loves me.'

Now, it was as though she was talking to herself.

'He does. In his own way. He just finds it hard to show it. And why wouldn't he with the childhood he had? Anyway, when he comes home from the War, it'll be different. *He'll* be different.'

Lewis didn't know what to do. Argue with her and risk even more anger or just agree with her and hope she would calm down.

'What do you think?' she suddenly said, looking up at him.

'Whatever's going to make you happy.'

It was the first thing that ran into his head and he thought it sounded limp, unhelpful. But, as the words hung there, he realised how true they were. That *was* all he wanted. He would have loved it if that had included him, but ultimately he just wanted her to be happy. She had a huge capacity for getting pleasure out of simple things – food, music, the sun and the beach and the sea. He just wanted to see her smiling and laughing all the time.

'Go back to him,' she said, definitely. 'Yes, that's what I'll do.'

'And you'll be happy to spend the rest of your days like that?' Lewis asked. 'Those would be happy days?'

Helen got up and went back to the sink, looking out the window towards the sea. She snuffled and found a handkerchief in her pocket and blew her nose. Her back was to him.

'We can't always pick what we want, can we?' she said. 'You of all people should know that, shouldn't you?'

'I should?'

'With the War, silly.'

She turned to face him and the way she had called him 'silly' sounded a bit like the old, affectionate Helen.

'You hardly want to go off to war, but you have to. It's your duty. Well, this is *my* duty.'

She faltered.

'This is my duty,' she said again, and as she did the tears began to flow again.

'This is my duty,' she said once more, but now the words were mangled in the tears.

He went to her and took her in his arms and held her. She sobbed and sobbed while he made soothing noises and stroked her hair. He could feel his shoulder getting wet where the tears were falling. After a long time her crying abated and she eased away from him.

'Thank you,' she said. 'And sorry for being so horrible to you a while ago.'

He shook his head.

'It was nothing,' he tried to say but the words came out as a whisper.

Then, knowing that he risked the whole thing flaring up again, he said, 'I'm sure Robert isn't a bad person. But he's bad for *you*. You know you won't ever be happy with him. You've found happiness here. You've done the hardest bit. Don't throw it all away. Hold onto what you've got. You need to go to a solicitor. Find one today. Get your divorce going and then you'll be safe.'

'I thought he was out of my life – Robert, I mean. I felt light, pure, somehow whole again. Bill coming here has sort of tainted all of that. Made it seem dirty.'

'You mean that thing he said about me being your lodger?'

'You were listening, weren't you?'

'Of course I was listening. I didn't know who he was. He was a big man, I wanted to make sure he didn't hurt you.'

'Oh Lewis, you're such a darling. If I was twenty years younger. Come here to me.'

She went to him and then said, 'Your shoulder's all wet.'

'You did that,' he said.

She put her arms around him and held him tight and they both began to laugh.

35

*O*ver the days that followed her brother-in-law's visit, Helen made no attempt to go to Fowey to find a solicitor. Several times he was going to say it to her. In bed at night he would rehearse different ways of saying it, trying to find a tactful way. Maybe he should phrase it like a reminder – acting as though she had forgotten. Or perhaps he should offer to go with her. When he was down the town he looked around and found a couple of names on brass plates. But, in the end, he said nothing. Better to keep the peace. Was that what his mother had done with his father? Gradually though, the tension eased as there was no reappearance from Bill Goddard. August turned into September.

As the leaves began to take on their first autumn colours, they gave up swimming and instead spent much of their time walking the lanes and pathways and cliffs. The ground, which had been iron-hard all summer, began to show signs of dampness. Dews were heavy and some days began with mist, though it pretty much always burned off by lunchtime.

Several nights, Lewis heard muffled sobbing coming from Helen's room. He would ask her about it – obliquely – the next morning. Had she slept well? Did she have any dreams? But the answer was always the same – that she had slept really well. He ceased to ask.

For Lewis, September marked the end of the seemingly endless book of summer. The world was starting to intervene again. There was so sign of the War ending so now it looked to be inevitable that he would go to France. And what of Helen? Once he left what would she do? Would she stay here or was it best to leave now, given that her husband knew where she was? Lewis had no sense of it and was edgy about asking.

And what of he and Helen? And what was 'he and Helen' anyway? The mother he hadn't known? A woman that he had offered to support when he was in France? He wanted to be her lover. There were times when he lay in his bed and ached to go to the room across the landing – or for her to come to him. Unless he was too tired and fell asleep straight away, these were always his last thoughts every night.

In his fantasy there was usually a thunderstorm, crashing loud and with lightning. His room would be dark but from time to time, sheets of lightning would blaze, lighting up the room like flares. Suddenly the door knob would rattle slightly and turn and she would be there in her long white nightgown. She would say something about being scared or cold and he would fold back the bedclothes, inviting her to climb in. Soon they would be wonderfully warm together, arms around each other, legs intertwined. They would kiss and they would gradually undress each other and then they would make love.

It wasn't just at bedtime that he had fantasies like this. He often thought about her when he was walking out from town or out running or any time he had a few idle moments. He often found that when he was reading, he was seeing the words but he wasn't taking them in. Instead she filled his thoughts.

The last day of September came. The sun was westering and Helen had gone into Fowey. The evening looked like giving way to a cold night, the first really cold one they had had. Lewis was outside chopping wood and loading up the log basket. They would keep the range hot for as long as possible because once the fire died, the house would get very cold and probably a bit damp. Lewis wondered whether Helen would survive a winter here if she did stay.

He finished filling up the log basket and carried it into the kitchen where he emptied it into a bigger basket which stood by the range. One more load. He carried the smaller basket back outside and was standing at the door for a moment, watching the setting sun which had started to paint the western sky orange, when he heard the sound of footsteps in the lane. He thought at first it must be Helen wheeling the bike back up the hill, but there was no sound of the bike and the footsteps seemed heavier, and of someone who was almost marching rather than pushing a bike. Curious, Lewis came round to the corner of the cottage from where he could see the gate. The hedge was over six foot high and so concealed whoever it was. A few moments later though, he saw a figure appear at the gate. The man was tall – over six foot – and wore an officer's cap and an unbuttoned greatcoat. He looked at the cottage for a moment, then bent and opened the gate. He stepped in, turned and bending a second time, shut it carefully behind him.

When he straightened up and turned round, Lewis caught a glimpse of an Army uniform and leather beneath the greatcoat. The man wore immaculately polished cavalry boots. With the coat hanging open he reminded Lewis of a khaki rook. Lewis knew who he was.

'Hello,' he said, 'can I help you?'

'Ah, hello, yes, I'm looking for Helen Hope,' said the figure.

There was a faint hint of the North or Midlands about the accent but Lewis thought that it was overlaid with a more posh accent, as though the man were trying to hide the original one.

'She's not here.'

If this was meant to deter the man, it had no effect whatsoever. He came towards Lewis and removed his cap. He had black hair flecked with grey and a black moustache. His eyes were hooded and his face was gaunt, almost cadaverous in appearance.

'Major Robert Goddard. And you must be Mister Friday.'

He extended his hand. There was something about the way

he said '*Mister* Friday' – as though Lewis were masquerading in some way. An actor.

Lewis had known this moment would come. He had often thought about it and in his head, it had always ended the same way, with him sending Helen's husband packing with a flea in his ear. Lewis would say a few cool, carefully chosen phrases and the man would leave, never to return. Lewis had never been quite sure what the things he would say were and now that the moment had arrived, he realised it was too late to try to work them out. He was lost for words, and weakly took Robert's hand. The handshake was firm, the skin dry and papery.

'When you say she's not here, she's left? Gone some place else?'

The voice was authoritarian with a hint of impatience. An officer addressing an enlisted man. Helen's husband was playing with him. Lewis didn't know whether or not to tell the truth. He opted for saying as little as possible.

'No.'

'No? No, she's not left. So she'll be back soon then?'

They stood looking at each other. Goddard spoke next filling the gap.

'My brother mentioned you. You met my brother, didn't you?'

Lewis nodded, almost involuntarily.

'So you're my wife's lodger.'

The words hung there like an accusation. Lewis was astonished to see the man actually look him up and down.

'You should leave,' blurted out Lewis. 'She doesn't want to see you. She told your brother that.'

'Ah, so she *is* here and she *will* be coming back.'

'Why don't you just leave now,' Lewis said. 'Leave her alone. She doesn't want to see you any more. She's finished with you.'

'How old are you anyway?' asked Goddard.

'Seventeen. I'll be eighteen on November. I'll be going into the Army then.'

'Can't be soon enough. We can use every man we can get. It's been damned hard going out there on the Somme.'

The words were conciliatory, spoken warmly, almost as if between a father and a son. Lewis remembered what Helen had said about Goddard having a staff job. There was another long silence. Goddard reached inside his coat and extracted a cigarette case. He clicked it open and offered one to Lewis.

'No thanks,' said Lewis.

'Mind if I do?' he said, but he was already lighting the cigarette anyway. He blew the smoke off to the side. Goddard looked around.

'Must be pretty bleak here in winter,' he said.

'It's a beautiful part of the country at any time of year,' said Lewis defensively.

'I'm sure you're right. Will she be back soon?'

Lewis hesitated again.

'My wife. Will she be back soon?'

'I don't know.'

'Gone into Fowey has she? I could always go and pick her up, I suppose. Surprise her on the road.'

'She doesn't want to talk to you,' said Lewis.

He realised he was just repeating himself over and over again. It sounded so lame. Goddard took another puff on the cigarette but then suddenly threw it, half-smoked, onto the ground and stubbed it out with the sole of his boot.

'Now listen to me, sonny boy. I've been pretty damn patient with you up until now.'

Goddard's face, which had been quite pale when he had first arrived, now suddenly began to show red.

'But I've had quite enough of you telling me how I should deal with my wife.'

Lewis wanted to say 'she's not your wife' but of course, she still was.

'So why don't you carry on doing whatever you were doing and when my wife gets back, you'll do me the courtesy of letting me speak to her in private. And I'm sure, if she were here, she would have had better manners than to leave me standing around out here.'

Lewis felt utterly defeated. The sun was gone and there was a real chill in the air now.

'I was just getting wood for the stove,' he said, as though that excused his rudeness in keeping Goddard out here. The remark hung there and Lewis thought it sounded ridiculous.

'I'm finished now,' he said. 'We can go in. It's this way.'

Lewis left the log basket by the woodpile and led the way round to the back door. They went in through the small porch and into the kitchen. The room was warm but Lewis felt cold. While Goddard hovered behind him, Lewis opened the door of the range and fed some blocks of wood into it. When he had finished, he turned to see Goddard looking around the room.

'I have to say it's a nice location for a house,' he said. 'Near the beach and everything.'

'Would you like to sit down?' asked Lewis.

'Very kind of you, thanks.'

'Can I offer you some tea?'

'Thanks. I'm dying for a cup. Long trip down from London.'

He was being matey now and Lewis hated him for it. He filled the kettle and put it on to boil. It seemed to take forever and while it did, Lewis busied himself with taking cups from the cupboard and putting the sugar bowl and milk jug on the table. Finally the kettle was steaming and rattling and Lewis took it from the range. As he did so, he heard the gate squeal open and the clanging of Helen's bike as she pushed it through the gate. He shot a glance at Goddard who returned an expressionless look. He saw her pass the window and a few moments later, heard her in the porch. She was humming.

'I'm home,' she called.

An instant later she entered the kitchen.

'Hello, Helen,' Goddard said.

The expression on her face was not so much of terror as of mortal sickness.

'You're looking well,' he said. 'The sea air must suit you. We'll have to see that you get more of it.'

Lewis went to Helen and stood beside her.

'I'm sorry,' he said. 'I —'

But he didn't know what to say so that he left the sentence hanging there, unfinished. Helen shook her head as if to say that it didn't matter, but her eyes were on Robert.

'What do you want?' she said.

She said the 'you' contemptuously.

'Excuse me Mister Friday, I wonder would you mind terribly if my wife and I had a chance to talk in private?'

Lewis looked uncertainly at Helen. She hesitated and then nodded.

'Actually, I've got a better idea,' said Robert. 'Would you like to come out to dinner, Helen? We'll find some place in town, have something to eat and drink and then we can talk.'

'It's alright. I'll leave you alone,' said Lewis.

'No, Lewis,' she turning to him. 'This is better.'

Then to Robert she said, 'Just give me five minutes to get changed.'

Helen turned and went up the stairs. Lewis watched her go. He hesitated and then said, 'Excuse me'.

'Of course,' said Robert with what Lewis thought was a sneer.

He followed her upstairs.

The door of her room was closed. Tentatively Lewis knocked on the door. She opened it a few inches and her face appeared. She had applied lipstick and it was strikingly bright against her face which was quite pale. Before Lewis could say anything she held up a forefinger and said, 'It's alright, Lewis.'

'But —?'

'No, really. I don't know why he's come but it's probably just as well that he has. We'll get it all worked out and then we can both move on. It's better this way.'

'But … but what if he hurts you?'

She smiled a weary smile.

'He's never hurt me, Lewis. At least not physically, I mean. And anyway we'll be in a public place. No, this is the civilized way to do it. It's how it should be done. No playing silly buggers or game playing or subterfuge or running away. Just let's get it sorted out for once and for all.'

'But —'

'But what if my resolve weakens?' she asked.

He nodded.

'It won't. Trust me. You'll see.'

'I can come with you. I don't mean with you, but maybe follow at a safe distance. Make sure you're alright. Get you home safely.'

'No, really Lewis. There's no need for that. This isn't a John Buchan spy story. This is real life. Grown-up people. I'll be fine. Honest.'

The words stung – 'John Buchan spy story' and 'real life' and 'grown-up people'.

'You go to bed,' she said, 'and I'll see you in the morning. Now, I really have to finish dressing.'

The 'go to bed' sounded like a mother speaking to a child.

He hoped she would kiss him goodnight as she always did, but instead she just closed the door gently. Lewis dithered on the landing, wondering whether or not to go downstairs. In the end he went to his room but left the door open. When he heard the door of her room opening, he emerged. She wore a dark blue skirt, a white blouse and cardigan and her good shoes. Her hair was tied up and she carried her bag and her coat over her arm.

'See you in the morning,' she said, and then, her shoes thunking on the wood, she went downstairs.

'You look beautiful,' he heard Robert say and Lewis hated him for it.

Helen clicked her way across the flagstones. The door to the porch opened and shut, followed by the outside door. Lewis heard their footsteps on the path that ran round the cottage and then crunching on the gravel. The small front gate squeaked as it opened and again as it was shut. Then their footsteps faded away into the night.

36

*I*t is about ten yards from their jumping off position to the British wire. As they start over the ground, firing breaks out from the German front line. There are small arms and the vicious, rackety sound of a machine gun – like some demented woodpecker banging repeatedly on a frail, wooden shutter. The men dive to the ground. Lewis feels his gut tightening. Random and not-so random bullets are flying through the night.

'Sir, the wire's not cut,' somebody shouts above the noise of the artillery barrage.

Oh, fuck it, thinks Lewis.

The whole movement forward has stopped. *This is not going right at all.*

Lewis lifts his head a fraction and looks along the thick belt of wire, like a long black animal in the night. It seems continuous in both directions until it fades into the gloom. Gunfire continues to spew from the German trench.

One, two minutes pass. Behind him British machine guns open up as they were scheduled to do on three minutes. The artillery continues to bang away, but it's all a bit pointless with them stuck out here in no-man's-land. *This wasn't the plan.* Now though, all at once, there is movement, away to the left. They are up, crouching and moving again. The German machine guns rattle away but it sounds like they are firing in the wrong place. At least that's what Lewis prays. Now he sees the reason for the movement. There is a gap in the wire about ten yards along from where the gap was meant to have been cut. He reaches it and passes through, following the men in front of him. He feels some wire beneath his boots and brushing his puttees but mercifully it doesn't snag him. He looks back to see that his men are following. The artillery and machine guns hammer away. Shells are bursting behind and off to each side of the German front line trench. In the yellow glare of explosions sandbags, clods of earth and other unrecognisable objects can be seen flying through the air.

They are through now and running towards the German trench. They only have to cover a few yards and, as they get closer, they see German helmets bobbing above the sandbagged parapet. German words are being shouted. Rifles are sticking up in the air or being levelled over the parapet. Lewis can imagine machine guns being swivelled, ammunition belts being refreshed and locked into position. *Hurry up. For Christ's sake, hurry up.*

Ahead of him several arms throw bombs. The helmets scatter. Then the bombs explode. There are screams. There is a roar from the British as the first of them reach the edge of the parapet and begin firing into the trench. The Germans are caught like rats in a barrel. Lewis arrives at the edge of the trench in time to see a couple of helmets and backs disappearing round a corner. There are dark forms on the floor of the trench. There is the smell of a butcher's shop.

The Covering Party takes up its station on the parapet and the ladders are placed into the trench. After the Right Blocking Party has gone in, Lewis leads his men down the ladders. Two Germans lie on the floor of the trench. One is deathly still while the other is making a wailing, gurgling noise. He sounds like he's very badly wounded – no use as a prisoner. Lewis steps over him and is conscious of being in a strange and alien place. The stench is mostly the same but the faint cooking smells are different. Everything looks unfamiliar. He goes to the end of the fire bay, to the first traverse.

This is perhaps the most terrifying thing about trench raiding – turning these corners and dealing with what you find there.

If this was trench *clearing*, they would merely throw grenades over the top or round into the traverse and then go and pick up the pieces. But here the objective is to find live Germans. There could be anything waiting for them round the corner. Men with rifles ready to shoot whatever comes round; men holding rifles with bayonets attached against which Lewis' pistol will be little protection; or maybe they will be met by grenades and have great big gobbets of flesh gouged out of them by flying, white-hot metal.

Some men reckon it is better to make a sudden jump round. Others to extend an arm or a hand to see if it gets shot at. The trouble with that is that it could result in a hand wound which some senior officer might well decide was deliberately self-inflicted. This, in turn, could result in a court martial and finding yourself before a firing squad in a cold dawn mist. Oh Christ, thinks Lewis wearily and as he does so, he half steps, half jumps from the fire bay into the traverse, with his pistol arm extended.

'Mercy, English, mercy.'

A German faces them with his hands up. In the starlight, Lewis sees his face under the helmet. He is little more than a boy and the helmet looks far too big for him.

'Mercy, English, mercy,' the boy says again and continues to repeat it like a prayer.

'Alright,' says Lewis, 'get him trussed and back to the Covering Party.'

The German is led away.

Two more. He needs two more prisoners. Lewis looks at his watch. It is one thirty eight. This has all taken far too long. One more. Lewis, Fraser and two men take a few steps further along the traverse. There is a piece of groundsheet hanging down one side of the trench and almost without thinking, Lewis pulls it aside. As he does so there is a split second when he realises that this could be a booby trap.

'Oh fuck,' he hears himself say.

Thankfully, it isn't. The groundsheet covers a rectangle that has been scraped in the side of the trench. There is a man in there and since the rectangle is only about two feet high, he is reclining like some bizarre Roman emperor. The man moves his rifle but he has no real freedom of movement. He is hauled out, his hands tied behind his back and marched off.

That's two. Just one more, thinks Lewis.

He can't believe his luck. This is turning out to be amazingly easy. Of course for some time now, they had been getting a sense that the fight was going out of the Germans. It looks like the last of it has gone. Lewis turns the next corner.

He finds himself looking into the round face of a beefy German soldier, about three paces away. Beneath his steel helmet, the man has a calm look on what Lewis thinks is a rather bovine looking face. The German is about the same height as Lewis but with a much stronger build. His tunic bulges as though his body is pressing against it. He holds a rifle with a bayonet on it, extended towards Lewis. The tip of the bayonet is no more than a yard from Lewis' belly.

37

*B*y midnight Helen had still not come home. Lewis, who had been sitting up in a chair waiting for her like an anxious parent, felt his eyes drooping. He went upstairs and lay down on his bed. Some time later there were voices from downstairs.

'Why did you come here anyway?'

The words were spoken contemptuously.

'I came for my wife to take her home.'

His voice was raised now too.

'I'm not "*your* wife". I'm not anything of yours.'

'Oh but you are, and now I've come to take you home.'

'This is my home now.'

Lewis got up and hurried downstairs. He was just in time to see Robert reaching inside his coat. Lewis thought for a horrified instant that he was reaching for his service revolver. But Robert merely took out a cigarette case, extracted a cigarette and lit it. He drew on it slowly and exhaled the smoke. It was as though he was blowing it towards the two of them. Nobody broke the silence. Robert took another draw on the cigarette. There was contempt in his eyes. Finally, Helen said, 'Get out of my house or I will send Lewis to get the police.'

Robert pulled back his left sleeve a fraction and looked at his watch.

'I *am* going to leave now. You will then have one hour in which to pack. I have a car and when I return we shall leave this wretched place and return home.'

'Don't be ridiculous,' she said. 'I'm not going with you.'

'No, you're the one that's being ridiculous. You – here with this boy. It's perverted, sick – bloody prostitute, that's all you are. As I said, I shall be back in one hour and I expect you to be ready.'

'I'll just lock the door,' she said, 'and have the police here.'

'Oh, I don't think you will,' he said. 'But perhaps I shall bring the police with me. Corrupting a minor.'

His eyes swivelled to Lewis.

'You're not yet eighteen, isn't that what you told me?'

Robert smiled.

'Yes – corrupting a minor, Helen. I'm quite sure that would involve jail. So – until we meet again, *au revoir*, as we say in France.'

Robert turned and went out through the porch and was gone. His boots were loud on the flagstones, then on the gravel. There was a pained squealing of the gate as he slammed it open. Then silence.

38

*I*t was some time before either Lewis or Helen gathered their senses; but at length, she seemed to shake out of a reverie. She ran the fingers of both her hands through her hair and said, 'Oh God, an hour. Only an hour. I have to pack. And you, Lewis – you must go.'

She spoke quickly, distractedly.

'Go? Go where?' said Lewis. 'What are you talking about?'

She didn't look at him.

'You must go so that I can go back with him. If I humour him, then maybe he won't do as he said. Oh, what was I thinking of – when I brought you in here?'

Helen took a step towards the stairs. Lewis intercepted her, caught her shoulders and turned her to face him. Then he held her upper arms in his hands.

'Listen to me,' said Lewis.

She was looking at him now but it was like she didn't see him.

'Oh God, oh God.'

'Listen to me please.'

At last she seemed to focus her eyes on him.

'The first thing is that I'm not going anywhere,' said Lewis. 'Leave you alone and unprotected with Mister Hooded Crow? I don't think so.'

The name had only just occurred to him, and he found the image mildly amusing. If Helen agreed, she gave no sign.

'But you must. You must go. We only have an hour.'

'No,' he said.

She struggled to break free.

'Look at me,' he said. 'Look, and please listen. I hadn't met your husband before tonight. But it seems to me that he's nothing more than a school bully. There were people like him in school and they're filth, scum. You have a happy life now and you're going to go on having a happy life. You'll get ready to go alright, but not with him. With me. We'll pack up, go to the station in Par and catch the first train in the morning. There must be a milk train that goes early.'

'But what if he goes to the police? What if he does what he says?'

'What – is it illegal for a woman to have a young man as a lodger? If that's the case then they'd better start building more prisons. Anyway, he won't do it. That's just him trying to bully you.'

'So why don't we just call the police ourselves? Have them here when he gets back?'

'We could. But do you think he'll let it rest at that, knowing that you live here? Let's go to some new place where he can't track us down.'

He looked into her eyes. They were glistening.

'What do you say?' he said, softly. 'Life is too short to be unhappy. You're too beautiful to be unhappy. This is your big chance. Take it. Please take it.'

She seemed to hesitate for a moment. Her face took on a serious, almost grim expression. She said nothing.

'Please,' he begged.

'Alright,' she nodded. 'You're right.'

'Come on then,' he said. Let's pack. One case only. We've got about three quarters of an hour but we'll do him yet.'

Lewis went to the door and locked it. Then they hurried upstairs.

'How do we know he's not waiting for us outside?' she said, as they reached the top of the stairs.

'We don't,' he said. 'But I reckon he's so cocky that he's scared the life out of you that he's probably in a pub somewhere having a whiskey and soda and warming himself while he savours his victory. He just thinks he'll be able to come back here and walk straight in. Come on, we have to hurry. We're in a difficult and dangerous position.'

A noise came from outside and Helen jumped.

'What was that?' she said.

'A night bird? An animal? Here, I'll go and take a look.'

Lewis edged along the walls to each of the upstairs windows in turn and looked out. There was the view to the sea, the front gate, but no sign of human life. They listened. The house was silent. Coals fell in the stove. In the distance the sea sighed. They listened for footsteps or any sound outside but there were none. Finally Lewis said, 'Come on. Pack as quickly as you can. Ten minutes – no more. I'll do the same. Clothes, wash things, your handbag. Probably best to leave the lights off.'

He emptied the wardrobe hurriedly and stuffed his things into his bag. On top he threw the three books and his diary, dealing them out like cards. Then he clicked the two brass clutches shut. He went into Helen's bedroom. It was the first time he had done so with her there. Her case lay on the bed. Lewis helped her to close and tie it.

'I'll write to Mr Jones, the landlord, to finalise the rent and organise to get the rest of our things.'

He considered this for a moment.

'It might be safer not to do that. Doing anything that involved a forwarding address could mean that he just picks up the trail again.'

Her face fell.

'Anyway, never mind that now,' he said. 'We can decide later. The thing now is to get out before he comes back. Ready?'

'Ready,' she said. Then, 'Lewis?'

'Yes?'

'Thank you,' she said, an exhausted smile on her face.

He touched her on the cheek with the palm of his hand and held it there for a moment. It was the first time he had ever done anything like that. He smiled back.

'When we go outside,' Lewis said. 'If he's there, drop your case and run. I'll try to delay him. Find your way into Fowey and go to Mrs Middleton's Guest House. I'll meet you there.'

She nodded. He checked his watch. They still had half an hour. He took both his bag and her case and they hurried downstairs. In the porch, they put on their coats and then Lewis opened the door and stepped outside. She followed, bareheaded, out into the gathering evening and the frosty fog.

They listened but there was no sound except for the sea and the croaking of some crows somewhere. The moon had not yet risen. Helen passed him the key and he locked the cottage door. Their bags were heavy but manageable – Lewis hadn't realised how fit and strong he had become since the day he had first arrived here on the bus. Then they followed the wall of the house to the first corner and he looked around. Nothing. Now they could see the small white gate. His eyes had adjusted somewhat to the darkness and Lewis scanned the open space they would have to cross. It appeared to be empty. He turned to her.

'Ready,' he whispered.

She nodded.

They crossed the twenty yards or so, Lewis leading the way. He found himself crouching down. As if that would help. Their feet, crunching on the gravel seemed incredibly loud in the silence. But then they were onto the rough grass and Lewis had opened the gate. By lifting it as he opened it, he was able to stop it from squealing. They stood out in the roadway, stopped and listened.

'So we're going to Par?' said Helen.

'Well we probably shouldn't go towards Fowey. I presume

that's where he's staying and where he'll come from. If we're on the road we'll run straight into him.'

'How far is Par?'

'About four miles. We've done much more on our walks.'

'Not carrying bags.'

'Let me worry about the bags. We'll find a place to stay and catch the first train out in the morning.'

'And what if he's at the station when we arrive?'

'Maybe we'll worry about that tomorrow. Or maybe we won't catch a train. We'll get a bus instead. Or get a ride somewhere.'

Lewis felt himself becoming exasperated.

'I don't know,' he said irritably. 'I just know we need to get out of here.'

They turned to the left, following the road uphill where it would eventually connect with a surfaced road that would take them to Par. They had only been walking a few minutes when Helen suddenly said, 'Oh my god, I have to go back.'

'Come on, don't be silly,' said Lewis. 'We've been through all that.'

'No, you don't understand. I've forgotten my money.'

'But you have your bag,' said Lewis, without slackening the pace. The cases were heavy and he didn't want to lose whatever momentum he had.

'I know,' she said. But all the rest of my money – my savings. When I sent Robert the letter telling him I was leaving, I took all of my money out of the bank and closed the account.'

Lewis had stopped by now.

'I don't know – I was afraid he might be able to get his hands on it or something.'

'So where is it?'

'Under the mattress.'

'Is it much?'

She nodded.

You wait here,' she said. 'I won't be long.'

'No, don't be silly,' he said. 'I'll be quicker.'

'I'm sorry, Lewis. I'm really sorry. I should have remembered but we were just so rushed.'

'Never mind,' said Lewis, looking at his watch. 'We still have time. You wait here with the bags. I won't be long.'

Freed of the cases, he hurtled down the hill. At the white gate there was so sign of anybody. He opened it and went in, crouching as he scurried to the cottage wall. Then, hugging the wall, he worked his way around to the corner before the porch. He turned the corner cautiously but again, there was nobody there. Looking around he put the key into the keyhole and turned it. He was ready at any moment to repel an attack but none came. He opened the door, stepped inside and closed it behind him with relief. He slipped the bolt and looked at his watch again. He probably had about fifteen minutes. It was enough.

He ran upstairs and into Helen's room. A faint smell of her perfume hung on the air. He touched the pillows and, on an impulse, picked one up and held it to his face. He touched the sheets and then pulled the covers back and smelt where she lay. Her fragrance was everywhere.

The money. Swiftly, he grabbed the mattress and upended it, throwing it off the bed onto the far side. There was a brown envelope that bulged. Quickly he checked inside. There was a large wad of banknotes rolled up and held together with an elastic band. He took the envelope and stuffed it into the pocket of his coat.

He was dithering about whether or not to put the mattress back when he thought he heard a sound outside. It was a very faint, very distant, low grumbling sound. He thought it might be a distant car or truck on the road from Fowey to Par, but he quickly realised that it was closer than that. He ran to the window in the gable end of his room. Outside the light in the hedgerow beyond the gate changed so that it seemed to move and dance. The grumbling sound had resolved itself into the sound of an engine and now the light on the hedgerow was a solid beam from the headlights of a car. It came to a halt outside the gate. The engine was turned off and the lights died. Lewis felt the sweat in his armpits and on his neck go cold.

Robert got out of the car and opened the gate. His heavy shoes crunched across the gravel and then clicked on the flagstones. Lewis followed his progress around the corner to the porch. Then he heard the handle being turned and the bolt rattling as Robert tried the door. There was a pause and then the door was kicked and finally, it sounded like a shoulder had been thumped against it. Lewis heard a sound that might have been 'bitch' and then the footsteps re-commenced, around the flagstones, across the gravel and back to the car.

The engine was restarted and then, the laneway being too narrow for anything else, Lewis heard the car being reversed at high speed back down the hill, the lights on the hedgerow eventually dying out. Lewis slipped downstairs, unbolted the door and eased it open. Then he slipped out, locked it again and was across the gravel and through the gate. He raced back up the hill to find Helen.

'You got it,' she said.

He nodded breathlessly.

'He came while I was there.'

Her eyes widened.

'Oh my God.'

'He's got a car, like he said. He tried the door and then went away again. I'd say he was cursing himself for not having stayed.'

'What do you think he'll do now?'

'Go back to wherever he's staying and try to get us in the morning. That's what I'd do. If I was him I'd be waiting at Par Station.

Anyway, I have an idea,' he said. 'We still don't know how we'll get out of here – by bus, by train.'

She nodded.

'And we don't know whether he'll be waiting for us – say, at the station. Or whether he's even by himself. Maybe he's got his brother with him.'

'Yes.'

'Well what if we don't go by bus or train? What if we don't go by land at all? What if we go down to Readymoney, borrow one of the boats that are always there and sail off somewhere. We don't have to go very far. We can even go up the Fowey. We'll just hole up there for a few days until they've gone. Presumably Robert has to go back to France some time. His leave can't last indefinitely.'

'Unless he's been posted back to England.'

'Even so,' said Lewis. 'Presumably he has to go back to work.'

'But we can't just steal a boat.'

'We're only borrowing it. And we don't have to go very far – just enough to get away. We can return it in a few days. You told me you learned to sail.'

'I did – when I was a teenager. I'm a bit rusty.'

'Can you sail it a bit out to sea and then maybe round the headland to Fowey?'

'Of course. On a night like tonight, no wind, no swell. That's easy.'

'Alright. Ready?'

'Yes,' she said.

They went back down the hill. Lewis felt lighter. The whole thing was developing into a bit of an adventure now. Who'd have thought that when he'd come here he'd be getting up to things like this? Chasing around the countryside with a married woman; hiding from her husband, stealing boats. And the night was still young. He was about to say some of this to Helen when he suddenly saw a shaft of light bounce off the trees straight ahead. Simultaneously, he heard the sound of a car engine.

'Oh Christ, he's coming back,' he said. 'Quick.'

The roadway was narrow with trees and dense undergrowth on both sides. The remains of a low wall were on their right. Lewis threw the bags over the wall and then he and Helen scrambled over. The ground sloped away sharply so they began to slide downwards but soon the thick underbrush stopped them. The squatted down, panting as the blazing lights of the car tore past them going up the hill.

The car came to a halt just outside the gate. The engine was turned off and the lights died. Lewis couldn't see what was going on – only the top storey of the cottage was visible – but he could hear clearly in the still night. A car door was opened and slammed shut and then a second one. The gate squealed.

'Reckon they've flown?

It was Bill's voice. So he was there as well.

'No, they're just playing silly buggers with the lights out.'

Their heavy shoes crunched across the gravel and onto the flagstones. Lewis was half-tempted to make a run for it but was afraid of the noise he would make scrabbling out of the ditch. What a pity he couldn't drive – they could have taken the car. They waited and listened to the cottage door being tried. When the two men realised it was locked, a voice – it was Bill's – said, 'They've gone.'

'Nonsense. They're hiding inside. Break open the door.'

'This is private property, Bob.'

'I don't give a damn,' said Robert angrily. 'Down with the door. If you don't do it, I shall do it myself.'

There was the thud of a shoulder put to the door. Then came what sounded like a grunt of exertion and a boot crashing onto the wood. There was a splintering sound and the sound of the door banging on the wall as it flew inwards.

'In, in, in,' said Robert.

Lewis heard footsteps downstairs and then the sound of boots rattling up the old stairs. Feet thundered on the planking of the floors and then the window of Lewis's room was flung open with a slam and a jingle of broken glass. A sleeve brushed broken glass from the window sill and then a figure leaned out, head and shoulders. The head moved slowly from left to right looking high out over the undergrowth. Lewis was sure they would be seen but if they were, the figure gave no sign of it. There were feet on the stairs and then there was the sound of heavy bootheels on the flagstones and the gravel again. The gate squeaked once more.

'They must be close by; they can't be far.'

It was Robert's voice.

'They can't just have disappeared,' he added.

'They could have had another place to go to. Guest house. B & B.'

'You're the damn policeman. What do you suggest then?'

Lewis was terrified that they would start to search for them, but then Bill said, 'Best to leave it until the morning now, Bob. We have the train and the bus times. We'll find her, don't you worry. They'll be trying to get out of Fowey. Not much chance of doing that this evening, I'd have said. In the morning we'll get to Par station first thing. If they're leaving by train they'll have to go there.'

'But they could leave by bus, on foot, on a bloody donkey and cart for all we know.'

Now it was Bill's turn to get angry.

'I don't know why you didn't wait at the bloody house when you had them. I go to all this trouble to track them down —'

He left the sentence unfinished.

'Alright,' said Robert. 'We'll wait until the morning.'

There was the sound of the car doors being opened and

slammed shut again. Then the engine started. The lights turned on and the car reversed down the hill as before and soon the sound of it had died away.

39

*L*ewis clambered out over the wall and then helped Helen out.

'Alright?' he asked.

'Yes.'

'I was sure he was going to see us that time.'

'Well, he didn't,' said Helen. 'Oh Lewis, I'm sorry I got you involved in all of this. Do you want to just pack it in now? We'll go back in the cottage and take our chances tomorrow. Or maybe better still, you should go back to Mrs Middleton and I'll just stay here and catch the train tomorrow. Who knows? The cottage might be our safest option now. They're unlikely to come back here again, are they?'

'Who knows?' said Lewis. 'I just think that as long as he knows where you are you won't be safe. And I'm not leaving you. You know I'm not going to do that. Let's go down to the beach.'

They began the descent to Readymoney. It was about a quarter of a mile. Over on their left the moon had begun to rise and was just clear of the Polruan side of the estuary.

'Anyway,' said Lewis, 'since I met you, I've been chased by irate husbands, I'm about to steal a boat, I don't know where I'll be sleeping tonight. I feel like I'm living the adventures of Mister Toad.'

She laughed. It was the first time she had done so since all this had started.

'I'm sure it's all good training for when I go into action.'

'Let's hope there are boats down there now,' she said.

'There are always boats there.'

Over on their right, over the underbrush and through the

trees, they could see the sea. The moon had just begun to shine on it, creating a shining pathway across the water. The laneway they were on curved to the left and as they came round it, Lewis thought he saw something that seemed out of place. It looked like a small, regularly-shaped splash of moonlight down at the bottom where the laneway joined the main road from Fowey.

Lewis, who was on Helen's right, was just about to say something to her when the world lit up. An engine roared into life and two large discs of light began to gather speed as they moved towards them. Lewis felt his heart jolt and he thought he heard Helen scream his name. It was hard to tell how far away the car was. Lewis thought it might be a couple of hundred yards. A quick glance to left and right confirmed that there were no places for them to hide.

'Go towards the car,' shouted Lewis above the roar of the engine.

'Towards the car? Are you mad?' she screamed back.

'No,' he said. 'Come on – and when I tell you to run to the beach, do exactly that. Alright?'

If she answered he didn't hear it. He dropped the bags and took her hand. Feeling her resist, he yanked it. This time she complied. It occurred to Lewis that seeing them hand in hand must be confirming everything that Robert had said – and must also be making him even more angry. Swiftly they walked towards the approaching headlights, blinded by the light.

The car, which had been gaining speed, slowed at first and then stopped altogether, the engine still running. Lewis heard the handbrake being applied. He moved to the left to try to get out of the glare of the twin beams. He was just in time to see the door being opened.

'Now,' he said to Helen. 'Quickly, run. I'll see you there.'

Helen ran past the driver's side of the car. As she did, the door had opened some more and Robert's head began to emerge.

In his peripheral vision Lewis saw the passenger door opening. Robert's ear was just level with the edge of the roof when Lewis lashed out with his right foot. His boot connected with the door and it recoiled straight away slamming back against Robert. The impact banged his head against the metal of the roof. Robert screamed but tried again to get out of the car. By now Lewis was abreast of the door. He shoved it as hard as he could with his shoulder and for a second time Robert's head cracked against the steel. This time he went down.

Bill had come round the back of the car and had his arms out to tackle Lewis. His burly figure seemed huge in the darkness. Lewis knew he wouldn't be able to avoid the tackle and once he was caught, he wouldn't be able to break free. But just then the driver's door swung open again and Robert collapsed onto the ground groaning. In the gloom, Lewis saw Bill hesitate for an instant, unsure of whether to catch Lewis or go to Robert's assistance.

'Help your brother,' said Lewis.

Bill hesitated further. It was only for a fraction of a second but it was enough time for Lewis to sidestep him.

'Fucking bastard,' he heard Bill say.

Then Lewis was past him and running as though his life depended on it. He was terrified that Bill would follow him but as Lewis lengthened his stride, he realised there were no footsteps pursuing him. He dared not look back for fear of losing speed, so he just kept on going.

There was no sign of Helen in the laneway. Lewis reached the bottom and turned right. Now he was running along the road that led from Fowey to Readymoney. The beach and the sea were over on his left and he saw that there were three boats drawn up on the beach. Amongst them he saw Helen.

40

*I*t really was like a *Boy's Own* adventure after that. They pushed a boat from the beach out into the water and jumped aboard. Taking an oar each they began to pull the boat away from the shore. Lewis remembered once on holidays having tried to row and not being able to master the coordination involved. This time, he had no problem. The blades of the oars bit into the water at just the right angle. They pulled back strongly and together and soon there was clear water between them and the beach. Away from the land there was a small breeze and it was enough for them to raise the sail.

Suddenly the boat began to rock. Lewis wondered what it was – it couldn't be a wave. The wind was only a light breeze and the sea had only the tiniest swell.

'Lewis?'

Helen was calling him.

'Lewis, are you awake?'

He opened his eyes.

Helen was sitting on the edge of his bed in the cottage. The room was in darkness but he could see her silhouette. He frowned in confusion.

'Lewis?' she said again.

'I was dreaming,' he said at length.

'I dreamt that your husband … that we had to escape. It was like *Treasure Island* – the pirates at the "Admiral Benbow".'

Lewis was still befuddled by sleep.

'Is he here? Downstairs?'

'No, don't be silly. Of course he's not here. He's staying in

Fowey tonight and then his leave is over. He's going back to France tomorrow.'

Lewis sat up and rubbed sleep from his eyes. He rested his back against the headboard. He was awake now.

'So what happened?' he asked.

'We never got to dinner. As soon as we left here, he asked me to come back. Now. Tonight. It was very upsetting.'

'And what did you say?'

'I said I couldn't. That I hoped we could always be friends.'

It wasn't what Lewis wanted to hear. He wanted the man gone from their lives.

'Did you tell him you wanted to divorce him?'

He saw her eyes look away.

'He asked me to leave it until the War is over. He said that if something happened to him that there would be no need for it then. Save a lot of expenses, he said. It made sense.'

'But you said he had a staff job. It's unlikely that anything would happen to him.'

'I'm going to leave it until after the War,' she said with finality. 'Please don't ask me about it again.'

Her hands were in her lap. Lewis reached out in the darkness and found them. She let him take one and hold it. They were both silent for a long time. Lewis was unsure what to say. Then Helen spoke.

'He said that he loved me still. That he would always love me. I told him he'd find somebody else, that there were plenty more fish in the sea.'

'And what did he say to that?'

'That he could never imagine himself loving anybody else. That he wouldn't want to. He was near to tears a lot of the time – and actually started crying once. He asked me if I knew that it's possible for a heart to be broken. I said I did and he said that his was. It was very difficult.'

'And what were you saying to him?'

'Not a lot really. I was mainly listening. There were several times when I nearly crumbled. It would have been so easy. I felt so sorry for him. He may be a soldier but he's not a strong man. I hope he'll be alright.'

'You couldn't go back to him just because you were sorry for him. That wouldn't be love.'

'I know that.'

'And it's not your job to make him happy.'

He saw her nodding in the darkness.

'I know that too. It's just that – well, I used to love him one time. You remember how it was, how you felt. The feeling that life was just glorious, that everything was perfect, that nothing bad could happen. How I used to long for the next time that we would meet. He would write me letters – passionate letters.'

Lewis found it hard to imagine the hooded crow being passionate.

'How did you get back?'

'He has a car. He had left it in Fowey. He drove me.'

'What time is it anyway?' asked Lewis, looking at his watch.

'After one.'

'Did you only just get back?'

'No, I've been back since about eleven. We got to the point where there wasn't anything more to say. I was downstairs. Outside.'

'Doing what?'

'Looking at the stars? Listening to the sea.'

'You should have called me. I'm sorry I fell asleep.'

'It was better that I was by myself. I needed time to think. To get it all out of my system. To make sure that I was making the right decision.'

'And are you?' said Lewis anxiously.

She paused and it was a while before she answered.

'I think so. Who knows about these things? Yes. I think I am. I hope I am.'

'I'm sure you are,' said Lewis. As he said it, he thought the sentiment sounded weak. Unhelpful. Pointless. He wished he could have thought of something wise or profound to say.

At length Helen said, 'Well, I suppose I'd better get to bed and let you go back to sleep.'

He didn't want her to go. He wanted to keep her here. To talk with her all night. To ask her into his bed. To spend the night in bed with her. After she had spoken she didn't move. It was like she was waiting for something. Or maybe thinking about something.

'Alright, well, good night then, Lewis.'

She leaned forward to kiss him.

Her lips met his but instead of the brief kiss he had been used to, he thought she pressed them against his. He responded instantly and they pushed their lips against each other till it actually hurt. He felt her tongue and as he opened his mouth, she slipped it in. Again he responded, mimicking what she had done. She moved closer to him and her arms embraced him, low around his back. He held her and stroked her hair.

Eventually they pulled apart. He looked into her eyes but in the darkness it was hard to tell what he saw there. Fear? Love? Desire? They kissed again. When they separated the second time, Lewis said, 'Would you like to stay with me tonight?'

'Here – in my bed,' he added.

She didn't say anything.

Instead, she slowly took off the cardigan she had been wearing. Then she sat up straight and her breasts pushed up and forward. To Lewis it was as though she was offering them to him. She looked into his eyes while, with shaking hands, he unbuttoned her blouse. She wore a white brassiere underneath and he could see her breasts heavy against its fabric. She stood up and undid the skirt at one side. She wiggled her hips as she pushed it down. Then it fell and she stepped out of it before kicking it backwards with her foot. She wore stockings beneath her knickers and placing first one foot and then the other on the bed she unclasped them, rolled them down and removed them. Lewis stared in wonderment. He couldn't believe that this was happening to him.

She lifted the bedclothes and slipped in beside him. The last time he had been in a bed with someone else it had been his mother. Helen's long legs stretched down the bed and lay against his. The night air had made her body cool.

'You're cold,' he said.

'You're not,' she said, cuddling up to him and wrapping herself around him.

Her breath smelt of toothpaste. He could smell her hair and the faint smell of the perfume she had put on earlier. *Shem-el-Nessim*. The Scent of Araby. He stroked her arms and, putting an arm around her, caressed her back. He touched her face, outlining her eyebrows, the bones underneath her eyes, her nose, her lips. He kissed her eyes.

'I can't believe how beautiful you are,' he said.

'Take this off,' she said, pushing her breasts forward to indicate the brassiere.

He reached behind her, found the clasp and undid it in one movement with one hand.

'That was very expertly done,' she said with laughter in her voice. 'Are you sure you haven't done this before?'

'With you? While you were asleep?' he joked.

'No, not with me, you fool. With somebody else? Some other lucky lady.'

He was suddenly serious.

'No, you know this is my first time, don't you?'

'Yes, of course I know,' she said. 'I was only joking.'

'Beginner's luck,' he said, and she laughed.

He lifted the brassiere away from her breasts. It caught for a moment and then the breasts slipped out.

'Here you are,' she said. 'These are for you.'

He took one in each hand as though weighing them and then kissed the nipples tenderly.

'They're beautiful,' he said.

'They're yours,' she whispered.

He stroked first one cheek and then the other against the nipples. He felt them become erect and go hard.

She reached down and touched his erection which was like a steel bar in his underpants. She stroked her hand gently up and down it, rubbing the fabric against it. Spasms of pleasure like little electrical charges darted through his body. Then she hooked a hand into the waistband of his underpants and said, 'Take these off'. It was an order, or at least she made it sound like that, and he obeyed.

He lifted his bottom, pushed them down and got one foot out. Then he used that foot to remove them completely and push them away. They disappeared somewhere in the bedclothes. She took hold of his penis and pushed down the foreskin. It was a tiny dart of pain and a huge surge of pleasure. He thought he would die it was so nice. He thought he was going to climax and was afraid that it would go all over her hand, but just then she stopped.

Lifting her bottom he felt her take off her own knickers. She was naked now beneath the bedclothes. They both were. She lay on her back.

'Give me your hand,' she whispered.

She spread out the fingers of his hand and placed it palm down on the curve of her belly, beneath her navel. Then she slowly guided it down until he felt the silky hair.

'This is the naming of the parts,' she said softly.

He felt her spread her legs. Then she took his middle finger and slid it into her. She was warm and wet.

'Push it in as far as it will go,' she said.

He did as he was told.

'What can you feel?'

'You. Your insides. It's all beautiful and wet.'

'Now bring your finger out gently and slide it up towards the front. Do you feel a sort of an upside down 'V' there?'

'Yes.'

The word came out sounding more like a breath rather than an actual word.

'That's my clitoris. It's like a foreskin. Touch it and I'll explode.'

He stroked it gently with a series of slow up-strokes. She closed her eyes and sighed each time he touched it.

'I want to see it,' he said.

'Do you want me to light the lamp?'

'No, just the candle.'

She reached back and found the box of matches. It rattled as she took one out and lit the candle that stood in its little metal holder on the bedside table. She lifted back a large triangle of bedclothes and he slid down the bed. His legs went out the end as he gazed on her open thighs. He kissed each thigh in turn and then the tuft of hair at the top. Then he kissed down the line of her vulva. He smelt its fragrance – her real perfume. The Scent of Helen, he thought to himself with a smile. He took the lips gently with each of his thumbs, parted them and began to lap at her clitoris with his tongue.

'Oh, Lewis,' she groaned.

'My goddess,' he whispered. 'I adore you.'

Her breathing became heavier, and she uttered little whimpers form time to time.

'Please – don't stop,' she said.

He didn't but continued to lick upwards with his tongue. The strokes were slow and deliberate. Her clitoris seemed to move with every stroke and it became like a game trying to centre his tongue on the 'V'.

She was groaning louder now and breathing hard. She was saying things but they were not really words – just little sounds. Then she began to buck and he licked faster, but then slowed down again suddenly. It was too much and she started shaking, vibrating, moaning loudly. Her thighs quivered like bowstrings. He licked her slowly, ever so slowly. He had no idea how long this went on but finally she clamped her thighs together. He tried to push them apart again with his hands but it was as though they had been glued together.

'Come on,' he said. 'More.'

'No,' she said. 'No more.'

'Yes more.'

'No. No more. Are you trying to kill me?'

He slid back up beside her, her taste and fragrance still on his lips and in his nose. He held her and she began to laugh softly. Her hair was damp and splashed across her face. She pushed it back with her hand.

'Dear sweet Jesus,' she said. 'Where did you learn to do that?'

'I didn't learn,' he said in all seriousness. 'I'd never done anything like that before. You know this.'

She opened her eyes.

'Don't tell me,' she said. 'Beginner's luck?'

He laughed.

'Maybe.'

She shook her head, her hair tangled across her face, laughing all the while.

Lewis rolled onto his back. The candle flickered. He pulled the bedclothes up around them to keep out the night chill.

'That was wonderful,' she said at length. 'But now, what are we going to do about this?'

She reached down and found his erection again.

'Come on, my love,' she said. 'It's your turn now.'

Later he entered her as she lay on her back with her legs apart and her knees up. He was wild with desire for her. Her skin, her hair, her smell, the feeling of being inside her. His penis rubbed against her lips as it pumped in and out, sending shattering tremors of pleasure through his body. He had never known anything like it. Finally he climaxed and collapsed onto her. She held him and he realised he was crying. She rocked him gently as she embraced him with her arms and her legs, uttering soft, soothing noises as one would to a baby.

'I love you, Helen,' he whispered.

41

*L*ewis fell into a deep sleep and it was late when he awoke the next day. As he opened his eyes he was glad to see that she was still there beside him, lying on her side and looking at him.

'Hello,' he said sleepily.

'Hello yourself,' she said. 'You slept well.'

'I did. It must have been the sleeping draught you gave me.'

'It was nothing like the one you gave me.'

She paused.

'You know I've only slept with one other man,' she said. 'But I've never known anything like that. Are you sure you haven't had a string of lovers?'

She looked deadly serious.

'No, honest, I haven't. I just … well, I did what I wanted to do – what I've wanted to do ever since I met you. You don't know how many times I've dreamed of doing that – of being down there. It's like it's the essence of you – of all women, I suppose. I just hoped it would be nice.'

Her face was laughing.

'Nice would be one word you could use,' she said. 'You're a very dirty boy, do you know that? And I mean *very* dirty.'

'My father was at sea,' he said, as though that explained everything.

A grey light filled the room and there was rain on the window.

'A day for staying in bed,' she said.

'Are you serious?' he asked.

'Of course I'm serious. Do you have a better idea?'

He shook his head.

He lifted the bedclothes and looked at her. The heavy breasts, the curve of her flank, her triangle of hair, her long legs.

'Reclining nude,' he said.

He was hard again.

'Greek god,' she retorted.

He slid across the bed and kissed her. He realised that he would never be able get enough of her body. He wanted to kiss every inch of it; to stroke it, to touch it, to explore the hidden parts of it.

'I love you, Helen. Will you marry me?'

'Whoa, just a minute there, young lad. In case you hadn't noticed, I'm already married.'

'But you're going to divorce him, aren't you?'

'Yes,' she said, 'I'm going to divorce him,' she said mechanically.

'So?' Lewis asked.

'So why don't we just enjoy today and tomorrow and the time we have.'

He fell back on the pillow.

'It's not fair,' he said. 'You see so many people who have all the time they want together, but they're not happy. They really don't want to be together. And here's us, we don't want to be apart. At least I don't want to be apart from you.'

She said nothing and they went silent. He moved closer to her so that his thigh lay against hers.

'I can't believe this is happening,' he said. 'I keep thinking I'll wake up from a dream.'

He turned to look at her. She was gazing up at the ceiling.

'I've been thinking,' she said. 'It was while you were asleep and I was lying there watching you. I'm going to become a nurse – you know, a V.A.D.'

She turned to look at him.

'Just until the War is over. This is what I thought: You're going off to the War and I'm fearful that something will happen to you. I thought that if I became a nurse it might act as a good luck charm. You would be there fighting and I would be helping to save some lives or at least make them a bit more bearable. Who knows – if you got wounded – I might end up nursing you. Only a little wound, mind you. Nothing too serious.'

'It's a wonderful idea,' he said. 'I would feel safe. I would feel like nothing bad could happen to me. You can get your divorce and then when the War is over, we'll be together. Won't we?' he said, turning to look at her.

'Lewis, I'm old enough to be your mother. What would people think?'

'What do you care what people think?'

'I don't but you might. Or you just might meet somebody else, somebody your own age. Or somebody more attractive. Somebody beautiful. A French woman while you've over in France. French women are all beautiful.'

'You're beautiful. You're the most beautiful thing I've ever seen.'

'But I'm the only woman you've ever seen – like this. And what about the difference in our ages? When I'm an old woman you'll be a young man. You'll get tired of me and start going out with young gals and having affairs and all that kind of thing.'

'Why are you saying all this?' he asked. 'Don't you feel the same way I feel?'

It was a long time before she answered.

'I felt – about Robert – I felt the way you feel now. I felt exactly that way. But something changed. I don't know whether it changed when we got married or when, but it changed. And it's gone. What we had is gone. And it won't come back.

For us – you and me – last night - I never thought that would happen for me again in my life. It's a pity that there are all these practical difficulties – our age difference —'

'That's not a difficulty —'

'Just let me finish,' she said softly. 'The fact that I'm married. The War, for God's sake, in case we'd forgotten about it. The bloody War. So here's what I'd say. We've got our plans. You have to join the Army, I'm going to become a nurse. We can't be together but we shall take care of each other while the War lasts. When I am tending other soldiers, it will be like I am tending you.'

'And how will I take care of you?'

'Won't you be fighting for me? Could any man do more? Not like Robert with his staff job. So we'll take care of each other. We'll get through it. And then, when it's all over – we can see. We may be two different people then. I don't think I shall be because I'm a long way down the path I've chosen, but you're only starting out. You're young. The War could change you in all sorts of ways. And young people change so quickly anyway.

Let's enjoy the time we have, Lewis. And the end of the War seems so far away. Let's not worry about any of that now. We have a rainy day in Cornwall, food downstairs, a warm bed and two beautiful bodies. Could anybody ask for more?'

42

$\mathcal{L}$ewis and Helen bought two one-way tickets, Truro to London Paddington, for Wednesday the eighth of November. He would be eighteen on Friday the tenth. Dad had wanted him to come earlier and have a week or so to get organised but Lewis had cut it as fine as he could. He had suggested that she come and meet Dad but Helen thought it was a terrible idea. He didn't push it. Instead he would go home and she would go to a hotel while she sought enlistment in a Voluntary Aid Detachment. She had seen a poster in a shop window in Fowey showing three women in the white V.A.D. uniforms with their blue sleeves. The poster said that V.A.D's were urgently needed – she assumed it had to do with the huge casualty lists from the Somme. Helen had telephoned and had an appointment for an interview on Friday the tenth. She hoped she would be successful and that she wouldn't have to spend too long in the hotel.

Their last week in Fowey, the weather was wintry with high winds and rain that lashed the cottage and the smell of the sea, strong in the air. Mostly they stayed in, only going out to bring in wood for the fire and one expedition into Fowey for food. While the rain rattled on the window panes, they listened to music and talked and cooked and ate and made love.

Helen had wanted to take him into Plymouth to buy things for the Front. Apparently it was possible to go into some of the bigger department stores and be kitted out with all 'trench necessities'. But Lewis didn't want to waste any of their precious time together doing that. As the Wednesday approached their mood became more and more gloomy. Their train ride, when it came, was made in almost complete silence. They finally parted at Paddington. While Lewis was walking home, the tears came. Luckily, Dad was still at work and calling a quick hello to Margaret, who was in the kitchen, Lewis went up to his room. He lay on the bed and cried until he fell asleep.

When he woke he felt like his heart had been torn out, bloody with bits of veins and arteries hanging off it. He remembered what Helen's husband had said about it being possible for a heart to be broken. Lewis too now knew that it was. It seemed hearts could do all sorts of things. They could be heavy; they could be light and – yes, they could be broken.

A few days later he had a letter from her. In it she told him that she had nominated him as her next of kin. She hoped he didn't mind, the letter said. Lewis was overjoyed at the implication of what she was asking. Essentially she was saying that there was no one else in the world to whom she was closer.

After that it would be almost exactly a year – November 1917 – before he would see her again.

He got a week and they spent it in a hotel in Brighton. He didn't tell Dad he was coming home for which he felt terribly guilty but there was so little time. The week was so like the final week they had spent in Fowey – the rapture of seeing each other after so long eventually becoming the long, painful Calvary of getting ready to return. They reassured each other that the spell was working – that because of the men she tended and the suffering that she eased, that he would survive. By then she was working at the one of the sixteen hospitals in Etaples, the huge British base camp on the coast of France.

They returned to France – on separate ships, the Army seeming to have a knack of arranging things that way.

43

'*Hande hoch*,' Lewis screams, indicating skywards with his free hand.

He knows the man won't obey. Why would he? He is stronger than Lewis. He holds a rifle with a bayonet attached. The German knows the British are looking for prisoners and so that Lewis won't shoot. All of this passes through Lewis' mind in an instant.

Time seems to slow down so that Lewis can see everything in startling detail. The German lunges with the bayonet. It is a training ground perfect thrust, launched off the rear leg. He also screams exactly as Lewis had been taught to do. Lewis tries to step to one side but the man seems to have anticipated this.

In a panic Lewis pulls his stomach back with an almost backbone-tearing jerk. *As though that would help.* Simultaneously he strikes in panic at the bayonet with his pistol hand. He feels the blade slice across the backs of his fingers and warm blood splashing out. His blow is pathetically weak in comparison to the power of the bayonet thrust but it appears to have been enough to deflect it. It drives into his Bomber's Shield just below his ribs. Lewis winces in anticipation of the blade entering his flesh, but the thrust seems to have run out of steam and gotten stuck in the layers of the Bomber's Shield. It has saved his life. The stupid thing has saved his life.

'Bastard!' Lewis screams. He steps back, extricating himself from the bayonet and then charges at the German. The duck-boards are slick and Lewis' feet slide on them for an instant. Then he is wrestling with the German. The rifle thuds to the ground, but Lewis knows that this is not good. The German is going to use his hands. For a moment they grapple together. Lewis tries desperately to maintain his balance and to push the German over. But the German is too powerful with the result that Lewis crashes down with the German on top of him. *This is not going at all the way it was meant to.* Lewis wonders where the others are.

Lewis tries to bring his pistol back around to point at the German but the man grabs Lewis' wrist and pinions his right arm through a layer of mud to the duckboards. He is dimly aware that his back and his legs have become soaked with icy mud or water. The German is unbelievably strong and heavy. He now puts his other hand on Lewis' throat and starts to squeeze. *Where the fuck are the others?*

The German's breath is foul and Lewis is suddenly filled with a deep, all-consuming hatred for this man. *Wife beater. Baby killer.* This bastard is not going to be the cause of Lewis' death. He screams, 'Get off me, you fucker!'

With a huge effort he lifts his pistol hand off the duckboards. He is hardly aware of the pain from the bayonet cut. His hand hovers a foot or so off the ground, the German trying to push it back down, Lewis trying to raise and aim it. Lewis hates this man, hates his ignorant looking face, hates his strength. But he is stronger than Lewis. He looks stupid but he is going to be the cause of Lewis' death. Lewis' pistol arms splashes back down again into the mud and now the man's hand tightens on Lewis' throat.

'Oh Christ. Oh Christ.'

Lewis hears the words gurgling out of him. He feels like his eyes are going to pop. He tries to move again but the German now has him clamped to the duckboards. The German adjusts his position slightly to get more leverage and power. Lewis' vision is starting to go red.

But then he hears a sound like something hitting on bone. The German roars more in anger than in pain and his grip eases somewhat. There is another dull sound. It is a kick, Lewis realises. The German roars again and dimly Lewis sees a boot crashing into the side of the German's head. There is another kick – this time more vicious and in the face. The German makes a stunned noise. All the strength and weight seems to go out of him. He relaxes his grip. Lewis gasps for breath and half rolls out from beneath him. In the gloom Lewis sees that it is Fraser, one of his men, who is doing the kicking. Fraser is tall and powerfully built. Lewis would have thought a kick from him would down a horse. Fraser drags the moaning German to his feet and passes him back to one of the other men. Then he leans down to Lewis and gives him a hand up.

'Alright, sir? Sorry about the delay, sir. Bloke popped up out of nowhere. Nearly done for me. Had to kill him.'

They have to shout to be heard above the noise of the continuing British artillery barrage. Lewis is gulping in lungfuls of cold, foetid trench air. It tastes like nectar. It is a few moments before he can speak. His throat throbs where the German squeezed it.

'Thanks, Fraser.'

Fraser grins.

'All in a night's work, sir.'

'No, really – thank you,' says Lewis. 'He had me there.'

'Somebody has to look out for you, sir. You're bleeding, sir.'

Lewis had forgotten about his hand, but he is suddenly aware of great pain where the bayonet sliced his fingers. His hand which is still wrapped around the pistol is sticky with blood and soaked in mud from when the German held it down. Lewis flexes his fingers and feels sharp stabs of pain. The fingers move, though. They can still hold the gun. It occurs to Lewis that the pistol may not actually be serviceable any longer after the soaking that it got in the mud. *Unarmed and running round an enemy trench. Jesus Christ!*

'Alright,' Lewis says to Fraser. 'Let's get out of here.'

A figure looms up out of the darkness. Lewis is so jumpy

at this stage that he is lucky not to shoot what turns out to be a British soldier.

'Blocking Party?' shouts Lewis, above the noise of the artillery.

'Yessir.'

'Whitby.'

It is the code word to withdraw. Lewis checks his watch. One forty one. They are way behind schedule.

'Whitby,' shouts the man to unseen people beyond him.

Lewis and Fraser turn round and hurry back to the entry point. Here they find their three men waiting. Up on the parapet there are several members of the Covering Party, kneeling down or crouching. The prisoners have already been sent out of the trench and back towards the British lines. Lewis is about to set off to find the rest of his party when the welcome figure of Sergeant Robinson appears out of the darkness. Robinson is carrying a satchel.

'Got some papers, sir. That should keep 'em happy.'

'Nice work, Sergeant. Everyone with you?'

'Yessir, all present and accounted for.'

'Alright, send somebody to tell the Blocking Party and let's get out of here.'

Robinson details a man called Wilson to do it. Lewis starts counting his men up the ladder and out of the trench. They are all out, with Private Jackson bringing up the rear, when Wilson returns.

'Sir, they've got a wounded man.'

Another bloody hold up.

Lewis hears the wounded man before he sees him. Three men materialise out of the night. Two soldiers half-drag, half-carry the casualty between them, his arms around their shoulders. The front of his chest is a mass of dark blood. His head lolls and he groans continuously, the groan becoming a scream when the two men jar him too much.

'Covering Party,' Lewis shouts up, 'we've got a wounded man here. We're going to need a stretcher.'

'Righto,' a voice calls back.

'Sergeant,' says Lewis, 'you and Wilson – up onto the parapet and get this man out.'

Robinson races up the ladder and Wilson follows him. As they do, Lewis sees one of the three ladders that the British lowered into the trench, being pulled back out. The Covering Party will lay blankets on it to use as a stretcher. The wounded man is brought over to the wall of the trench and placed with his back against a ladder. The two men who carried him lift him under his thighs and simultaneously, Robinson and Wilson lean over and haul him up by the arms. The man's screaming becomes ear-splitting above the continuing artillery bombardment and the racketing of the machine guns.

Come on. Come on. Lewis looks at his watch. One forty four.

Finally, the wounded man is up, out of the trench and onto the improvised stretcher. *Nearly there. Nearly there.* Now it's just a question of getting back.

Lewis hurries up the ladder where Sergeant Robinson waits for him.

'The men are all on their way back, sir.'

'Well done, Sergeant.'

Lewis' party has sustained no casualties. Three prisoners and documents. They are almost home. Almost home. Almost home. They find the tape and begin following it to the wire, crouching and running as fast as they can. Behind them they can hear the men of the two Blocking Parties. The Covering Party, on the German parapet, will be the last to withdraw.

But then, suddenly, everything goes quiet. The ear splitting noise of the bombardment ceases and Lewis is conscious of a ringing in his ears. It is what he has been dreading. The extra time that they spent trying to find a gap in the wire meant that they were behind schedule going into the German trench. Now, the artillery – believing the raid to be on schedule and thus, over – stops firing. The British machine gun fire continues but the artillery is stopped. Lewis and Robinson, along with most of the raiding party, are still on German side of the wire.

The momentary silence is deafening. A voice from somewhere behind Lewis says, 'oh, Christ.' Then the Germans open up with rifle and machine gun fire. Everyone dives to the ground. There is a crackle of small arms fire as the Covering Party, still between Lewis and the German front line, fire back. The stinging sound of bullets seems unbelievably close.

Lewis is panting and his heart is beating in his chest as though it would burst. He is coated in icy sweat. The German fire, which initially sounded reasonably light, is now starting to intensify as more Germans realise what has happened. It's only a matter of time before they call up artillery fire. When that happens the British in no-man's-land will be blown to spots.

'Come on,' says Lewis. 'We can't stay here.'

Lewis counts to himself – three, two, one. He stands up. Sergeant Robinson is up now too. The sound of bullets is all around them. Lewis hunches his shoulders in anticipation of one in the back. *Let it be clean. Don't let me be paralysed.*

They begin running towards the gap in the wire, hunched down and conscious that behind them all the other men are doing the same. There is the sound of bullets stinging by. Lewis doesn't understand why the Germans haven't called up artillery. But then, as if reading his thoughts, Robinson says, panting, 'I found some wires, sir. Phone wires by the look of them. Cut 'em all, sir.'

Lewis grins at Robinson. He could kiss him. They are pounding through the gap in the wire. Lewis hooks his boot on some barbed wire, trips and falls. He puts his hands out to brace himself, forgetting about the wound to his fingers. The pain is excruciating as his hands and knees land on the barbs, and are then shredded as he gets up again and disentangles himself.

Just as he stands back up, a shower of green flares suddenly goes up from the German lines. This is the signal for their artillery. Now it all depends on where the first salvo will land. If it lands on the British side of no-man's-land they are done for. He hears the distant crack of an artillery piece followed by several more. No-man's-land is full of running men.

The first shells come whistling in. They explode in yellow flame and black smoke and showers of dirt and stones on the German side of the wire. Lewis reaches the sandbag wall at the British trench. As he does so, he realises that the British artillery barrage has started up again. Somebody has been clever enough to grasp the situation and telephone the artillery to resume. Lewis blesses him whoever he was. That should give the rest of the men a chance to get in.

Lewis throws himself onto the sandbag wall and, on all fours, tumbles over it and down into the trench. He lands on the fire step where strong arms suddenly catch him. A voice that sounds gentle, even though it is shouting above the noise of the artillery, says, 'We've got you, sir.'

44

*I*t was nearly five by the time Lewis had calmed down enough to sleep. By then, the wounded man that had been carried back, had died. Two other men, caught out in the open by the German barrage, were also killed and three more seriously wounded. All of Lewis' men got back safely. Lewis had his hand dressed but was told it would be impossible to stitch and that it should just heal by itself and come back to normal. The raid was judged to be a success by whoever decided these things.

Lewis fell into a deep sleep and it was just after eight when he emerged from the dugout. Later that day he received a letter from Helen. It was like so many others that she had sent. She talked about her work at the hospital, dwelling on the lighter moments, obviously hiding the darker ones. She did the same things Lewis did when he said things to her like 'We have a little job to do tonight, but don't worry, it is nothing serious.' He loved her for that. Some day, he was sure, when they were together again, they would talk about what the War had really been like for both of them. But this had been a way to get through it, to lighten the load, to keep the dark forces at bay.

She said she was longing to see him and hoped that the War might soon be over. It was closed with 'Much love'. 'All my love' was the other phrase she used. She had never said, 'I love you', as he did. She had sent so many letters to him, writing every couple of days, that he had a huge collection. Most of them he had sent back to her in batches for safe keeping; but he always kept the most recent ones in a waterproof bag in his pack. He added this one to it after writing a reply.

The rest of the day was quiet. During the afternoon Lewis remembered Byrne and the quote from *The Wind In The Willows* about 'matchless valour, consummate strategy and a proper handling of sticks.' Lewis found himself smiling – he should tell Byrne when he saw him next.

But it was a different runner, a man Lewis didn't know, who brought a message that evening. Lewis asked the man if he was likely to see Byrne later. The man hesitated and then replied, 'Sorry, sir, Byrne was killed this morning. Shrapnel, sir.'

Aimlessly, Lewis returned to the dugout. He wished he had some whiskey; he felt like getting well and truly drunk. To take his mind off Byrne, he took out the photograph of Helen. 'Thank you, for keeping me safe, my darling,' he said. 'I love you.' He wrote and asked her what she had done for her birthday.

But it was a question that would never be answered.

Lewis wrote several more letters in the days that followed but none of them received a reply. Finally, towards the end of October, he received them all back, held together with a rubber band. On each of them somebody had written, in blue indelible pencil, 'Not known at this address'.

His first reaction was the she had been killed or died. It couldn't have been shelling – Etaples was far, far away from the front line, but had it been bombed? Or had she had an accident or caught something – hospitals weren't exactly the healthiest places in the world. He was her next of kin, so there followed more agonising days that killed whatever joy or relief he might have felt at the Armistice while he waited to receive a War Office telegram. But none came.

She was alive. But where was she? And why had she stopped answering his letters? Was there something he had said or done? He tried to remember his last letter to her. Had there been anything untoward in that? But no, it had just been the usual love letter that he had been writing to her since November 1916.

The following year, in June 1919, Lewis was offered demobilisation from the Army. Since he could think of nothing better to do, he signed on for another two years. He was given a month's leave and arrived back in England on the twenty ninth of June. He spent a day with Dad in London on the thirtieth – Lewis hadn't seen his father since just before he had been posted to France in Easter 1917. Dad looked older, greyer, a bit more well-fed. He would be retiring from the Navy and, a bit like Lewis, was unsure what he would do. They had lunch and both seemed to be of the opinion that 'taking some time off', 'a bit of a rest' was the best thing for both of them now. Lewis was able to put Helen out of his mind for a few hours but by the time he went to bed, he could think of nothing else.

The next morning, as he had planned, he went to Paddington.

Part 2

45

*T*he omens were good. It was exactly the same date as the day he had begun his journey three years ago. The weather was remarkably similar as well, promising a day of blue sky and heat and no clouds. He had dressed in civilian clothes and taken the Tube to Paddington. He felt he had already picked up her trail.

The station looked different, of course. Three years ago, with the Somme offensive only a few hours away, and the action off Jutland less than a month old, the predominant colours in the station concourse had been khaki and navy blue and white. Today, even though it was a Monday, the place had a holiday feel about it as families caught trains to places on the coast – all the Mouths, Sidmouth, Bournemouth, Teignmouth, – and places further west. The women wore brightly coloured pastels, the men grey, black and white. It was as though one of those new coloured films had somehow become spliced in a strange way with an ordinary black and white one.

And the papers had been different too. Then there had been so much about the War. Today, if there was any recognition of it being the anniversary of the opening of the Somme battle, he hadn't seen it. The big story was the airship R.34 flying to America and back. How things had changed.

He remembered the women with the white feathers. 'Can I suggest, my dear ladies, that you take your feathers, shove them up your pretty little bottoms and fly away home?'

Lewis bought a single to Truro and carried his pack to the platform. It was the pack he had carried with him all through the War. In it, shaving tackle, a couple of changes of clothes, and his

1919 diary. Porters and passengers hurried by, the tea and coffee shops and food stands were busy, the noise of it all echoing off the great glass ceiling of the station. There was the odd sailor or soldier but nothing like there had been during the War years. It was as though somehow, the War had never happened. Could it really only be eight months since it had finished?

The train was already at the platform. He boarded and found an empty compartment. He put his luggage on the rack and sat by the window. The compartment filled up. A young father, an incredibly thin and childlike mother and two children under ten, a chubby boy and a tall, pretty girl; an older couple. The children chattered excitedly. The parents apologised for their high spirits – they were going on holidays. The older couple smiled indulgently. Lewis said something about us all having been children once. The mood in the carriage was light and festive. Lewis' heart was broken.

People used the expression glibly but now Lewis realised what it meant. Strangely enough, it had been Helen's husband who had first said it in a way that he understood. It was something that Helen said he had said the night they went into Fowey to talk. 'It is possible for a heart to be broken.' Lewis knew this now. It *was* possible for a heart to be broken. He knew all about it. He could describe – in minute detail – the symptoms.

It began when you were separated from the person whom you had loved. There was the ache of not having them around, of not being able to do and say all of the things that had been possible before. Then, added to that, hope was taken away – the hope that you might ever see the person again.

But some things were also given to you. Gifts. Poisonous gifts. You were given all the memories of how it had been. The sweetness. The laughter. The happiness. And you weren't just given them. They were sharpened, intensified. Wine tasted sweeter, music sounded more beautiful, the colours of sunset were more vivid, lovemaking was more intense, flesh felt and smelt more perfect. And they weren't all given to you at once. It was as though some were injected into you at unsuspecting moments, so that you could be engaged in some entirely innocuous pursuit and suddenly a memory would find its way to your brain and to your heart. And the torture would be more intense for its unexpectedness. This was a broken heart. It was worse than a death. A death was final. This just went on and on and on.

Apart from his memories he had so few physical things to remember her by. The photograph that he had gazed at countless times. The final bundle of letters that had come back to him – she had the rest of them. So that they wouldn't be lost, he had said. So that their children would have a record of their parent's relationship, had been what he had thought – though he hadn't said this to her. Instead he had said it was for the book he would write about his wartime experiences – a book that he would never write – could never write – now.

There was the stocking she had sent him, the fragrance of the perfume she had sprayed on it long faded. It was in his pack. He sometimes touched it with his fingertips or held it to his face, trying to inhale the scent of her and call her back. This stocking had held her leg, the top had encircled her thigh. How could all that closeness and intimacy be gone from his life?

His plan was simple. Or stupid. He wasn't sure which.

He was certain she wasn't dead. Somebody at Etaples or the War Office would have told him if that was the case. So she was alive, but for some reason she didn't want to see him or be in touch with him any more. Had she met somebody else? Had she gone back to her husband? That seemed the most likely explanation. She had always stalled about getting a divorce so maybe she had just returned to him. Or maybe he had been wounded as she had feared he would be and she had gone home to nurse him. The irony there would have been in that. She had become a nurse with all of that talk about nursing Lewis if he was wounded. How cruel it would have been if she had ended up nursing her husband.

So assuming she was alive, he would track her down.

The sensible thing to do might have been to go to Etaples and begin the journey there, but the place was already being wound down and eight months was a long time. A lot could have changed in the time since she had sent back – or caused to be sent back – his letters. A trail beginning there would be cold. No, his hunch was that she was gone from France. She was in England, he felt. The two most likely possibilities were that she had gone back to Fowey or home to Shropshire.

And there was another way to view all of this. His whole relationship with Helen had begun when that landlady of his in Fowey – Mrs Middleton - had asked him if he was going to church. Such a small thing but if that hadn't happened – if Mrs Middleton hadn't seen him that morning; if she hadn't been interfering or solicitous of her guests (depending on how you saw it); if he hadn't felt so guilty that he thought he'd better go to church to keep Mrs Middleton happy – then he wouldn't have been in the church that day. And if he hadn't done that he would never have seen Helen.

Yes, he might have met her some other way but, as far as Lewis was concerned, there was an almost mystical inevitability to their story. This wasn't just normal life. Some force had been at work that day that had made it all happen. Two years ago he would have ridiculed these thoughts, but war had a way of making the most rational of men superstitious or spiritual – whichever you preferred. So he would try to tap into this force again. That was why he was going back to Cornwall. He would go to Fowey where it had all began. He would go on exactly the same day, and retrace his steps. He would pick up her trail and track her down. He didn't know what had happened, why she had gone.

He just knew that she haunted his dreams, that thoughts of her filled his days, that he longed for her, that he couldn't picture a life without her. He had had eight months of it and it had been unbearable. He would go to Cornwall and somehow, he would be guided to her. He would be guided just as he had been guided safely through the War.

Lewis had done one final thing. It had occurred to him last week. He had sent a letter to Helen c/o No. 24 General Hospital, Etaples with 'Please Forward' loudly emblazoned on the front and back. In it he told her that he loved her, that his life was empty without her and that he just wanted to see her so that they could talk. He didn't know where she was but he had a suggestion. He was planning to go to Fowey on the first of July. He would arrive there that evening. Next day, the second he would go out to Readymoney and he would be at the spot where her bicycle got the puncture all that time ago. He would be there at the same time, which he suggested must have been about five thirty in the evening. This would allow her more than enough time if she was coming from London that day. Would she come too? Would she meet him there on the second? Please, would she come?

The train slipped out of the station and began to pick up speed. How dreary the suburbs of London were. But soon they were behind as the train hurried along. The War had changed how Lewis saw things in so many ways. In some ways it had ruined the world for him. A hilltop crowned with leafy trees appeared in the distance and hurried towards them. There was a time when Lewis would have just seen its beauty or perhaps wondered what birds lived within its foliage. Now he saw the landscape as an infantryman saw it. No cover for the attackers and a steep climb. That hill would have been a bastard to take. They had taken worse.

Lulled by the rhythm of the carriage and with tummies full of sandwiches, the holidaying children had settled down somewhat. The boy had fallen asleep while the girl was reading. There was a map on the wall of the compartment above the seats beneath the luggage rack. Lewis followed the train's journey – Reading, Taunton, Exeter St David's, Newton Abbot, Plymouth North Road, Devonport. He thought of the oceans of tears that had been spilled at these stations and hundreds of others like them all over the country during the last four years. He looked at the buildings as the train sped past. Churches, houses, halls, shops – they would still be standing long after their occupants had gone. Had it all been for a collection of buildings? Was that what the War had been about? Was that what England was?

Then came the Cornwall names, Liskeard, Bodmin Road, Par, St Austell and finally Truro. It was just after four when Lewis stepped onto the station platform into a tawny, golden afternoon. By six he had arrived at the Fowey Hotel.

46

*H*is room overlooked the estuary. This was the hotel where – ten or fifteen years ago – Kenneth Grahame had begun to write *The Wind In The* Willows. Lewis wondered whether Grahame had ever stayed in this room. That world of *The Wind In The Willows* and all those childish things seemed to belong to another age now. Yet, *The Wind In The Willows* had been part of the complex spell that had saved him. That piece where Ratty arms the animals, he had read or written it out so many times before engagements and it had protected him as surely as any creeping bombardment or advancing behind a tank. Perhaps it reminded him of what he was fighting for – England, its countryside and riverbanks, innocence, that other boys wouldn't have to do what he had done. Maybe. But he wasn't so sure. These sentiments seemed too noble, too jingoistic almost, to be his. Were these words a link to the world of innocence and childhood and to the woman who had first read it to him?

He came down to dinner early, through the double doors with their frosted glass panels and into the dining room. Only one other table was occupied and the maitre d'hotel gave him a table by the window. A few moments later the kitchen door swung open and with a shock of recognition, Lewis saw the same portly man that had served him and Helen on the night they had come here, celebrating the fact that she had sent the letter to her husband. Presently he came to take Lewis' order.

'Good evening, sir. Have you chosen?'

Lewis found himself momentarily at a loss for words.

'Good evening. Yes, I have. I say, I hope you don't mind me

259

saying so, but I was last here three years ago and I remember you from then. You served us that night, myself and my … my friend.'

'I'm delighted that you remember, sir. Yes, things don't change much down here in Cornwall. It's one of the things I like about the place.'

He took Lewis' order and shortly returned with the wine. The man had short fat fingers like sausages but he opened the wine expertly and poured it with care. Lewis held the glass under his nose. He had tasted so much terrible wine in France that this was like someone had opened a flask of sunlight and flowers. He tasted it and it ran down his throat like velvet and honey.

'Good, sir?' asked the waiter.

'It's *very* good,' said Lewis, looking up at him. The waiter had a sun-tanned bald head with a tuft of hair around the back and sides, twinkling blue eyes and a ruddy face as though he enjoyed a drop himself. Lewis thought of Mr Pickwick.

'I don't know much about wine but I've had some pretty bad stuff over the last few years. I think they were getting rid of all the rubbish and saving the good stuff for when we left.'

'You were in France, sir?'

Lewis nodded. He didn't really want to talk about this.

'At the Somme, sir?'

'No, I was too young for that. I didn't go in until November 1916. But I was at the Somme in 1918, when they tried that last push.'

'I'll just go and see if your soup is ready, sir.'

The waiter returned with the soup and left Lewis to eat it. When he came to retrieve the bowl, Lewis said, 'The Somme? You had somebody there?'

'Yes, sir. A son.'

The blue eyes switched from Lewis to looking out onto the estuary.

'He died, sir. On the first day. Today, sir. It'll be three years today.'

That stupid first day. The number of times Lewis had heard people say this. Nearly twenty thousand dead. Nearly sixty thousand casualties in total. In *one* day. Because the Staff had thought that volunteer soldiers couldn't be taught to do anything other than walk towards the enemy carrying impossible burdens and that a sufficiently long barrage would guarantee a walkover. Stupid bastards.

'I'm really sorry,' said Lewis.

Despite himself, he felt guilty. He wished there was something he could do, something he could say. But he had written too many letters to parents about their sons. That well was dry.

'His mum took it hardest,' said the waiter. 'He was an only child.'

The man shook his head and ambled off slowly to the kitchen. From the back he looked terribly old. Defeated. How many families were there like this all over England? And what had it all been for? What had been gained? In comparison to what had been lost.

Later, when the waiter was pouring the coffee, Lewis heard himself saying, 'I'll be going back to France before too long. Do you know if your son has a grave?'

'Oh yes, sir. We know where he's buried. They were very careful to tell us that.'

Yes, thought Lewis, they *were* very careful about organising things like that. Pity the stupid bastards couldn't have been a bit more careful organising the battles that had caused all of those graves.

'Well then, if you – or his mother – wanted to, I could put something on the grave. Flowers. A letter. Something …'

It sounded hopelessly inadequate.

'Oh sir, we couldn't impose on you like that.'

'Really, it would be no trouble. I have a camera – if you wanted to, I could take a photograph of his grave and where he's buried. I don't know if you'll get out there yourselves any time soon' – Lewis knew that they probably never would – 'so until then, this might do.'

In the end it was all agreed. Lewis was staying one more night. The man whose name was Henry Harris, would go and talk to his wife. Tomorrow evening he would bring the details of the location of their son's grave plus whatever they wanted to leave there.

As Lewis went out on the balcony for a smoke after dinner, he felt that it was another good omen. It had been a good thing to do and tomorrow, it would all come right because she would be there. They would meet and it would be as it was before. They would hold each other and the reason for her disappearance would not matter now because they were together again. They would go back to the hotel. They would bathe – together – and have dinner. They would have wine and there would be time for talking and explaining and laughing. Henry would give Lewis his mission and then he and Helen would watch the sun set from the terrace. Later they would go up to bed and make love and the following day they would begin their new life. Maybe she would come with him to France while he served out his two years. What a way that would be to begin again. He had always thought that he would revisit the places where he had fought, but to do it with her – and to see where she had been. It would be a trip that would lay whatever ghosts needed to be laid. It would bond them together for the rest of their lives.

Lewis woke with a start. He was sweating. He had been having a nightmare but already it was fading from his consciousness, like water slipping through his hands. The dreams often ravaged his night's sleep.

He lay in the dark and stared up at the ceiling. This quest was ridiculous. She would not come and he would never find her and life – the life that had been handed back to him, after being held hostage for over a year and a half – would be empty. He would slide down to death uncaring. Coming to Cornwall in the hope of picking up her trail? That wasn't a plan. That was the sort of plan that the Staff put together – bombard the enemy trenches, send lots of men over the top, fingers crossed and see what happens.

When he'd gone to bed last night, he'd felt confident that it would all work out. The gods – or whatever he believed in – that had brought him safely through the War were smiling on him. Surely they would restore the life he had had; make up for what the War had taken from him.

Now, he knew it wasn't so. Maybe the fact that he had come through the War when so many others hadn't, was as much as he was going to get. It was a hell of a lot more than many others had been given. Now it began to dawn on him until it became an incredible certainty that he would never find her, that he would never see her again. He turned on his side, drew his knees up to his chest and began to cry uncontrollably.

47

*I*n the morning, Lewis had a quick breakfast, picked up the sandwiches and a couple of bottles of beer which he had ordered the previous night, and headed out to Readymoney. The day was fine and he had thought of going for a swim but he didn't want to be all wet and tousled when he met her. So instead he brought a book – he had just started *Under The Greenwood Tree* by Thomas Hardy. The beach was crowded when he arrived. He found a spot that was shady and settled down to wait.

The sun shimmered on the water and spears of light danced from its surface. A couple of people walked along the water line and stopped. Their silhouettes were black against the dazzling water and he had a sense that their bodies were about to melt. After a while they moved on. He closed his eyes and immediately everything went red. He listened to the seagulls. A long way off – or so it sounded – children were calling. Lewis breathed in lungfuls of the pure air. He picked up some sand in his hand and let it slip through his fingers.

It occurred to him that this was the second time in his life that he had waited for a woman he loved to come back to him. He remembered the night of his mother's funeral; the wardrobe door; the nights that had followed until gradually the realisation had dawned that she wasn't coming back at all. How strange that he was in the same situation now. Did the gods do this as a joke? Hardy had a book of poems called *Time's Laughingstocks*. Was that what he was?

But wasn't there also something about how life kept sending you the same challenges until you did the right thing about them?

Actually, it was Helen who had told him about this. What had he done wrong then as an eight year old that this situation had not been resolved and had reappeared in his life? Had wanting to see Mum one more time, to say goodbye, been the wrong thing to ask for? And what should he do this time? Surely it couldn't be wrong to want to be with someone you loved so much? Was it because she was married? Or older than him? Is that what made it wrong?

He switched his mind to other thoughts. He wondered if she would get here early. It all depended, he supposed, on whether she had travelled today or yesterday. But that was assuming she was coming from London. Maybe she was already here. That hadn't occurred to him and he suddenly wondered, with a jolt, whether she was already at the cottage. Had she rented it again? What a perfect surprise that would have been – to suddenly see her walking down the beach and hear her say, 'What are you doing down here, silly? Tea's ready.'

He wasn't really that convinced that she was there but he thought he should go and check anyway. Putting his things into his pack, he stood up and hurried up the beach. It was after midday now and very hot. He could feel the sweat on his face and pooled in his armpits. He approached the cottage up the narrow lane and realised that his heart was pounding. Eventually he saw its chimney through the summer foliage and then its roof and then he was standing outside it.

The hedge had grown considerably in the three years. There had been no attempt to trim it and so he had to look over the small wooden gate to see in. The white paint on the gate had flaked – it looked like it hadn't been touched in the intervening time. The cottage itself was much as they had left it, although – as far as he could see – the vegetable garden was gone to ruin. The windows were open so there was obviously someone inside. Lewis heard the sound of the head of a brush knocking against something wooden – a table leg perhaps. The smell of cooking came to him on a whiff of breeze. He realised he was holding the top timber of the gate tightly with his hands.

But then he heard a scream. It was a scream of delighted fear and two small children appeared round the side of the house. They looked to be both under five, one girl and one boy. The girl carried a ball and was running away with the boy in pursuit. She screamed again, doubled back, wrong-footing the boy. Then he turned and they both disappeared round the back of the house. So she wasn't here.

He returned to the beach. He set out his towel again, and sitting on it ate his sandwiches. He began to fret about whether his letter to her had arrived. But he realised there was no point in thinking about that. He had learned the lesson in the Army. If you couldn't influence it then no point in worrying – just get on with it.

The sun tracked on. People came and went. The water was crowded in the mid afternoon. Lewis kept looking to the spot where people coming from Fowey first became visible, expecting to see her appear there. But it was always somebody else. A biplane flew overhead at one point and Lewis remembered how the infantry in the trenches had envied the fliers the cleanliness of their war. He tried closing his eyes, holding them shut and saying to himself, 'She'll be there when I open them'. But she never was.

The beach began to empty and the heat from the sun became a little less intense. The wavelets broke ceaselessly on the shore. They arrived, fell on the wet sand as though exhausted, spread out and slid up the beach. Then they withdrew, whispering gently away. Now that there were less people in the water, a couple of gulls had come down. They ran about in the shallow surf, the water surging around legs that seemed impossibly thin to hold such powerful bodies. Several boats were beached by their owners. Lewis turned his back to where she would come from and imagined her hand landing softly on his shoulder like a bird, and her soft voice saying, 'Hello, Lewis'.

He tried to think about something different. After he finished his remaining time in the Army, what then? The more he thought of going to university the less he liked the idea. He pictured Oxford or some place like that. She would be working and he studying. They would be living in a small rented house. They would spend all day apart and then he would come back in the evenings to food and firelight and making love. But no, he didn't want that. He wanted to be with her all the time. So maybe they could buy a plot of land, maybe down this way somewhere, maybe here in Cornwall. They would work together. They would raise something – he didn't know what – but maybe crops, not animals. He had seen enough slaughter and didn't want to have anything more to do with it. Herbs, maybe. Or flowers.

He liked this idea. They would live and work together, growing their own food. Their days would be full of laughter and happiness and work would seem like fun rather than work. Perhaps she might have a child, his child. And their nights would be nights of starlight seen through lozenged windows and warmth under bedclothes and nakedness and holding each other.

He had been reluctant to check his watch but he did so now. It was just before six. A spasm of anxiousness rose in his belly but he quietened it. There was still time. If she was catching the train from London, the bus from Truro – there were all sorts of possible delays along the way. Even now she could be hurrying out of town to meet him.

There were only a few people left on the beach. It was strange, he thought. All of these people were enjoying the simple pleasures of a sunny day by the sea. They were swimming, making sand castles, eating their picnics and unaware of the huge drama that was being played out here. He wondered. Maybe there were other dramas happening here as well. Between husbands and wives. In children's minds. Maybe love affairs were starting or finishing or people were tormented by love or basking in it. He looked around to see if he could get any sense of these things anywhere, but suddenly found he didn't care. Not about these people. Not today.

The minutes crawled now as he constantly looked at his watch, willing her to appear, not wanting to have to leave this place without her. He remembered the morning after that third night in bed when he was eight – the feeling of emptiness, of loss, of huge, overwhelming grief. The feeling that he had lost everything that mattered and that he would never be happy again. He could feel tears smarting in his eyes. If she came he would have to tell her that they were tears of happiness.

It was at eight that he decided that she wasn't coming.

'All the day dreams must go; it will be a wearisome return.' He walked back to Fowey through the honey light of evening. A phrase had begun going around in his head. 'Yes, but under very different circumstances from those expected.' It chased around his brain, cannoned off the inside of his skull, refused to stop. 'Yes, but under very different circumstances from those expected.' He looked down the long tunnel of the years ahead and saw nothing but emptiness. Loneliness. Desolation. How would he be able to get up tomorrow and begin another day without her? And the day after that? And the day after that? What would he find to fill his days? He might have been able to bear it had she been dead but to know that she was alive. People would see her, meet her, speak with her, be friends with her. They would hear her voice and her laughter. They would enjoy her company and love being with her. 'Yes, but under very different circumstances from those expected.'

At the hotel he checked at the reception desk but nobody had left any messages for him. He wanted to just go to bed and never get up again, but he had to go and get the things from Henry, the waiter. Steeling himself, Lewis went down. He made an excuse about not having dinner, saying that he had had 'a bad night'. He had to say no more than that – Henry understood.

He gave Lewis a small canvas bag and a piece of paper. The bag contained an aged bouquet of roses, brown and dusty and an envelope.

'This was his mother's wedding bouquet,' explained Henry. 'She kept it all these years but now she'd like you to put it on his grave. The envelope has a letter from the pair of us to him. If you could leave that at the grave too, it would be much appreciated.'

'Would you like me to read it to him?' asked Lewis.

Henry's eyes brightened.

'I think that would be a really nice idea, Mr Friday. You wouldn't mind doing that? You wouldn't – I don't know, feel awkward or stupid —'

'Henry, I'd be proud to do it.'

'These are directions as to where his grave is. I copied them out from the letter the War Graves people sent us.'

'Will you give me your address?' asked Lewis. 'Then I can send you a picture of the grave.'

'But we're imposing on you too much, sir —'

'It's nothing. He died a hero. They all did. We have to remember them. To recognise what they did. Your son died. What are a few photographs against that? Just put your address on here.'

Lewis handed him the piece of paper and Henry wrote the address with his waiter's pencil. When he had finished, Lewis read it aloud just to make sure he had it correct. Then he folded it carefully and put it in his inside jacket pocket. They shook hands and Lewis headed up the heavy staircase. In his room he took off his shoes, lay on the bed and eventually fell asleep.

He woke some time in the middle of the night. For a few moments he wasn't sure where he was but then he remembered and the huge crushing boulder of loss rolled back onto him. It couldn't be true. This had to be a terrible dream from which he would wake. Why had he survived the War just to end up with this? He tried to go back to sleep but it was hopeless. His mind was too full of everything he had lost. Little scenes of his life with her kept coming back into his mind and refused to be banished. He would stop one but then another would suddenly appear, playing out like a little film. He would rip that reel from the projector but another would start up from another projector. He wondered if he was going insane.

Later, he became aware of the first brightening of the sky. His mind seemed to slow down, to become a little quieter. He heard the first birdsong of the day. Slowly – very slowly – he began to think about the situation. Do what he had done in the trenches. Do what had helped him to survive. Try to solve the problem.

She had not come. So either she didn't want to see him or she hadn't known about the rendezvous. He found it hard to imagine her not wanting to meet, given everything they had shared together. Surely she would have come – if only to draw a line under it, to close the circle. Anyway, logically, there was no point in thinking about that. The other possibility was that she hadn't known about the rendezvous.

If she hadn't known about the rendezvous, then she hadn't received the letter. So now he would have to go to France. He would go to General Hospital No. 24 and either find her there or, failing that, pick up the trail. Maybe she was sick in Hospital No. 24, maybe that's why she hadn't been in touch. Or lost her memory or had a breakdown due to the stress of the kind of work she was doing. There were all sorts of possibilities but there was no point in thinking about them now. The important thing was to get there. He felt easier. He had a plan. People didn't just disappear. He would find her.

48

*L*ewis packed for a trip of a week and caught the steamer from Dover to Calais. It was a day of yellow sun and blue sky but there was a strong wind on the Channel. He sat in the lee of the ship's superstructure and read. From Calais he took a train to Amiens arriving there towards evening. The city was crowded with visitors. It was three years since the Somme battles but the first year when civilians had been able to come here. They had come in their droves. There was a sad, lost air about many of the people he passed – middle-aged couples, lots of women in black, singly and in groups of two or three.

He managed to find a room in a small hotel in Rue Amiral Courbet. The window had a view of the spire of the Cathedral. Having dumped his pack, he went back downstairs and asked at reception whether it would be possible to hire a bicycle tomorrow.

'*Mais bien sur*', came the smiling reply from the strikingly beautiful blonde girl behind the counter. It would be here for him in the morning. She had brown eyes. Her shining hair was tied up in a pony tail and was in stark contrast to her black dress with sleeves that came down below the elbows. Her arms were white and she had long fingers. She was thin with no breasts to speak of and her lips pouted in the way of almost all French women. He thanked her and going out, wondered what it would be like to lie in her arms, to be naked with her.

'I miss you so much, Helen,' he murmured, as he turned right, out of the hotel and up the street towards the Cathedral.

The signs of the War were everywhere. Roofless shells of houses; piles of rubble and timbers neatly swept to the side of the street; lone walls – all that remained of some houses – looking decidedly shaky; shell-battered buildings with weeds and bushes growing wildly from them, boarded-up buildings. And then almost as if by a miracle, a lone house or the odd tree that had escaped damage. There were also signs of rebuilding. Scaffolding around houses, masons or plasterers or carpenters whistling cheerily or calling to one another. There would be work here for the rest of their lives.

Lewis hadn't been here during the battles on the Somme – he had spent that summer and autumn with Helen. Back then it had been like the capital of the British Army, a hectic, bustling place where civilians still lived and earned a living from the British and their allies. When Lewis had been posted to France, there were still one or two men in his platoon who remembered that time. Amiens had boasted restaurants, shops, brothels, they told him. Here men with a little bit of time off could lorry-jump and find a few hours of civilized living. There were hotels where they could get a bath if they were early enough and the hot water hadn't run out. There were streets of shops with unbroken plate-glass windows. Civilians walked about. There were women and children – women who might smile and look away sadly if you caught their eye.

Always these men had money to spend – 'bought it' in the front line having an entirely different meaning. And so they bought little things that they could carry back to the line as presents for wives or girlfriends. Perfumed soap, stationary for writing letters, a print to stick on the wall of a dugout. Lewis got the impression that it was the normality of going into a shop and buying something, rather than the thing itself that was what made the expeditions so special. And, of course, there were always girls behind the counters. They would smile or your hand could touch theirs when the money was exchanged. Or if you were really daring you might ask their name and they would say

'Helene' or 'Odile' and it would be an excuse to say *'Enchanté'* and reach out and take their hand.

And there were other pleasures to be had. *'Bonsoir, mon capit-aine'* a girl would say out of the shadows. *'If fait froid, n'est-ce pas?'* It's cold, isn't it? Would you like a little love? *Un peu d'amour'.* Lewis was sure he would have gone himself if it hadn't been for Helen. It was hard to imagine how men could resist even a few minutes of softness and femininity and sweet fragrance. Especially if, earlier that day, they had been under harassing fire or living through a gas wave or lying in mud and shit and piss and bits of bodies as shell splinters and machine gun bullets flailed the air above them.

Lewis first came to Amiens at the beginning of April 1918. By then the place had been evacuated of all its civilians by the French military authorities. He thought it possibly the saddest place he had ever seen. During the War, extensive measures were taken to protect the Cathedral. The stained glass windows were carefully removed and stored; the great west door was screened from bomb-splinters by sandbags piled high. Inside, sandbags were stacked high in the nave and around the sanctuary and some of the windows. The sandbags were gone now and the interior of the place echoed with the footsteps of visitors.

It was strange but also, in an odd sort of way, comforting to be back. Lewis sat in a seat towards the back and followed the tall columns up to the impossibly high roof. Light spilled in through the arched clerestory windows, candles flickered in the shadows. He thought of all the men who had come here during the years of the War – the figures who had walked around here and were ghosts now.

Later he found a restaurant and had something to eat. Then, when it was dark, he went back out and down towards the river, the Somme. He wanted to be with the ghosts. The moon wasn't up but there was a certain luminescence off the water so that he could see as he walked along the quayside. The last time he had been here, the sky north and east had been quivering with flashes of white light like summer lightning and the guns had been thundering. It was all quiet now. The night was clear, the stars were out and since the street lighting in Amiens hadn't been restored over most of the city, they were as bright as diamonds on black silk. The air was starting to cool after the heat of the day. The place had a certain stark beauty about it. He crossed the river and looked back at the Cathedral, high and beautiful above the silhouettes of the huddled ruins of Amiens. He could see its pinnacles and buttresses faintly against the inky night.

Lewis felt empty, numb, fearful. He was glad that tomorrow he was going to Henry's son's grave. The next day would be the trip to Etaples. He was longing for it and dreading it. If she wasn't there or if she was there but didn't want to see him or wouldn't come with him or he couldn't find any trace of her. He had been so confident after she failed to appear at Readymoney. Now here, in this place that looked like the end of the world, when the resolution of all of this was only a matter of hours away, he feared that his world was coming to an end too.

49

*L*ewis had had his forebodings about the bicycle but it turned out to be an almost brand-new, touring machine. The blonde receptionist explained that she was expecting to have many more tourists who would want to visit the battlefields, and so in future, she intended to buy a number of cycles for just such a service. Lewis had thought she worked there. From the way she spoke, it sounded like she owned the place. After breakfast he took the road up the Rue Amiral Courbet, past the railway station and over a little stone bridge along the road to Querrieux.

Lewis was struck by how far away from the front line the town was – this was where Rawlinson, the architect of the first day on the Somme, had made his headquarters. Like most front line soldiers Lewis had never been to any of the generals' headquarters. But those few who had, had brought back stories of what it was like. Headquarters, any headquarters, was a world apart.

Usually, the generals picked chateaux or fine old houses in grand parks with fields. GHQ, the overall headquarters of the British Army, was in Montreuil, an old walled town on a steep hill with views out over richly cultivated lands. Here it was the world of light opera with clean, sharply pressed uniforms, medals, decorations and much saluting. Elderly generals with fine, carefully trimmed moustaches, middle-aged colonels and majors, young officers all wearing red hat-bands and red tabs on their uniforms.

But for the uniforms, it might have been an insurance company or some other paper-intensive enterprise. Men came and went looking important and carrying sheaves of paper or files. A man carrying a single piece of paper with a purposeful stride and glancing to neither right nor left, had to be even more important. Men scribbled notes in the margins of papers. 'I agree' or 'Please copy Colonel So-and-so'.

These were the men who masterminded the campaigns. What a heavy responsibility they bore and it could be seen in the worried frowns and lines on their faces as they passed up and down corridors and from one office to another. Such warriors needed some diversion in the evenings and so they would change into a different and perhaps even more grandly decorated uniform, with polished buttons and crossed swords. Their boots would be gleaming as they came noisily down marble or wooden staircases to a dinner of rich food and wine. They would chat over dinner of inconsequential things or of the latest intrigue or scandal. At night they slept in beds with deep pillows and clean sheets.

Despite the heavy food and the good claret that washed it down, they sometimes found themselves unable to sleep or would wake in the middle of the night. Perhaps it had been too much good coffee. 'Bloody artillery,' they would curse, while twenty miles away men were being clubbed to death or eviscerated with steel blades or drowned in mud or gas or atomised by the selfsame artillery that disturbed the officers' dreams.

Lewis continued along the *Route Nationale* to Albert. The sky was a pale blue that promised another warm day. A lark was singing somewhere. Lewis remembered that the road ran like a ribbon over a series of long, slow rises and falls. The climbs would be stiff on a bike but the downhills would be exhilarating. It had been different three years ago. Men weary – even after a rest period – and carrying sixty pounds or more of equipment, found the climbs brutal. The toil turned calf muscles to bars of rolled steel and there was no mercy in the downhill because the next ascent could be seen in front, waiting. The men sang to try to forget their fear.

After only a few minutes, a British Army truck pulled in ahead of him and stopped with its engine running. Lewis cycled up to the cab. The sergeant in the driver's seat had a Bairnsfeather's Ole Bill moustache and told him he was going up to Albert if he wanted a lift. Lewis was happy to accept and went round to the back to stow his bike. As he lifted it over the tail board, he saw that it contained a great heap of wooden crosses, newly made and smelling of wood preserver. Lewis went up to the passenger side and climbed in.

The sergeant had a cigarette permanently in his mouth and rested his elbows on the steering wheel. On the dashboard was a large scale map of the area. Between them, on the truck's single seat, lay an open folder holding a sheaf of forms. The top form had been completed in type but then there were pencilled corrections to it. The form was headed 'Burial Return'. Then it had a series of columns headed 'Row', 'Grave', 'Map reference where body found', 'Was cross on grave?' The next column was called 'Regimental particulars'. There was one entry in this column that said '2 / Scottish Rifles' but all the rest of them had 'Unknown British Soldier'. The final two columns said 'Means of identification' and 'Were any effects forwarded to Base?'

'Working for the War Graves people,' the sergeant explained without being asked.

'That must be a tough job,' said Lewis.

'Pays well,' said the sergeant. 'But it's unpleasant, that's for sure. And dangerous. A lot of unexploded stuff still out there. We lost a fellow only yesterday.'

For a moment, it seemed to Lewis that he was back in the War again and that when people said things like this, you just shrugged, if that. But it was peacetime now. He remembered that there were certain niceties that had to be observed.

'I'm sorry,' he said.

The sergeant's cigarette had burnt right down. He put his

thumb and forefinger around it, took one last pull and threw the butt out the open side of the cab.

'We're under a lot of pressure apart from that,' he went on. 'The Froggies want to get back onto their land, rebuild their houses, plant crops, start getting on with their lives. Can't blame 'em really, I suppose.'

The road had been repaired in the sense that all of the shell holes and craters had been filled in. The trees on either side were still stumps though, like bits of giant pencils driven into the ground. The land on either side was pretty much as the War had left it. Greenery grew in profusion in shell pits, long rolls of brown marked rusting barbed wire. The land was a study in a deep red brown, and an intense shadowy green. From the cab of the lorry it was possible to get a sense of the zig-zags of trenches hurrying in this direction and that. And everywhere there were shell holes, with who knew what ghastliness in the bottoms of them.

'Ain't a pretty sight,' said the sergeant. 'Even on a day like today.'

'Think it'll ever recover?' asked Lewis.

'It'll recover,' said the sergeant with complete certainty. 'Nature's a wonderful thing.'

Lewis wasn't so sure.

'Where there's plenty of greenery growing,' said the sergeant. 'That means there are bodies there. We also use this.'

The sergeant reached behind him and from the back pulled forward a long piece of metal, thin like a rapier, with a handle on it. Lewis recognised it as a cleaning rod for a machine gun. He looked quizzically at the sergeant.

'Push it down into the ground,' he said. 'Then pull it out and smell it or touch it and see if it's sticky.'

The sergeant turned to look at him.

'You soon know.'

In Albert children played over the heaps of rubble which lined the streets. It was hard to imagine that houses could be destroyed in such a multiplicity of ways. Houses with the tiles swept off the roof; houses that were little more than a skeleton of rafters and beams and laths; houses where the front had collapsed as though it had fallen on its face; houses where the back or the side had fallen off; houses with large, roughly circular holes in the sides where shells had crashed through, houses that were just empty shells so that it was hard to imagine how life had ever gone on in any of these places.

The sergeant stopped in the square in front of the Basilica. The Basilica tower was still there, more or less intact and rising out of a mound of rubble. Behind it, only the walls stood. The Golden Virgin which had stood on top of the tower was nowhere to be seen. Lewis had never seen the famous statue. Before the War, it had stood on top of the Basilica and had been visible for miles around. The image was of the Virgin holding the infant Christ aloft as though offering him to God. Whether it was covered in gold or made of gold, Lewis never knew. Repeated shelling during the early part of the War had caused the statue to tip over so that eventually it lay slightly below the horizontal but still attached at the base. The result was that the Virgin looked like she was diving – offering her child as a sacrifice to stop the War, some of the more fanciful said. Eventually, during the German Spring Offensive in 1918, the British, knowing that the tower would make a good observation post, had deliberately targeted the tower and blown the statue down. Lewis thanked the sergeant and retrieved his bike.

The road south east out of Albert wound through more devastated countryside. The patching of this road had been more rough and ready, so that Lewis had to steer carefully to avoid damaging his tyres on flints or bits of metal. Soon on his right, amidst a clump of blasted trees so that it could easily be missed, he found the cemetery. The wooden crosses with the little metal tags on them were in straight lines. Lewis guessed that the dead had been buried in an old section of trench.

He wandered up the first line and then back down the second one and soon found the grave he was looking for. He stopped and unslung his pack. Out of it he took the bouquet of flowers which he had carefully placed in a small square cardboard box to avoid damaging it. These he carefully placed in front of the cross. Then he took out the envelope from his jacket pocket and tore it open. The ripping sounded loud in a countryside disturbed only by birdsong. He unfolded the paper and read.

'Our dearest, darling, son James.

This kind gentleman, Mr Friday, has said that he will bring this letter to you & read it. It is a chance for us to say goodbye.

We miss you, darling boy. It is impossible to believe that you will never be coming back to us again. Remember those times when you used to come in from work in the shop? Such stories you had about the customers. You used to have us in stitches. Your father always said you should have been on the stage. Your commanding officer wrote to us after you died & said you were exactly the same in the Army, keeping them all laughing with the jokes you used to tell.

So farewell our darling until we meet again.

With all our love.

Mum and Dad.

Lewis was in tears when he had finished. He placed the letter back in the envelope and slipped it down between the blooms of the bouquet. Then he took some photographs of the grave and of the views in each direction. When he had finished he sat on the ground and looked off to the south across the rolling, destroyed ground.

So now there was nothing else for it. Tonight he would stay

in Amiens and tomorrow he would go to Etaples. And there he would see what he would see. He had done a good thing in coming here and, in general, he thought, in his life he had tried to live a good life and not hurt people. Yes, it was true he had killed men in the War, but he had also saved some lives. The gods were balancing the scales now. He hoped he wouldn't be found wanting.

50

*T*he following morning Lewis, dressed in his best uniform, took the train to Etaples. He sat by the window, staring out but not seeing anything. A taxi took him to No. 24 General Hospital. The sentry at the gate directed him to a building that was sign posted 'Administration'. Here, a mousy French girl behind a hatch with a sliding glass pane directed him to a room down a feebly lit corridor. The corridor felt cold after the warmth of the sun outside. The sign on the door said 'Administrator'. Lewis knocked and a voice commanded, 'Come in'.

A well-built woman sat behind a desk. She wore no makeup and her hair was perfectly done. Her face didn't look like a happy face or a face that smiled or laughed that often. On the desk in front of her were a glasses case, a leather blotter with an unused sheet of white paper in it, a pen holder, a black telephone and a wooden nameplate that said, 'R.A. Armitage'. Whether this lady actually was R.A. Armitage, or whether she was just using the office to intimidate, Lewis never found out because she never introduced herself. Instead she addressed him as lieutenant, politely asked him to sit and inquired what she could do for him.

'My name is Lewis Friday,' he began. I'm here because I'm trying to track down somebody —'

'Who was a patient here?' asked the woman, in a please-get-on-with-it way.

'No – who used to work here.'

'Ah,' said the possibly R.A. Armitage. 'And may I ask her name? I assume it is a she?'

Her tone had the merest edge of distaste about it. Lewis found himself wondering if she was a virgin.

'Yes, it's a she. She may have used her maiden name, Hope or her married name, Goddard. Late thirties, blonde —'

'Yes, I remember Mrs Goddard.'

Lewis felt a surge of joy, but it was immediately tempered by the fact that she was still using her married name.

'She's not still here?' asked Lewis, thinking what an incredible thing that would be.

'No, she's not still here. She left.'

'Left? Went to some other hospital? Here in France ... or she went back to England?'

'No, she left. She gave up nursing.'

'Gave it up?'

Lewis realised he was repeating everything she said. He must have sounded like a fool.

'That's right.'

R.A. Armitage, if that's who she was, wasn't giving much away.

'Er, do you know why?'

'Personal reasons. That was what most of them used to say when they did.'

'Personal reasons?'

Jesus, there he was doing it again.

'Unfortunately, Lieutenant Friday, I'm really not authorised to say any more than that. These are peoples' private lives, you understand.'

Lewis wasn't sure if R.A. Armitage had a better nature. He doubted it, but he thought he knew enough about her now to know what not to say to her. He leaned forward in a gesture that said, confidentially, just between the two of us.

'May I be frank?'

He had been about to add 'Miss' or 'Mrs', but unsure of which one to say, he just left the four words hanging there. He noticed that R.A. Armitage bent forward slightly.

'You'll remember the Zeppelin raids on the east coast during the War?'

She nodded.

'My parents and brother and sister were killed during those raids. Mrs Goddard was my aunt, my mother's sister. She is now the only surviving relative I have. I've lost – we've all lost – so much during the War. Please don't let me lose this as well. All I ask is that you could give me the last address you had for her. With that I might be able to track her down. Please – we were a very close family. And maybe she thinks I am dead. It would such a joy to her to know that I'm still alive.'

R.A. Armitage looked at Lewis as though sizing him up. Outside a truck revved as it went past. Then silence returned to the room. Lewis' heart was pounding.

Finally, she said, 'Please wait here'. R.A. Armitage got up and went out a side door into an adjacent room. Lewis heard the drawers of a filing cabinet being slid open. It didn't take her long. She returned with a manila folder, extracted some glasses from the glasses case and opened the folder. If Lewis had been hoping to read the folder upside down, there was no chance of that – she held it in one hand while her plump fingers turned the pages of onion skin paper.

'The address we have on file for Mrs Goddard is "The Oaks, Shrewsbury, Shropshire". I'm afraid that's all I can tell you.'

R.A. Armitage closed the file. Then she got up, saying, 'Now, if there's nothing else you'll have to excuse me.'

Lewis felt stunned. A terrible fear began to creep into his mind but he had no time to put a name on it as he followed R.A. Armitage's lead and stood up. Mechanically, he thanked her and left the room, walking down the depressed corridor, past the mousy girl and back out into the sunlight. Hands shaking, he found a cigarette and lit it.

It couldn't be true that Helen had gone back to her husband. 'Personal reasons'? What did it mean? Of course, her husband could have died and she had gone back to deal with his estate and inherit the house. But supposing he had only been injured so that she had gone back to mind him. 'Personal reasons'. Did it mean she was pregnant? That's what R.A. Armitage seemed to have been implying in that disapproving way of hers. If so, it couldn't have been his baby. It had been a year before the Armistice that he had last seen her. So pregnant with somebody else's?

The sun shone on Lewis as he smoked, first one cigarette and then another. Gradually he calmed himself down. He would have to go to Shropshire and find where she lived and confront her. No, 'confront her' wasn't the right term. He just wanted to see her, to see her face again, to hear her voice, to hold her in his arms. Then she would explain what had happened. The whole tangled mess would be unravelled. And once they had done that everything would be out of the way and they would be able to start again.

If she had gone back to her husband, if she was minding him – it was alright – Lewis could put up with that if he had to. They could come to an arrangement. They could be lovers, their lives a chain of clandestine, hurried meetings. It would be exciting. They could be friends – if that was all she wanted. But what he couldn't bear was the thought that she might not be in his life at all.

51

*L*ewis returned to London and stayed overnight in Horn Lane. According to Margaret, Dad was up north in Scapa Flow. Lewis unpacked, repacked, slept, washed, shaved and next morning was on an early morning train to Shrewsbury. In the late afternoon, a taxi dropped him at the entrance to 'The Oaks'.

The house was invisible from the road, screened by a belt of oak trees. A heavy wooden gate, painted white, was open and Lewis walked in. The drive turned almost immediately to the left and the house came into view. It was a fine place – an old farmhouse originally, Lewis guessed – build of red brick, with bay windows on the ground floor to either side of the imposing front door, over which a portico had been added. The thought that she was in there made Lewis' heart race. He could feel his face and limbs warming as the blood pumped faster. Simultaneously he was terrified that this would not turn out as he had intended.

He was about to walk up the drive to the front door, when he heard a car out on the road. It was slowing and Lewis realised it was going to come into 'The Oaks'. Quickly he slipped into the thin belt of trees that surrounded the house. A few moments later the car passed him, crunched up the packed-dirt driveway and stopped at the front door. The driver got out and, as he did, the front door of the house opened. A wheelchair was pushed out and, even though it was over a hundred yards away, Lewis recognised the cadaverous face of Helen's husband, Robert. Despite the fact that it was going to be a hot day, he wore a heavy tweed jacket, a cap and had a woollen blanket stretched tightly over his legs. Moments later, Lewis saw that Helen was pushing the wheelchair. He only saw her for an instant before his view of her was blocked by the car. However, he could see what they were doing – she and the driver were loading Robert into the back seat. Once this was done, Helen wheeled the wheelchair back to the front door, where a maid took it. Then Helen turned and waved as the car pulled off. She went back inside and shut the door. So that was it. She had gone back to him. He had been wounded, lost the use of his legs and now she was minding him.

Lewis wasn't that surprised. Ever since the day in Etaples, he had gradually gotten used to the idea that it would be something like this. Helen was a gentle, tender and caring person. It was just the kind of thing that she would have done. His guess was that her husband was going for some kind of therapy or treatment, so presumably he would be gone a few hours. Lewis stepped out of the trees and continued up the gently sloping drive. In a couple of minutes he had reached the front door. He pressed the bell and heard it ring somewhere deep inside the house.

*A*s he expects, it is a maid who opens the door.

'Yes sir, can I help you?'

'I'm looking for Mrs Goddard, please.'

'And who shall I say is calling?'

'Lewis. Er, Mr Lewis.'

'Just a moment sir, please.'

The maid leaves the door slightly ajar. The seconds pass. He is sweating and wipes his forehead with his sleeve. His heart feels like it is going to burst. He doesn't know whether it's from love or fear. He hears footsteps in the hall – heels on wood flooring. Then the door begins to swing open and she is there.

The last time Lewis has seen Helen is November 1917, more then a year and a half earlier. Her face doesn't seem to have changed but there is something different about her. It is something to do with her clothes and her hairstyle. Her hair is shorter than it was when he last saw her. It strikes him as a 'sensible' style – easy to manage and quick to wash. Her clothes have the same sensible feel to them. She wears a dark green skirt, straight and ankle length and a white blouse, but she wears pearls with them. He has never seen her wear pearls. And she has pearly earrings. Lewis never remembers her ears having been pierced. And she wears make-up. Her face is powdered and she has applied fresh lipstick. He knows she will be forty in December but she looks older than that now by several years.

He sees a momentary lack of recognition in her face followed, moments later, by something else. He thinks it might be an urge to shut the door on him. He thinks he may have seen a reflex movement that would have been the beginnings of her hand reaching up to shut it. But if there is, she stops it. And he could be wrong anyway. All of this happens so quickly.

'Lewis,' she breathes.

She looks completely beautiful. Even so it is a Black Dog moment – the look of a woman who sees a ghost. Lewis feels a moment of satisfaction at having surprised her but that quickly gives way to something else. He feels sorry for her, sorry that he has had to do this to her. He wouldn't hurt her for the world.

'Hello, Helen.'

'How —?'

But she is unable to finish the question. She seems to be having difficulty speaking.

'May I come in?'

She is as one in a daze. She makes none of the normal gestures that people make as a sign of invitation. She merely stands aside and Lewis steps into the hall.

'In there,' she manages to say and nods towards a reception room on Lewis' left. He goes through the door and she follows him in. The room has a couple of armchairs, a sofa, a fine fireplace and French windows that look out onto a pretty garden with a very green lawn and lots of flowers.

She seems to recover a little.

'Are … are you staying somewhere close by?'

'The Prince Rupert.'

She nods.

'We could … I could come and meet you there this evening.'

For a moment his heart leaps. But then he realises – she is trying to get him out of the house before her husband returns.

'You didn't come and meet me in Fowey. Why should I believe that you'd come tonight?'

'Because I will. I promise.'

She is more composed now but she can't keep the note of anxiousness out of her voice.

'You just want me out in case *he* returns, isn't that it?'

'No Lewis, that's not it. I want a chance to explain. Explain everything. I need time to do that.'

'You stopped writing,' he says simply.

He has rehearsed this sentence and this scene many times in the last few weeks and had hoped to make it sound just like a statement. But it comes out sounding like an accusation. He hadn't wanted that.

'I thought it was for the best.'

The colour is completely gone from her face but she is as beautiful as ever. The short blonde hair doesn't suit her. It makes her look too old. The face is still the face of an angel. If it were to smile now, it would be like the sun had entered the room. But she is not smiling.

'We were in love,' he says.

'Tonight Lewis, in the Prince Rupert. I'll come there at seven. We can have something to eat or go for a walk. Whatever you like. I can explain everything.'

There is the tiniest hint of desperation in her voice. He loves her so much.

'You won't come,' he says. 'You're just trying to get rid of me.'

'I'll come. I promise I will.'

'You got the message about meeting in Fowey?'

She nods.

'And that didn't mean anything to you either?'

Lewis nearly starts to cry as he says, 'You know that twice in my life I've waited and been disappointed?'

'I know that, Lewis and I'm so sorry. So terribly sorry. But I'll come tonight. I swear it. I swear.'

He is unsure whether he can believe her, but now that he has spent a few minutes with her, he knows that he wants more time. He is like a man who has crossed a desert and found water. He is gulping it down and cannot imagine himself ever having enough.

'Seven?' he says.

'She nods.

'You promise?'

'On my life,' she says.

53

Lewis waits in the street outside the front door of the hotel. He fantasises about her showing up with a bag packed and them leaving tonight. He looks at his watch. It is before seven. Suddenly he sees her turning a corner in the distance. She is early.

She wears a calf-length skirt that is faded red and an ivory blouse with a deep V-neckline over a white camisole. Her lipstick is the same shade as the skirt and she carries a small evening bag. The skirt is like that she used to wear when he first knew her and he experiences again the almost physical ache he has for that time. When she reaches him he hopes that she might kiss him, but she stops in front of him.

'You came,' he says, trying to keep the relief and gratitude out of his voice.

'I said I would.'

The words are said simply, almost tenderly.

'You look beautiful,' he says.

'Thank you.'

'I thought we might go for a walk,' he says.

She nods. It is a warm evening and the heat from the day lies in the narrow streets between the half-timbered buildings. Lewis sees the spire of a church over the rooftops.

'I don't really know my way around here,' he says. 'Over that way looks nice.'

'It is,' she says, and they set off.

There is so much he wants to say but he has no idea where to begin. Eventually he utters the same accusation as earlier.

'You stopped writing.'

'I did, Lewis and believe me when I tell you that for that I am truly, truly sorry.'

They are walking side by side, looking ahead. Now he turns his head and says, 'Why?'

'I thought it was for the best.'

'The best for who?' he asks, and he can feel anger rising.

There is a long pause before she begins to reply. It sounds like something she has rehearsed.

'Robert was on the staff. He wasn't a real soldier. Not like you were. He had no sense of *real* fighting.'

'I wasn't aware that any of them did,' interrupts Lewis bitterly.

She ignores this.

'So that when the final advance began he was off one evening looking for a place that his general could use as a headquarters. There were some soldiers with him – real soldiers.'

She keeps saying 'real soldiers'. She sounds like she is trying to butter him up.

'I suppose they were bodyguards really. But they found this place – a chateau of some sort. Robert rang the bell. The Germans had booby trapped the bell so that when he rang it a bomb inside the door exploded. The two soldiers were killed and he was paralysed.'

Typical luck of the bloody staff, thinks Lewis.

'It was what I had always feared.'

She turns to look at him.

'Remember I said it to you that first time I talked about myself. That if anything like that happened to – that I would have to come back. To take care of him.'

'But he's rich. He could hire nurses, people to take care of him.'

Lewis thought he sounded like an unhappy child.

'No. It's not those things he needs. He needs somebody to love him. He told me that if I hadn't come back, he just wouldn't have wanted to go on living.'

'That's just blackmail.'

'It's not blackmail. He's not as strong as you or I. He needs somebody.'

'And what do you need, Helen?'

'This is my duty. I'm his wife.'

'So this will make you happy?'

'It's for the best. It's the right thing to do.'

'You're not answering the question.'

She says nothing. They continue walking. They are passing by the church whose spire they saw earlier.

'Did you have a baby?' he asks.

'What?' she says, with shock on her face.

'You heard what I said.'

'No, I didn't have a baby, Lewis. We were very careful, if you remember and Robert ... well ... he can't now.'

'Is it because of the difference in our ages? If I was older, would we ...?'

'No, it isn't that,' she says.

She seems happier to be on this safer territory.

'But you must admit it would have been a problem,' she says.

The use of the past tense is like a blow.

'What about when I would have met your friends?' she continues.

'I don't have any friends,' says Lewis. 'Any friends I had were killed in the War.'

'And your father – what would he have said?'

Lewis tries to keep the discussion in the present.

'I told you. He'll like you. He'll probably fancy you like hell and start flirting with you. I'd have to watch him.'

It is a weak attempt at humour.

'You'll find somebody else, Lewis. Somebody your own age. There are lots of women now who are looking for men.'

'Plenty more fish in the sea, eh? That's what you said to him, to Robert, that night in Fowey.'

She doesn't reply.

'And that's meant to make me feel better, is it? Helen, we were so happy. We were made for each other. The age difference – it was like it wasn't there. You were as young as I was and now – well now, I'm as old as you. Older in some ways. We can't throw this away. How many people do you know that are in happy marriages? Ours would have been extraordinary. It would have been everything that marriage should be.'

She looks at him and he can see that her eyes are wet, glistening.

'Oh Lewis,' she said, 'can't you see – I have to do this. Don't make it more difficult for me than it already is.'

'You could walk out of here now, tonight – into a life of fun and laughter and happiness and tenderness. Don't you want that?'

'It's not what I want. It's —'

'It's what then?' he says angrily.

'It's what's right.'

'*This* is what's right. To come with me now.'

'That's not right, Lewis. You know it isn't.'

'I know it *is*, Helen. It *is*. Look – I've seen things. I've seen how brief life can be. I've seen lives wasted. Lives that were full of promise. Snuffed out. We have that promise now. Let's not lose it. Let's seize it with both hands. Oh please, Helen. Please.'

They have come to a bench that sits in the grounds of the church. Helen stops and takes a handkerchief from her handbag. She had begun to cry. He goes to comfort her. She turns away at first, turning a hostile shoulder towards him. But when his hands touch her arms and then encircle her, she relents and turns back. He holds her in his arms and she sobs. He can smell her scent. The perfume is new, different but the smell of her hair is just as he remembers it. The whole feeling is just as he remembers it. His body remembers how it was when he held her. It all seems so familiar – the press of her breasts against him, the feel of her body beneath his hands.

She is sobbing now and he holds her and strokes her hair. He touches her hair with his lips. It is a long time before she separates from him. When she does, the handkerchief is still in her hand. She blows her nose and smiles through the tears. It is the first time she has smiled since she arrived. He thinks he has never seen her looking more beautiful. They stand close to one another in front of the bench. She blows her nose again and wipes her reddened eyes.

She looks at him. She is weakening. He knows it. She is going to relent.

'If I did this,' she begins slowly, 'I should never be happy. Oh, I know you think we would just go back to the way we were. But we wouldn't. I should be thinking about Robert all the time, wondering how he is. I should be permanently guilty. There would be no happiness in that for me.'

Lewis goes to interrupt but she holds up the hand that contains the balled-up handkerchief.

'No. Please. Life wasn't meant to be a bed of roses, Lewis —'

'Our life was.'

'Lewis darling, please try to understand. It's me. It's just the way I am. I know it sounds wrong. Maybe it *is* wrong. But it's me.'

'People can change,' he says.

'But that's just the point, don't you see – I don't want to. I want to do this.'

'More than you want to be loved? Loved like nobody's ever been loved? I would dedicate my life, you know – dedicate my life to making you happy.'

'I know you would, my love. But some things are just not meant to be.'

'I – I could come to live here. Close by, I mean. We could meet … see each other.'

She shakes her head.

'No,' she says.

'And if Robert were to die?' he asks.

'No more, Lewis,' she says. 'Please, no more.'

'Did I not love you enough?' asks Lewis.

She looks up at him.

'Of course you did. You know you did.'

'Then why?' he asks simply.

'Because he needs me.'

'And me?' he says. 'Maybe I need you too. And maybe you need me.'

She just continues to cry. Her eyes are swollen, her face red.

'Can I ask you a question?' he says.

His voice is loaded with bitterness and anger.

'That night … in Fowey … when he came and you went out with him. And then you came back and you got into my bed and we made love. Why did you do that? If you felt this way, if you knew it was always going to end up like this, why did you do that? Why did you offer something like that only so that you could take it away again?'

'I know, I shouldn't have,' she says.

'Then why?'

'I suppose I was trying to convince myself. To act the way I would act if I were free. I was trying to draw a line under my relationship with him. I thought that if I was unfaithful to him then that would be the end of it. If nothing else it would give him a reason to divorce me. I was trying to end my relationship with him.'

Lewis absorbs this.

'For you it may have been the end of something. For me – I thought it was the beginning.'

'I shouldn't have,' she says limply. 'It was wrong. All of it was wrong. I was stupid.'

'No,' says Lewis. 'You were in love. You're still in love.'

Helen sits down slowly on the seat. It is like she has crumpled. Lewis finds himself standing over her.

'You know what will happen, don't you?'

She continues crying. Lewis ploughs on.

'It will be just like what you said happened to my mother. Your unhappiness will make you sick.'

'Oh stop Lewis, don't wish that on me.'

He sits down beside her. He reaches out and puts his hand to her cheek, turning her face towards him.

'I'm not wishing it on you, you know that. But it's what will happen. You know it better than I do. And I don't want you to die. To die unhappy. When you could have so much else.'

'Stop, Lewis. Please stop.'

He can see that he is hurting her and he doesn't want to.

'There was a time,' he says. 'When I knew nothing about you but I longed to know so much.'

He smiles. It is a weak, tiny smile – the most that he can manage.

'Do you know that I still feel that way? I wanted to spend the rest of my life finding out all about you.'

She seems to suddenly decide on something. She blows her nose, dabs at each of her eyes in turn and then returns the handkerchief to her bag. She stands up and extends a hand.

'Goodbye Lewis. I hope you find all the happiness in the world. You deserve it.'

He refuses to take her hand. Instead he stands up too. She looks at him steadily for another moment and then she turns and begins to walk away slowly. He calls her name once. Twice. But she doesn't turn round. He thinks he should go after her, and actually makes a move to do so, but then he stops. She reaches a corner and he wills her to look back. To change her mind. But she doesn't. Instead she disappears round the corner and out of sight. He knows with a terrible finality that he will never see her again.

Little images of their time together race through his mind. The first time he saw her in the church. And then on the beach. The evening he repaired her puncture. The first time he came to tea and listening to the music afterwards. The first time they made love. He sees her face in sunlight, smiling, laughing, happy, her blonde hair flecked with strands of gold. His skin remembers the sensation of her skin. His fingertips touch her face, stroke her nose, trace her lips, outline her eyebrows. His palms touch her cheeks and stroke her hair.

Lewis realises that ever since his mother died, he has been alone. Apart from that few months he spent with Helen in that long ago summer, it has always been this way. Foolishly he thought that when he was away in France she was with him; that he was travelling with her, that they were on a journey together. But he realises now that it is a fallacy. They were never together. He was always by himself.

He finds himself wondering whether this is the way of the world – that everyone goes alone. But he knows it isn't so. People travel in pairs and in merry groups and in great caravan trains. But somehow, for some reason, he has been fated – cursed – to travel alone. Because he knows now that is the way it will always be for him from now on. This is how he will make the rest of his journey.

Swallows are swooping over the roof of the church. Further away he hears the sound of children playing in the summer evening. He can smell onions frying as somewhere normal life goes on. Despite the warmth of the evening, he feels cold. Cold as though he were dead.

Part 3

54

*D*ecember 1919.

'Come on,' lads,' a voice said firmly. 'Time to get up.'

Lewis tunnelled out of a deep sleep and eventually broke the surface to see the canvas over his head. The tent was freezing. Outside he could hear Sergeant Wilkes's voice becoming more insistent along with groans and curses as the men stirred themselves. Lewis had been awake most of the night and then had fallen into a dead sleep, what seemed like only a few minutes ago. He got out of bed into the arctic air and pulled on his uniform. Then he stepped outside into the frigid day. It was just after dawn and a heavy frost had fallen. The grey and seaweed-green world had been dusted with white. He wasn't sure which were worse – the summer days when they had to stop at noon because of the smell or the freezing cold ones where digging was so backbreaking.

There were seven tents pitched on a flat, bare site that had been a Casualty Clearing Station. The thirty two men in the squad occupied four tents, the cook slept in the supply tent, the two sergeants, Wilkes and Crawford, shared one and Lewis had a tent to himself. It contained a cot, a small portable writing table and a folding chair. It had been a cold, clear night last night and he had sat outside looking at the stars until the cold had driven him in. He had forgotten to bring in the chair and now it had a thick layer of frost on the canvas seat. Jenkins had already boiled water, and seeing Lewis, brought him some in an enamel bowl. He shaved and by the time he'd finished, the air was full of the smell of frying bacon.

Lewis' unit was a so-called 'Flying Squad'. While other units were working their way methodically across the battlefields of Northern France and Belgium, Lewis' unit was called to areas not yet swept, if bodies were found during rebuilding or cultivation work. They had gotten the call yesterday. A French farmer, clearing his land of barbed wire, had come across something. After breakfast they boarded the trucks – three Type J lorries with canvas covered rears.

Wilkes drove the lead truck while Lewis, with a map on his lap, gave directions. After about twenty minutes, they pulled off the main road onto a narrower one that had been freshly gravelled. Then, further along, was what had probably been a farmhouse, of which only one wall remained standing. Several tarpaulins, tied together with string, had been attached to the single wall and hung over a frame to form a roof and walls. Sheets of corrugated iron leant against the sides to hold them down against the wind. There must have been a hole in the roof because a thin stream of brown smoke rose vertically upwards in the still air.

'There they are,' said Wilkes.

There were two men in flat caps standing on the side of the road. Wilkes changed gears and slowed as the Frenchmen flagged him down.

Lewis and Wilkes shook hands with them. Lewis had picked up a bit of French since coming here in July, so he got the gist of what they were saying. The farm had belonged to their eldest brother, but he had been killed by the *sales Boches* – they both spat as they said the words – at Verdun. They had now inherited the farm and it was urgent that they clear the field and plough it. They had families to feed and the house had to be rebuilt. They pointed at the place with the tarpaulins. Then they turned and indicated the grassy, shell-hole pitted ground that dropped away from the road. Pools of murky water, scattered across the field, reflected the dirty white sky. There was a muddy stream in a ditch at the bottom where the field levelled off. '*Ici, ici*,' they said.

The French brothers led the way down the field through the frost-covered grass and vegetation. About half way down they stopped at a cleft, a couple of feet wide, in the ground. It was hardly visible because there was so much grass growing over it. Lewis pushed the grass aside with his stick. In the cleft was a discarded British helmet. But then, as he looked more closely he saw the white of a leg bone protruding from the soil and then what looked like a shoulder and an arm in a rotting tunic.

'I'd say it was a trench, sir,' said Sergeant Wilkes. 'Used as a grave by the look of things and then filled in.'

Lewis nodded. In halting French, and waving his arms a good deal, Lewis explained that they would have to search the whole field, not just this patch. At this the two men groaned and looked up to heaven and threw their arms in the air and blew through pouted lips. '*Non, non, ce n'est pas possible.*'

'*On va essayer de travailler aussi vite que possible,*' said Lewis. We'll try and get it down as quickly as possible.

It was a line he had become used to using. He asked them where their boundaries were and after a bit more rapid fire French and gesticulation, these were established. Lewis explained that what his men would have to do then would be to clear the area within the boundaries. There were more groaning and loud exhalations. But once it would be done, it would be done, Lewis concluded. Then they could get on with their lives.

'*D'accord?*' he asked them.

'*D'accord*', they agreed, somewhat huffily.

The brothers then offered to help, to speed things up, but Lewis explained that his men had been doing this for a long time and they had a *systeme*. The brothers should keep gathering in the barbed wire while Lewis' team went to work. It was agreed. As they headed off, Lewis called a reminder to them that if they found any *munitions*, not to touch them but to call him straight away.

Lewis and Wilkes went back up to the road where the men stood around smoking. A white disc of sun was trying to break through the cloud cover. The two sergeants lined the men up on the edge of the road. They were in one long line with a man every six yards or so, facing down the field. Lewis took up a position at the end of the line, furthest away from the ruined house, Wilkes was in the centre and Crawford at the near end. Most officers didn't take part in doing the actual work, but Lewis liked to do it. It took his mind off other things. Each of them carried a steel rod and a handful of dirty wooden stakes. Every second or third man had a hammer for driving the stakes into the ground. The steel rods were like the one that Lewis had seen that day last summer when he had gotten the lift from Amiens to Albert. Lewis' rod actually *was* a machine gun cleaning rod. Some men had these too; others used whatever they had been able to pick up in the course of their work.

Sergeant Wilkes gave the order and they began to advance down the field very slowly. Wilkes and Crawford shouted at the men not to bunch. The command brought back chilling memories to Lewis. It was the same one he had shouted each time they had gone over the top.

He looked for all the telltale signs they had been taught. The easy ones were rifles or posts bearing helmets or equipment, usually placed at the heads of graves. There were no rifles or posts here. Remains or equipment upon the surface or protruding from the ground. Rat-holes, sometimes showing small bones or pieces of equipment brought to the surface by rats. Discoloration of grass, earth or water. The grass was often a lush, vivid, bluey-green colour and pools of water turned a greenish black or grey. And finally there was the rod method – 'poke and sniff' as the men called it.

During their training, the officers had been told to impress on the men that the work was of vital importance given the number of men still missing. Officers were to encourage the men to work carefully so that they might be able to not just find, but also identify missing men. In reality, Lewis had found that the men hardly needed any encouragement. They seemed to have an almost religious desire to do the work as well as they could. During a day's work there were often moments when there was a whoop of delight because somebody had found something to identify a body. A pay book or a letter or a notebook or some identifying object that would now make its way back to a devastated family and perhaps ease their pain a little.

The line of men worked their way slowly down the field. Each time they found something, they drove a stake into the rock-hard ground. By mid-morning the field had been swept. Twelve spots had been staked, though the number of bodies could be several times more than that. Now the work began. Lewis estimated that, at most, they would be able to recover twenty bodies today. Accordingly, a dozen men under Sergeant Crawford were dispatched in one of the lorries to the nearest cemetery which, according to Lewis' map, was half a mile away. There were so many that it was rarely a long journey. At the cemetery, these men would dig a trench sufficient to take twenty bodies. The remaining men were divided up into parties of four with shovels, rubber gloves, canvas, rope, Cresol disinfectant and stretchers. Then each party took a staked spot and began to dig.

The work was slow. The battlefields were covered with a thick, luxuriant layer of rank grass and nettles, in places almost waist high. Often, when this was cleared away, further bodies or traces of bodies were discovered. In addition there were chunks of elephant or corrugated iron, barbed wire, stakes, discarded kit and all the other material the Army had used to fight the War. Finally, of course, there were the unexploded munitions.

Thankfully it was happening less often now, but a shovel pushed with too much force into the ground could still strike metal, and that unexpected ring of steel upon steel could be the second last sound that the owner of the shovel ever heard.

Lewis wondered if they would get a second pass through this field. There were rumours of the Graves Exhumation Units being disbanded. The War was becoming more and more of a distant memory. The French were anxious to get on with their lives. Yes, the British had lost hundreds of thousands of men – some said it was more than a million. But the French had lost even more. And the War had been fought on *their* soil. Life had to go on. People had to eat and make love again. Houses had to be built or rebuilt; crops sown and harvested. How much longer would the living have to wait before the dead would make way for them? Hadn't there been death and dwelling on death for long enough? Time to move on. He suspected that they would only get one shot at this field and after that, anything that remained would be lost forever.

Lewis didn't do any digging himself. When he had started he had wanted to and on his first day, he did. He found the rhythmic movement dulled his brain and tired his body. But the two sergeants had come to him saying that it wasn't really the thing, and the men disapproved, saw it as demeaning and that it diminished his authority. Reluctantly Lewis had stopped and then had contented himself with going from digging party to digging party. But he had stopped doing that too as he felt he was treading on the two sergeants' toes. It was perhaps a better use of his time to look for more bodies. And so he would sweep the ground again, from a different direction. Or he would do more poke and sniffs. Or, towards the end of the day, he would stand with a low sun at his back and see if it showed up anything on the ground. He almost always found more bodies.

The men worked steadily through the morning. They were

instructed not to dig too closely to the bodies. This made the work easier but also prevented disturbance of the bodies and, most important of all, revealed whether more than one man was buried in a particular spot. They were taught to disinfect their hands and gloves generously with Cresol, not that they needed much reminding. If nothing else, the smell of the Cresol masked the other smells.

Like most of them Lewis had been appalled at the nature of the work they had to do. Despite the fact that he had volunteered for it, it seemed scarcely endurable. But this had only lasted a week or two. After that men just seemed to get hardened to it. Strange as it seemed, Lewis felt also there was a large amount of tenderness in the work. Men felt that each new body could have been them and that each body, particularly those that were identified, represented not just a man but a family. Fathers, brothers, children.

By mid-afternoon there were ghastly parodies of bodies lying on sheets of canvas all across the field. There was also a small pile of rusted shells of different calibres. These had been carried up to the roadside and placed as far away as possible from the ruined house. French engineers would come along in due course and take them away to be destroyed. The sun had given up trying to break through and the off-white clouds blanketed the sky. What the bodies looked and smelt like depended on when they had been put in the ground. Some looked like piles of grass, earth, stones and bones. Some were grinning skulls attached to rotting, compressed clothing. Some – those that had been buried on the bottom of a pile of bodies – looked almost like boards made of a blackened, compressed material.

Each of the bodies was searched carefully for any effects which might lead to identification. Lewis remembered how these burial parties had been conducted at the time. He had never known whether it was better to take the identification or leave it on the body. His first reaction had been to take it, as well as noting carefully the location of the grave, so that the news could be passed on to the next of kin. But then what about the body? Shellfire was always disturbing bodies, throwing up previously buried ones and scattering gobbets of them all over the place. With some bodies it happened countless times. And taking the identification didn't guarantee anything because the man who took it could be killed the next minute. In the end, though it wasn't always possible, he had come to the conclusion that it was better – if possible – to do both, take something and leave something on the body.

But it had never been quite as neat as that in practice. He would ask his men to do this but there was no guarantee that they would. Most of them just wanted to get the burial fatigue over with. And as 1917 progressed, the number of bodies became so great that such niceties were simply forgotten. At Passchaendale burying bodies had been the furthest thing from anybody's mind.

Today, all the bodies were British. They found a couple of pay books and some identity discs, so that it looked like they might be able to identify four or five of them. The rest of the bodies would be recorded as 'Unknown British Soldier' on the Burial Return.

When the General Service wagons, each drawn by a pair of mules, arrived from the cemetery, the men began to move the bodies from the field up to the road. The remains were wrapped in the sheets of canvas which were then tied up. A brown paper butcher's label on a string was attached to each one. Any personal effects found were placed in a ration bag and this too was tied to the canvas. Where more than one body had been found in a particular location, the bodies would be sent to the cemetery together. This was because it was often possible to identify unknowns from the fact that they were known to have been buried with men who *could* be identified. But this would be a job for somebody else.

Lewis went round to each of the bodies in turn and wrote out the labels. For each group of bodies he marked them with a particular letter of the alphabet, followed by a number giving the order in which they were to be buried. Then he signed each label. In the end, there were seventeen bodies from today's work but more remained. At the very least, they would have to return tomorrow which wasn't going to make the French brothers very happy. Still, there was nothing else for it.

The canvas-covered bodies were placed on stretchers and loaded onto the wagons. The French brothers, their wives and a gaggle of children, stood in front of the ruined house and watched silently. Even the children were quiet. Each time a new body was placed on a wagon, they crossed themselves. Each wagon could take five loaded stretchers, four laid across the top from one side to the other and a fifth underneath on the wagon's floor. There was a large Union Jack in each wagon and, once the stretchers were installed, the driver shook out the flag and draped it over the canvas covered bodies.

There were four wagons and now they lined up in a row, their mules waiting patiently with alert ears and sad eyes. Four men were detailed, one for each wagon. Their job was to walk behind the wagon as it made its way to the cemetery and ensure that nothing fell off the wagon or slipped out of the canvases. Lewis told the Frenchmen that they would be back tomorrow and was pleasantly surprised to not get any more disagreement from them. They were strangely subdued. Maybe they were glad to be getting all of this horror off their land.

The train of wagons, each with their follower set off down the road towards the cemetery. Cemetery duty was regarded as the cushier of the two types of work and most officers rotated from exhumation to cemetery. Like all the others Lewis had been offered this rotation but he had declined. He preferred to do the exhumation work. It seemed to have become his mission to recover every lost body in France. It was as though each time his men identified a body, he reduced the ocean of sadness that the War had caused by maybe a teaspoonful.

As the wagons disappeared from view, the men finished their cigarettes and went back to do another hour's digging. It was just after three when Wilkes suggested it was time to pack up. Lewis agreed and the men stopped, brought their tools and equipment up to the road and put them into the backs of the two remaining lorries. Lewis took a walk around the field to make sure that nothing had been left behind. Then they got into the lorries and drove to the cemetery.

The stretchers had been lined up beside a newly dug trench about six feet deep. The men who had dug it stood around, leaning on their shovels and smoking. A French priest was there in a white surplice with a heavy black coat over it against the cold. It was a dreary scene. The cemetery officer, a lieutenant called Timpson that Lewis had met before, had worked his way along the line of stretchers. He was on the last one. He squatted down, examining the personal effects in the ration bag and comparing them to the label attached to the body. He made some notes in a notebook.

'Any problems?' asked Lewis.

'Don't think so,' he said, without looking up and continuing to write. 'There are a couple that I've noted that we might be able to identify from battalion records. Apart from that, nothing else.'

He finished writing and looked up.

'Just get on with it, I suppose,' he said.

He had a lantern jaw, a firm mouth and deep set eyes. Lewis asked Wilkes to form the men into a hollow square with the men on three sides and the grave on the fourth. While this was going on, two of Timpson's men jumped down into the grave. Then two others went to the first stretcher in the line. Slowly, they lifted up the end of the stretcher furthest away from the trench, causing the canvas shrouded body to slide forward slightly. Then, as the stretcher was raised more, the body slid down into the trench to be caught and guided by the men there. They lowered it to the earthen floor. Lewis was always taken by the great gentleness, the almost reverential way in which they did this. As the stretchers were emptied they were taken away where they would be washed in Cresol and returned to the wagons.

When the last body was lowered into the grave, the priest who had been standing on the thrown up earth, delivered a short and fast, committal service in Latin. He seemed anxious to get away and get in out of the cold. When he was finished he shook hands with Timpson and hurried off, obviously with thoughts of a warm fire and a hot drink. Meanwhile the men were hammering wooden crosses in at the head of each grave. Each one had a little strip of tin plate attached to it into which had been pressed details of the soldier in the grave. Sometimes the tin strip gave the name, initials, number, rank and regiment of the soldier. More often though it just said 'An Unknown British Soldier'.

55

*T*impson asked Lewis if he'd like to go into Amiens that night, but he declined. Lewis found such evenings tedious beyond belief. Instead, he ate his dinner in his tent, and afterwards lay on his cot and read. The evenings and nights were the worst. Then there was nothing to occupy him, to keep him busy and the thoughts and feelings came flowing in until they swamped him.

He had no real memory of what had happened after Helen had said goodbye or how he had come back from Shropshire. It was self-evident that he had but he could not recall the smallest detail of those few days. He assumed he must have gone back to his hotel and spent the night. He must have checked out in the morning and gone to the station and caught the train to London. But he remembered none of it. All he knew was that by the time he was walking up Horn Lane towards home, he had decided he would volunteer for the Graves Exhumation Units. Now that everything that was best in his life was dead, being with the dead seemed like the only logical place to be.

In fact, the truth was he *wanted* to die. Why hadn't she done this while the War was raging? Then dying would have been so easy. But he thought he still might be able to do it with the Graves Exhumation Units. There would be unexploded shells all over the battlefield. Hadn't the sergeant who had given him the lift to Albert told him that somebody had been killed only the previous day? So maybe this was a way that he could go.

He vaguely remembered a talk with Dad where he explained what he planned to do – not that he told him anything about Helen. Dad was less than pleased, saying that if he planned to make a career in the Army, then the Graves Exhumation Unit was hardly the place to do it. They had had an argument, as far as Lewis could recall, but it didn't matter. The next day he returned to barracks and within a couple of weeks had been transferred as he had requested.

He started at the worst possible time – high summer. The stench and flies were unbelievable and the armies of rats, who had come to regard the deserted battlefields as their domain, took time to be persuaded otherwise. Rat bites were common. One man in another unit died from one. But by starting early and finishing early, so as to avoid the worst of the day's heat, they managed to make it a bit more bearable. By the end of the summer when the weather was starting to cool, they had settled into a well practised routine.

What he remembered most from those first couple of months was the feeling that Helen had been cut from the world. It was like a great hand had come down and taken her away. He would never speak to her again, never hear her voice, hold her, touch her, hear her laugh. He thought about her as if she was dead, but of course she wasn't. He felt that in some ways, had she died it might have been easier. There would have been a finality about it. But to know that she was still in the world, that he could have written to her, gone to her, talked to her, this was perhaps the most unbearable of all.

In those early months he was often tempted to contact her. Untold times, he had taken out paper, written all or part of a letter, telling her how he felt, pleading with her to change her mind. But all the letters had ended up in the fire. What was the point? He should be trying to put it behind him. But he found it impossible.

He remembered the first night he dreamt about her. In the dream they were sitting up in her bed in the cottage talking and she was laughing. Lewis was so surprised to be with her that he woke with a start. But then came the shock of finding that she wasn't actually there.

He would go into Amiens with some of the others. He would try to put a brave face on it and he must have been fairly successful because only once did anyone say that he seemed to be 'feeling a bit down tonight'. He got drunk. He went back to a prostitute's attic room one night, climbing endless flights of creaking steps. But once he got there and she took off her blouse and her brassiere and he saw her bare breasts, he just threw the money on the table and fled back down the stairs.

56

*J*anuary 1920. Lewis was given a weekend's leave. He normally just ignored these things but he had grown weary of their encampment and the smell of decomposition which he never seemed to be able to get out of his nostrils. He thought he would go to Amiens. He'd only been in the city a couple of times since he'd joined the Graves Exhumation Unit but suddenly, the thought of a couple of days in a hotel, hot baths every day – or even twice a day – some decent food , was too overwhelming to resist. But what to do in Amiens all day long after a bath and before it was time for the next meal? He feared time on his hands – empty spaces in which to think, to brood.

Then he had an idea. He had decided he would stay at the hotel he had stayed in last summer when he had gone to Henry the waiter's, son's grave. But now he had an even better idea. He would take a bicycle and revisit the grave, take some more photographs, write a letter to Henry and tell him he'd been there again. He realised there was no particular point to this. It would just give him a little project to do, something to keep his mind off other things.

It was Friday evening when he rode into Amiens on the lorry that was taking a group of leave men into the city for the weekend. He found the hotel in Rue Amiral Courbet and the blonde girl in the black dress was still there behind the counter. He was pleased when she said that she remembered him.

'*C'est gentil,*' he said. '*Merci Mademoiselle.*'

It was *her* hotel, he asked. It was. And she ran the hotel by herself? Yes, she did. She had bought it with her husband before

the War. But then he had been called up and gone off to be a
soldier and never come back. She had hoped he might be a prisoner in Germany but all hope of that was gone now. It was hard
being a widow and having to cope with the entire place by herself.

'*C'est dur*,' she said.

Lewis was astonished to hear that she was a widow. He had
her as a *mademoiselle* of nineteen or twenty. Her story put her
more in her mid to late twenties.

He set out for Albert the next day, wearing a brown Army
waterproof cape over his uniform. It was a wet, grey day after
a night of heavy rain that had stopped around dawn. Low bal-
looning clouds were like the roof of a tent as the tyres of the
bike swished over the wet road. The air was cold but clean and
newly-washed.

By mid-morning he had arrived at the cemetery. The rem-
nants of the flowers were still there, little more than a brown
soggy mess now. The letter was long gone, dissolved by rain or
taken by the wind. He had brought some fresh flowers, placed
them on the grave and took a couple of photographs. It was
while he was wondering how he was going to spend the rest of
the day that the idea occurred to him that he would ask the girl
at the hotel if she'd like to have dinner with him. The notion that
there had been a time in his life – indeed, not so long ago – when
he would have been terrified to do this, made him smile. But it
made sense – neither of them had much in their lives apart from
the work they did. It would be good for both of them. And if
she declined? He shrugged. He didn't care one way or the other.
How did you say it in French? *Je m'en fiche.*

Around noon he ate the lunch that she had provided for him
and then he cycled back to Amiens. It was a downhill run and
easier – almost exhilarating at times as he freewheeled along.
She was at the desk when he came in. He told her that he had left
the bike in the courtyard and then he asked her. The surprise

on her thin face became a smile and she said that yes, she would like that very much. Her friend Cecile, also a widow, could bring over her children and mind the place for a couple of hours. What was her name, by the way – he was sorry, he didn't know. It was Sandrine.

They went out just as it got dark. She had changed into a different dress – still black – and shoes with heels. She had put on lipstick and her hair was up. They turned out of the hotel and went in the direction of the Cathedral. He asked her if she knew some place and she said that she had heard there was a very good place that had just reopened. They found it – essentially the living room of a house that still had new timbers showing and smelt of fresh paint. The husband did the cooking in the kitchen while the wife waited the tables. There was no menu, just three courses that her husband was cooking tonight. The wife knew Sandrine and they spoke in machine gun fire French for a few minutes before she left to pass on their order to her husband.

It turned out to be a really enjoyable evening. Sandrine had picked up a little English from the British soldiers who had stayed in the hotel during the War. Lewis' French was modest but he made up for it by not caring if he made a fool of himself. They smiled and laughed and urged each other on and there were also a few puzzled silences and lots of frowns and requests for '*Encore?*'

She had heard in June 1917 that her husband was missing and Lewis wondered if he had been involved in the French mutinies after Nivelle's disaster on the Chemin Des Dames. Lots of the mutineers had been executed. But he said nothing of this to her. She asked him if he was married and when the answer to that was that he wasn't, she ragged him. Surely he had a girlfriend. He shook his head.

Outside the restaurant, he offered his arm and she took it as they walked back to the hotel through the dark streets. They were silent. Helen tried to push her way into Lewis' thoughts.

Normally he allowed her, welcomed her, but tonight he closed that door. He realised it was the first time he had been able to do that.

'Do you have more things to do now when you get back?' he asked her.

He could only see the vague outline of her face it was so dark.

'No, Cecile should have done everything. Just lock up and go to bed,' she said.

And so they did.

57

*L*ewis began to come to Amiens every chance he got. If he could only stay a night, they would go to dinner and then return to either his bed or hers. He always insisted on renting a room saying she needed the money. If he came for a weekend, he would help around the hotel so that after a few weeks it felt like they were a couple running the place. Each night they slept in either his bed or hers.

Sandrine was very independent, her own woman and Lewis liked that about her. She and her dead husband, Jean-Jacques, both had family but they lived in Rouen. It was a long way. Sandrine didn't see them very much. Lewis' French improved as did her English. They had no disagreements of any description. Sandrine was always happy to see him and he her. She rarely spoke about Jean-Jacques and he told her nothing of Helen. Though one evening, as they were eating, she said to him, 'There *was* somebody, wasn't there?'

'There was.'

He didn't know what else to say and, after a long silence, she said, 'It's alright, you know. You can tell me if you want to – when you are ready'.

And then they talked of other things.

Their lovemaking was genuine and passionate and adventurous. It wasn't serious or mournful. There didn't seem to be any ghosts in the bedroom, neither Jean-Jacque's nor Helen's.

One evening, over dinner, he told her about Helen. When he had finished, Sandrine said laconically, 'She sounds complicated.'

The remark stayed with Lewis for the rest of the evening.

Later, during the night, he woke and it was still there. Lewis had always thought that the only thing complicated about his relationship with Helen had been their age difference. He hadn't seen her marriage as a complication. She didn't love her husband and so she would divorce him – simple as that. And Lewis and Helen loved being together – that was what really mattered. She would divorce her husband and she and Lewis would be together. But now he realised how profoundly accurate Sandrine had been. And it wasn't just Helen that had been complicated. Lewis realised that he himself had been complicated – or maybe confused was a better word.

His relationship with Helen hadn't been simple at all since – simultaneously – he had wanted her to be mother and lover. And for her it had been even worse because, at different times, he was the son she never had and her lover *and* she already had a husband to whom, despite all her protestations, she was bound.

He saw it clearly now in a way he had never done when he had been in the midst of it. She had never left her husband. Not really. Those things that Lewis and Helen had shared together in Fowey had been just strange anomalies. Married to her husband was her normal state. My God, all the time she was writing to Lewis, while he had been at war, she had been married to her husband. Who knew? Maybe she had been meeting him, sleeping with him, especially after she had been transferred to France and the distance separating them wouldn't have been that great. Lewis realised that her relationship with him had been in her head. It was an imaginary one conducted by an imaginary version of her that never really existed. She had pretended to be a person that she wasn't.

But she had had no malicious intent – he knew that. She had just not wanted anybody to get hurt. But looking back on it all now, somebody was always going to get hurt. And it had turned out to be him. But he couldn't hate her for it or feel angry – not any more. Given how mixed up he was at the time, it must have been a thousand times worse for her with the added complication of Robert. Her head must have been about to explode a lot of the time with all of the conflict going on there.

Lewis wondered if she was still like this or had she managed to find some peace. Had she been able to put him out of her mind and her heart in a way that – up until now – he hadn't been able to? He found himself hoping that she had found some happiness. And he realised that this was something he had not felt before. Up until now he had been tormented by the thought of her sharing her life with somebody else. That idea had been like a terrible nagging ache that never left him. Tonight, for some reason, it didn't seem to bother him – it seemed remote and far away.

And what about Sandrine? There were times when he thought that being with her was what he wanted. That to settle down with her, to get married, to have children would be the finest thing in the world. But then, at other times, he couldn't picture himself growing old as an hotelier. Whatever else about his life so far, it hadn't been conventional. It had had colossal highs and lows. He had spent the last couple of years living on the edge and while it hadn't been pleasant, there had been something about it, some whiff of danger that appealed to something deep inside him. He knew that he definitely didn't want to live that close to extinction again, but neither did he want the kind of extinction that he sometimes thought being an hotelier would bring with it.

By the spring came confirmation that the Graves Exhumation Units were indeed going to be disbanded. Whatever bodies had been recovered were recovered; whatever remained would now be left to chance or to French farmers or builders. Even though he had known for a while that it was coming, the decision was still a shock to Lewis. The unit had become like a family to him. Indeed, for a long time, before Sandrine, it had been his whole world. Now, in July, his enlistment would be up and he would be demobilised. What would he do then?

He was no nearer an answer to this question when he spent the following weekend with Sandrine. That Friday evening, as he rode on the lorry into Amiens, he found himself wondering again if his future lay here with her. Was that why she had come into his life? Maybe he should ask her to marry him and he could live here and help her run the hotel. As a business it was clear that it had a future. Every month there seemed to be more and more people coming to visit the battlefields. The hotel was busier than it had ever been. She would need help. And he enjoyed being with her. He was sure she had her dark moments, just as he did, but they seemed to understand each other, understand each other's sadness. They didn't ask about it – just took it as a fact of life. They were solicitous of each other and tried not to take each other for granted. It seemed like a very solid foundation for a future together.

That evening they ate in the small apartment she maintained for herself on the ground floor at the back of the hotel. She had prepared the food herself which was unusual because normally, when they ate in, she just got food from the kitchen. The remains of dessert lay on the table and their coffee cups were half full. Apart from the two tall candles which had burned half way down there was no other light in the room. The heavy furniture in dark wood seemed to have merged into the walls. She reached across and took his hand, but this was something one or other of them often did when they went out. She looked at him with her brown eyes and then with a little smile on her face, she said, very softly, the words that had never passed between them before.

'Je t'aime, Lewis. Je t'aime'.

58

*L*ewis stood outside his tent smoking. The spring evening was warm with a smoky orange sun sinking beyond the green rolling countryside, making long shadows of the men as they moved around the encampment. The smell of onions and grilling meat was in the air.

'Mail, sir.'

Sergeant Wilkes passed Lewis a handful of letters. The first was from Dad – he would read it later – there were two bills, one for shirts that he had bought when he had reluctantly gone home on leave at Christmas, the other for books he had had shipped from Foyles. When he saw the handwriting on the last letter it was a moment before he recognised it. Or perhaps he recognised it straight away but it was a moment before he believed what he was seeing. Thick, expensive white paper. The back-sloping hand in blue fountain pen. The obviously feminine writing. Helen.

The letter had been posted to Horn Lane and re-directed in Dad's handwriting. Before he realised what he was doing Lewis smelt the letter. Stupid fool. An old habit. He turned it over and read the return address. It was the one in Shropshire. So, she was still with *him*. Or had he died? Was that what this was about? With trembling hands Lewis tore open the letter, ripping the envelope apart in his urgency. It was one small sheet of heavy white paper folded in two with the same return address on it and written in the same blue ink. His eyes raced over the words.

Dear Lewis,

I have made up my mind to leave Robert & will be doing so in the next few days.

I wanted to meet you. There is so much I want to say to you.

I don't know what your circumstances are. Maybe you are married & if you are, I hope that it has turned out to be everything you would have wished for. I don't know where you are or even if you'll get this. But if it does & you would like to meet, I would come to wherever you are, no matter where that is.

I know that I have hurt you beyond belief & perhaps you are standing by a fire getting ready to burn this.

But I hope you will not & I can get a chance to see you. You can reply to this address & don't worry, if you do, your reply will reach me.

Yours, Helen.

He collapsed into his camp chair and for a long time sat there, reading and re-reading the words. He searched for signs of affection. The 'dear' and 'yours' were bland, things one might write to a friend. She wanted to meet him. But for what? To say what things to him? She was still with Robert and he was still alive and she hadn't left him. She had said everything she had to say the last time. What else was there?

Yes, he would meet her. He would be delighted to meet her. There was much he wanted to say to *her*.

He wrote a reply straight away. It was an equally bland letter that began 'Dear Helen' and ended 'Yours sincerely'. He told her that he was in France – he left it as vague as that – that he got leave every other weekend and that if she wanted to meet he could meet her the weekend after next. He wrote his reply on Monday, it went in the post on Tuesday and would have arrived in England Wednesday. He had a reply by Friday.

Yes, she would come to France on that weekend. Where should she meet him?

He replied telling her that he would meet her outside the main door of Amiens Cathedral at 6 pm on Friday March 19.

59

*T*he Wednesday before he was due to meet Helen, Lewis went into Amiens. He hadn't told Sandrine he was coming so that when he came in the door of the hotel, her face lit up.

'Lewis! *Quel surpris.*'

She leaned across the counter and he kissed her on the lips, but he knew it was a half-hearted kiss.

'Is somesing wrong?' she asked?

She always spoke in English when she wanted there to be no doubt about what she was saying.

'No, nothing's wrong,' he said airily. 'It's just that I won't be able to come and stay this weekend.'

Her brown eyes met his. He looked away with a kind of reflex action and then looked back again.

'She's come back,' she said. 'Hasn't she?'

He felt ashamed, guilty, he wasn't sure what exactly.

'It's just something I have to take care of,' he said in French. 'I'll probably see you that weekend after all. I just won't be able to do it on the Friday night.'

'Don't say things you don't mean,' she said in English.

'I'll be back,' he replied in English. 'I promise.'

'Or make promises you can't keep,' she said.

'*Je dois partir maintenant.*' I have to go now.

He hesitated, unsure whether or not to kiss her goodbye. She made the decision for him.

'Goodbye, Lewis,' she said.

Spoken in a French accent the two English words sounded like the shutting of a door and the turning of a lock.

They usually finished early on Fridays, so by four o'clock, he was back in camp. He washed, shaved and changed into a uniform that he'd had freshly laundered in the nearby village. The leave lorry deposited him outside the Cathedral just after five thirty. There were still a couple of hours of daylight left. The square outside the Cathedral was busy with people returning home after the day's work, or going into the great church. The smell of evening meals being prepared was in the air.

There was no sign of Helen, so he went into the Cathedral and found a pew near the back. He sat in the cool, dim, vaguely incense-scented interior trying to calm his thoughts. The lights of candles twinkled in the side altars and the stained glass windows were still boarded up. His heart was racing. He didn't know whether he wanted her to appear or not. He didn't know what he would say if she did. He didn't know what he wanted or how he hoped this meeting would end.

He had never been religious, not since he had been a child and Mum had first knelt down to say night prayers with him. In his teens he only went to church to see Victoria and Sophie. During the War he had found himself turning to God in moments of extreme terror. And the last time he had prayed had been after Helen had gone out of his life and he had begun to pray again to get her to return. After several months of that he had given up.

He slid from the pew onto the kneeler and covered his eyes with the palms of his hands, welcoming the warm pools of darkness. What a life, he had had. Why had he survived? What was the point of it all? He felt like he was going to cry. Outside were the faint sounds of traffic. Pews creaked as people got in or out of them. Somebody dropped a coin into a box which had been emptied. It made a hard wooden thud as it hit the bottom of the box. Feet trudged or shuffled up and down the aisle. But then he heard another sound. It was the clicking of heels, walking slowly on the flagstones. He took his head from his hands and looked up.

Helen was coming down the aisle and was about mid-way between the altar and the door. She wore a floral dress that stopped above her ankles. It had short sleeves with a white collar and a matching hat. Her coat was draped over her arm. She saw Lewis at the same time. He stood up slowly and stepped out of the pew.

'Hello, Lewis,' she said softly, and like a tidal wave, it all came back to him, falling on him at once in a great rush. The line of her shoulders, her arms, her hands, the smell of her hair, her laughter. And how she looked when she was naked – vulnerable and powerful all at once. Her back and her buttocks, her magnificent breasts, her thighs, her feet which he had kissed.

He thought she looked a little older, or maybe it was just that she looked tired. But everything else was as before. The dress was a different style but it reminded him so much of what she had worn that first day in the church in Fowey.

'Shall we go outside?' she whispered.

He turned and they walked out together. Walking down the aisle and leaving a church – he was struck by the irony of it. Outside, the sky was a bit more orange and the air was a little chillier. She turned to face him.

'You look well,' she said.

'So do you,' he said, inadequately.

'Shall we walk?' she asked.

'We could go down by the river,' he offered.

'Is that the Somme?'

He nodded. She began to put her coat on and he helped her into it. She thanked him. They went north across a little bridge and down the cobbled Rue du Hocquet. They walked slowly, in silence, almost like lovers. Eventually, Helen took a deep breath and said, 'When I met you, I ... I was a mess. Oh, I didn't realise it at the time. I thought I was ready to start a new life. But I realise now that I wasn't and the result was that I hurt you really badly.'

She halted and turned to him. She put her hand on his arm to stop him.

'For that, dearest Lewis, I am really, really sorry. I know that saying sorry is so inadequate but it's all I can do. I thought when I left Robert that first time, that I could just turn off my feelings. But I wasn't able to. It wasn't that I still loved him – that was long gone. But I felt guilty. I pitied him. And especially after he was wounded. Those are strong emotions. At least they were strong in me.'

'Stronger than love?' asked Lewis.

She looked into his eyes.

'At the time they were,' she said.

She turned and continued walking.

'I was very angry,' he said.

'You had every right to be.'

'But then – recently – I realised that I was messed up too,' he said. 'I realise that now. I didn't know whether I wanted a mother, a girlfriend, a lover or what.'

'But at least you didn't hurt me,' she said.

'Someone was always going to get hurt,' he said.

'But it shouldn't have been you. You were nothing but kind and generous and loving. You're a good man, Lewis. A good, strong, caring man. You don't find too many of them. At least I haven't come across too many.'

They walked on in silence.

'It turned out exactly as you said. It was killing me. If I'd stayed with him I would have been dead in a few years. In the end, I had to leave – for my own survival.'

'So you really have left him?'

'Yes. I've rented a place a few miles away. I still go over there every day —'

His voice rose slightly.

'So you haven't really?'

'No. I have,' she said quietly. 'We're in the process of making alternative arrangements. Then, I won't go so often and eventually it'll probably become just a couple of times a year. Holidays, birthdays, that sort of thing. I've already met with a solicitor and the divorce proceedings have been started now. I suppose that's all less complicated now, she said, since … Robert can't … well, we're not really married, not like that, any more.'

'So what are you going to do now?'

'Decide where I want to live.' she said, 'Go back to teaching the piano. Get an income is the first priority. Independence. That's one of the things I learned from you, Lewis.'

They were silent again.

'And you – you stayed in the Army.'

Lewis told her what he had been doing.

'At the time it felt like everything good in my life had died, so being amongst the dead seemed like the only place to be.'

'And will you keep doing that?' she asked.

He shook his head.

'We're going to be disbanded in a few weeks. My enlistment is up in July. I don't know what I'll do. I don't know where I'll go.'

They had come to the river, smooth as glass, and turned right along its bank. After a long time, he said, 'Why did you get in touch with me?'

'To apologise. To close a circle. There was a lot between us that had been left unsaid.'

'And now you've said it?' he asked.

'Some of it.'

'What else is there?'

'Have you met anybody – a woman, I mean?'

He told her about Sandrine.

'She sounds like she would be good for you,' said Helen. 'A

nice quiet life in a small city like this. It could be good for you after everything you've been through.'

'I don't know,' said Lewis. 'I can't really picture myself as an hotelier.'

'No,' she said, and there was a smile in her voice, 'neither can I.'

Then, after a pause, he said 'And you – have you met anybody?'

'Don't be silly,' she said. 'That would be the last thing on earth I would want right now.'

The way she said 'silly' reminded him of the way she used to call him 'silly' – 'What are you doing down here, silly?'

'So what do you want now Helen?' he said, stopping and turning to her.

'I just want to be happy,' she said and then, as he was about to interrupt she added, 'I was happy when I was with you.'

She smiled.

'It was so unlikely. *We* were so unlikely. But I was happy.'

'And what about all that about our age difference?'

'Do you know, Lewis, maybe there was a time when that would have mattered. But one of the things I realised is that you can't worry about the future. We only have today. Now.'

'I learned that in the War,' he said. 'I think it was how I got through it.'

'We've both had to learn it the hard way,' she said, 'although I think yours was a lot harder than mine.'

'So what are you saying?' he said. 'Why have you really come here?'

She took a deep breath. It sounded more like a sigh.

'Maybe,' she said. 'When you get out of the Army, we could try again.'

Whatever he had been expecting, it hadn't been this.

'How do you know you're not just afraid of ending up on your own?'

'Lewis,' she said. 'I've been alone most of my life. When I was a child, when I was married. Being alone holds no fears for me.'

'If we did start again, it would only be a few weeks and you'd be wanting to go back to him.'

'That's not what would happen, Lewis.'

'Of course it is,' he said. 'Isn't that what was happening all the time we were together? You were physically with me but in your head you were with him.'

'Things change, Lewis. People can change. I've changed.'

'How can I know that? How could I ever be sure of it?'

'You want some kind of guarantee?'

His silence was a yes. She shook her head slowly.

'I can't give you that. Life's not like that. I'm saying that this is the way I feel and this is what I would like to do. I love you, Lewis. It's taken me all this time – all this wasted time, all this heartache I've caused you, to realise this.'

She had said the words. They were the first time he had heard them from her lips.

'Maybe it sounds stupid to you. There's this bloody age dif-ference. Maybe you now think of me as a sad old woman, and that's alright if you do. But I don't think I'll ever find anybody who's as good as you – who's as good for me and to me as you were. I'm just so sorry it's taken all this to make me realise that.'

They had nearly reached a bridge with three arches. Dusk was descending slowly onto the river bank and the sky had become a very deep blue. Across the river, along the partially rebuilt far bank, lights were being lit in the houses. He could see the tables and tablecloths of a restaurant through its plate glass window. The lights threw splashes of yellow like paint onto the inky blue of the Somme. That terrible name.

'And if the age difference worried you,' she said, 'we could go and live in a place where nobody cared. It doesn't have to be England. France maybe. Greece. It would be an adventure …'

She tailed off and then she said, 'But now you have to say, Lewis. You have to say what you want.'

'I just want things to be as they were,' he said.

'And they could be,' she said, and for the first time, he thought he heard some of her old passion.

'They couldn't,' he said, with great sadness. 'It's too late for that now.'

'How can you know?' she said. 'If this is what you want, surely you should try.'

'You know,' he said. 'Maybe that actually isn't what I want.'

'So what then?'

'I don't want to be alone any more. I'm tired of it.'

'We're all alone, Lewis. The only person who's with you your whole life is yourself. It's just that sometimes, on the journey, if we're lucky, we meet other people. We team up with them. I was lucky enough to meet you. I was lucky and I was stupid because I didn't realise how lucky I was.'

He heard what she said but another feeling was dawning on him.

'It's not being alone either. It's not that. I know what it is now. I just want a woman to love me and I want to love her back.'

'Like you did with your Mum, before all that was taken from you?'

He could feel tears smarting in his eyes. He nodded, unable to speak. She looked into his eyes.

'What we had … what we did in Fowey? Is that what you mean? For you … was that love?'

Lewis didn't know what to say. He didn't know what he was feeling. It was all hopelessly complicated. Mum, Helen, the War, Sandrine, Helen again. Life as he knew it would be ending in a few weeks. What would he do? Where would he go? And no matter what he did or where he went, what was the point of it all? Before the War it had all seemed so clear. Since it ended nothing was clear.

'I don't know,' he said.

They continued on in silence. It was dark now and cold. There would probably be a mist on the Somme tonight. If not here in Amiens then certainly upstream where it joined the Ancre and on up to dismal Albert where so many had suffered and died. The silence lengthened until eventually, she broke it by saying, 'I suppose I should be getting back.'

He said nothing. She turned and began to walk back the way they had come. With just a few steps she had almost disappeared into the darkness. A star had become visible. The spire of the Cathedral rose into the blackness on the left, a diffuse black needle against the backdrop of the night sky. Lewis walked after her and caught up with her.

'When are you going back to England?'

'Tomorrow. There's a train about ten in the morning.'

They were walking more briskly now – whether from the cold or because they were people whose business had been concluded. A horse clip clopped across the bridge ahead, the cart it pulled trundling behind it. On the far bank, somebody – maybe the cook in the restaurant before his shift started – smoked a cigarette, the red tip the only thing visible in the darkness.

'It's been really good —' she said.

'Could I take you to —' he said.

They spoke together and then both stopped.

'I was going to ask if I could take you to dinner,' said Lewis. 'That's if you wanted to eat.'

'I haven't eaten since breakfast – and that was only coffee. I've been sick about meeting you.'

'We could go across there,' he said, indicating the restaurant on far bank.

'That would be nice,' she said.

He took her hand – it was cold – and together they walked

up towards the bridge that would take them across the Somme towards the light.

Acknowledgements

I am deeply grateful to Andy Robertshaw for the meticulous care he took in reading the manuscript and pointing out a number of inaccuracies. Any errors that remain are my responsibility alone.